DESPERATE HUSBANDS

(What Men Think, Want and Need)

By

BRITTEN WILDER

Premier Publishing

Printed in USA

To the Reader

Although this novel is a work of fiction, it contains actual places and people; facts, news, events, statistics, occurrences and stories; as well as clinical research and information that can enhance your marriage or relationship. Any other reference to actual people, events, business establishments or organizations is only an attempt to give the story a sense of credibility, reality or authenticity. Other names, characters, places and incidents are either a product of the author's imagination, used fictitiously, or used in admiration, humor, and respect.

Acknowledgment

Behind every successful author, there are also people whom deserve praise.

To God, from whom inspiration and greatness come, I give glory, honor and praise.

To my family, thank you for your sacrifices and unconditional love: Thomas L. Wilder, Sr., Amy Wilder, Thomas L. Wilder, Jr., his wife Mechelle and my sister Lt. Colonel Angellum Wilder, Uncle Sammy Wilder, Aunt Emma Wilder and nieces and nephews – Charas, Kendra, Thomas and Gilia.

To singer/activist, Stevie Wonder and the staff at KJLH in Los Angeles, thank you for your love and support.

To Dr. Karen Wise, thanks for your input, motivation, spirituality and always having a kind word when the going got tough. This book could not have happened without you.

To Natalia Porche and Claude Baudin, Diamond Bar California, your friendship has been priceless.

To E. J. Major, at All God's Children Day Care, Atlanta, Georgia, thanks for your encouragement and the development of generations to come.

To Dr. Sharon Jordan, your friendship and dependability is one of a kind. Much love and success.

To Oscar winner, Jamie Foxx, your friendship has been priceless.

To the "Bad Boy of Radio" Michael Baisden, thanks for the love. The African American community is grateful to you for spearheading the "Jena Six" release.

To author/lecturer, Dr. Rosie Milligan, in Los Angeles, California, thanks for the never-ending support.

To Barbara Walters and the ladies at "The View," you're the best. Thanks for making "Understanding the Games Men Play" a best seller.

To Dr. Patrice Boddie, thank you for the encouragement.

To BET, thanks for always making me feel like part of the family.

Much love to Meredith Vieira of the "Today Show."

To Ed Crisanti, Phil Freelander and Phil Mathenia, Coleman, Florida, thanks for the critique.

To Dwanda Farmer for being a friend and reading this manuscript with love when you should have been working on completing your Doctorate.

To Miss Burk, at the Medical Department, Coleman, Florida, you bring so much joy to the people you help. You are a blessing to the medical profession.

To Tavis Smiley, thank you for the love.

To V-103 Radio, thanks for your never-ending support and special thanks and much love to all the disc jockeys, radio stations, magazines and television shows around the country that made my other releases best sellers.

Much encouragement to Zarina Aurah. There is a great story inside of you waiting to be told.

A big shout out to Paulette Andwele. You are one of a kind.

Felicity Neely Deno, thanks for the positive energy and encouragement. You are a credit to the real estate profession.

And much love and a special thanks to directors, Spike Lee and Tyler Perry, actors Brad Pitt and Angelina Jolie, and all other participants committed to the rebuilding of New Orleans and the Gulf Coast. Together, we can do the impossible.

Other books by author Britten Wilder

"Getting and Keeping Your Mate Trained, Whipped, Faithful and on a Leash"
(Self-Help)

"Understanding the Games Men Play"
(Self-Help)

"Is It Love or a Big Misunderstanding"
(Self-Help)

Get your advance autographed copy of the author's upcoming release "A God-Fearing Man" (When Life, Love and the Lord Aren't Making Sense) – A Novel

Part of the proceeds will be sent to assist the victims of Hurricane Katrina.

Message from the Author

...Before you divorce, always remember there are five sides to every story, not two; a man's side, a woman's side, the in-laws side, the lawyer's side and the truth.

...I often tell single women, you are spoiled when you have a closet full of designer shoes. You are mature and ready for a mate when you trade them all for at least one pair of shoes that don't hurt your feet.

...I often tell men, your mate will have her days and her ways. When a woman marries you, she often unsuspectingly, marries three different people; the person you pretend to be, the person you really are and the B-I-T-C-H she becomes after she's been married to you.

...Young men, relationships are seriously out of order. It used to be 'Mary and Johnny sitting in a tree K-I-S-S-I-N-G. First comes love, then comes marriage. There goes Mary with a baby carriage.'
Now, it's 'Mary and Johnny sitting in a tree K-I-S-S-I-N-G. First comes love, then comes baby. There goes Johnny with another lady.'

If you're single or over 40 or 50 and not a man in sight...sometimes instead of waiting for your ship to come in, you need to row out and meet it.

...If you miss one bus, don't worry, a Mercedes is on the way. Who in their right mind wants to jump on another bus?

...Men, pay your child support. Parents, be there for your children, they are the people who will one day decide which nursing home to put you in.

Newlyweds, make sure you are on the same sheet of music. He's thinking 'Now that I have a wife I won't have to work so hard.' She's thinking, 'Thank the Lord for giving me a husband, now I can quit my job.'

...The secret of having a long-lasting relationship is to put God first, accept your differences, concentrate more on your similarities, keep the romance alive, compromise, and have open honest communication about what you both want and need.

...You cannot change your past, but couples everywhere can change their future.

Prologue

Hi, I'm Quentin Banks. It's 6:30a.m. in Atlanta, Georgia. The sun is coming up over a beautiful spring morning in the city labeled "too busy to hate."

The dogwood trees are in full bloom. As the bumble bee makes its way from petal to petal, the city looks like a Norman Rockwell painting, full of greenery and flowers, in a rainbow of colors. Or, maybe a scene out of "Gone with the Wind," capturing miles and miles of beautiful daisies, tulips, lilies, honeysuckles and dandelions. As the sun rises over the Westin Peachtree Plaza, Atlanta's tallest hotel, it changes from fiery orange to a bright yellow. Maids and butlers run around whipping their employer's homes into shape. The sound of lawn mowers and the scent of fresh cut grass fill the air. Household pets make nuisances of themselves running around barking at the lawn mowers. A Mexican immigrant and his Cuban friend talk about America electing the first African American President, Barack Obama. They gleam with pride.

"Emilio," he shouts triumphantly, "I still can't believe it. I didn't think it was possible. America finally elected an African American to be the Commander and Chief of the United States."

"*Tambien* (me too), Jose," Emilio replies.

"That goes to show you Emilio, anything in this great land of ours is possible. Before long, it will be the Latinos' time."

As the sun rises higher and higher, more homes come into view. Some look like pictures out of *Southern Living*. Spring always brings a rebirth and freshness to the city. Although you just washed your car, pollen is everywhere, taunting you with its reappearance as soon as you finish washing it away the first time.

"Achoo! Excuse me. Pollen always gets to my allergies."

Highways I-85 and I-285 are filled with the hustle and bustle of the 8 to 4 and 9 to 5 working stiffs. As the traffic moves at a snail's pace, most folks are busy trying to find alternate routes, or listening to their favorite DJ giving them the rundown on Atlanta's crazy traffic.

"Come on! Get out of the way, buddy!" I shouted. Got to get a move on, rent is due and baby needs a new pair of shoes. But, damn, why does baby's new shoes have to be so darn expensive? Have you checked out the price of gas lately; it's up and down like an old man on Viagra. I have more gas in my stomach after a good Mexican meal than in my automobile's tank. Let me check out the radio and see what the new day will bring."

"Good Morning Atlanta!" the DJ shouted. "It's going to be a beautiful day in the A-T-L. Brace yourselves for another pollen filled day folks. For all you commuters on your way to work, traffic is at a standstill. So you had better call your boss, because you're going to be late, late, late."

"Tell me something I don't already know," I mumbled.

The working stiff and the unemployed are oblivious to Georgia's bluebloods; the rich, powerful and privileged. And get this, in Buckhead, baby rides around in a new Mercedes convertible. So, why in the hell does he need new shoes? He damn sure isn't walking or catching M.A.R.T.A. (the city bus).

Buckhead is the ritzy part of Atlanta. Even though the sun shines bright in the good, old A-T-L, it always seems to shine a little brighter in the 30305 zip code and it goes nova in the most desired area of West Paces Ferry. You can say it's our own little Beverly Hills with its own dirty secrets, star studded cast, issues, therapists and plastic surgeons. Its residents include the Governor of Georgia, entertainers, athletes, communication moguls, politicians and a host of uptown doctors and high-powered lawyers. Oh, I almost forgot, even Rap artists have that exclusive zip code attached to their diamond-studded, gold-plated grills, sagging pants and bling bling. Oh well, there goes the neighborhood. That damned "Affirmative Action!" The next thing you know, we'll be having pedigree dogfights. Atlanta is split on the recent election, but the city holds a strong republican loyalty.

On any given morning the country club, tennis courts, shopping malls and therapist couches are filled with bored, unfulfilled and overweight housewives. "Let's see, the country is in recession and your biggest problem is your husband is only a millionaire. Your mansion is fabulous; you have around-the-clock servants, now you complain your husband doesn't spend enough time with you. Your life has no meaning and you are unfulfilled. Very interesting!"

"Talk to some of Georgia's homeless and unemployed? That will be $1000, and I will see you next week." Boohoo, you poor thing! I had the same sentiment for hotel heiress Paris Hilton, when she tried to dodge spending 45 days in jail. Oh yes, that was a great day in American history. Yeah, the justice system works.

Buckhead residents enjoy the best of the best; shopping malls, restaurants, schools...the list goes on. Every day, luxury automobiles are parked outside the glitzy, highlife and trendy spots. If you're up and coming, it's most definitely the place to be seen. If you are new money, old money, or a baller, this zip code is a must. If you are a baller on a budget, visit this place on the weekend or come back when your money grows up because Phipps Plaza or Lenox Mall does not offer a lay-away plan. Or you can just fake it, until you make it.

But when the sun goes down, the mask comes off. Respectable couples stop playing musical beds and the doors and gates of Buckhead's "Who's Who" are opened. You'll discover the making of any good soap opera and keep the church house packed.

Okay, okay, I'll stop hating. Who am I kidding! A while back my wildest dream was to rub elbows with that exclusive and elusive bunch. And when opportunity knocked, I dove in headfirst. But as the sayings goes, "be careful what you wish for, you just might get it" and "all that glitters is not gold."

Now, just sit back, relax and let me tell you how a one time, down and out, unemployed writer and his friends, Assistant Pastor Donald Reynolds, Jeff Montgomery, Antonio Fernando, and Peter McCallister became members of Buckhead's rich and famous and in the process how we all became "Desperate Husbands."

$$1$$

One Year Earlier

QUENTIN

"Stop it Tyra! Leave my pants alone! You don't know me like that! Beyoncé and I are still married!" As I continued to push Tyra Banks off me, she pawed and pleaded.

"Come on Quentin. Why am I the last girl to get a piece of you?"

I finally gave in. Just when she tosses her Victoria Secret panties out the window, a loud buzz sounds.

BUZZZZZZ....BUZZZZZZ! A look of fear and horror comes over her face.

"What's that?" I ask trembling.

"My man!" She looks at the door.

"YOUR WHAT?" I scream, scrambling to straighten my clothes, "I thought you were single!"

The loud buzzing forced my eyes open. I was dreaming. Her clutching thighs were the sheets wrapped around my waist.

"Damn, DAMN,!" I yelled in frustration. I sat up, attempting to untangle myself from the embrace of the stupid sheets.

"Let go of me! NOW!" I am pathetic. I'm arguing with my sheets. I fell back against my pillows in abject surrender and grabbed the fricking alarm clock by the throat. I returned to my own tired, demented, little world. I thought to myself lying there, "Man, why can't my fiancée, Bridgett, be like the women I dream about?" I contemplate the injustices of the universe, but the practical part of my mind insists I'm probably not the type of guy Bridgett dreams about either. I mentally give my practical side a swift kick.

I lay there, drifting off, hoping Tyra would return. The buzzer sounded again. I gave the clock a good hard whack. "Buzz that!" I said with satisfaction. I focused on the clock face. The digits 10:30 stared back at me. Damn, I just laid down!

I pull myself out of bed, wrestling some more with the sheets. The sexually frustrated sheet made one last grab at me as I got off the bed, tangling with my foot and almost tripping me. I tamed the thing by kicking it away and cracking my toes on the bed frame.

"Ouch!" I shrieked as I hopped around clutching my foot. I flopped down on the bed and was rewarded by the insane cackling of the local radio station.

"Hi, this is Frank Ski," the DJ said.

"And this is Wanda Smith," the other DJ echoed. I glared at the radio.

"You're listening to Frank and Wanda in the Morning!" they said in unison.

"Our topic for today is 'Sex and Scandal in the Pulpit.' You may remember not too long ago, one of our most respected and trusted DeKalb County clergy, Earl Paulk, was caught with his pants down," Frank said. "While so many are under investigation because of their lavish lifestyle, others are creating controversy, like President Obama's former minister, Reverend Wright."

"Since then, the phones haven't stopped ringing," Wanda highlighted. "Women across the country are wondering whether they can trust their ministers any more..."

"What's the world coming to?" I said sarcastically as I sat staring at the radio. I began searching for something heavy to kill the radio with. I just wanted it out of my misery.

I half listened to Frank and Wanda banter back and forth for a few minutes as I commiserated with my throbbing toe. I reached over and flipped off the radio.

"Oh boy," I muttered under my breath, "Everybody knows how to make headlines, except me."

I looked around my tiny apartment. Dirty dishes were piled in the sink and clothes were scattered on the floor. The bed was unmade. Okay, I was sitting on the bed. But it wasn't made when I got home and it won't be made when I leave. Wadded piles of typing paper surrounded the trashcan. But, at least, the trashcan was empty. The kitchen table was filled to overflowing with open mail. It would be welcome if it were from adoring fans, praising my writing. But they all said the same thing, Past Due-Collections-Delinquent-Very Delinquent. There was even a couple of letters offering condolences on my deceased state.

MTV Cribs will never set foot in this place. Instead of looking like something out of *Better Homes and Gardens*, the place looked like the Air

Force had used it as a bombing range in preparation for Desert Storm. As I looked around, I sighed and thought about getting a maid. Then the masochist side of my brain reminded me that the only maid who would set foot in this disaster area was my mother. But, I haven't paid her lately.

In anticipation of a New York publisher buying my latest manuscript, a burst of energy coursed through my body. I looked down to see if I was standing on a naked electrical wire. Just checking.

TODAY IS THE DAY! I can feel it in my bones. Today those stuffy, New York publishers and the whole world are going to realize my greatness! THEY WILL REALIZE I'M THE NEXT JOHN GRISHAM!

I've been turned down by 22 different publishers. But that is all in the past and I'm not going to let it get me down. THAT WAS THEN...THIS IS NOW! Even a blind squirrel is guaranteed to get at least one nut. Okay, don't examine the metaphor too closely. Just go with it.

I peeked between the folds of the curtain. Where is that stupid mailman? Why does he have to pick today of all days to be late?

"Nooooo..." I said aloud. "Don't do this to me!"

I looked at the clock. It was 10:35a.m.. He always comes by 10:00a.m.. Lazy, good for nothing civil servant. No, wait. Wait just a minute. I see someone walking up the sidewalk. I see a blue hat. I see a blue uniform. It looks like...YES! It looks like the mailman!

"OH YEAH, MY MAN, THE MAILMAN!" I shouted. I threw open the living room curtains, then pulled them closed as I remembered that I wasn't wearing anything.

"BRING DADDY THE GOOD NEWS!"

I jumped over the coffee table in the best "Track and Field" style and frantically looked for something to put on.

"AHA!" I exclaimed as I grabbed the robe from under the kitchen table. The doorbell rang. I hesitated a moment as I put the robe on, wondering how it ended up under the table. Never mind! I MUST RECEIVE MY DESTINY! I walked to the door and started to grab the knob to throw open the door to my much deserved fame.

The man on the other side of the door began banging on the door. I hesitated. I've heard of opportunity knocking, but this was a little ridiculous.

"QUENTIN BANKS, I KNOW YOU'RE IN THERE!" the voice yelled. I jumped back. Wrong uniform. Not the mailman. It was the sheriff, who also happens to be my big, strong and mean landlord.

"Oh crap," I thought and searched for a place to hide. I backed from the door as if it were a nest of cobras. He pounded on the door again.

"OPEN THIS DOOR," he yelled. Yeah, like I'm going to do that. I jumped behind the couch.

"YOU HAVE UNTIL NEXT FRIDAY TO PAY THE RENT! IF NOT, YOU'RE OUT OF HERE!"

He banged on the door a few more times for effect, then turned and walked away.

I cowered for a few minutes, waiting for the walls to stop vibrating. I eased out from behind the couch and peeked out the window. He was driving away.

How long could I keep this up? If I don't get the rent by Friday I will look like Beetle Bailey after the Sarge gets through with him. I've gone from the heights of ecstasy to the depths of despair.

First, I quit my six-figure job. Stupid. Then I give up my comfortable house to suffer for my art. Stupid. Now I'm about to get evicted and really, really suffer for my art. Stupid.

Just because I live in Atlanta's 30305 zip code, one should by no means think I'm rich. I'm the poorest guy on West Paces Ferry Road.

Sometimes I think the only reason I'm able to live here is because of affirmative action. Not that "Affirmative Action." Politicians, entertainers and sports figures live within a stone's throw. Either they took a vote one day, or they all took a bunch of hits off the same marijuana joint and voted to let a poor guy into their exalted ranks.

Peter McCallister is my girlfriend's godfather. I needed a place to stay. Peter knows Mr. Jenkins, a/k/a Sheriff Jenkins, a/k/a Big Foot. He owns this apartment and owed Peter a favor. He rented me this small apartment in his basement.

Someday, I hope to be able to afford my own house in the 30305 zip code, and rub elbows with Atlanta's rich and powerful elite. But for now, I'll have to continue to rent here providing Big Foot doesn't dropkick me out next Friday.

I look at the clock on the wall. 11:00a.m. What's keeping that stupid mailman? I decided I might as well relax. He'll get here when he gets here. I sat down on the couch. I thought I heard someone walking across the sidewalk. I jumped up and peeked through the curtains. It was the neighbor's big ass dog. I tried to get a handle on my nerves. I'd take up smoking to calm down, but I'd probably burn the house down with the first cigarette.

I went into the kitchen, opened the refrigerator, took out a carton of orange juice and took a deep drink. No glass for me, straight from the carton. I only punk out and use a glass when Bridgett's around. She doesn't get mad; she just gets this disappointed look on her face, and then withholds sex. She's really great about that. If all the women in the world withheld sex from their husbands and boyfriends for about a week, peace would break out everywhere

By the way, I leave the toilet seat up. I figure she can put it down just as easily as I can. I don't know why women make such a big deal out of it anyway. Maybe it's Freudian. I don't know. Maybe women just have a bad case of penis envy.

Don't mention that to Bridgett, okay.

I took a few more sips and the doorbell rang. I choked and spilled the orange juice all down my chin and on my robe...Damn!!! The sheriff is back...RUN FORREST RUN. He's coming to get you. I dove behind the couch. The doorbell rang again and my heart started to pound. I'm going to jail! I'm going to be somebody's bitch!

The caller knocked on the door.

"Quentin Banks, it's Stan, the mailman. Open the door. I know you are in there. I saw your broke down hooptie outside."

I silently rejoiced. "The mailman!" Well, let the man in. WAIT, suppose it's not Stan. Suppose it's a set up. Suppose it's the sheriff disguised as the mailman. I crawled over to the window and looked out. I saw Stan's mail truck parked outside.

"Yeah boy!" I screamed. "It's the real McCoy."

I rubbed my hands together. This is it, the moment of truth. Fame and fortune are waiting for me at the door. I'm so broke I can't even pay attention. Still cautious, I peeped through the peephole. Blue uniform, blue hat, no gun, or handcuffs. NOPE! It's not the cops. Let me open the door.

I quickly unchained the door threw it wide open. The sun was shining and the spring flowers threw color everywhere. Stan the mailman was standing right in front of me, smiling broadly.

"Hello, Stan! Isn't it a beautiful morning?"

He laughed. "It's okay Quentin." He looked in his bag and gave me a big smile. He pulled out a huge stack of mail. He began to tease me. "You have a lot of mail. Most of it's from New York publishers." He started to turn them over to me one by one.

"I think I have a letter from Oprah Winfrey and Jay Leno."

"For real?" I said excitedly. "Give it here, give it here." As he fumbled around in his bag, my eyes bulged. He pulled out a yellow envelope.

"Oprah Winfrey!" I said excitedly, snatching the mail from his hands. "Hell no! Bam, it's from the gas company. Pay up or get turned off!" He laughed hysterically.

"Ha, ha, everybody's got jokes," I said snidely.

"Laugh now, Stan. He who laughs last, laughs the loudest...When I'm rich and famous, I'm going to take my first check and buy you a personality, some class, and some lotion for your dry ashy legs."

I slammed the door in his face. I took the stack of mail and sat down at the kitchen table.

Let's see what we have, bill, bill, bill, bill... Okay here we go, Simon and Schuster, Random House and Harper Collins. Just think; if a New York publisher picked me up, Bridgett and I would be on our way. I will buy her one of those Kobe Bryant diamonds. You know the one he bought his wife when he got caught up in the Colorado love scandal.

Afterwards, we will have one of those lavish Star Jones-Reynolds weddings.

After my book comes out, Oprah will be dying to talk to me. I'll be able to tell her to have her people get with my people. When I finally get there, I will show my ass like Terry McMillan. You know how she acted when she found out her 21-year old stud was gay. Or maybe I'll jump up on her couch and act a fool. I mean, like Tom Cruise. I'll scream at the top of my voice…"I LOVE YOU BRIDGETT!"

Okay Quentin, back to business. Don't count your chickens before they hatch. Open the letters. Let's see what Random House has to say…

Dear Mr. Banks,

We have received your manuscript "Confessions of a Married Man." Your manuscript shows promise, but after careful consideration, we cannot offer you a publishing deal.

Please keep us in mind for your next submission.

Sincerely,

Submissions

Ah, man, what a downer. I took a deep breath. Okay, Quentin, don't get bent out of shape. Keep your chin up. Don't get discouraged. Let's see what Simon and Schuster have to say…

Dear Mr. Banks,

Thank you for your submission, "Confessions of a Married Man." Although it's informative, we don't feel its right for us.

Take a few more writing classes and try us again in a year.

Sincerely,

Submissions

Okay, no big deal. One man's trash is another man's treasure. Let's see what Harper Collins has to say...

Dear Mr. Banks,

Don't quit your day job. Don't call us - we'll call you.

Sincerely,

Submissions

Ah, man, that's cold. I didn't want them to publish my book anyway. I opened the remaining letters. They basically said the same thing. I stink as a writer.

I've officially set a record. I have now been rejected 30 times. Maybe I should get my own reality TV show. I can call it *How Not to Get Published.* I took a deep breath, let out a big sigh and started to pace the floor.

That's it...QUIT! You must have a stopping sense. "For richer or poorer" is something people say in their wedding vows. But very few people really mean it. And very few people think it could happen. Why should I bring Bridgett to ruin with my pipe dream? She deserves something better. She deserves the finer things in life. Why should she hang in there with me? Why should she be the best-dressed woman in the homeless shelter?

Although she's pressing me for a commitment, reality hasn't hit her. If we get married now, we can take turns holding up signs on the freeway. There are exit ramps all over Atlanta. She can take the morning shift, and I'll take the evening shift. Her sign will say:

"WE THOUGHT LOVE WAS ENOUGH
NOW WE WORK FOR FOOD"

My sign will say:

"WHY LIE, I NEED A BEER"

"Man, what was I thinking?" I mumbled. I had a nice cushy job once upon a time. I worked at a prestigious investment firm. I had respect, admiration. I was their number one broker. I had all the VIP clients...the Falcons...the Braves...and the local entertainers.

But, I wasn't satisfied with it. I guess I was tired of eating three hot, nutritious meals a day. I guess I was tired of paying my bills on time. I guess I was tired of driving a new black BMW 850 convertible.

My other self must have said, "Quentin, why don't you ride the bus? Quentin, you are putting on weight, but quit the gym. Running from bill collectors will help you lose the weight."

Life was too perfect, so what can I do to screw it up, because I have no right to be happy. Why should Bridgett and I get along so well? Why should I have the perfect woman, the perfect relationship? I shook my head...stupid, stupid, stupid.

Man, I thought I had talent, skill. I was going places. I thought I was going to be the next John Grisham or Stephen King.

The experts say the number one thing couples fight about is money. Now I'm a believer. When I first quit my job, Bridgett was very supportive. She encouraged me to follow my dream. "Follow your heart," she said, "love is enough. Love will keep us together. I got you babe. It's, you and me against the world." But, the moment she got closer to 30, the marriage and maternal bug bit her. She flipped the script. Now she's my probation officer.

"Where have you been?"

"Did you look for a job today?"

"Did you pay the bills?"

"How many resumes did you send out today?"

"What's your five year plan?"

"Do we have a future together?"

"Am I wasting my time with you?"

Well, she's right. I'm going to the soup line. I wonder if the volunteers are feeding the hungry tonight.

Every bill in the house is past due; electric, phone and cable. I told Bridgett I would take care of them. She is going to flip when she finds out I haven't paid any of them in three months. I've been calling everyone, making payment arrangements

Look at this tiny apartment. It's a mess. I don't know what to say about a man who can't keep an apartment the size of a horse stall neat. I'd better clean up before Bridgett gets here. She's so anal-retentive. Everything must be neat and in its place, perfectly aligned. I'm double knit, she's Prada. I'm Yin, she's Yang. I paced the floor.

Face it Quentin, you might as well forget about being an author. There is nothing sexy about a broke man. Like the man said, "don't quit your day job." Maybe I can get my old job back. Go ahead Quentin, swallow your pride. Pride and ego don't pay the bills.

I walked over to the telephone and slowly punched in Mr. Gill's number. My finger stiffened with each number I pressed. The call connected and I gritted my teeth. I can't do this. I can't go crawling back. I was so happy when I threw my resignation letter on his desk. All those other working stiffs were so envious. Quentin Banks was the man! He was getting out of the rat race. He was going to control his own destiny. Even the female executives looked at me with admiration. I couldn't do it. Before I could react, a voice came over the phone. I did the only thing I could do...I hung up.

Within seconds the phone rang. Caller ID showed Gill's number. Damn, he hit redial. I picked up the receiver.

"Quentin Banks, did you just call me?"

"Oh yeah," I said, trying to play it off. "I was just going through the many letters from New York publishers and thought of you. Man, I can't believe what they are saying," I said pretentiously.

"Has Oprah called you yet?"

"No, not yet," I replied, "I've been so busy I haven't checked my messages. Mr. Gill, speaking of jobs, what's going on with my old job?" I tried to slide this in casually. "I was your number one broker. I was a real tiger. My sales figures were hard to beat..." I chuckled, trying to sound off-handed.

"Well, Quentin, I thought I wouldn't be able to replace you, but it's funny, the same day you quit I had twelve more hungry tigers standing in line. Think about it Quentin, I hired two additional brokers for what I was paying you! My boss was so pleased he gave me a fat bonus and a raise. My team is doing great!"

I was deflated. I let out a sigh and said, "That's great. Every company needs some new blood."

"You are right," he interrupted. "In fact, they both have surpassed your numbers. They are real go-getters. They are how you used to be before you got bit by the book-writing bug. An author..." He teased. He was not going to let me have the last word.

I regrouped. "Man, that's great. I'm happy you found someone. I just called to make sure I didn't leave you shorthanded. You weren't just my boss, you were my friend."

"Oh no, Quentin. I have other lions on the chain. If those two don't work out, I have ten more waiting anxiously in line," he replied confidently.

"That's a load off my mind. If you need me, just call. Hey, man, I've got to go," I said scraping my ego off the floor. "I just got a call on the other line. It's probably my agent. Fame and fortune await me."

I hung up the telephone...damn. I could hear the sarcasm in his voice. I bet he can't wait to spread the news. Quentin Banks called me begging for his old job back. Quentin Banks made a mistake. Quentin Banks is on skid row.

I gritted my teeth. I clenched my fists. Someday! Somehow! The world will know my name!

I spent all morning trying to come up with something fresh and exciting. But unfortunately, I had no luck. Hoping to take my mind off things, I called Peter McCallister.

Peter is one of Georgia's richest developers. His fortune is estimated to be about 700 million dollars. He was in his mid-fifties, Caucasian, very distinguished, suntanned, with a full head of hair with touches of gray in his sideburns. He reminded me of the movie idol, George Clooney. Just like Clooney, the older he got, the better looking he got. Peter is always impeccably dressed. Italian suits, French cuffs, monogrammed shirts oozing wealth, class and charm. But, in spite of his megawatt smile, his southern politician charm and professing to be a liberal, we watched closely, secretly believing him to be a sexist and a closet racist.

If you wanted to get something done, Peter was the man to know. He has contacts around the world. If he likes you, the world is your oyster. But if you got on his bad side, you needed to watch your back. Of course, everyone wanted to know Peter. Everybody wanted to be in Peter's circle. For me, being around Peter was both good and bad. It was good because I had a goal to be more like him. It was bad because he only reminded me of how poor I was. He gave Bridgett gifts that I couldn't even afford to pronounce. Just by knowing him there were privileges. So, everybody went out of his or her way to keep him happy.

The telephone rang forever. Finally Peter picked it up.

"Hello." Peter said.

"Hey Peter," I said in a depressed voice.

"Hi Quentin," he replied in his deep southern drawl. "How is it going?"

"Not so good." Before I could say another word he interrupted.

"Hey, Big Guy, let me call you back in a minute. My secretary is gone and the phones are ringing off the hook."

"Okay Peter, but I really need to talk to you."

"Hold your horses, Big Guy. I'll buzz you back shortly."

PETER

"I'm going to be late," I shouted to no one in particular. "I have to get a move on!"

As the telephone continued to ring, I dashed out of my posh Buckhead office and jumped into my new $400K Rolls Royce, drop-head coupe convertible.

I checked the messages on my cell and there are twenty-one fucking messages from my wife, Jan.

"Man why did I ever get married? What was I thinking? What was I smoking? Was I drugged?"

I put the phone on speaker and listened to the messages:

Message #1: "Peter, I saw a new red 500 SL Mercedes at RBM and it has my name written all over it. I'VE GOT TO HAVE IT! Please call."

Message #2: "I want to go shopping, please call...I need to raise the limit on my credit card to $100,000.00."

"$100,000.00." I thought out loud, "What is she buying, a politician?"

Message #3: "The boys need money to pay their rent...please call."

Message #4: Britten Wilder's play, "A God-fearing Man" is at the Fox Theater. Everybody is talking about it! It's a must see! Don't forget that tomorrow night is the party for your friend, Antonio and his wife Liana. It starts at 8:00 p.m. You need to be home by five. Does your tux need cleaning?"

I keyed off the phone. All the rest of the messages would be the same...something she wants...something she wanted me to do...or something I forgot to do. Is this it? Is this as good as it's going to get? What do men get out of marriage? Oh, I almost forgot, we get sex; but only if she's in the mood.

Then when she is in the mood, you better perform on cue. Perform for hours and be a contortionist. Now days, they want you to be the acrobatic man. Just think, once I was single, broke and happy. Now I'm married, rich and unhappy. Why couldn't I just settle for single?

But, I believed the myths. You probably know them. That bullshit you hear everyday from Dr. Phil. You have a better chance of being successful if you're married; you live longer; marriage is so fulfilling. Bullshit. Whoever is doing the PR for "Love, Marriage and Relationships" is doing a damn good job. Men everywhere are falling for it hook, line and sinker. Trust me, don't believe the hype.

I once overheard a little girl and boy talking in the park about divorce. The little boy was asking what a divorce was and the little girl told him that a divorce was when the mommy wasn't happy and the daddy was the last to know and then they moved to different houses and the mommy told everyone what a bastard the daddy was. When the boy offered the little girl candy, she took it and told him that knowledge wasn't cheap.

Well that's for damn sure. It took me thirty-two years of marriage to learn my lesson. First, you voluntarily give the woman your candy, then the judge gives her the shirt off your back. Well, no use whining about it now, I'm stuck. I didn't have a pre-nuptial agreement. So like the song says, "it's cheaper to keep her". I started the car and pushed the convertible button to let the top down. I put the car in drive and soon hit Georgia 400, on my way to the club.

When you hear "The Club," you probably think of a ritzy country club in some posh part of the city. But "The Club" is a code word for a strip club. The fellows and I came up with the code just in case our mates were present.

To keep our little charade going, we would even keep a set of golf clubs in the trunk of our cars for a prop. We've been doing it for years and our mates have never suspected a thing. It is the only place we can get any peace. It is a place where a man can truly wear the pants. But, once we return home, we may be wearing the pants, but our wives will tell us which pair to wear. As I made my way to the freeway, I stopped at the GA 400 toll bridge. Looking in my console, I found fifty cents and threw it in the tray.

"Thank you, Mr. McCallister, have a nice evening," the attendant said.

"Thank you, Darlin'," I replied as I mashed on the gas pedal.

I am stuck in rush hour traffic before I got 100 yards down the road. Where in the hell are all these people going? Not so long ago, Atlanta was an up and coming city and everybody and their brother wanted to move here. Real estate prices once soared through the roof. Now the country is in a recession and prices have dropped like a rock, but the highways are still one big parking lot. I thought about real estate being the very reason I am rich. So what am I complaining about? Just buy up all the foreclosed property you can find and wait for the market to change again.

The cell rang and I took a quick glance at the caller; damn, Jan again. With a devilish grin, I finally answered the call.

"Hello Jan."

"Hello, Peter. What took so long for you to answer?"

"I was talking with a client." I knew I was lying but it keeps peace in the household.

"Peter, you always put everyone else before me," Jan whined.

"I'm sorry Darling. What was I thinking?"

"I don't know, Peter, but you are becoming so selfish."

I rolled my eyes.

Jan continued to whine. "I've been trying to call you all day. Didn't you get my messages?"

"I got them, I just haven't had time to return your calls."

"The main reason I called was to remind you of Antonio Fernando's party. All of our friends are coming. We want to make a good impression. Did you tell Antonio's wife to speak English? When she speaks Spanish, she speaks too fast. I can't understand a word she says. This is America, not Saturday night in Tijuana." She attempted to poke fun.

"Oh, that was a good one Jan." I said sarcastically.

Ignoring me she continued, "Peter, today I was passing by RBM Mercedes and I saw the new 500 SL convertible. I must have one! This time can you make sure you get the color right? I want red. What good is it to have a new Benz if the color clashes with your clothes? As my therapist says, and I certainly agree, "a gift is not a gift unless it's well received." I told the salesman you'd be there Saturday with a check. It's a steal at $125,000.00."

"I'll make sure you get it, Dear."

I sighed heavily and listened to Jan run on and on about nothing.

"Peter, that Ashley Reynolds is such a bore. She called me this morning bragging about the new mink coat Donald bought for her. If I weren't such a sweet person, I would call PETA right now and turn her in. In fact, just between you and me, I was one of the people who dropped a dime on Falcon quarterback, Michael Vick a while back concerning that illegal dog fighting."

"Jan, you didn't," I said.

"Oh, yes I did. I even got rid of those Freaknickers. I threatened the Mayor that Buckhead would secede from Atlanta if those college spring breakers, with their sagging pants, didn't leave Buckhead. If we aren't careful, we will have an epidemic of illegal dog fighting and drive-by shootings in Buckhead. Keep it in the hood and the woods where it belongs. Well, anyway, enough of that. Back to that Ashley Reynolds. She really thinks she's the shit since Donald bought her that mink coat and that Harry Winston diamond ring. The stone is flawless. It almost out blings mine. How can they afford it? Her husband is only the assistant pastor at Holy Faith Church. You see what happens when President Obama tries to redistribute the wealth? Those damn Democrats. After a while you won't be able to tell the "real money" from Joe, the damn plumber..."

I couldn't Jan's voice in my ear anymore. It all became a repetitive buzz in my ear, so I made up an excuse to hang up. How can anyone talk so much without taking a breath?

"Jan, I've got another call, got to go!"

"Okay Peter, make that money. Will you be home for dinner? Maria is planning on whipping up your favorite."

"Ah, Sweetheart, I'm sorry, I've got to meet some VIP's at the club tonight. I'm sure I will be getting home late."

"All right then, that'll work." Jan responded. "I was on my way to Adrian's Beauty Salon. My hair is a mess. I have a hat on. I hope nobody recognizes me. I'm supposed to pick up the girls. Darling, do you think I need a new hair style?"

"No Jan, your hair is fine."

"Do you think I need liposuction?"

"No Jan. You don't need liposuction."

"What about a tummy tuck?"

"No."

"What about Botox or a facelift?"

"No, you don't need those either."

"When you come home tonight, do you want me to dress up like Cat Woman and screw your brains out?"

"No Jan. That won't be necessary." I imagined my very overweight wife in a Cat Woman outfit and couldn't help but cringe.

"What about I pretend to be a stripper and do the Booty Clap. I have a lot of junk in my trunk."

That was for sure. I yawned, uninterested. "No Jan. No, that won't be necessary."

"Peter!" She screamed into my ear. "You aren't paying attention to me!"

"Yes I am, honey. You are always the first thing on my mind."

"Are you happy Peter?"

"I'm very happy Jan. Why do you ask?"

"Every since I started going through menopause, I've been very insecure about our marriage. My mood swings are like a roller coaster ride. One minute my body is fine, the next, I'm the queen bitch. Thanks for being so patient with me. You are so sweet. I don't see how you put up with me."

"Don't worry Jan, it will soon pass. Hot flashes are part of being a woman. Well, I've got to go Jan. Don't wait up for me." I hung up the phone.

Oh, God, I don't know how much more I can take of that woman. She was moody and selfish even before menopause. Calm down, I told myself, you're not off the clock yet. I have money to make and people to see. Like Jan's therapist says, "go to a happy place." I am going to a happy place~the strip club.

The traffic finally started to move. I tried to make up the time. I quickly increased my speed, hoping I wouldn't get a ticket. I set the cruise control at 75 mph and remembered that I hadn't called Quentin back. Let me give that wannabe John Grisham a call right now. I wanted to know how his writing gig was going. I quickly punched in his number. A sad voice answered the phone on the fifth ring.

"Hello, hello...Is this Quentin Banks?"

"Yes, this is Quentin," the sad voice replied.

"Is this Quentin Banks, the famous author?" I asked trying to cheer him up.

"Famous! Definitely not!" He answered in disgust. "This is Quentin Banks the broke, busted and disgusted writer."

"Stop being so modest. I know you're the next New York Times best-selling author."

"I don't know about that. Today makes a total of 30 publishers that have turned me down. I might as well face it. I suck as a writer. Things are spinning out of control. The bills are due, Bridgett is pressing me for marriage, her birthday is coming up and she's anxious to start a family. Peter, I'm really down in the dumps. I feel worthless. I can barely support myself. How can I support a wife and family?"

"Okay, big guy, things are going to get better. You're not going to keep striking out. You're just in a slump. Keep swinging and you are bound to hit a home run."

"I don't know Peter. Poverty is as low as you go. Maybe I'm destined to be in the minor leagues. I might as well throw in the towel."

"I won't hear of such a thing Quentin."

"Peter, I became so depressed today that I broke down and called my old boss."

"What happened?"

"Mr. Gill took great joy in telling me that twelve people lined up for my job when I left. He said he was able to hire two people with the salary he was paying me. Can you believe that? Those backstabbing trainees."

"Quentin, everybody wants their shot at the American Dream. Don't take it personally. It is just business."

"Man, I made a career booboo. What was I thinking? I should have left well enough alone. Sometimes you need to know when to quit."

A brief silence passed between us. "Are you still there, big guy?"

"Yes, Peter. I haven't gone anywhere. I was just wondering if Calvin at McDonald's is hiring. I can whip up some mean pancakes. 'Hi, my name is Quentin. Welcome to McDonalds. Would you like some fries with that shake? What! Blah...blah...blah! Can you understand the words that are coming out of my mouth?'"

I snickered in amusement, "Sir is that with or without cheese?"

"With my luck Peter, I'd probably write down the wrong order and Calvin would end up firing me. He would write me this great recommendation and tell me to go work for Wendy's."

"Cheer up big guy. It's not that bad. I tell you what, Quentin, I have some friends in the right places. Let me give them a call. I'm sure they can hook you up."

"I appreciate the offer Peter. I know Bridgett is your goddaughter, but I want to make it on my own. I'm so disgusted. Just think Peter, I let a six-figure job with benefits go down the drain for this. Man, I put 'starving' in the phrase 'starving artist'. To add insult to injury, I was on I-285 and I noticed a wrecker following me. Everywhere I went he was there. When I switched lanes, so did he. Tired and frustrated, I pulled over. I got out of my car and walked back to him and asked him why the hell he was following me. You know what he said Peter?"

"What Quentin?"

"He said, 'I'm sorry sir, I mean no disrespect. Your car is so old I knew it was only a matter of time before it broke down. Thought you might need a tow. My wife just had a baby, so I wanted to get a jump on the competition.'"

"No, he didn't Quentin." I roared.

"Yes, he did. Peter, I'm a desperate man."

"Well Quentin, hold your breath and hold your head up high. It's Peter to the rescue. The reason I'm calling is because the fellows and I are meeting at the club. We would like to invite you out. We want to cheer you up."

"I don't know Peter. I don't know whether I would be good company after today. I'm really depressed."

As Quentin and I went back and forth, I finally broke him down.

"Okay Peter, maybe a few beers and a little fun won't be too bad. See you at eight."

DONALD

I sat at my desk writing my Sunday sermon. Writing? Okay, I was trying to write my Sunday sermon. The only thought running through my mind was how I managed to get to this point in my life. Married to a woman I thought, a long time ago, that I loved, living in a huge, expensive house I can't afford and hating the direction my life has taken. How did I get here?

My serenity was interrupted when the love of my life and the source of my problems intruded on my solitude. Unfortunately, or maybe fortunately, both entities occupied the same body.

"Donald," Ashley whined, "Why can't I live like the other Buckhead wives? I feel so embarrassed when the girls start bragging about their extravagant lifestyles. All the girls flew first class to the inauguration and I had to fly coach. Michelle was dressed to kill in a designer gown by Isabella Toledo and Jason Wu and I had to wear my old Chanel suit. There were three other women there in the same suit."

She stuck her left hand out at me and continued, "look at this wedding ring. I can barely see the stone. I often ask myself if I married the right man."

She gave me one of her patented disdainful looks. "Oh, I can't stand it. Michelle Obama is so lucky. She married a president!"

At that moment I lost it, but spoke as patiently as I could. "What do you expect from me? I'm an assistant pastor at Holy Faith Church. I don't make a lot of money. I just bought you a mink coat and a diamond ring. Wear that instead of your engagement ring if you want. We're over extended right now. Every penny I make or borrow is spent trying to make you happy. What might be left over goes to keeping this Buckhead monstrosity up."

A loud sigh filled the room. "And your point is…" she whined. "You're the man. You need to figure something out. A pastor's wife should look prosperous." She sounded as if she were trying to explain something to a five year old.

I shook my head in resignation. Same battle—different day.

"I need to go," I said cutting off anything else she might have to babble about. "This conversation is going nowhere!"

I grabbed my briefcase and started out of the house.

"Where are you going?" She yelled at my retreating back.

"I'm going to meet a member of the congregation. I really need to lay hands on her." I replied over my shoulder without stopping. "We'll talk later."

I slammed the door, cutting off any reply. I got into the car and angrily hit the steering wheel with my fist.

"Damn," I exclaimed flinging my hand back and forth to take the sting out of it, "Lord give me strength."

I picked up the cell and scrolled through the list of names until "Angie" flashed up. As I hit the send button, I looked at the clock on the dashboard. It said 8:46a.m. I hoped it wasn't too early. After several rings, a sleepy voice answered the phone.

"Hello?" she asked. She didn't sound like she was altogether sure who she was.

"Angie, this is Pastor Reynolds. I didn't mean to call on your day off, but something's come up and I need your expertise."

"That's okay. What can I do for you?" She sounded more awake now.

"I need you to meet me at the Westin at 10:00. We have some very important business that has to be attended to right away," I said.

"Okay," she answered, "I'm always happy to lend you a hand. I'll be there."

I arrived at the Westin and checked in. I went to the suite and settled in. I thought to myself that wives were so ungrateful. That explains why so many husbands are unfaithful. When a man cheats on his wife, you can be assured the woman he's with is the opposite of his mate.

The suite's door opened slowly. All thoughts of my wife and her morality disappeared when Angie walked into the room carrying a small suitcase. Angie was definitely easy on the eyes. At 5'7" and 28-years old, she was beautiful. She had an hourglass figure on which even jeans and a demure blouse looked sexy. She had beautifully expressive, soulful brown eyes and full, beautiful, almost pouty lips. Her complexion was tanned and not blemished by anything so rude as a tan line. Angie's hair was long, fine and molded itself to her body hanging all the way to her butt.

And that small, tight butt was to die for. Her breasts were high and tight with nipples that showed through the material of her blouse, telling everyone that, though she was a good church-going woman, she didn't feel her breasts should be contained by anything as vulgar as a bra. The jeans she was wearing hugged her body like a second skin.

Angie's lovemaking skills were from another planet. It was out of this world. When I was with her, I was no longer ordinary. I WAS LEGENDARY! This beautiful woman should wear a red cape and have a giant "S" between her lovely breasts. With her I was like a Man of Steel! Hard! Indestructible!

We came into each other's arms and squeezed each other tightly. Moans filled our luxurious Westin suite. We were on the fiftieth floor, high in the sky. I had pulled the curtains back so all the world could see us. The spring sunshine turned Atlanta golden.

I was cheating on my wife, and DAMN, IT FELT GOOD! We kissed, our tongues flickering in each other's mouth. I slid my hands down her smooth back then up under her blouse. Her skin was so soft and she felt like she was on fire! She was mine and I loved every bit of her!

I couldn't wait another minute to see all of her. I began kissing her and moving my hands to the front of her blouse, releasing the buttons one at a time and kissing the exposed skin. I knelt in front of her like I was worshipping at the feet of a goddess.

My tongue roamed everywhere on her skin. Each kiss, lick, and caress brought a satisfied moan from her lips. I unbuckled her belt, unzipped her jeans and reverently moved my hands to each side of her hips and slid the jeans down her long sexy legs.

Angie smiled and stepped out of them. I gazed upon her naked body, breath catching in my throat. Gorgeous! Absolutely GORGEOUS! I must have done something right in a previous life to get this kind of reward.

I took her in my arms again and began kissing her, moving my tongue from her lips, across her cheek, nibbling at her earlobe.

"I've been waiting for this moment all week. Running laps, doing sit-ups and crunches," I whispered.

"Why do you do that, silly boy?" She asked as she ran her hands down my body. Almost like magic, I found myself naked. I don't remember getting undressed. It just happened. She molded herself to me and moved her hand between us until she encircled what she was looking for. She could tell I was really, REALLY happy to be here.

I sucked in my breath as she stroked me. "I knew making love to you would be like an Olympic event. I'm going for the gold," I said.

"Okay, Mr. Olympic Contender," she whispered back. "Let's see just how well you do in the Pelvic Thrust Competition."

The comment to my wife briefly flitted through my mind. I really was laying hands on one of the congregation. Angie wrapped her legs around me as I picked her up. She guided me to her wet, waiting, warm channel and slowly slid down on me. She sighed as we came together and she kissed me passionately as I slid deeper into her. It seemed our bodies were made for each other. Separate, we were harmless. Together, we were like gasoline and matches, we were explosive.

I thrust deeper into her. Her body temperature seemed to rise with our passion. As she reached the boiling point, she clawed my back and screamed, "DO IT HARDER!" I thrust into her faster and faster, harder and harder until all of me was in all of her.

She moaned breathlessly. "I want it doggy style."

Without stopping we repositioned. Her beautiful breasts filled my hands as she rested her head on the bed. I squeezed her nipples between my fingers. She moaned with pleasure. I moved my hands from her full breasts to her perfectly rounded derriere. The bouncing globes filled my hands. I slapped first one cheek, then the other until both were a bright red.

"WHO'S YOUR DADDY? WHO'S YOUR DADDY?" I yelled.

"YOU ARE BABY! YOU ARE!" She kept repeating between each slap.

"WHAT'S MY NAME?" I roared.

"DONALD, DONALD REYNOLDS!" She screamed.

The sounds of our bodies slapping together echoed through the room. Our ragged breathing, moans and screams filled the air.

I screamed, "I'M THERE! I'M CUMMING! OH SHIT! OH GOD! I'M CUMMING!" as I spilled my seed inside her.

She arched her back and moaned loudly, the breath catching in her throat. Time stood still. The earth moved. We fell back to earth and onto the bed together. She smiled at me through the tangled mess that her hair had become. We lay sweating, totally drained and trying to catch our breath.

"That was wonderful," she said softly. I could almost feel her purring. She reached down and cupped me. "I want it again, and again, and again, and again." Each statement was followed by a delightful squeeze of her hand.

"Your wish is my command." I responded, rising to the occasion.

We lay there exhausted after the third, or was it the fourth time? I felt like I had swallowed Kryptonite. Angie lay next to me curled into a contented ball. We kissed and she ran her tongue across my lower lip.

"So great," she said with a catch in her breath, grinning. "Just one more time, baby, please."

I looked at her in shock. "Do it again? I can't baby. I need water. I need rest. I need Viagra!" I moaned throwing my head back on the pillow.

She reached down and took my lifeless little friend in her hand and squeezed gently. I could only moan. Pride wanted me to rise again, but reality raised its ugly head. Reality bites!

"That was only a silver-rated performance," she stated with a chuckle and a squeeze. "If you want the gold..."

"Sorry baby, but I have to rest. I couldn't get it up now if I had a crane," I apologized.

"Bet I could get you ready again," she said impishly.

"Angie. Baby," I pleaded. "If we do it again, I won't have anything left for my wife."

The temperature in the room suddenly dropped to sub-zero. Angie jerked her hand away like she'd received an electric shock. She sat up and stared at me in astonishment and anger. She moved away from me like I had leprosy.

She shouted, "ANYTHING - LEFT - FOR - YOUR - WIFE!" Each word was punctuated with a jab at my ribs. "I thought you didn't like making love to HER scrawny ass?"

"I don't," I stammered, trying to protect myself from the stiletto fingernail she was jabbing into me. "But, if I don't want her to be suspicious, I have to make love to her at least once in a while."

I tried to take her into my arms, but she moved to the edge of the bed. "Baby, you know I love only you." I sounded pathetic to my own ears.

Placated, Angie leaned against me and twirled her finger through my chest hair. "Donald baby, who makes love to you the best, me or your wife?" She asked in a low voice.

I can recognize a minefield when I walk into one, and unless I was very, very careful, I might blow myself up. "Baby, there is no comparison," I said, kissing her neck just the way she loves. "You have her beat hands down. Making love to my wife is like 'Now N Later' candy."

" 'Now N Later' candy?" she asked with a chuckle.

"Yeah," I answered with another kiss. "I can take her now or later. Since I met you, it's now much, much later."

"Yeah, right. Tell me another one."

"For real," I said trying with everything I had to convince her.

She kissed me lustily. "You're not just saying that, are you?"

"Nope. Not a chance. Would I lie?" I asked, trying to look as trustworthy as possible.

She smiled at me. "You're so full of crap."

Another minefield disaster averted.

"Baby, I'm for real. All Ashley does is complain and try to keep up with the Joneses. Every penny I make is spent trying to maintain our lifestyle. It's been weeks since we made love. Before I came over here, we had the worst argument."

"What about?" she asked.

"What else? Money. I stormed out of the house and over here."

"Well honey, I'm here to relax you. Just sit back and let me take good care of you," she said seductively.

She moved behind me and pulled me back against her soft, warm body. My head rested between the pillows of her breasts. She tilted her head and kissed the side of my neck.

"That's the spot," I moaned while tilting my head forward to give her better access to anyplace she wanted. Her hands circled around me and began massaging my chest. "Beat me. Make me write bad checks. But don't ever stop loving me," I said softly, purring like a kitten. "That feels so good."

"Baby, you're starving for love," she laughed. "Let me be your private all-you-can-eat buffet. Tonight I want to do something special." She continued to kiss my neck.

"Special? Like what?" I asked curiously, looking back at her face.

She nodded her head to the corner of the bedroom where a chair held her little suitcase. She unfolded her long legs, got up from the bed and moved to the bag. She unzipped it and removed a small camcorder and tripod. I sat up like someone had just walked in with a cattle prod with my name on it.

"Ohhh, Nooo!" I objected. "No way! No how! Not in a million years. NEVER!"

"Ah, come on baby," she pleaded, "Don't be a party poop. Be wild and adventurous. Let's make an X-rated movie. Later, we can watch it together. Then, when you're away, I can watch it and masturbate."

I looked at the camera with all the trepidation of a mouse staring at a snake. "Honey, we can't. When it got out, and don't shake your head, it will get out, it would be a scandal like that other DeKalb County minister." I tried to reason with her.

"Let me have my fantasy," she pouted. "It's not going to end up in the wrong hands. I promise, I'll guard it with my life." She crossed her heart. "I'll keep it safe and secure."

"These kinds of tapes always get out. Paris Hilton didn't think her tape would get out. So did Rob Lowe and Pamela Anderson Lee. But somehow they always do. What if your husband finds it?"

I kept objecting and trying to reason with her. She kept insisting. I put my foot down, but she knew just how to lift it right back up. She began licking my nipples. Then she moved down, smiled up at me, and without taking her eyes off me, took my penis into her mouth and slid it down her throat. My brain told me not to give in, to show her who was the boss. Unfortunately, the brain in my big head wasn't in charge at the moment. The little brain was screaming, YES, YES. Life returned and I grew hard in her mouth.

Embarrassingly enough, not only did she convince me to lift my foot up, but I gladly put both of them down on the floor and walked my happy little ass right over to the camera and set it up. I was about to become the next great porn star.

I connected the camcorder to the 42-inch TV. I was aroused again as our naked bodies flashed across the screen. She started out dancing in front of the camera. I'm in love with a stripper; all she needed was a pole. Ride baby ride! Ride it like the Lone Ranger rides Silver. Excitement moved through me watching her sensuous body on the screen. Damn, a stripper's got me whipped. Work it baby, Work it! Rent is due and baby needs a new pair of shoes.

I watched us on the TV and then looked back at her. I felt like I was making it with twins.

I got into the act, forgetting about the camera. I was free as a bird, acting out my own fantasy. I was no longer Donald Reynolds, Assistant Pastor. I WAS DONALD REYNOLDS, **PORN STAR**!

I pulled her up to me and kissed her, as I rolled her over onto her back. Then I positioned myself between her legs. I watched myself as I fucked her. I pushed deeper and deeper into her warm, wet body. She sighed under me, quivering with anticipation. Like an idiot I waved at the screen and mouthed, "Hi Mom." I was an animal...a beast...a WILD MAN! I wanted to experience and devour every inch of her luscious body for the camera.

She looked at herself on the TV screen and pushed me off her. She climbed on top, took me in her hand and made sure she was filled again. She ground down harder and harder.

"Whose dick is this?" she screamed.

"Yours, IT'S YOURS!" I screamed, fondling her breasts.

"WHAT ABOUT YOUR SWEET LITTLE WIFE?" she screamed.

"FUCK HER!" I screamed, "I ONLY CARE ABOUT YOU!"

She slapped me across the face and screamed, "LOOK INTO THE CAMERA, TELL IT TO THE CAMERA!" She turned my head towards the camera.

I screamed, squeezing her breasts hard. "I DON'T CARE ABOUT MY WIFE. I ONLY CARE ABOUT YOU! I ONLY LOVE YOU!

"WHAT'S HER NAME?"

"Her name?" I asked in confusion. She tightened her muscles. "ASHLEY!" I yelled.

I was confused, but the little brain was driving the wagon now.

"TELL ASHLEY YOU DON'T LOVE HER. TELL HER YOU LOVE ONLY ME!"

"ASHLEY, I DON'T LOVE YOU!" I screamed into the camera, "I ONLY LOVE ANGIE!"

As our rhythm increased and our bodies continued to slap together, she became a wild woman. Sweat shimmered on our bodies. My body suddenly convulsed. I thought I was having a heart attack. My body jerked like I was having a seizure.

I felt her squeeze me tightly inside her. We both climaxed. She fell on top of me. We both were breathing heavily.

"Angie," I stammered between breaths, "You're trying to kill me... I can't take any more!"

She gave me a very sexy, seductive look, kissed me gently, then slid off me and cuddled at my side. "You're so scandalous, Donald. If people only knew." She chuckled.

"Only knew what?" I asked nuzzling her hair.

"If people only knew how scandalous the Assistant Pastor of Holy Faith Church really was," she said with a grin.

"Darling," I said with a sneaky grin, "They will never find out."

We both laughed and began to caress each other. We lay there quietly catching our breaths. As we cooled down, we drifted off to sleep.

My cell rang. I checked the clock; about an hour had passed. We both jumped off the bed.

"Who can that be?" Angie asked, annoyed.

"I don'. Help me find the phone." We pawed around, following the ringing to its source. I moved her shirt and my pants aside and finally found it. I looked at the caller ID.

"Uh-oh," I said looking around nervously, "It's Ashley. Quick put some clothes on."

Angie looked at me like I was the village idiot. "Aren't you going to answer it?" she asked. "It's just your sweet, faithful wife. I'm sure she just wants to know what you want for dinner. Tell her you've already eaten, you had a fur burger!" She picked up a shoe and threw it at me. I retreated to the bathroom and slammed the door so Ashley wouldn't hear the invectives that rained down on my head from the bedroom.

"Men are all dogs. I thought it would be different with a preacher," she screamed through the door at me, and then proceeded to call me every name in the book. She used even a few I'd never heard before.

I took a deep breath and opened the phone. "Hi baby," I said sweetly. "I was just thinking about you."

"I've been thinking about you too," she said just as sweetly. "What are you doing?"

"I'm laying hands on someone," I responded in a sincere voice. I looked over my shoulder at the door. It was awfully quiet in there all of a sudden.

"Well, keep doing the Lord's work, honey. Your reward is sure to come."

"I certainly hope so." I replied, wondering if I dared stick my head out of the bathroom.

"Just one more thing buttercup, and then I will let you get back to the Lord's work. Forgive me for the argument this morning. I don't know what came over me. All those Buckhead wives are always bragging about their fabulous lifestyles. It just went to my head, I guess. I'm sorry."

Accepting her apology, we whispered sweet nothings to each other. We were acting like two lovey-dovey high school sweethearts. Sometimes I can be sickening sweet when I try.

I closed the phone and focused on gathering my composure. I had to bring my raging pulse back under imminent heart attack levels.

I opened the door to the bedroom, calling to Angie, "I've got my second wind and I feel like the Energizer Bunny..."

The room was empty. The camcorder was gone. So was Angie.

I felt another minefield exploding before me. This was definitely an "OH SHIT" moment. I mentally put on the brakes as all the possible scenarios played out in my mind. What if she posts the video on YouTube, or sends Ashley or Pastor Cash a copy? Suppose she tries to blackmail me. Whoa! She's been a member of the church all her life; she loves me; she wouldn't think of blackmailing me! If I'm so safe, why do I feel like someone just walked over my grave? I'm such a putz.

I paced the bedroom floor mulling over what I might do to mitigate any damages that might arise from the tape getting into the wrong hands. I told myself to stop tripping. It wasn't going to get in the wrong hands.

The day was playing down, when the cell rang again. Caller ID told me it was Peter, so I quickly answered the call.

"What's up Peter?" I said, feeling honored that he'd called me.

"Well, Donald, Quentin is feeling a little down in the dumps. He just got another batch of rejection letters, so I thought it would be nice if the fellows got together to cheer him up. Are you busy tonight?"

"Well no," I said with a smirk in my voice. "Well, not really."

"I was thinking about taking Quentin to the club so he can forget his problems. Do you think you can make it?"

"What time do you have in mind?"

"About eight?"

"Well, I know Ashley is expecting me for dinner. I told her I'd be there at six. Yeah, I can make it." Hey, it's Peter McCallister on the phone, I'm sure not going to turn him down, so Ashley will just have to understand. "I'll see you guys at eight then."

"Meet me at the club. It's going down!" Peter said.

10

JEFF

"Happy Birthday darling," I shouted as I walked in the door. Beverly was sitting in the living room. I pulled a dozen red roses from behind my back.

"Ah Jeff, you shouldn't have," she said with delight in her eyes.

I showered her with kisses. "Baby, I couldn't wait to get home to you!"

As Beverly admired the flowers, I knew she was putty in my hands.

"Jeff, the flowers are beautiful!" she said in admiration, burying her nose in the soft petals. As I swept her into my arms, she jumped up and wrapped her legs around my waist. I caressed her curvaceous body and began to get turned on.

"I'm so lucky to have you baby," I said with joy. I kissed her softly. "Out of all the men who were dying to marry you, you chose me. The day we got married, was the happiest day of my life."

"I love you too, Jeff. You are so sweet, so wonderful!"

We kissed passionately, and as I carried her toward the bedroom, I tried to sneak a peek at my watch. At that moment my cell rang.

"Jeff, don't even think about," Beverly warned.

The enchantment was broken. Beverly slid down my body, touching her feet to the floor. I pulled out the phone to answer. The spell was broken. I'd turned from a prince to an insensitive jerk. She stared at me quietly. I knew what she was thinking. Make a choice. It's either me or the phone. I gently broke the silence.

"Baby, you know I love you, but it could be the airline. You know, as a pilot, I must be accessible when they call."

"Can't you forget that freaking job just once? Can't you forget the telephone? Money and meetings? Can you for once concentrate on your wife? For God's sake, it's my birthday! I only have one of those a year. Even though I want to forget it myself, I still can't ignore it."

"Don't worry baby. Let me take this one itsy-bitsy call, then it's all about you." Beverly gave me "THE" look and walked into the bedroom, slamming the door closed.

I looked at the caller ID. It was old money bags himself, Peter McCallister. I flipped open the phone.

"What's going on, Peter?"

"Nothing, Big Guy. What are you doing?"

"I just got in from L.A. I had to come home early. It's Beverly's birthday."

"Tell her happy birthday for me. Also, remind her about Antonio's party tomorrow night."

"I will Peter. So what's up?"

"I called because Quentin is depressed. I was hoping you could join the fellows at the club. His writing aspirations are not going well, so I decided it would be great if the fellows could take him out and cheer him up."

"Ah, Peter, man, I would love to, but tonight, I can't. It's Beverly's birthday. With the pilot strike and the Transco bankruptcy, I've been spending a lot of time in the air." Silence filled the phone.

"I understand Jeff. You've got to keep the wife happy. Tonight I really wanted to talk to you guys. I'm about to recommend a few people for membership in our secret society. I just wanted to give you guys a head start. Other than that, I thought a few beers and a lot of tits and ass would be good for all of us. It's nothing out of the ordinary," he added in a sneaky tone. "But if you can't make it, you can't make it."

A lump rose in my throat and I hesitated. "You said you were going to give us a scoop on membership?"

"Yeah, Big Guy," he said nonchalantly. "With what I tell you tonight, it will guarantee you a spot in the 30305."

Silence filled the phone and my ambition reared its ugly head. This could be the break I've been looking for. I slyly looked around. I whispered, "Peter, count me in."

"Count you in?" he said in surprise, "What about Beverly? It's her birthday. She will be mad as a wet hen."

"Let me worry about that," I said pretending to be the man. "I can handle my wife." Please God; just get me into Peter's group. "I'll be there at eight on the dot!"

The moment I closed the phone, I walked to the bedroom. I had to find a way to get out of the house. I couldn't tell Beverly I was going to a strip club for her birthday. That would lose me 99 and ½ cool points — not to mention my nuts. I will do what every all American male has done before, especially when the truth wouldn't work. I'll lie. The truth won't set me free, but it will set me up. Okay, I'm going to march right in there and tell her I have to leave because it's work related. Hey, it's the number one lie men tell their wives when they are cheating or doing something equally slimy.

Obviously, I couldn't just spring it on her. I've got to sugar coat it. I felt in the pocket of my jacket for the jeweler's box I'd picked up on the way home. I opened the elegant box. A diamond bracelet glittered among its nest of satin. Diamonds are a girl's best friend and it will keep the husband out of the doghouse.

I gathered my composure and opened the door into the bedroom. Beverly tossed me an angry look, arms folded across her chest. I knew it was time to put on the charm. I gathered her in my arms and gave her a 100-watt smile. "Darling, you are so beautiful."

"Thank you sweetheart," she said reluctantly.

I kissed her passionately.

"Jeff, I am looking forward to spending a romantic evening at home. You are always gone."

"I know honey, maybe this will help." I reached into my pocket and pulled out the black velvet box and opened it.

"A diamond bracelet!" she exclaimed. "Oh, Jeff, it's so beautiful. It's what I've always wanted. You are the most wonderful and thoughtful husband in the world."

For a brief moment I believed my own press. I knew I was about to burst her bubble.

"Beverly, could you please have a seat? I have something to tell you." I took her hand and we sat on the bed.

"Sweetheart, you know I love you and nothing in life is more important than making you happy." She gave me a piercing look.

"Jeff, it's my birthday, don't bring me any bad news."

I kissed her gently. "Sweetheart, you know I spent a fortune on your breast implants, liposuction and plastic surgery."

She arched an eyebrow at me, "Your point, Jeff."

"It costs to stay so beautiful. I have to work night and day for it. So baby, I just got a call from the airline...I have to go to a union meeting."

"What!" she choked out. "You have to go back to work?"

"Yes, baby."

"Go back to work?" she repeated. "On my birthday? What kind of husband works on his wife's birthday? I bet Obama at least took the day off for his wife's birthday."

I tried to hug her, but she threw my hands off. "Don't touch me Jeff, just don't touch me. You are not fooling me. I know the real reason you don't want to spend time with me. You've got another woman haven't you?"

"Another women?" I said surprised. "Sweetheart, I don't have another woman. You are the only woman I will ever want or need."

"Bullshit Jeff. Do you think I'm stupid? Do you see stupid written across my face? I am not a ditzy model, without a brain. Right now the only thing I want to hear about is the wine you brought home, and how tonight you want to start a family."

I grabbed her hand and began to stroke it. "Baby, you know how iffy Transco is right now. Not only is Transco in financial trouble, we are too. We are in debt all the way up to your pretty little ass."

"Jeff, I don't care about money or material things. All I want to know is why you don't want to spend time with me?" she yelled uncontrollably.

"Calm down sweetheart. Calm down. I do want to spend time with you. I do love you. I'm just trying to keep food on the table and a roof over our heads." I kissed her gently on the mouth and then her neck.

"Stop, Jeff stop! You are not going to get off the hook. It's my birthday and I'm pissed!" She began to cry.

"Don't sweetheart. I promise you I will make it up to you. When this is all over, I will take you on a long cruise. We will start a family."

She got up to get a tissue from the dresser. She wiped her eyes.

"It's not just your job, honey. It's everything. It's my entire life."

"What, your life?" I said in surprise. "You're a model. You were the toast of Milan, Paris and New York."

"That's the problem, Jeff, I *was*. You know my telephone has not rung in months. I know what the other models are saying. 'Beverly Demoor's name used to be on everyone's lips. She was the pride of

Louisiana, now she can't get arrested. Even her husband doesn't want to spend time with her. He's always gone. He's probably cheating. I bet his mistress is younger and prettier. His 32-year old wife is over the hill." Tears formed in her eyes.

"Jeff, I knew I couldn't model forever, but I thought I had a few good years left. I call my agent everyday. It's always the same. 'Beverly, maybe you should think of retiring.' Hell no!" She shouted. "Everyone reinvents themselves. Everyone can have a life after modeling. Look at Tyra Banks, Elle MacPherson and Cindy Crawford. Even Naomi Campbell has reinvented herself. She stays in the spotlight by being a diva and keeping up shit. Maybe that's it. Maybe I need to get arrested. Maybe I need to go to jail, or at least wear an ankle monitor."

"Get arrested, go to jail, ankle monitor?" I repeated amused. "It's not that serious."

"I'm not kidding," she said, giving me a mean look, "Bad girls and divas are in. Nice girls and over the hill models and actresses are out!"

All attempts to diffuse the situation failed. Beverly was on a roll.

"Every other model has got it going on except me! Everyone has gone on to bigger and better things. Look at Kimora Lee Simmons, Brooke Shields, and Iman."

"Baby, don't let it get you down."

"Jeff, my career is over!" She shouted. "And the only family I have is you. I want to have a baby, NOW! But I'm even too old to do that. Advertisers, designers and everyone are constantly reminding me of how old I am."

"Baby, fame and fortune could be just around the corner."

"Fame and fortune, my foot! It's always the same thing. They all want younger women, with a fresh face and a new look. Jeff, do you think my butt is too big?"

"Beverly, your butt in not too big!"

"Maybe I need more plastic surgery. Maybe I need bigger implants, a smaller butt and Botox."

"Don't be silly, your body is fine."

"I don't know Jeff. I can't tell anymore. I feel I'm over the hill. Washed up. A has-been."

I got up and put my arms around her. "You are not a washed up, has-been. You are still the most beautiful and sexiest woman I have ever laid eyes on. I still feel I'm the luckiest man in the world. Remember, you chose me over all the men you could have married."

She smiled up at me. "Jeff, you sure know what to tell an old lady..."

"You're not an old lady," I said interrupting her flow, "You are a beautiful swan."

"You mean that Jeff?" she said dabbing at her eyes with the tissue.

"I sure do. In fact, when things settle down, maybe you can get your own thing going. Maybe you can open up your own modeling agency, or coach other aspiring models. Or, maybe you can design your own clothing line. Nobody knows fashion better then Beverly DeMoor."

"You think so?" she asked excitedly.

"Baby, I know so. You're smart, you're creative and you have a way with people. Come to think of it, that should be your next move." I looked at my watch. "OK, baby, we'll talk more about it later. I've got to go now."

We had moved into the living room and she excitedly hugged me. She picked up the flowers. I kissed her passionately, crushing the blossoms between us.

"Happy Birthday Beverly, you are not getting older, you are getting better!"

11

ANTONIO

"Antonio, I am so proud of you," Liana said as she squeezed me tightly. We looked at the breathtaking view of Atlanta from our penthouse balcony. "I can't believe it, my Antonio is a congressman. Maybe in the future, a US Senator or the first Hispanic President of the United States. Just think, not so long ago, we were wondering how we were going to make it. Now you are the hope and dream of Latin people everywhere."

I smiled and kissed her gently. I poured her another glass of Cristal and said, "Let's propose a toast."

"What should we toast to?"

"To us. To success. To President Barack Obama. To the American Dream." We raised our glasses in a toast, linked arms and took a little sip of champagne. I gazed proudly at my wife as a news flash came across the television screen in the living room.

"Thousands of Latinos are marching in the streets of Atlanta this evening..."

"Turn it up Antonio, turn it up," she said like a child at Christmas. I grabbed the remote and turned up the sound.

"Hi, this is Amanda Davis with a news update. Thousands of Latinos are lining the streets, protesting Senate Bill 529. If this bill passes, it will make felons out of thousands of illegal aliens. The bill will also target employers who hire them. According to the INS, the United States has about twelve million illegal aliens..."

As Liana watched, the camera panned on thousands of Latinos packed into Centennial Park. Tears came to Liana's eyes.

"Antonio, I feel so sorry for our people. All they want is the opportunity to live a better life. It's not like Latinos are taking jobs from American people. We get the jobs no one else wants. We pick the fruit, we work in their fields, we cut the grass and work as maids in homes, hotels and businesses. The *gringos* pay Mexicans and other Latinos far less than any other minority. We are not asking for a handout, just a hand."

She gave me a series of small kisses. "Antonio, I know you will make it all happen. I know when everyone votes you will do the right thing. I know you will vote against that bill. Everyone knows that you hold the deciding vote in the house. Everyone knows the Governor listens to you. In the Latino community, you are the spokesman for our people."

I walked back to the balcony. I took a deep breath. "I love this country and I love this city, but..."

"But what? What Antonio?"

I stood, quietly contemplating the postcard perfect view of the Atlanta skyline. The silence stretched between us.

Finally Liana spoke. "Antonio, I know you. We grew up together. I know when you are not telling me everything. Baby, you don't have to play that macho role with me. Be straight, what are you hiding?"

Still I could not speak. I took a long swallow of my drink.

"Antonio!" Liana pleaded. "Why is it the *gringos* are putting you on front street?"

I let out a deep sigh. "Well, Liana, a lot of very rich and powerful people want this bill to pass. But they don't want to publicly be for it, or publicly against it."

"Why should they straddle the fence?" she asked.

"Liana, it happens all the time in politics. Nobody wants to look bad. Nobody wants to offend anyone. If the politicians publicly announce they are for Senate Bill 529, they lose a lot of Latino votes. Latinos are now a very powerful group. We are now the number one minority. If the politicians say they are against the bill, people born in this country would get upset. As a result, they would accuse their congressmen and senators of selling out to the illegal immigrants. So to save face and try to keep everyone happy, they picked me to do their dirty work. They want me to be the bad guy."

Liana moved close to me and put her hand on my shoulder. "Antonio, I didn't know. I didn't know the pressure you were under."

I ran my hand through my hair. "Liana, people say that illegal aliens are not loyal to this country. Americans say they use the system, send their kids to public schools, take public assistance, but send all their money back to their native countries. The *gringos* want me to sell out. They want me to be a Latin Uncle Tom. They want me to be Alberto Gonzales."

She put her head on my chest. "Antonio, what are you going to do?"

I shook my head. "I really don't know, Liana. The Buckhead crowd, the 30305 crowd, carry a lot of weight. I have ambitions of my own. I have plans and dreams for us. But, if I cross Peter's friends, then I'm dead politically. If I vote for the bill, a lot of hardworking Latinos will be kicked out of this country." I dropped my head, resting my cheek against the top of Liana's head, breathing in the fragrance of her hair. "I don't know what to do."

She took the glass from my hand, and sat it on the table. She put her arms around my neck and tilted her head back and looked into my eyes. "Antonio, you have to do the right thing."

I shook my head. "I don't know what the right thing is anymore. Things are not just black and white. There is a gray area. Politics is about money, power and favors. Everyday major decisions are made in private settings. Politics and careers are made and destroyed at a posh country club, over a game of golf or a nice dinner. Liana, we want to stay rich. They want to maintain the status quo. You spend your life trying to get in, and then you sell your soul to stay in."

"Liana, I wasn't elected to Congress on just the Latino vote. The *gringos* like me too. I had to make a lot of promises to get elected. Peter's friends hand picked me from my law firm and groomed me for this job. I thought I was securing our future, but in reality, they were securing theirs."

"They knew that one day illegals would be a problem, so they sat back and put their plan together and just waited until the problem came to light." I gave a long sigh.

"Liana, when you want to control a race of people, you don't do it with someone from a different race, you get one of their own. I believe men like Martin Luther King. Jr. and Nelson Mandela are gone. Politicians of today do what is in their best interest, without thought for the masses. Thank God Barack Obama came along."

Liana moved away from me and leaned against the balcony rail. The lights of Atlanta created a halo around her. "That is so sad, Antonio. If you get a person of the same race to oppose his own people, it gets the job done. No one is the wiser and no one can scream racism or discrimination."

"That's the plan in a nutshell," I said. "Sad to say, it has worked for so many years."

"Antonio!" she interrupted angrily, "If you knew what they were up to, why didn't you just quit."

"If I quit or fail, it would just make it that much harder for the next Latino. I'm sorry, Liana, I've got to ride this one out. Furthermore, I'm sure they wouldn't let me off the hook that easy. I'm sure there would be repercussions. They've invested a lot in me. They hand picked me to fulfill a plan. Now they want that plan executed, regardless of who gets hurt. Look at what happened to Attorney General Alberto Gonzales during the Bush administration. His sins came back to haunt him."

She grabbed both my hands. "Antonio, I hear what you are saying and I understand your predicament, but you must do what is right. Vote against that bill. Your loyalty is to your people."

"No, Liana," I said angrily, "My first loyalty is to us, and to secure our future. I can't do that as a disgraced congressman."

"I'm surprised at you Antonio. I don't know who you are. You are not the Antonio I once knew. The Antonio I first met was presidential, he had principles. He had courage. He had a heart and a conscience, and that Antonio would not sell out. Every since you were elected to Congress, you seem to have lost a piece of yourself. You are not the same man I married."

"I'm still the man you married," I said angrily, "I just wised up. Everything is a compromise now. Everything is give and take."

"Give and take!" she screamed. "If you don't do something our people will be herded up like cattle. They will be shipped back to Mexico and to starving third world countries. Families will be torn apart. They have a right to be here."

"A right to be here!" I screamed back, "Illegal aliens have no rights. They are just a bunch of uneducated wetbacks. They won't be missed."

Liana gave me a slap that made my ears ring. "What do you mean illegal aliens have no rights?" She got in my face. "Don't ever call honest, hardworking Latinos a bunch of uneducated wetbacks. They worked the fields to put food on our table. They almost died crossing the Rio Grande so you could be born in the United States. I dropped out of school and worked day and night at Adrian's Beauty Salon just to send you to law school. Now that you've achieved the American Dream, to hell with everybody else?"

She snapped her fingers in my face. "It's finally coming out. It happens everyday among minority men. You become more successful and the first thing you do is drop the woman that stood by your sorry ass. Now you want a white girl? I guess I'm not pretty enough or classy enough for you. Is that right? Well OJ, I guess I'm just another wetback!"

"Are you accusing me, Liana, of being like that?"

"If the glove doesn't fit, you must acquit!"

I took a deep breath and said, "I'm sorry, I didn't mean it that way. I love you and no, I'm not looking for a white girl. Sweetheart you are one of the smartest people I know. If you hadn't spearheaded my campaign, I would never have been elected. You made me believe in myself. Hell, I would have never gone to law school if you hadn't encouraged me. You and I are a team. Right now, I'm just caught between a rock and a hard place."

The fight had gone out of both of us. I picked up my champagne glass and took a long swallow. The phone rang.

Liana moved toward the French doors and said, "I'll get it."

"Don't worry about it sweetheart. I'm closer." I went inside. Caller ID identified Peter. I took a deep breath and picked up the phone.

"Hello Peter. What's up?"

"Hey, Big Guy. Just calling to check on the man of the hour. Are you alone?"

"Sort of. Liana is on the balcony. We were just having a political discussion."

"Those are the best kind. I hope she is talking some sense into you. She knows a good thing when she hears it. She knows opportunity when it's knocking. Your vote for Senate Bill 529 to pass in the house is securing both our futures."

"Uh huh...uh huh..." As Liana looked at me, she rolled her eyes. She knew it was Peter on the telephone. She knew when he called I went from Congressman to errand boy. But she doesn't know that Peter spent millions getting me elected to office.

"The reason I called is because Quentin is singing the blues. He got another batch of rejections today. He's about as far down as a fox circling a locked hen house. The fellows and I are going to the club to cheer him up. We wanted to know if you could join us. And, tonight I'm giving you all a heads up about getting into my little circle."

I quickly forgot all about Liana and our discussion. I whispered to Peter, "Hey man, that is the news I've been waiting for!"

"Oh, by the way," he interrupted, "Antonio, don't forget that Jan and I are throwing a little party for you and Liana tomorrow night. It will be at my mansion. All the right people will be there."

I frowned as he sneakily interjected, "The senate bill vote is coming up on Monday. Everybody is depending on you to do the right thing."

I glanced over at Liana. If looks could freeze, I'd be an iceberg about now.

Peter continued in my ear, "Be at my house about eight. Have Liana looking her best. Also, one more thing, Big Guy..."

"What's that Peter?"

"We are just good old country Georgia folks. We don't understand a lick of Spanish. So can you please tell Liana not to speak it? I would hate to keep calling my cook to interpret."

I gave him an appropriately ingratiating laugh, but clenched my teeth and held my tongue from telling him what I really wanted to say.

"Okay, Peter, I will relay the message. See you at the club." I cradled the phone.

When I stepped back onto the balcony, Liana let me have it. "Antonio, where is your pride, where are your *cajones* (balls)? You are definitely not acting presidential. When that rich *gringo* calls, you go out like a punk. It's 'yes, Peter' this and 'yes, Peter' that. Aren't you tired of dancing to his music? For once in your life put your foot down. Be a man. Say no!"

"Liana, I really don't need your attitude tonight. What I need is your support and understanding."

"You have that, but you are not supporting yourself. You are not supporting your people. I don't understand what you are doing?"

"What I am doing is securing our future." I replied a lot more calmly than I felt. "Do you like our home? Our Mercedes? The money we have, the clothes?"

"I don't care about any of that! They mean nothing to me! All I want is the man I married. We can live in a ditch. I would be happy there with the man I love."

I looked at her coldly. "Take it from me, a ditch ain't happening. I've been there and it sucks!"

She shook her head.

I told her about meeting Peter at the club, implying country club, and that I'd be gone a couple of hours. "It's a very important meeting, Sweetheart," I concluded unconvincingly.

"Go ahead Antonio," she spat out, "Go out with your bourgeois friends. I hope you have a good time."

"Liana, don't do this. I don't want to argue with you."

"I'm not arguing. I'm just telling you how I feel."

"One more thing," I said as I began to walk out. "Don't forget that tomorrow night, Peter and Jan are throwing a party in my honor at his mansion. He expects us at 8:00p.m. Let's not be late."

"I won't Mr. Congressman," she said sarcastically, "Anything else?"

"Well, sweetheart, a lot of Peter's friends are old money, southern, so if you can remember, please chill out on the Spanish."

She rolled her eyes. "You *pinche joto* (fucking faggot). I thought you were a real man."

"I've got to go. See you later." I responded.

12

QUENTIN

When I arrived at the Cheetah Club, the parking lot looked like an exotic car showroom. There were Ferraris, Mercedes, Bentleys and Jaguars everywhere. The valet had already parked the fellows' luxury cars. The moment I arrived in my beat up old hooptie car, Oscar, the head valet attendant snickered, "The ballers on a budget are out tonight."

Pissed off, I thought I might get some respect if I looked hard. I decided to roll up like a gangsta rapper in the videos. I pulled my pants down sagging and showing my underwear. "Hey Dawg, park my ride next to Peter McCallister's Rolls."

"You got to be kidding, homie," he replied, smiling.

I gave him a hard stare. "I'm rolling with Peter's crew. You got a problem with 'dat, fool?"

"Please, pull up your pants. I see your Winnie the Pooh underwear."

"Dawg, I'm about to go off. Don't be dissing my ride."

"Sir, you are not dangerous, but your car certainly is."

"Ha, ha," I said. "Everybody wants to do stand up. Can you park this for me?"

"We don't have space available."

I looked around. "Sir, there are three spaces right in front."

"I certainly can't park your hooptie there," he said arrogantly, "There's no way."

I looked at him angrily. "Why not? It's out of the way, not blocking traffic. Give me one good reason why you can't park my car in front."

"Okay!" He screamed, throwing his hands up, "You twisted my arm. Your car won't block any traffic, but it will give the club a bad name. I'm on a roll tonight! I'll tell you what, Mr. Baller on a budget, I got the perfect place for it. It's out of the way, I'll keep an eye on it and I won't charge you a dime."

"Okay, dawg, that's what I'm talking about. Show me some love." I gave him my keys. The moment I turned my back, he grabbed a large sign from inside the key stand and jumped in my car. Before I knew it, my car was parked on the shoulder of 285 with a large sign in the window that read *See What Happens When You Drink and Drive. Friends Don't Let Friends Drive Drunk!*

"No respect," I said, shaking my head, "No respect."

I turned and walked into the club. There were curvaceous and flawless bodies everywhere. Peter and his fellows quickly spotted me. The hostess escorted me to their table. The music blasted and the fellows greeted me with high fives and a "What's uppppp!"

I'm a lamb in a field of wolves. I'm 35 and just your average Joe. I just want to be a successful writer and have people read my books. I believe in marriage, commitment and fidelity. I'm looking forward to getting married. I just want to make sure I'm doing the right thing. I'm a Grady baby. That's a person born and bred in Atlanta, Georgia. I've lived in Atlanta all my life.

Atlanta is a unique city. They don't call it Hotlanta for nothing. This town has as many strip clubs as it does churches. People live secret lives here. The city is full of single women. It's also full of gay men, bisexual men, and men on the down-low. I don't have anything against an individual's personal lifestyle. Some of my best friends are gay, but get real...as far as your sexual preferences are concerned, just come on out of the closet. Give the other person a choice. The only thing more astounding than a man's secret life is a man's private thoughts. It would curl your hair to hear what men say about their mates behind their backs.

As for me, I'm 100% heterosexual. I'm the man with the slow hand. I'm the man you call to cry on his shoulder when you are in love with someone else. I'm the guy you want after The Player and Mr. Wrong has done you wrong. I'm the one you describe as too nice or a good friend. I respect women and want to be faithful.

When I first started dating my fiancée, Bridgett, I only wanted to kiss her, not jump her bones. It is said that men only kiss women they are interested in for real. Kissing is very intimate. Sex is not. You can have sex with a lot of women, but you will only have intimacy with a woman that's marriage material. A man will never kiss a prostitute. I was a virgin until I met Bridgett. Bridgett was my first and only sexual experience. Please don't tell the fellows.

13

Jeff saw an attractive waitress coming toward us. "Hey baby!" he yelled at her. "I'll have a Screaming Orgasm or maybe Sex on the Beach."

Jeff Montgomery is 40 and epitomizes tall, dark and handsome. He's a pilot for Transco Airlines out of Hartsfield-Jackson International Airport. Women generally swoon at his feet. I don't know if it's just his good looks or the uniform. Women do like men in uniform. His charm and calm voice bring women to their knees. Somewhere between "Fasten Your Seatbelt" and "Let Me Unfasten Your Bra" unsuspecting women become another notch in his belt.

"In your dreams," she said with a smile as she sauntered on by our table. Jeff can sometimes make a complete ass of himself. He called a stripper over for a lap dance, and said, "Hey baby, this is your lucky day. Don't settle for a minnow when you can have Jaws."

I shook my head at his tired lines and he looked at me past the swiveling hips of the dancer and grinned.

"Baby, as long as I have a face, you will always have some place to sit," he said as he tucked a twenty into her g-string.

The waitress arrived with a pitcher of beer and glasses. As Peter poured he said, "a toast." We all raised our glasses. "To The Club," he said with a broad grin.

"To The Club," we saluted.

"So, Quentin, how is the writing coming?" Jeff said.

"Well, not so well. Today I've now been turned down by 30 publishers. I'm about to give up. I might as well face it; I suck as a writer." The fellows gave me sympathetic looks.

Antonio interjected, "Hey man, don't be so hard on yourself. Rome wasn't built in a day. Don't worry. Some things take time. Look at me, I grew up picking strawberries."

Antonio is 38 and one of those success stories we love to read about. His parents were immigrants from Mexico, who came to this country with nothing but a baby in his mother's belly and a few bits of clothing on their backs. They picked fruit all their lives to give him a better life. Antonio made them proud. He pulled himself up by his own boot straps to become Georgia's first Hispanic congressman. Now he's a household name and faced with the ultimate decision; stay loyal to his people or stay loyal to Peter.

Peter looked at him proudly, "With my friends and me behind you, there is no telling how far you can go — maybe the Senate or the White House."

Antonio eye's gleamed with ambition. "Yeah, a Senator, the next Attorney General, President, the sky's the limit."

Antonio looked over at Peter. "Hey, I can't stay out too late. Bill 529 is on the table. You know, in the House my vote is instrumental to the life or death of this bill. Remember, the early bird gets the worm."

Peter gave him a smirky grin and said, "But the man who sleeps late probably owns the worm farm."

"Now since we are on the subject of illegal aliens, Antonio, I don't have anything against your people. I know the decision to kick illegal aliens out of the country is a hard decision. I'm as liberal as the next guy. I'm an equal opportunity employer. I have a Mexican gardener. My cook is from Guatemala, and I pay your people a few cents above minimum wage."

I gritted my teeth. "Peter, you are a real American."

"And, Jeff, you know I don't have anything against African Americans. When Tiger won the Masters, when Venus and Serena won at Wimbledon and when Barack Obama won the democratic nomination and went on to become our 44th president and the first African American president, didn't I pull out a big plate of fried chicken and collard greens to celebrate. Didn't I also instruct my yardman to take up all the black lawn jockeys in front of my southern mansion?" Peter burst into hysterical laughter. We gave each other a dry smile.

"That was a good one Peter," Antonio said, sucking up.

Peter gave us a solemn look. "America is changing. We didn't see Obama coming. He slipped through the cracks. But at least we finally got OJ's ass." Peter continued his teasing. "You give us one, we give you one."

Then Peter turned serious, and said, "You know, Antonio, if you vote to get that immigration bill passed, you can write your own ticket to the top. Just think about it, Antonio Fernando, the first Hispanic Senator from the great state of Georgia."

Antonio smiled and said, "The first Hispanic Senator. I like that. It's got a nice ring to it."

"Let's propose a toast to Senator Antonio Fernando."

I cut in, "Antonio, don't achieve your dreams on the misery of others. The manner in which you achieve a goal is just as important as achieving the goal itself. A lot of Hispanics are not criminals. They just want a hand, not a handout. They came here for a decent life."

All the fellows, but Peter, clapped and cheered. "Bravo, Quentin!"

Peter rolled his eyes. "I hear what you are saying Quentin, but sometimes in life you have to make the tough decisions. Sometimes you have to piss off the party and your people. You can't always be popular. Look at the bigger picture. Antonio, you are a Democrat and I'm Republican. Sometimes you have to give a little to get a little."

Peter continued, "Guys, I'm no fool. All eyes that are closed are not asleep. Face it, the only reason you hang out with me is because you want something. You want to be members of the club."

He then looked at Jeff and Antonio. "Hispanics are where African Americans used to be in the 60's. I watched both your people march in the streets. But with all the abuse African Americans endured, they produced a President of the United States. But, there is one thing you have to remember."

"What is that Peter?" Antonio asked cautiously.

"Black is beautiful, tan is grand, but green is always the color of the big boss man! Sometimes you have to take matters into your own hands. Jan and the Daughters of the South started Buckhead 30305 for that reason. Sometimes you have to bleed on the American flag to make sure the stripes stay red. Nothing happens in Georgia without our say so and we make sure we put the right people in the right place. We were all split about whether Obama was the man for the job, but we had to put our pockets over our prejudice. When white America's money is in jeopardy, fuck the color. It's time for a change."

Peter looked at all of us as we listened intently. "The question is what would you do for your lifelong dream? Before it's all over each one of you must answer that question."

A grim silence fell over us in spite of the blaring music.

Peter looked at Donald and said, "You are the Assistant Pastor at Holy Faith. It's no secret that Ashley likes the finer things in life, and I'm sure you have your own ambitions. Jeff, you are the spokesman for your union. With Transco's uncertainty, you'll never be sure whether you will have a job next year or not. My group of friends can take you to the next level. A nice executive job with a fat salary and perks will be just what you need. And what about you Mr. Goody Two Shoes? Quentin, if you get any broker, you'll be holding up an "I'll Work for Food" sign. The question is how far will you go to make your dreams come true?"

He took a sip of beer. "Take it from a millionaire, never say never. The very thing you say you'll never do is the very thing you will be tempted by. You won't be tempted when you are strong, it will hit you at your weakest moments."

I couldn't help but contemplate what Peter was saying. All of us had a dazed look on our faces.

Suddenly, Peter shifted gears. "Hey fellows, are we here to have a good time, or what? Let's not get all serious and philosophical. We're here to cheer up Quentin." Our glasses and the pitcher were empty and he snapped his fingers at our waitress, Savannah.

"Ya'll ready for another round?" she asked.

"Yes ma'am, and here's a fifty for your trouble."

"Thanks Peter," she said as the fifty disappeared and she flounced away.

Donald finally came to life and said, "Quentin, don't ever get married. The moment you say I do you are done."

Donald Reynolds is 50 and an Assistant Pastor at Holy Faith Church. Donald came to Holy Faith after numerous scandals at his old church. He is struggling between his faith and demons of the flesh. Donald has his eye on becoming the next Senior Pastor at Holy Faith, making him one of the most powerful men in Georgia. He knows Peter could make all his dreams come true.

"Amen to that," Peter agreed. "I don't know what I was thinking. I got married without a pre-nup."

"You mean to tell us Jan caught Georgia's richest developer slipping? I didn't think it was possible," Donald said in dismay.

"One night Jan put a good one on me. She got pregnant and before I knew it, I was married like a motherfucker. I've been married 32 years and unhappy for 31 years. I must admit, there is some truth to the old saying that a man's brain is between his legs."

"I'd like for any one of you to name three married couples that are happy. Can you?" Peter said looking at Jeff.

Jeff immediately jumped in. "Man that's easy. Tom and Susan Stevenson; they've been happily married for twelve years."

"Guess you didn't hear about the Stevensons." Donald intoned, "They got divorced last month. She traded in Tom for her personal trainer. She took the house, the car and the kids. It's all over Holy Faith. Pastor Cash is counseling Tom weekly."

"OK, what about Steve and Paulette Harvey?"

"They separated last week." Antonio advised.

"What happened," Jeff asked surprised.

"Well, according to somebody who knew somebody, Paulette came home from work early and found Steve in bed with a male somebody."

"Stop lying Antonio."

"Man, I'm for real. Steve is on the down low. He's open about his affairs with women, but hides his thing for men."

"Didn't Steve retire from the NFL?" Quentin asked.

"Yes, he did. What's your point?" Antonio asked.

A grim silence rimmed the table. Donald rebounded and gave us hope again. "What about Michelle and Barack? They've been married sixteen years and have two beautiful daughters," he said proudly.

"Hell yesssss!" We gave each other hopeful high fives.

"That's the kind of woman I need," Donald continued. "Not a walking ATM machine like Ashley."

Donald lifted his glass in a toast and we followed suit.

"To Michelle Obama," Donald yelled, "A one of a kind woman!"

"Fellows, I hate to rain on your parade, but the Obama's are only one couple. The question was can you name three?" Peter interjected.

He had us there, but we all thought long and hard. We tossed around names of everyone we knew. Then it was over. We couldn't come up with three couples that were happily married.

"Fellows, do you remember that movie, *Lord of the Rings?*" Peter asked. In case you didn't see it, the story centers upon the magical ring. Whoever possesses it will have their soul taken over, and it makes them do evil things. Is it just me, or did that ring look just like a wedding band?"

"Ah, man, you got down on that one," Jeff screamed.

"I kid you not fellows. I'm telling you Quentin, when you get married. It is not about you anymore. The woman automatically controls the ring. You will do a lot of things and you don't know why."

"Like what?" I couldn't help myself. I had to ask.

"Like going shopping and watching her try on 50 pairs of shoes and not buy a single pair," Jeff said wisely.

"Like the unrealistic expectation women have that men should be strong, but also be sensitive and anticipate her every need," Donald added.

"Like make a ton of money, but be home at five each night for dinner," Peter inserted.

"Like sex on demand, but you only get sex if she's in the mood," Jeff complained.

"And how! Some days, she's just angry for no reason and the harder you try the angrier she gets," Peter said.

"Why would she do that?" I asked. "I've been taught there is a reason behind everything people do."

"Earth to McFly!" Peter said loudly, "Her reason is because she's Lord of the Ring. You're not listening. The ring comes with certain privileges. She is the queen and your job is to make her happy."

The fellows all looked at Quentin and Jeff said, "You're doomed, get out while you can!"

"Turn back," Donald warned. "After the wedding, her horns will come out. Turn back, or you will perish."

Jeff gave me that Vincent Price laugh. You know the one on the Michael Jackson video, "Thriller"?

I gave the fellows a condescending grin. "Fellows, I believe in marriage. Marriage is a good thing. I can't wait to wake up to the same person for the rest of my life."

"McFly," Jeff said jokingly, "You can't wait to have sex with the same woman the rest of you life? Are you crazy?"

"I'm not going to let you discourage me. I think getting married is the best decision a man can make other than buying life insurance."

Donald cut in, "So Quentin, you're saying a man should prepare for a wedding and a funeral right from the start." The fellows all cracked up, stomped their feet and pounded on the table.

"Think about this, Quentin," Peter said, "If it's so good, why do 50 to 60 percent of all marriages end in divorce?"

"Well, burned out husbands of the 30305, marriage is not complicated," I replied, "You make it complicated. The key to having a happy and successful marriage is to put God first. Accept your differences, concentrate on your similarities. Never stop dating each other. Make compromises and have honest and open communication about what you both want and need. And, keep your thing in your pants!" I concluded.

"That's it Quentin?" Peter said drunkenly. "You are out of this club. You are turning into a real little punk.

"Quentin, for someone who is not married, you sure seem to know a lot about relationships. That's for damn sure," Jeff said giving me the third degree. "Come to think of it, I heard before you met Bridgett, you were a virgin."

"A virgin!" Peter exclaimed in shock, "Ah man, tell me it's not so."

"I was a virgin?" I squeaked defensively. "Who's been spreading those vicious rumors about me?" I grabbed my crotch. "I've had a lot of sexual experience."

"Quentin, a blow up doll or a jar of Vaseline and your hand is not a bonafide sexual experience," Antonio blasted. "That is definitely not considered a ménage a trois."

"Maybe it is," Peter teased. "It's a geek ménage a trois, a geek threesome!" The fellows roared.

"Damn, Quentin, you are rolling like that?" Jeff asked, adding fuel to the fire.

Donald started laughing so hard beer came out of his nose.

"Peter, I heard that before Quentin met Bridgett, he and his blow up doll were running off to Jamaica so he could get his groove back." Jeff roasted me. It was now open season on me. The fellows were laughing and punching each other.

Jeff slyly looked around. "Fellows, have your ever had a threesome?"

"Not me," I said, not believing my ears, "I went to Catholic School."

"Not me," Donald blurted out with a drunken slur.

"I have," Antonio admitted, "but I was too drunk to remember."

"What about you, hotshot pilot?" Antonio asked.

Jeff sat there with a condescending smile on his face. "Of course I have. I've had several in the cockpit!"

"Whatttt!" we all yelled out in amazement. "For real!"

"Would Jeff the Pilot lie?" Jeff said, placing his hand over his heart, "This is your captain speaking, we are experiencing a bit of turbulence. Please fasten your seatbelts." He snickered. "It's amazing what you can do at 30,000 feet."

"Don't you have to fly the plane?" I asked.

"Man, no, everything is computerized. You put it on autopilot and go about your business. Hey, Quentin, you're not the only author in the house. I'm going to write a book called *How to Have a Threesome*. As a matter of fact, I've slept with most of the flight attendants in my crew."

"Stop lying!" Antonio said in astonishment.

"I kid you not. You can ask anybody," Jeff bragged.

My eyes bulged when I realized that Jeff was talking about going to bed with two women, but the fellows were right in there, hollering and jumping out of their chairs. "That's what I'm talking about. Jeff you are the man!" they yelled.

I took a deep breath. "I'm the only one here that is not tainted or has issues about marriage. When Bridgett and I get married, we will have the perfect marriage. It's all about trust, honesty and communication."

The laughter stopped as they all turned to look at me.

"I think women's problems are Freudian," Jeff said trying to sound intelligent.

"Freudian?" Antonio said in disbelief.

"Yes, Antonio, Freudian! Women have penis envy."

"Touché!" The fellows toasted comically.

"Jeff, why would women have penis envy?" I said defensively. "Especially since the world revolves around the vagina." I had everyone's attention now. "Check this out fellows. Not so attractive women can get sex anytime, anyplace. Can an unattractive man boast the same thing? That's excluding him from being a rich or powerful man."

I gave Peter a sly glance.

"I know you young bucks are not throwing hints at me," Peter comically replied. Then he started to think about my claim.

I continued. "Check this out fellows. Men come out of a vagina. Most men spend their last dollar trying to get back into one. If you don't believe me, look at all these horny men in here. They are spending their last dime and the 'baby needs new shoes' money trying to get laid."

"He's got a point," Antonio said.

Totally unimpressed, Donald yawned, and said, "Quentin, you are totally whipped."

"Whatever, Donald, whatever," I said sarcastically, "A woman will take a lot of crap trying to keep her relationship together. If we put as much energy and creativity in keeping our women happy as we do cheating the divorce rate would go down." Silence once again filled the table.

Jeff leaned toward me, and out of the blue, pimp slapped me upside the head.

"Ouch!" I yelled grabbing my head, "What was that for?"

"For all the divorces in America."

"Fellows, isn't this country about free speech?" I responded, rubbing my head.

"Hell no," Peter said with an intimidating tone.

"Won't the truth set you free?" I asked.

"Hell no. The truth will set you up. Just the same as in a marriage, when your wife says 'if you tell me the truth, I won't get angry.' It's a set up and you'd better lie," Peter warned. "If she didn't see you do it, you're not guilty. Trust me marriage is just like the Feds. Your past will be used against you."

"Quentin, are you sure you're not gay?" Jeff said.

"I'm not gay," I protested. "Fellows, a woman wants a man who will do the right thing, even when she isn't there. She wants a man who will check himself even when he knows he can get away with something. Furthermore, cheating husbands — a woman needs to know she can believe in her man."

Antonio yawned, and pretended to ignore me, but I continued to press my point. "Part of loving someone is to reveal and surrender your secrets, your past and your hang-ups."

"Oh hell no!" Jeff protested.

"Zip it Jeff," I said angrily. "It's giving a woman a fair chance and a clear picture of who she is involved with. If you haven't done that then your secrets and past issues will eventually surface." I paused and gave them all a judgmental stare. "The truth will always set you free. But I warn all of you, lies and dishonesty will set you up."

Donald leaned over and pimp slapped me again.

"And what was that for?"

"McFly, that was for going against the team."

I rubbed my head, but was determined to make my point. "Fellows, cheating hurts a woman not just because you gave away the intimacy, but because the person she has been faithful and devoted to didn't hold the relationship and her feelings in the same regard.

Jeff stopped, choked off a laugh and gave me a bone chilling warning. "Get out while you can. You are doomed and you will end up like us. A shadow of the man you used to be. Run, Quentin, run!"

"Jeff, either you have been flying too much or not getting enough oxygen," Antonio said with a laugh.

"I'm lucky to have found Bridgett. Before I met her, I kept meeting bitter, divorced, bisexual women with serious father issues."

"For real?" Jeff said probing. "I thought you were my boy, Quentin? Why didn't you hook me up? Every man wants an easy score."

The fellows roared hysterically.

14

"I won't dignify your juvenile remarks with an adult response." I was getting pissed off and really wanted to crack their heads together. I, once again, tried to take the conversation to a higher level.

"Ok, guys, all jokes aside. I would like to ask you a serious question."

"Fire away," Jeff responded, struggling to be serious.

"I'm getting ready to get married. I really need some good advice from experts. But since I can't afford them, I guess you guys will have to do."

"No, he didn't say that!" Jeff shouted. "Richie Cunningham doesn't have jokes. I bet he's one of those sensitive guys who likes to cuddle after sex!"

"I do! You should try it sometime. It would work wonders for your marriage."

"Oooooh, Richie Cunningham struck me with a hater arrow. Oh attitude, attitude!"

"Speaking of attitude," Peter interrupted, "two husbands were cheating and one husband looked at the other and said, 'Do you talk to your wife after great sex?' The other husband looked at him and said, 'I sure as hell do. What kind of husband do you think I am? I call my wife the moment I leave my mistress's house.' "

They burst into laughter again and I just sat quietly and shook my head.

Antonio looked at me suspiciously. "Quentin, are you sure you aren't wired?"

"I'm cool. I just want to make sure my marriage lasts a lifetime. I don't want to be another statistic."

"Okay fellows, calm down. Quentin asked a reasonable question." Antonio looked at Peter, Donald and Jeff. "If you knew then what you know about marriage now, would any of you marry your mates over again?"

The fellows pondered the questions, then almost at the same time they said, "Let me get back to you on that one!"

"What about you Peter?" I asked. "You've been married the longest. Give us some wisdom from your vast experience."

Peter took a sip of beer, leaned back in his chair and cleared his throat. "Fellows, I've been married for 32 years and 31 years have been unhappy ones. I don't care what Dr. Phil says, the shortest time in history is the phrase 'I'll love you forever.' What I have learned is, instead of marrying a woman you love and who loves you, grab the bull by the horns and marry a woman you can't stand. Then just give her your house."

"Peter, that makes no sense." I said.

"Hear me out. After the honeymoon is over and a few good years of marriage has passed, you'll both end up hating each other anyway. And the judge will give her the house. So, why waste time?"

"Damn Peter!" We all roared with laughter.

Our waitress returned to our table and inquired, "You gentlemen ready for another pitcher?" Peter circled his index finger around the table as he finished off his glass of beer.

Jeff studied her swaying hips as she moved around the table, tidying up and said, "Hey sweetheart! Can I have your phone number and some fries to go with that shake?"

She gave him a polite smile and said, "Sorry, I don't date the customers."

"Don't date the customers? Honey, I'm a pilot. I make a lot of money."

"Well, that's great for you," she said smiling sweetly, "But it looks like your plane is going down in flames, so you need to bail out." With that, she turned on her heel and left the table to bring them some more beer.

"Player down!" Antonio screamed. "And there were no survivors! Just think we almost took your lame advice."

15

"Men and their large fragile egos," I said, shaking my head, "So back to my original question. Peter would you marry Jan all over again?"

Peter cleared his throat and put his hand to his temple. "Putting all jokes aside, I would advise any man to get married, but get married for the right reasons." He gave me a meaningful look. "The only way I would marry Jan again is if I were stranded on a deserted island, like Tom Hanks in the movie Castaway, and I had to choose between Jan and Wilson, the damn volleyball."

"Wilson the volleyball!" Jeff roared as tears rolled down his face."

"At least Wilson is a few pounds lighter!" Peter wisecracked.

"Quentin, you will be lost forever. Men go down the road of matrimony, but a vegetable comes back," Donald warned. "A few years from now the only thing you will see are dead people."

They continued to tease each other, but Jeff grew quiet. I looked at him curiously. He looked back at me and laughed without humor. "Ninety-five percent of your time in a marriage will be spent trying to make your wife happy. For me to capture Beverly's heart was an expensive proposition. I used to buy things I didn't need with money I didn't have to impress people I didn't like. A diamond may be a girl's best friend, but a good divorce lawyer is running neck and neck.

"Touché." Peter commented, raising his glass drunkenly.

They continued to behave like Boys Gone Wild, but suddenly Donald went rigid.

"What Donald?" Antonio asked perplexed.

"Man, a scary thought just hit me," Donald said.

"What's that?" Antonio asked.

"Fellows, what would happen if you got busted cheating and later on the woman you were cheating with tells you she's pregnant...with twins no less?"

"Damn!" We all shouted in unison. A scary silence filled the table.

"Man, that would be really fucked up," Peter supplied morosely. "How in the world would you explain that to your wife?"

"I'd explain it long distance," Jeff blurted out. "I mean long ass distance, like from a Rio police station." Jeff shuddered. "Because once she hears it, there would certainly be a homicide."

"Quentin, why are you so against a pre-nup. It's the safest thing to do to protect yourself?" Antonio asked.

"Antonio, right from the start you are telling your woman that you don't trust her. That you don't think the relationship is going to last and that you have to protect yourself against her. How do you think that's going to make someone you love feel?"

"Bravo, Quentin," said Peter. "I like where your head is. I may not agree with it, but don't let us burned out husbands give you our marriage blues. Do you think Bridgett feels the same way?"

"I certainly do," I said with confidence.

"What about if she hits the lotto and wins 100 million or more?" Peter asked, giving me a sly look that I didn't understand.

"It still wouldn't matter, Peter. Money doesn't buy happiness. What's mine is Bridgett's and what's hers is mine. I'll bet my life that Bridgett feels the same way."

"Well, Quentin, I'll leave that one alone for now," Peter slurred, leaning back in his chair. "Okay fellows, now down to business. It's time for your induction. My first question is what movie title reminds you of making love to your wife?"

Donald and Jeff looked perplexed. I thought about it, and Antonio was smiling at Peter as he said, "I have one in mind. *Terminator!*"

"How does the *Terminator* remind you of making love to Liana?" I asked, not really believing my ears.

"Man, when I'm finished, I have to tell her..." he dropped his voice and tried to assume a German accent, "I'll be back."

"Damn," Jeff roared, "You rolling like that? Okay, my turn. With Beverly it'd have to be *Gone in 60 Seconds.*"

"Man, your lady is a ten. She's a supermodel." Donald said enviously.

"Yeah, she may be all that, but she's a two in bed. She just lies there like a log. So I'm gone in sixty seconds. Tonight's her birthday and here I am with you guys."

A looked passed across Donald's face that I couldn't interpret. All he said was, "Man, that's cold."

"So what about you Donald?" I asked.

He shook his head as if waking up from a deep sleep and said, *The Sixth Sense.*

"Why?" Peter asked simply.

"Because after fifteen years, I see dead people!"

"Damn, Donald, you got it bad. Just think, you could've had a V8," Antonio said.

Peter, delighted in his little game, looked at me, "Okay, Quentin, spill your guts."

I hesitated, embarrassed, but said, *"Definitely Maybe."*

"Why?" Peter asked.

"Man, Bridgett is inexperienced at sex. She's all over the place. What really drives me crazy is that she's so anal retentive that in the heat of passion she'll jump out of bed and neatly fold her bra and panties."

"Stop lying, McFly!" Jeff roared.

"I kid you not!"

"Hey, Quentin, that's my goddaughter you're talking about," Peter noted. I looked at him and smiled innocently.

"Well, you asked," I replied.

"Okay, Peter, it's your turn," Donald pointed out. "You've heard our stories. What about you?"

He smiled drunkenly, enunciating each word very carefully, "Mine would be *Titanic,* because I'm sinking fast."

We all roared with laughter, jostling each other.

"Okay, Peter, you got it baaaaad!" Jeff yelled.

"Okay, okay," I said, raising my hands, "I've heard you all complain, but none of you have said what you want out of marriage."

"That's easy," Antonio jumped in. "Respect, admiration, appreciation, emotional support, peace of mind and great sex!"

"I'll drink to that!" the fellows cheered.

"So what do you want when you walk in the door at night?" I asked.

"Number one, peace," Peter slurred, weaving about in his seat, "and not a list of things to do or things that I forgot to do."

Antonio said with a frown, "Cave time."

Jeff tossed out, "Man, when I come home from a flight, I just need time to unwind. The moment I walk through the door, Beverly wants to talk and talk and talk and talk. She doesn't know when to be quiet. She doesn't know how to make her point and let it go. She keeps on and on and on. It's a power thing."

Peter interrupted, "By not letting you have the last word, she's showing you she is liberated and won't be pushed around."

"That may be so Peter, but no man wants to go toe to toe with an emotional woman. The only thing having the last word will do is push me away, or make me tell a lie to avoid an argument," Jeff added.

"I agree," Antonio said, "Not many men want to keep being beaten up with their shortcomings."

"I know that's right," Donald agreed.

"Now, after I cool off," Jeff continued, "I want a home cooked meal. But instead of having dinner ready, the supermodel wants to visit every five star restaurant in Atlanta. I tell you, if you took a microwave away from a woman, she'd be totally helpless."

"What I want is appreciation," Donald said. "When I come home Ashley throws so many things I'm not doing in my face, I'd like for once just to hear what I'm doing right."

"I feel your pain, man," Jeff sympathized. "For once in my life I would like Beverly to initiate sex. I am tired of always having to be the one to bring it up. I'd like to act out her fantasy, but it just isn't there."

"I like to be treated like a king," Antonio said as he reared back in his chair, cupping his hands behind his head. "If I'm the bread winner, and the man of the house, I want to be treated special. Traditionally, Latin women cater to a man. Liana's pretty good at that part. Dinner's ready unless we're going out. Man, I got it pretty good compared to you guys. I just wished she'd slow it down and realize I'm working for our future. I wished she'd stop judging me and accept that what I do, I do for her."

In defense of women everywhere I said, "Fellows, men are always talking about what they want, but what about what she wants? Women are forced to be the man and the woman too. Maybe they feel overworked and under-appreciated."

They all looked at me in silence, so I forged ahead. "Peter, you would probably receive more if you gave more. What about when Jan gets home. Do you lighten her load by making sure the house is in order? Do you pamper her? Not just with things, but with time, understanding, attention or affection."

"And Jeff," I continued. "Women relieve stress by communicating. If you need time to unwind, tell her. Women aren't mind readers and you would certainly get more sex with romance. She's got to feel that sex is given freely, instead of out of demand and expectation. Acting like a spoiled brat or pulling the duty card is not exactly a turn-on for a woman."

"Antonio, anybody would have an attitude if all they did was give. Is it asking too much to have a romantic dinner ready for her when she gets home?"

I thought I finally had made a point, but leave it to Jeff. He was not going to take any responsibility for his marriage. He said, "It's a dark day for relationships when we take advice from a therapist with a blow up doll."

He stopped and took a long pull of beer, then said morosely, "Beverly is pressing me to have children."

"You got something against the patter of little feet?" I asked. "Doesn't every man want someone to carry on his name?"

"Depends on the individual," Jeff exploded. "Once a woman gets pregnant she controls all the cards."

"Shouldn't you have thought about that before you laid down with her?" I asked.

He set his glass down on the table very carefully. "Hell yeah! But, it's up to the woman to protect herself. A man should be given a choice about fatherhood. I don't want a woman making that choice for me. That's the very reason I pull out or use a condom when I have sex with Beverly."

"A condom with your wife," Donald said disbelievingly.

"Fellows do it all the time. I'm enjoying my life. I'm not ready to become a father."

"Come on Jeff, what kind of woman would trap a man with a child?"

"It happens every day in the Latino community," Antonio added.

"And it definitely happens in the white community!" Peter declared.

"I must admit the sisters aren't above a little deception," Donald added.

"I guess one child wouldn't be so bad, but Beverly wants twins. They run in her family."

"No one can determine if they are going to have twins," Donald corrected. "Twins wouldn't be so bad if you wanted children."

"I'm just not ready to be a father. I'm having too much fun," Jeff whined.

I looked at him in disgust, and then looked at the other fellows. I really couldn't understand why they hated their wives. I said, "Fellows you all have beautiful, devoted women. Why do you cheat when you have a good woman at home?"

"We do it because we are men!" Jeff stood abruptly and smartly saluted every man in the club. "Didn't you read the Constitution? Men have certain inalienable rights like life, liberty and the pursuit of happiness. Translated - all the pussy you can get. It's in our job description."

"Quentin," Peter said compassionately, "when men finally say 'I do' cheating is the last thing on their mind. Most men are just like women. We want to believe that our marriage will last forever."

"But most men ignore the alarming divorce statistics," Antonio contributed.

Donald added, "We walk into marriage thinking we will defy the odds. But far too often, once married, things change and we are stuck. As far as why men cheat when they have a good woman? Sometimes it's ego, sometimes it's boredom, a man wants adventure or variety. Some men are always looking for something a little bit better, younger or prettier than what they have. Some men need to be constantly validated by someone other than their mates. That's Donald Trump's problem, and Hugh Hefner's. Some men cheat because they can never be satisfied," he looked pointedly at Jeff, "Some men are just dogs, Scooby-Doo."

"Marriage is boring. You work, worry, pay bills, you die. It's the same day in and day out," Jeff said. Some of the fire seemed to go out of Jeff. His chin rested on his chest and he seemed to be contemplating his navel.

"I disagree!" I said, slapping my hand down on the table, "Sometimes the people in the marriage are boring. If you fail to reinvent yourself or your love, it's going to lose its appeal. You can be on the most exotic vacation, but if you don't come out of your room and explore all the options, you'll be bored in paradise."

"Listen to Quentin," Antonio wisecracked, "Mr. Relationship Expert."

"I agree with Quentin," Peter said in admiration. "But, I guess I too, let temptation get the best of me. I guess the reason I started cheating was because Jan and I couldn't communicate. I also didn't feel appreciated. Regardless of how hard I tried, my best was never good enough. Fellows, it is very frustrating to give your best and not be appreciated."

"But women feel that way all the time," I commented. Everyone gave me an angry stare.

"Whose side are you on, Quentin?" Antonio questioned.

"I just want you guys to be fair!"

"What does fair have to do with relationships? It's the three C's: catch, conquer and control," Peter spat out angrily. "I don't know why women feel if they complain they will get more. Complaining only makes a man want to do less."

"Well, my story is quite the opposite," Jeff said, "Beverly was all that and I still cheated because far too many women believe the myth that there is a shortage of good men. Of course, as men, we exploit it. One secret that I hope women will never find out is that a man will do only what you allow him to do."

"But a woman shouldn't smother a man," Donald threw in, "A man needs space."

Peter chuckled. "Some men cheat because their marriage is lacking something or their mate is lacking something as a person."

The fellows nodded in agreement.

Donald said, "Let me tell you about the downside of cheating."

"Stop playing Donald," Jeff teased. "You just want us to stop cheating so you can have all the women for yourself."

Donald shook his finger at Jeff. "That's it, you dirty dog."

"Let's be real. What kind of drawback comes with X-rated, uninhibited sex, appreciation, no complaining, being catered to and having someone there to please you 24/7?" Jeff asked.

"You're missing the point," I interrupted. "Fellows, a woman's mind, heart and body are usually a package deal."

"Un huh, uh huh," Jeff said with a yawn.

"You bunch are so thickheaded. A woman gives her body when she gives her heart!" I bellowed in frustration.

"Okay, okay," Antonio said, motioning with his hands for us to be a little less loud.

"The drawback, my horny friends," Donald said knowingly, "is when the other woman becomes emotionally involved and wants to become your wife; or she wants to confront your wife."

We roasted each other, called for another pitcher of beer and Jeff got diarrhea of the mouth worse than usual.

"A man will only do what his woman will let him do? Check this out. A man will let a woman know he's cheating."

"How can she tell?" I asked Jeff.

"He leaves signs everywhere, like when you start asking for more time for yourself. That would be okay if you were spending 24/7 together. But it's a telltale sign if you only see each other a few days a week. Another give away is if you're always working late but not making any more money. He's finding excuses to get away from his woman. Another clue is he's rarely in the mood for sex. Or he suddenly becomes critical of you and starts comparing you to other women."

"I do that to Ashley all the time," Donald reflected.

"He tries to start an argument over trivial things then storms out of the house angry."

"That's me again," Donald said, sinking lower and lower into his seat.

"He develops a certain interest in new things, or has a roving eye."

"I reckon that's all of you," I said sarcastically.

"You notice an unfamiliar fragrance in his hair or on his clothes."

"That one has gotten me busted for years," Peter said lifting his lapel to sniff it.

"He can't look his lady in the eye when she asks him point blank if he's having an affair."

"That's me," Donald admitted. "Man, these women are taking the fun out of cheating! First, you got that show called *Cheaters*, and now that angry woman on the loose. It's hard out there for a pimp!"

"Man, if Liana ever caught me cheating, it would be my ass. Come to think of it, didn't a man have his thing cut off by an angry wife, in some sort of love triangle?"

"Yeah, what was her name?" Jeff said, "Lorraina something!"

"Lorena Bobbitt!" I supplied. "After that happened, cheating went down and church attendance went up. Men became as faithful as puppies. Imagine life without your thing."

"Damn!" Donald cringed and crossed his legs.

"Come on fellows, let's change the subject," Jeff said with a tremor in his voice.

"Hey Quentin, why should you care anyway. Ain't nobody going to cut yours off. You don't use it. In fact, it's collecting dust." Antonio roasted me. The fellows howled.

I was getting pretty tired of being the butt of their tired old jokes so I fired back, "Well, I hope you all learned something from these stories."

"Like what?" Donald asked, with innocent dignity.

"Like don't get caught," Jeff tossed out.

"Like protect the family jewels," Antonio said.

"Like women have penis envy," Peter said seriously.

"No, you juvenile delinquents, the moral of this story is honesty is the best policy. And what's done in darkness will come to light."

"Will someone please slap Billy Graham up side the head?" Peter said drunkenly, "He's blowing my high!"

Jeff slapped me up side the head. "Ouch!" I yelled and the fellows gave him high fives.

"That's what I'm talking about; give him one for the team. What a sellout!" Peter cheered.

"Okay!" I yelled. I cleared my throat and caught my breath. "I'm sure you fellows have your reasons for feeling the way you do, but I want my marriage to last forever. I will not be a statistic."

"Speaking of statistics, fellows, what do you think the real reason for the high divorce rate is?" Jeff inquired.

Peter immediately jumped in, "People get married for all the wrong reasons. Sometimes, it's for our own selfish interest; money, power or prestige."

Antonio came to life. "Men have forgotten how to be romantic and women have forgotten how to be appreciative."

"I totally agree!" Donald said fuming.

I said, "Couples are not committed to making their marriages work."

Jeff rebounded, "couples now give up so easy. A big marriage killer is so many women believe that a man can make them happy. A man can't make you totally happy. A man can only add to or take away from the happiness that you have created for yourself. A lot of women come into a relationship with unresolved hang-ups and baggage."

"When Beverly and I met," he continued, "She had so much baggage I thought she was Samsonite. By the time I broke down her defenses, I was almost burned out and was losing interest."

"Hey man, you are preaching to the choir!" Donald chimed in. "A lot of couples don't have a belief in God or a higher power. Sometimes life is going to throw you a curve ball. The only thing you have to rely on is your faith."

"Slow your roll, Donald," Peter said comically. "What I also learned is that a lot of couples feel that love is enough to make them happy."

"I thought so too," Donald said.

"Well, it's not."

"What?" said Antonio. "I've always heard that all my life. I thought as long as you loved each other, that was enough."

"Sorry to inform you fellows, but that isn't necessarily true," Peter intoned.

"O Great Peter McCallister, enlighten us," I said stroking his ego.

"Fellows, love must be accompanied by capability. Being at the same place at the same time and wanting the same thing. Love is hard work. It takes total commitment and a willingness to forgive."

"Run, Quentin, run," Donald said in a scary tone. "It's too late for us, but you still have a chance."

"Peter, you make it sound like a tough job with little benefits," I said.

"Marriage is a job," he re-emphasized, "but the benefits are great. That is if you marry the right person, on the other hand, marriage can be hell."

"Tell us something we don't know," Jeff said slapping his forehead.

"Marriage can turn into a nightmare." Peter continued, "Especially when your friends, material things, or your job become more important than your marriage. Love also begins to fade when your attention is not given from the heart, or when your affection is given out of demand, expectation, anger or just to pacify."

"I have one more question," I threw in.

"What now Quentin?" Jeff asked exasperated.

"How long did you date your wife before you popped the question?"

"That's a no-brainer," Jeff jumped in. "From the first time I laid eyes on Beverly, I had to have her. I popped the question in three months."

"It took me a year to pop the question to Ashley," Donald added.

"Six months for me," Peter said in a jovial tone. "Now, thirty-two years later, I wonder what the hell I was thinking."

We all looked inquiringly at Antonio. Antonio made a noise in his throat. "How long Antonio?" I asked.

"Oh, about twelve years."

"Man, I heard of cold feet, but iceberg feet are ridiculous," Jeff howled at his own joke.

"I knew Liana since we were children."

"Hey, how long should a woman wait on a marriage proposal?" I asked.

Jeff, of course, had the first opinion. "When a man meets a woman, he puts her into one of five different categories; wife material, bed buddy, friend, sugar mama or Miss Right Now."

Donald took the stage. "Knowing this, if a woman is really serious about marriage and she's between twenty- one and thirty, the maximum time she should wait is two years - over thirty, one year."

Peter interjected as he raised one finger, "Especially if there are no extenuating circumstances like he lives in another city, or he just came out of an ugly divorce or he's unemployed. If there are extenuating circumstances, she needs to start looking somewhere else. The guy is probably putting her into category five, Miss Right Now. Someone to date until something better comes along."

The fellows pretty much said in unison, "I'll drink to Miss Right Now."

I looked at my watch and it was 12:45a.m. "Hey Peter, it's getting late."

"Quentin, don't be such a party pooper. Since the fellows and I are getting plastered, you need to be the designated driver. We will be the designated drunks." Peter took another swig and put his glass down with a thump. He gave each of us a serious look. "Okay, here it is. I know you are all dying to get into my little group, but the other members and I must feel that we can really trust you."

"How do we go about earning your trust?" Antonio said anxiously.

"The main thing that has bound us all together for so many years is dirt and scandal. Dirt and scandal is the glue that keeps everyone in check."

"It's worked in Washington, DC and corporate America for years," I said.

"Okay, so what do we have to do?" Jeff asked hesitantly.

"Nothing out of the ordinary," Peter said with a sly grin. "Just give up your first born."

"Just kidding!" he said happily as he watched us start to squirm. "Don't get your knickers tied in a knot."

We all let out a collective "Whew!"

Peter looked at all of us one by one and added, "Putting all jokes aside I'm going to ask you a second question to get into our club. Now, here's the question. What is your deepest, darkest, most scandalous secret?"

As we sat in stunned silence, Peter snickered under his breath and said deviously, "Now who's first?"

17

JEFF

Drunk and trying desperately to impress Peter, I spoke up. "I'll be your guinea pig. I got balls the size of Texas. Now all of you know my wife is a former super-model."

"Yes, we do," Donald said annoyed. "You have told us a thousand times."

"You also know my best friend, Dean. Well, my senior flight attendant, Clarissa and Dean were planning to get married. The day they chose was the day after New Year's Day."

Donald broke my flow by asking, "Isn't Clarissa that brunette with the tight ass and those giant ta-ta's."

"The very same one. Well, anyway for years I wanted to jump her bones, but since she was my boy's girl, I wouldn't think of it. I kept my thing in my pants. I just sat at home and masturbated and kept my fantasy to myself. As time passed, I discovered to my surprise, Clarissa had a crush on me. But, we both kept it professional and lusted after each other from afar. Well, two years ago, desire got the best of us."

"So what happened, you dog, come on spill it!" Antonio shouted. "You tapped that ass?"

"Well it was about 11:30 p.m. and we were flying to Rio. Clarissa had been working non-stop to get everyone settled and the passengers, crew, and my co-pilot had gone to sleep. Clarissa opened a bottle of champagne to relax and before I knew it she'd had one too many. She was twirling around in the aisles with a party on. I'd put on the autopilot and gone to see what the commotion was all about when I heard a party horn blow. It was Clarissa starting the party early. I told her to be quiet, not to wake the passengers. She looks at me flirtatiously. She said she wanted to bring in the New Year with a bang, and asked if I had any suggestions. She started unbuttoning her blouse and backed me into the cockpit. I was in shock and asked her what she was doing. She smiles at me and says 'I'm doing something I wanted to do ever since I laid eyes on you. I'm going to fuck you."

"I tried to reason with her, told her she was drunk. She told me she knew perfectly well what she was doing as she slowly stripped off her blouse and undid her bra. I protested, reminded her about Dean and how she was getting married in two days. She said that was two days from now and this is the here and now. She was winding herself all over me and pushed me down against the nav console and straddled me, running her tongue over my lips. She pushed her breasts in my face. She was hitting me with them like the LAPD was hitting Rodney King. I tried to get away and I was screaming that I was Dean's best man..."

"She what?" Donald begged.

Jeff quickly changed the subject. "Fellows, any one want a beer?"

"Hell no, we don't want no damn beer. Man, get back to the story!" Antonio yelled.

"Okay, now where was I?"

"You were at the part where she pistol whipped you with her boobs!" Donald said licking his lips lasciviously.

"Oh yeah, she slapped me."

"Slapped you? Come on man, what happened?" Antonio smirked, not believing him.

"Stop hating Antonio. She slapped me and told me she'd decide who the best man was. She told me I was acting like a wimp. She started grinding into my thing. I mean, what was I going do? My pants were bulging so big it hurt. She started loosening my tie and unbuttoning my shirt. Then she went to work on my zipper."

Donald lifted his glass to his face, pressing the coldness against his forehead.

"Fellows, I did think about my friend Dean, I looked her straight in the eye and told her point blank I couldn't do this to my best friend."

"Yeah, you told her you couldn't do that!" I said disbelievingly.

"She gave me a tonsil touching kiss. She pulled away and slapped me again. Told me to stop acting like a punk. She told me if I didn't give it to her, she'd wake up Chuck and screw him. She looked at me with those beautiful eyes and pleaded. 'If you can't fuck a friend, who can you fuck' she said. Being the good friend that I am I couldn't let her screw a stranger. What kind of friend would I be to Dean if I let her fuck the first Tom, Dick or Chuck she met?"

"Jeff, you're quite a guy." Donald said, cracking up. "The mayor should give you the key to the city."

"Shut up Donald, get on with it Jeff" Antonio said.

"Well, her perfect boobs were bouncing up and down and I tried to think of every reason I had to hate Dean. He wouldn't give me his last Oreo cookie in the first grade. He drank the last glass of Kool-Aid thirty years ago."

"Those are good reasons to hate him!" Donald put in.

"Anyway fellows, Clarissa took her bra and tied my hands behind my back. Now I was a complete slave to her lust. She pulled my pants down around my ankles and took my throbbing penis deep into her throat. When I was right on the edge, she straddled me and forced me to suck her breasts, one by one."

"She forced you?" Donald said.

"Yeah, she forced me! Those flight attendants are strong, man. They should be tested for steroids. I looked at the clock at it was 11:55 p.m. I increased the rhythm and she said for me to slow down, she didn't want to cum before midnight. I couldn't help but think she had to be kidding. She kept gripping me tighter and tighter. I didn't think I could make it last, 11:58 p.m. was the max, but I fought it down, I even thought of every ugly girl I ever slept with. The more I fought to hold back, the harder she rode me. My heart was beating like a drum. The minutes ticked by. I used every trick I could think of. I looked at the clock again. It was countdown time. She saw me looking at the clock and looked over at it too. It was 11:59 and 50 seconds. We both increased the rhythm and counted down, 10, 9, 8, 7, 6, 5, 4, 3, 2, 1...we both screamed out, 'Oh shit, I'm cumming, oh fuck!' We both came and there I was speechless, breathing heavily and two quarts low and wondering how in the hell Chuck slept though it. We cleaned up, got dressed and she walked out the door and blew me a kiss. She then woke the passengers up and wished them a Happy New Year."

"Player, player!" Antonio and Donald yelled.

"Two days later, she got married and Dean never suspected a thing."

18

ANTONIO

"Man, why doesn't anything like that happen in coach? Okay fellows, here's my little something. While I was in law school, my roommate and I were pulling an all nighter for a final. About 2:00 a.m., he noticed me rolling my head from side to side. I was trying to relieve the strain on my neck. He came over and began massaging my neck. It felt so good and I was purring. Slowly his hand moved down to my chest. He started gently stroking my nipples."

"Stroked your nipples?" I said in surprise.

"Damn Antonio, he propositioned for a booty buddy!" Jeff teased. "Come on out of the closet with it. Throw your pink panties in the air!"

"I got your pink panties right here Jeff," I said grabbing my crotch.

"Let him finish his story," Peter interrupted calmly.

"After Bill's homosexual pass, I was shocked. I looked at him and asked him if he was gay. He gave me a sly grin and said 'who wants to know' sort of coyly. Well, I told him as a friend and roommate I wanted to know. He told me he wasn't 100 percent gay so I asked him what is 'not 100 percent gay?' Maybe like being a little bit pregnant? He told me he liked men and women, but didn't advertise that he liked men, he kept that part a secret, said he was on the down-low. I never guessed, so I guess he was very discreet. We used to shower together after soccer practice. He could have been checking out my butt and I never knew it."

Peter teased, "Are you homophobic?"

"Fellows, I don't have anything against gays. I think a man's sexual preference is his own business. But you need to let a woman or your buddy know. Well anyway, one night after that discussion, Bill's fiancée came over. We started drinking. They ended up on the bed making out. I watched them, I admit it. I was getting turned on. Before I knew what was happening, she was down on the floor in front of me unzipping my pants. Next thing I knew, we were all three in the bed together and getting it on. After we climaxed, we drank more wine and began round two. I was totally shit faced. She left and Bill started kissing me."

"Oh gross!" they all chimed together.

"Two big, hairy men, bumping and grinding and kissing," Jeff said.

"Ah, Antonio," Peter teased, "You are so gay."

"I'm not gay," I said defensively. "Just because a person has one homosexual experience, it does not mean that he is gay. Does it Peter?"

"Let's just say you are on the waiting list," he joked. All the guys started laughing and jumped up to sing. Of all the "real man" songs they could have chosen, they chose YMCA by the Village People.

Young man, are you listening to me?

I say young man, you can fulfill your dream.

It's fun to stay at the YMCA! YMCA! Say it loud.

Then Jeff screamed out comically, "*They have everything men enjoy, you can hang out with the boys at the YMCA!*" They all roared at their performance.

"Shut up!" I demanded. "If you breathe a word of this, especially to Liana, you will all be playing checkers with Jimmy Hoffa."

They sat back down and looked at me, trying to get their laughter under control.

"Don't worry Antonio, we won't tell a soul, will we guys?" Quentin commented.

"Antoinette," Jeff said, flipping his wrist.

I clenched my fist. "My name is Antonio and I got your Antoinette, waiting list and YMCA right here." I grabbed my crotch with my other hand and shook my fist in his face.

"Don't be so sensitive," Donald snickered. "The fellows are just funning you. Your sexual preference is your business."

"I'm not gay!" I shouted, jumping to my feet. I then noticed customers and strippers looking at me. I could just see this getting into the news.

"Shh, cool out Antonio, it's not that serious!" Quentin said, coming to my rescue. "Forget what the fellows think."

19

QUENTIN

The fellows continued to roast Antonio, but I held my ground. "Let it go guys, get off Antonio's case." I said as threateningly as I could. "It's my turn now. Let me tell you guys my little hidden secret."

"Quentin, we already know your business," Jeff teased. "You date blow up dolls."

"Jeff, a mind is a terrible thing to waste," I said angrily. "Now, here's another riddle for you. If you are supposed to be an intelligent man, but you keep saying stupid things, does that make you a jackass?"

"Oh, Jeff, you got punked!" Antonio said gleefully.

"Whatever, Quentin, whatever," Jeff said, flipping his hands at me.

"I also have a reputation to worry about." I said.

"What reputation?" Donald blurted out. "You don't have any reputation. You need to get one first, before you can worry about it."

Ignoring him I continued, "Anyway fellows, don't you breath a word of this."

"Mums the word," Peter said yawning.

"Here goes rated G and made for Nickelodeon," Jeff warned.

"All right, shut up guys." I insisted. "My scandalous secret happened years ago, when I worked at Baby Doe's Restaurant."

"Wasn't that the restaurant that hung off the cliff over 285. The one that closed mysteriously," Peter inquired.

"The very one," I confirmed.

"That was one of my favorite eating places," Peter added.

Trying to get them back on track, I said, "Have you ever wondered why women go to the bathroom together when only one of them has to pee?"

"Can't say I have," Jeff answered, "Seems like there are more pressing issues, like the economy, the troops in Iraq, world hunger, peace. We don't have time to wonder or care what the co-pilot does when only one woman has to pee. But since you brought it up..."

Donald interrupted, rescuing me from one of Jeff's long-winded diatribes, "Let him finish his story."

"Okay, I used to notice that on certain nights at Baby Doe's, some of Atlanta's hottest and most beautiful women would congregate in the bathroom. After they came out, they were as happy as singing Smurfs. La, la, la, la."

"Quentin, I was just joking about Nickelodeon. You know the theme song from the Smurfs?" Jeff interrupted again.

Ignoring him, again, I returned to my story. "I was waiting on tables one night and curiosity got the best of me. I just couldn't take it anymore. The next night I got to work an hour early and sneaked upstairs and drilled a hole in the wall adjacent to the ladies room..."

"No you didn't!" Donald exclaimed.

"Yes, I did."

"You are such a Peeping Tom! If that's not a geek move I don't know what is. You're as bad as George McFly," Jeff said.

"Why do you keep calling Quentin, McFly?" asked Antonio, "Who the hell is he?"

"George McFly was Michael J. Fox's father in the movie *Back to the Future*." I was really getting irritated with Jeff's interruptions.

"May I continue with my story?" I asked.

"By all means, continue," Jeff said, aggravated.

"Okay, what I discovered will astound you. The reason some of Atlanta's hottest women were hanging out in the bathroom together is, other than the fact they were making sure no one had toilet paper stuck to their shoes, they were getting it on with their lesbian lovers."

"What!" Jeff came to life on that one. "Stop lying."

"I'm not. It really tripped me out to see some of the hottest and most influential women doing the nasty with each other. I even made a tape. I would go home and masturbate. Fellows, give me five!" I put up my hand.

"Oh, hell no." Jeff protested, wiping his hands on his pants leg. "Ain't no way I'm touching that without disinfecting it."

Peter shook his head, "Quentin, that was too much information."

"You know it makes sense, though." Jeff snapped his fingers. "I thought it was me."

"What makes sense, and what about you?" Donald asked baffled.

"I knew one particular anchor woman that hosted the evening news. I was dying to get in her pants. But, she wouldn't give me the time of day." Jeff smirked. "I would see her at Baby Doe's all the time. Now it makes sense. She's gay. Speaking of hotties, that Robin Meade on CNN's Morning Express is a cutie. But that Nancy Grace scares the hell out of me." We all laughed at the expression on Jeff's face.

"Quentin, I'm dying to see those flicks..." Peter said.

"Come over anytime and we'll make a night of it."

Peter caught himself. "I can't believe what I'm doing. I'm dying to get a Peeping Tom into our little club. Talk about affirmative action."

As the fellows went back and forth roasting me, Donald came to my rescue. "Hey, get off Quentin's case. Plus, Jeff, you aren't the only one boning a supermodel."

20

DONALD

"Trust me, women don't just want a preacher after they've had their share of Mr. Wrong. Take it from me, minister's are the first choice. The truth of the matter is, what women we don't want, we pass over to you."

Everyone stopped sipping their beer and looked at me quizzically.

"What?" they asked.

"How can a minister be a Bad Boy? Aren't you guys supposed to be celibate or like a monk? Aren't you supposed to run from temptation? In fact, Donald, what are you doing at a strip club, and why are you drinking?" Antonio wondered.

I just gave the fellows a foxy, all knowing grin. "What we are supposed to be and what some of us actually are, is two entirely different things. Man, I could tell you some stories that would make your hair stand up."

"Well, don't stop now." Peter said, "The more scandalous it is the more I trust you."

"All right, fellows, hold onto your seats. It's no secret that Holy Faith Church has some of Atlanta's most beautiful women attending. Every Sunday I look out at the congregation and have to shake my head. Sometimes women would purposely wear their dresses extra short to flirt with me. You know about the attraction women have for ministers?

"No," Quentin said.

"A man who professes to know the Lord is sexy. A woman wants to be led. Most men lack the leadership qualities, so they come to us. Where we lead them is up to how serious we are about the Lord."

I shrugged my shoulders. "One such single woman was a sixteen year old by the name of Angie Brown."

"Sixteen!" Peter said in surprise. "That's jail bait. Donald that's too young!"

"Age ain't nothing but a number."

"Well, a sixteen year old is against the law!" Quentin protested.

"Against the law?" Donald said deviously, "It's only against the law if you get caught. Angie was the first baby born in my first church, Divine Baptist. The moment she turned sixteen, I coerced her into having an affair with me. It lasted about seven years."

"Man, you are an undercover R-Kelly. The boy has no shame," Jeff protested.

"Eventually one of the sisters of the church found out. She kept quiet and later on introduced me to Ashley. Ashley was from a good family. She was everything a man could want. After I got married, I broke it off with Angie. I even introduced her to a doctor. They fell in love and were married six months later. Shortly after, the two of them started having problems, so Angie and I rekindled our affair."

"Donald, I can't believe it. Who would have thought!" Peter said, surprised.

"Oh, it gets worse, or better depending on your view point. After a couple of years I broke it off again. I found another cutie in the church and had an affair with her, then Angie and I started back up. Now I've found out they are both pregnant."

"Damn, Donald. Their husbands never suspected any of this?" Peter asked.

"Every penny I make that Ashley isn't wasting goes to keeping them quiet. That's why, Peter, I need to make some real money with you and your friends."

I looked at the other guys and said, "Fellows, Pastor Cash must never know of this. Pinky swear."

They all wrapped their pinkies around mine swearing to take my secret to the grave. Everyone was a bit shocked, never having guessed that their assistant pastor was a wolf in sheep's clothing.

Savannah wandered over with a couple of the other strippers and gave us a lap dance. Every once in a while we'd look at each other and knew what the other was thinking. Now we wanted to know Peter's deep, dark secret, but was afraid to ask. After the strippers finished and were tipped, Peter finally got the message.

21

PETER

"All right, my friends, don't think I've been trying to pull the wool over your eyes. I know you have been kissing up to me. I know you want to be a part of my club, and I know you all think of me as a closet racist. But, that is the farthest thing from the truth. The person we project in public is not always the person we are, especially behind closed doors."

The fellows sat there. The perplexed expressions on their faces told me they had no clue where this was leading. Inside the blare of music from the sound system we had our own little bubble of silence. I looked at each one of them.

"What I'm about to tell you must never go beyond us. It's a secret that must be taken to the grave. Don't even tell your wives."

The guys looked at each other uneasily.

"If anyone ever found this out, it would not only upset my unhappy little home, but would cause McCallister stock to plummet."

I plead with them, "If you don't care about me, think about yourselves. Look at it from a selfish standpoint. If I'm exposed, we will all be kicked out of the 30305 Club. Your ambitions for fame and fortune will cease to exist. You will be in disgrace, just like I will be."

They all looked at each other again, their hearts pounding. They knew their dirt could get them into trouble, but they also suspected it would be nothing compared to what they were about to hear. I stuck out my pinky, "I want each one of you to pinky swear again."

"Peter, we are with you man. We promise we won't breathe a word of it." Each man locked his pinky around mine, one by one and repeated, "This secret will be taken to the grave."

I put my elbows up on the table and leaned in. "Fellows, I am not who I pretend to be. I'm not a closet racist. I'm a coward."

"A coward?" Quentin asked.

"Shhh, Quentin," Jeff said.

"A coward," I repeated. "I'm afraid to face the truth. The reality of it is I'm a closet Thomas Jefferson."

"Peter, you're losing us..." Donald started to say.

I waved my hand and took a gulp of beer. "Ahhh." I said wiping my mouth. "All of you know how unhappy I am, but you don't know why I married Jan, and why I won't divorce her.

"As the song goes, it's cheaper to keep her. You see, when I met Jan, I was just a struggling real estate developer. Jan was married to a prominent lawyer. They had two boys, Perry and Carlton. She and the Daughters of the South started the 30305 Club. I was young and ambitious and Jan took a shine to me.

"Although she was married, we had an affair. She's always had a thing for younger men. Maybe she wants to get her groove back or something. Shortly after we started our affair, her husband passed away. We then became a couple. Everyone thought we were the perfect couple. She introduced me to her rich and powerful Buckhead friends. Soon, I had more business than I knew what to do with. McCallister Enterprise's stock soared. I had real estate holdings all across Georgia, even outside of Georgia.

"I was so happy; I thought I'd found my soul mate. We went everywhere together, Paris, Rome, the south of France. She told me she was pregnant. That was the happiest day of my life. I've always wanted a family. I grew up in an orphanage."

"An orphanage?" Donald asked in surprise. "Man I thought you were a blueblood."

"No, I'm the product of drug-addicted and alcoholic parents. Jan is the blueblood. She's from a rich Boston family. She's been pedigreed all her life. She doesn't know what it means to struggle. I was so in love and so anxious to get married after I found out she was pregnant that I didn't even think about a pre-nuptial agreement."

"So she caught you slipping," Jeff said dryly.

"No, not really. I don't believe in pre-nups. Marriage should be sacred. Jan and I married very quickly. After a few months the fangs came out. I found out she wasn't pregnant at all. She couldn't even get pregnant. After Carlton was born, she'd had a hysterectomy. I was devastated. Her deceit didn't stop there though. Her bills started coming in. Her extravagant spending had bankrupted her dead husband. Now I had to bail her out.

"I couldn't even be mad at her though. We used each other. She used me for my youth, ambition and money. I used her for her contacts. Still, two wrongs don't make a right."

"But two wrongs do make you even," Donald interjected.

"Anyway, as the years passed, the marriage went downhill. Jan not only used sex as a weapon, but as punishment and reward. Back then I was a faithful, church going husband. But as the first year of marriage passed, I became so unhappy that I started spinning out of control. To relieve my marriage blues I started hanging out at the strip clubs."

"Strip clubs! Have you no shame?" Jeff tossed in trying to lighten the moment.

"Damn, don't you have any morals or decency?" Donald added. I couldn't tell if he was being judgmental or trying to make a joke. Quentin leaned over to Donald and reminded him that we were in a strip club. Donald looked around as if he'd woken from a 20-year nap and said, "Oh, I was wondering what all these naked women were doing in my room. I knew it was either a strip club or Bill Clinton was back in the White House."

Nobody laughed, so I continued with my story. "Two of my favorite clubs were Club Cheetah and Magic City. One day, Jan and I had a major blow out. She packed her bags and flew back to Boston with the kids. In the past, when we fought, I was always the one to apologize, whether it was my fault or not. She knew I would do anything to keep the family together. She always used this as leverage. But that day, I didn't care anymore. I was fed up with her insecurities and excessive spending. I wanted out. But, she knew she had me by the balls. Half of my money would be gone before the ink even dried if I tried to divorce her. I was so trapped, like a lion in a cage. I was king of the jungle, but I had to ask the queen's permission to roar.

"Peter, we feel your pain," Antonio said sympathetically.

"When she walked out the door, I was so hurt and angry. I drove straight to Magic City. I was sitting at my usual table when this beautiful, dark-skinned stripper came towards me. She was about five foot seven and her skin was as smooth as a baby's bottom. Her stage name was Eye Candy. I must admit, the name perfectly described her. She had the most beautiful breasts I've ever seen. She had a butt that looked like two basketballs."

"Damn, Peter, you are the man. Did you jump her bones?" Jeff asked.

"Well, no."

"Damn, Peter, were you having an equipment malfunction? I got a friend that can prescribe some Viagra," Jeff said.

"My equipment works just fine and I don't need any damn Viagra. I was sexually attracted to her, but after talking with her, I went past the visual part. I became attracted to her emotionally, spiritually. I loved her personality."

"So, Peter, did you tap that ass?" Donald blurted out. "Or did you just like her personality, or you were attracted to her mind."

"I guess I did like her mind. This one time I kept my dick in my pants. Sometimes the worst thing you can do is sleep with someone before you really get to know them. Sex clouds things. Sex brings on false feelings of hope."

"Hey man, tap the ass first," Jeff said acting like a buffoon, "Then like the Reverend Jesse Jackson says 'keep hope alive.'"

"Carla and I became friends. I loved that she was so attentive and she made me laugh. She was totally different from Jan. What so many women don't realize is that philosophically a man is attracted to any woman that makes him feel good about himself. Her race or color doesn't matter. Your soul mate can be anyone, any color."

"I'll drink to that," Antonio slurred. Antonio raised his hand in the air. He was so drunk he didn't realize his glass was still sitting on the table. He looked at his hand. "Where's my glass?" He slurred. "Jeff, did you take my glass?"

"Why would I take your stupid glass? Oh, I know why you are asking me. It's because I'm black. The black man is always the number one suspect. Your stupid glass is on the table right in front of you. If you weren't so drunk, you'd know it."

"Sorry Jeff." Antonio blasted beer breath into his face. "The glove doesn't fit, so I must acquit. I love you, man." They hugged each other.

"I love you too, man."

"Now, ain't that sweet. An Oprah moment," Donald said shaking his head. As Antonio drunkenly lunged to hug him, Donald reared back.

"Will you please let Peter finish his story," Quentin said.

"Okay, Peter, you have our totally divided attention." Antonio warbled.

"That's our undivided attention," Quentin corrected.

"Whatever man, please continue Peter," Antonio said graciously.

"The longer Jan and the boys stayed in Boston, the closer Carla and I became. I would come to the club every night. After she got off, we would have a late dinner. We would talk for hours. She was a very classy woman. She was working at the club to help support her family and send herself to medical school."

"Peter, I know you didn't fall for the old 'I'm stripping to pay for my tuition trick.'"

"Call me a punk, but I actually believed her."

"If you believed that," Donald teased, "I've got some swamp land in Florida I want to sell you. We are building condos for the alligators. And those AIG executives will give you half of their golden parachute money for the orphans and widows."

Peter rolled his eyes and continued, "I did believe her. She never asked me for anything. I offered to pay her tuition and help her take care of her family, but she refused."

"Peter, forget that women's integrity stuff," Jeff persisted, "I want to know, did you tap that ass? Again, my self righteous, horny friends; my philosophy about women is to get to know her after you get her in the sheets. If you do it that way, you know whether she's a keeper! Communication is so overrated."

The fellows giggled like six year olds that just saw their first boob.

"I'm with you Jeff. Sensitive men get no sex! Look at George McFly, I mean Quentin," Antonio said, joining the fun.

"I was more interested in winning Carla's heart than getting in her pants."

"Check please," Jeff said loudly, swiveling his head around. "You can't be serious, Peter. Hey, remember our pact. Peter, are you on dope or dog food? Are you trying to rewrite male/female relationships? Men are hunters and we screw. We hunt for something to screw."

The fellows high-fived each other enthusiastically.

"All I know is that the more I got to know Carla, well, something unexpected happened." I took a sip of beer. "We fell in love."

"Damn, Peter, no, no, no. I never knew you were that sensitive. I see you in a totally different light."

"Me too!" Antonio said in disbelief. "A stripper has the great Peter McCallister whipped. Peter, I don't know whether I want to be a member of this wimp club."

Everybody shot Antonio an angry look. He hung his head and mumbled an apology to me.

"Apology accepted. Now, where was I?" I snapped my fingers. "The more time I spent with Carla, the less I thought of Jan. Normally, when Jan left I'd be so lonely I would do anything to get her back. Well, one night, I invited Carla to my yacht for dinner. I prepared a romantic dinner. We danced by moonlight, and we made love."

"Finally!" Jeff said with a big smile. "You finally tapped that ass."

"We made love, Jeff. It was the most beautiful experience I ever had. Making love to Carla consummated our love. But, a few weeks later, she found the Lord."

"Found the Lord!" Donald shouted in awe.

"Yes, fellows, she loved me. But, her belief in God wouldn't allow her to continue to date or have sex with me. I was crushed, devastated. Shortly after that, Jan decided to come home. But, I didn't feel the same way about her. She knew something had happened. Carla had my heart and soul. I didn't want to make love to Jan."

"Amen," Donald exploded. "You got a bad case of jungle fever."

22

QUENTIN

As we sat in awe of Peter's story, he continued and the story got even juicier.

He said, "Two months later, Carla called me crying. She told me she was pregnant. She had thought about an abortion, but was torn. Her faith couldn't allow her to terminate a pregnancy, but her heart wouldn't allow her to keep a child conceived in sin."

"Man, Peter," I replied, "Oh what a tangled web we weave, when first we practice to deceive."

"Shut up, Quentin," Donald threatened. "If you don't, we'll stab your blow up doll. What did you do Peter?"

"I couldn't let her terminate the pregnancy. I always wanted a child of my own. I felt I would never get another chance. After we went back and forth, I finally convinced her to have the child."

"You have an illegitimate child?" I asked, "Boy or girl?"

"Girl.," Peter stated proudly. "We had a beautiful little girl. She was a fair skinned copy of her mother, though some people say she looks like me. The day my daughter was born, I set up a trust fund for her until she turned 30. After Carla finished medical school, she was ashamed to have even contemplated getting rid of the baby. She became obsessed with the treatment of children around the world. She joined the Peace Corp. She was sent to Darfur, Africa. It's a city not too far from Sudan."

"Sudan," Jeff said. "Man, that's drama to the tenth power. Genocide and abuse is everywhere."

"I know Jeff, but, I had people keeping an eye on her. She was always safe. She wanted to take our daughter with her, but she was happy living with her aunt. Carla didn't want to uproot her. To this day she thinks her father died in an automobile accident."

"Peter, I would never have guessed. I thought you were a racist," Jeff said.

"I'm not a racist, Jeff, I'm a coward."

"Peter, what's your daughter's name? My curiosity overcame me.

It was a sight to see. Tears came to Peter's eyes. He looked at me intently and put his hand on my shoulder and began to stutter. "Mmmmy dddaughter's name is Bridgett Mmmoore."

I know my eyes became as big a saucer's as what he said penetrated my brain. "My Bridgett? My fiancée is your biological daughter?"

"Yes, she is Quentin."

"I knew you were very protective of her, but I never in a million years expected that Bridgett was your daughter!"

The fellows sat in stunned silence. Peter took a sip of beer and swallowed hard.

"Fellows, for once in my life I am going to follow my heart. On Bridgett's 30th birthday, she will inherit my entire fortune. Seven hundred million dollars has been transferred into an account in the Cayman Islands that I set up in her name. She will become the CEO of McCallister Enterprises."

"Don't tell me anymore, Peter. This is too much to absorb." I said putting my hands over my ears.

"Listen, Quentin, get a hold of yourself. You promised to marry her for better or worse. I'm depending on you to keep quiet about this until I can tell her. Okay?"

"Peter, she'll turn thirty in a few months!"

"I know that. All of you have to keep it quiet. Please."

"Peter," Jeff said in a reasonably sober tone, "The heir of your empire is an illegitimate daughter you fathered with an African American stripper. Talk about an equal opportunity employer..."

I gave Jeff a sharp elbow to the ribs. "Ouch! That hurt, Quentin!"

Donald gave him a 'you'd better know when to shut up' look. They all looked at me. Suddenly their attitude changed.

"Quentin, you are marrying an heiress. You are going to be rich!" Jeff said, unable to keep his mouth shut.

"Quentin, Bridgett must never find out. I will tell her when the time is right. I just don't know how to undo so many lies."

I downed the last of my beer. I felt a terrible weight pressing on me. We figured Peter's secret was scandalous, we just didn't know the depth. I guess Peter is a closet Thomas Jefferson.

"Please, fellows, not a word of this. If it got out before I was ready, the change in CEO would cause a stockholder panic. It would affect Wall

Street. The last thing we need is another failed fortune 500 company. Thousands of people would be unemployed.

"I've been grooming Bridgett for years. She's ready to handle it. Once it's all done, I will be free to marry the woman I've always loved."

Still unable to process what he'd told us all I could say was, "Damn."

Savannah noticed our pitcher was empty and hurried over and smiled at us flirtatiously. "Another round boys."

We looked at Peter. "No, I think we've had enough for one night," he said as he opened his wallet and flipped three hundred dollars bills on the table.

As we stood and stretched, Antonio said, "Remember, we made a pact and we will all honor that pact. We will also add to our pact that we will never let a woman come between us. Not even our wives."

Jeff, true to form, gave a lustful chuckle and waggled his eyebrows like Groucho Marx. "Unless it's a ménage a trois."

We all agreed and had an Oprah moment, embracing and slapping each other on the backs.

"I love you, man."

"I love you, too."

"See you next week, Savannah."

Jeff smiled at Savannah and said, "Next week Savannah, I'll let you take me home. But tonight's my wife's turn." He gave her a lewd wink.

We rolled our eyes and I said, "Jeff, have some pride."

Savannah walked away with a loaded tray.

23

As we walked out of the club, the fellows staggered around. I looked at the fellows' drunken state and cautioned, "Hold it right there. I'm calling cabs for all of you. Friends do not let friends drive drunk."

"Or pick up ugly women," Jeff breathed beer fumes all over me.

The valet walked over, "Should I bring your cars around gentlemen?"

"No, Oscar, we've had a little too much to drink." Peter answered, "Could you call us a cab, please."

"Don't worry Mr. McCallister, I'll call right now. Your car will be safe here tonight."

Peter then turned to us. "Fellows don't forget about the party tomorrow night." He turned his wrist up and looked at his watch, "Oh, actually tonight. It's black tie. See you at eight."

A cab pulled up, Peter opened the door and turned to us before getting in. "Don't forget, mum's the word." With that he slid into the cab, closed the door and was gone. Other cabs arrived and one by one the fellows departed, leaving me with Oscar.

"You want your contraption brought around?"

"Yes, I'm ready for my car," I said with my nose in the air. The valet ran down the hill to the highway and zipped up the exit. He removed the sign as he exited the car and put it under his arm. I asked what the sign said.

"Oh! It just says VIP client," he said lying through his teeth.

"Yeah, right. Sir, you have treated me shabbily tonight. I will not refer any of my friends to your establishment." I still had my nose in the air.

"You mean all the wreck yards are closed?"

I rolled my eyes and tipped him with my last dollar.

"Oh, one dollar," he said, snapping the dollar in and out. "A big baller, one whole dollar. Wow! I just might have to go on a shopping spree!"

"You'd better use it to buy yourself some personality and class."

"Okay, Mr. Big Spender, I'm on my way right now." He laughed and slapped his knee at his own joke.

"Very funny." I got in my car and I slammed the door in his face and roared off in a cloud of smoke.

My car started misfiring on I-85 West. Come on baby! Just make it home. As my car and I puttered along, I thought about the revelations of the night. I couldn't believe Bridgett was going to be an heiress and that Peter was her father. I wanted Bridgett and me to have the perfect marriage. No secrets, no lies, no deception, only honesty and openness. I liked the fellows, but listening to their marriage woes; they truly sounded like a bunch of desperate husbands. Desperate husbands, I like that. I burst out laughing. At that moment, a stupendous idea hit me. That would make a great title for a book. It could be a sitcom, a stage play, and a movie. It would be a great book! New York publishers would love it. Hollywood would love it. I know it would sell. It's fresh. It would be scandalous and women would love to hear what their husbands are saying behind their backs. Just one thing missing, I don't know any juicy *Sex in the City* tales.

Traffic had come to a standstill. The city was working on the highway again. It was backed up like it was six in the evening, not like one in the morning. Well, it was a good time to think about my book. I looked for my little tape recorder. I keep it to record my ideas when they hit me. I felt around under the junk on the seat, I leaned over and searched through the trash on the floor. I slapped my pants pocket. I smacked the breast pocket of my jacket. There it was. I pulled it out and the red light was on. Man, I must have accidentally left it on. I started the recording over to see what was on there. I didn't want to erase any ideas.

"Angie was the first baby born..." Donald's voice floated out. I ran the recorder forward. "...then I found another cutie..." I ran it forward again. "...are pregnant..." I stopped the recorder. Bewildered, I ran it forward again and pushed play, "...once in my life, I'm going to follow my heart..." Peter's voice said.

Oh, my God! I had everyone's confession on tape! I must have accidentally hit the record button when we were horsing around in the strip club. I held the recorder up and looked at it. Lives could be ruined if the tape fell into the wrong hands. I really needed to erase this. But, I thought I'd just listen to it all the way through first. I rewound and an evil thought hit me. Man, from a journalistic point of view, these will make great stories. These stories are better than any soap opera. They are so juicy it would almost guarantee a best seller. I thought about the money that would come rolling in. I could buy a new car and a big old diamond ring for Bridgett. No, I can't do that. That would be a betrayal. Some things money can't buy. Like friendships and promises. It's not cool. It's not ethical. I pinky swore for God's sake. I tried to put the thought out of my mind. I stuck the recorder back in my pocket, but I didn't erase it.

Traffic has started moving and I was crawling towards my exit. The puttering sound turned to a grinding sound and then the engine died. I guided my car to the shoulder. I beat my head against the steering wheel, wondering how much more I could take. I turned the key in the ignition, but the car remained silent. I patted her, I coaxed her, I talked sweet nothings to her. I turned the key again. Nothing. I cursed her, I smacked her dashboard. I turned the key. The car finally started with a cough of smoke that blocked my rear vision.

I engaged the gears and we were off. I smoked, sputtered and bucked to within two feet of my driveway when the car cut out again. Thank God the driveway was down hill. Momentum took the car on in and we made it to our usual parking spot and there the car gave one final wheeze and died.

"You piece of crap," I yelled, as I kicked the back tire. "I hate you! When I'm rich and famous, you're the first thing I'm going to get rid of. There's a Mercedes or Bentley just waiting to take this spot. Your days are numbered!"

I unlocked the door to my tiny apartment and went inside. I opened the refrigerator. No food, but I had a box of Arm and Hammer Baking Soda, a cool breeze and a burned out light bulb. I took off my jacket and removed the recorder from the pocket.

I sat down on the couch, thinking. I rolled the recorder over and over in my hand. Why couldn't I use these stories? I could just change the names and some of the details. Walter Mosley does it. Sidney Sheldon does it. Stephen King —wait a minute. Ain't no way in hell that weird ass stuff he comes up with is based on his friends' lives. If it is, he needs to get a better class of friends and dump the drug addicts and mental patients. After reading some of his stuff I can see why they outlawed LSD.

A desperate need replaced my caution. It wouldn't be like I was selling them out. They'll never even know it's them. I'll put a different spin on it. Names, I need names for my characters.

Antonio could be Ricardo Santiago and Jeff will be Bob. Bob, the pilot. That sounds good. All pilots are named Jeff, Bob or Chuck. Donald can be Pastor Hayes. And Peter, Winston Dillingsworth sounds like a rich guy's name. What should my name be? No one must ever guess it's me, since I'm the sensitive guy. Lance Shelton sounds good. That sounds like a great name for a writer.

Okay, now I need names for the wives and girlfriends. Carla could be Kathleen Cole. Jan will be Buffy. Ashley will be Carol. Beverly needs something exotic. Giovanna McNeal works. Liana can be Alexis and Bridgett will be Summer Baldwin.

I spent several hours listening to the tape in its entirety. I made notes on the characters and made a rough outline of the plot and the theme. Before I knew it, I had roughed out two chapters. I was dog-tired, but couldn't put it down. But, I needed to hide the tape. What about the safe? Yeah, I'll put it next to my money, stocks, bonds and jewels. That's how tired I was, I didn't even remember I didn't have a safe. I eliminated all the obvious spots, like under the mattress, in case Bridgett wanted to clean house. I looked in the closet, the one place Bridgett tries to ignore. The golf clubs Peter gave me were in the back corner, dusty from disuse. My stinky golf shoes were pushed up against the bag and partially covered with the shoes Bridgett never wears. If I put the tape in the bag I'd have to pull it out to get to it, so I opted for the shoes. I tucked the tape down in the toe of the left shoe. Bridgett would never look there. Those shoes could keep vampires away. They could send Jack Bauer, from the TV show '24' and the CSI people in and they'd never figure it out.

Tired and yawning, I went into the bathroom and brushed my teeth. I couldn't help but smile at myself in the mirror. "Quentin, you are going to blow up. You are going to be rich and famous. After a while, you won't have to jump through Peter's hoops. You can hand him a million dollars and tell him to buy a personality." The man in the mirror stared back, but didn't say anything.

I felt like now I could tell Peter to have his people get in touch with my people if he wanted to talk to me. I was so excited and wanted to shout from the rooftop. I got the theme, I got the plot and I got the characters. Look out New York; Quentin Banks is in the house.

24

Later that morning I called several of the publishers that had turned me down. Everyone was very excited. They knew I had a winner. Every publisher I called ended up competing for my manuscript and promised me the world; a whopping up front advance, bigger royalties, cars, etc. I decided to go with an Atlanta publisher, Premier Books, because I would still own the rights to my book. Besides, the New York publishers turned down my first manuscript, and made one snide remark too many to me about my writing ability. To celebrate my potential best seller, I dusted off the one credit card that wasn't over the limit and about to be confiscated, and went shopping for some new threads and stopped by Adrian's Beauty for a fresh haircut.

Adrian's is located in the ritzy Atlantic Station, a mini city within the city of Atlanta. It is noted for shopping areas, restaurants, movies, posh condos and fabulous nightlife. Adrian was Atlanta's hottest and trendiest salon. Atlanta's Who's Who went to Adrian's, the place to get the latest cuts, style, fashion and gossip. If you were doing anything crazy in Atlanta, Adrian knew about it. Part of coming to his shop was, Adrian Johnson himself, the clown prince of scissors.

In his early 30's, Adrian was an African American, gay man noted for his hyper personality and the way he sported his over the top hair creation of the day. Because of his lifestyle, the phrase "why don't you join the church," was a phrase uttered with dire consequences. He had fifteen top-notch stylists, but everyone wanted the Adrian touch. Besides getting the best styling job possible, the thrill of going to Adrian's was listening to him talk trash and toot his own horn about his own highly exaggerated life. Every time he made a point he would snap his fingers and roll his neck sister girl style. The wives and girlfriends of the 30305 Club regularly attended Adrian's. There they could get their weekly fix of Adrian's own unique therapy and latest gossip. Adrian teased his "girls" unmercifully, but they loved him and kept coming back for more. Each insult made them a little more special.

The fellows and I have known each other for about five years. We all met at Holy Faith Church and are members. We differ in personalities, but each has something the other admires. Once we got to know each other, we were bound to the core. The wives became friends, as well. The girls are a different breed, I admit. They will fuss and fight, gossip behind each other's back, and they were at times down right catty. But when the chips are down, they have each other's back. When egos arise and tempers flare, we men back up and don't take sides, because within hours the girls have usually sorted it out. But if we got in the middle, we'd probably end up with our heads on a plate.

Bridgett would turn 30 in a few months. She's extremely anal retentive and has her own special quirks about how things must be neatly ordered and organized. Adding to that, she is very naïve and innocent. She's also very insecure and caught up in the fantasy of marriage. She's also the only woman I know that has "Here Comes the Bride" for a ring tone. To me, Bridgett is a beautiful woman, but looking at her objectively, she has a boyish figure and has nothing of the 'drop it like it's hot' you see on rap videos. Our sex life is boring and predictable as well. Bridgett is inhibited and never thinks outside the box. If I was lucky enough to get sex, it was always in the same place, at the same time and in the same way. A blowjob is definitely out of the question. Bridgett couldn't blow out the candles on a birthday cake. But, I have hopes that time will work all that out. I love the woman, what can I say? It amazes me that women will often make jokes about their men being inadequate, but what they don't know is that men say the same things about them. I wonder what Bridgett says about me?

Peter's wife, Jan, is as conservative as they come. Having started the 30305 Club and being blue blooded, she's very appearance and image conscious. However, her weight has ballooned to huge proportions over the years. Only Adrian knows her true size, hair color and age, and she threatened to cut his tongue out if he ever spills the beans. We know she has to be at least in her 60's but no one knows for sure. But expensive skin care and a good haircut have kept her looking elegant in spite of her weight. She's had several plastic surgeries and Botox and has constantly sought the attention of younger men. On other women her age, it might look silly, but some how she manages to pull it off.

Jan is a socialite, very charming and the perfect hostess, but if you cross her she can be as devious and cunning as Peter. You know revenge is coming, you just don't know when or how. When it comes to extracting revenge, she and Peter are two peas in a pod. Jan spent most of her life sheltered by old Boston money. She is clueless about the woes and worries of the average Joe, and she has a special talent for not accepting the obvious if it doesn't suit her plans.

Then there is the lovely Beverly. Ooh, la, la. Jeff is a lucky man and Beverly has us all drooling. She's a former supermodel with black, silky hair that spills down her back. She's definitely eye candy. She's African American, 5'10" flat footed, with green cat eyes and an hourglass figure. She's 32, but looks 25. She has large breasts, a perfect derriere and seldom wears panties.

Beverly is overly sensitive about getting older and insecure around younger women. Although Jeff attends church regularly, Beverly has consistently refused to attend. She refuses to discuss her reasons, which we all find confusing. The other girls are always trying to get her involved, and she has alienated most of the 30305 Club by her refusal to even step foot into the church.

Then there is Liana. She isn't bad on the eyes either. She and Beverly are pretty much neck in neck in the looks department, but Liana is a traditional Latina beauty. She's about 5'6"; with dark, curly hair that falls just below her shoulders and her skin is a smooth, coppery color. She favors very tight clothes that reveal a curvy, luscious figure.

She's from Tijuana, Mexico, hot-blooded, and full of attitude. Antonio often wishes Liana would tone down her mouth; she says exactly what she thinks. Her lack of inhibition in the bedroom and the use of that same mouth on his throbbing penis more than makes up for the arguments. In truth, the fellows love to hear about Antonio and Liana's sex life. It beats *Sex in the City* any day. Liana used to be a stylist at Adrian's. She's as faithful to Antonio as a puppy and very proud to be Latina.

Then there's Ashley. She's a rail-thin, repressed, prim woman. Ashley is a very fair skinned African- American, in her late 40's. Ashley makes a very good preacher's wife. You can count on Ashley to be wearing the biggest hat in the congregation and that the hem of her dress will be properly below the knee.

She is very concerned about her status in the church, but is also very eager to keep up with the Jones, or the McCallister's as the case may be.

I think she sees Jan as some sort of competition, so she's working on spending as much of Donald's money as possible, in as short of time as possible. I've heard that the women of the 30305 Club think Ashley is a secret drinker. She has convinced herself that everything is perfect between her and Donald, and since he is dedicated to doing the Lord's work, it has earned her a special place in Heaven that the other members of the 30305 Club will never obtain.

Regardless of our status, or outward appearance, when the sun sets on Buckhead, our masks come off and we are just one big, not so happy, dysfunctional family.

25

BRIDGETT

"Are we late Adrian?" Jan said as she burst through the door, wearing an Atlanta Braves baseball cap. "Liana has to look extra sharp. She and her husband Antonio are the guests of honor at my house tonight. Peter and I are throwing them a pa-tee tonight. Pardon me for being late. I had to park the 'ka.'" She said in her thick Knob Hill accent.

"Jan, your accent cracks me up. Pa-tee and ka indeed. This is not Boston, down south we say party and car." Adrian looked at the clock. "You desperate housewives are right on time. One o'clock on the dot."

"Oh good," Jan clapped her hands and let out a big sigh of relief. "I had to park the Mercedes in a handicapped space."

"Jan, you didn't!" I said in disbelief.

"Don't get your panties in a wad," she said, flapping her hands at me in a dismissive motion. "I'm sure they won't mind. I don't know why they have so many parking spaces set aside anyway. In fact, some guy in a wheelchair outside was really tripping. It's not like he was tortured during the war or taken captive like John McCain. If he did have a brand new red Mercedes, I'm sure he couldn't afford the gas."

"Why are you wearing that hideous hat, Jan? You think you're A-Rod or something?" Adrian asked sarcastically. "Girl, you gotta let go of the Sarah Palin starter kit. Your hairstyle is #1 on my "No Ma'am List!

Adrian has a large, brass bell hanging on the wall of the lobby. When he gets ready to do his 'orientation', as he calls it, he rings the bell and we come to attention. He reached over and rang the bell. We all sat and turned to listen. Adrian positioned himself center stage.

"Welcome to Adrian's Beauty Salon, where we take a bad situation and make you look, three words, Fa-Bu-Lous—" He stopped short in the midst of his orientation and peered closely at Jan. "Jan, you have put on so much weight I thought you were twins." He looked at all of us from head to toe with a critical eye.

"Excuse me, I'm sorry. It's not the Desperate Housewives; it's the girls from the 30305 Club. Lights, Ms. Insecure. No Action, Red Hot

Chili Pepper and it's newest member, The Preacher's Wife, a/k/a, No Sex in the City."

Adrian let out a cackling laugh and slapped his hip. "I really crack myself up!"

"I got your Red Hot Chili Pepper right here Adrian," Liana said angrily. "Believe me, it's *muy caliente* (very hot)!"

We all delighted in Adrian and Liana's love/hate relationship. Adrian continued to roast Jan.

"Jan, why do you look so sad? Did the President try to balance the budget by raising the price of Twinkies? Word around town is that the only thing hot in your life is your hot flashes."

Embarrassed, Jan dropped her head and took off her hat.

"Lord, what did you do that for? Ahh, Jan. What's up with your hair? It looks like a terrorist starter kit with a second bomb getting ready to go boom!" He shrieked and looked closer. "On the other hand, your hair looks more like a Hurricane Katrina starter kit, and believe me child, it's a category five." He snapped his fingers and rolled his neck.

Jan let out a breath of relief and smiled. "It just needs a little touch up Adrian. But it's not that bad!"

"Not that bad! Child, your hair looks like Buckwheat in rehab!"

Jan burst into tears. "Adrian, don't tease me, you know I'm going through menopause. Each birthday that passes, it only reminds me of how old I'm getting. I'm so sensitive."

"Child, age ain't nothing but a number. You're only as old as you look. I mean as old as you feel. If you feel down and out, you've come to the right place. Adrian's Beauty Salon is guaranteed to make an ugly duckling feel and look Fa-Bu-Lous, before long you will be dancing with the stars."

He gave Jan a big hug. "Jan, you know I love you. That is why I tease you. I only insult the people I love."

"I love you too," Jan replied with a big sniff.

"Regardless of how old you get Jan, you will always be my number one customer. Right now, I want you ladies to sit back and relax. Chill out for a second, while I get you something to drink."

"Stand by ladies and get ready for your free massage, manicure and pedicure," The hostess yelled out. Adrian pointedly looked at Jan, and then at Beverly. mumbling under his breath. "Judging by the wrinkles in your face it's not a moment too soon."

"Wrinkles!" Beverly shrieked. "Did he say wrinkles? Bridgett, I thought you were my friend. Why didn't you tell me?" She dashed to the mirror. "Ah, what is that on my face? Is that a zit? Are those crows' feet? Oh my God! I'm aging by the second. Call P. Diddy. I need some ProActive. Tell them to make it a six-pack!"

"Chill out Beverly. Adrian is just kidding. You're still a spring chicken. If you stop acting so nutty, you might get asked out to the prom. Now sit down and cool out!" I said.

Beverly gave me a crazed look. "It's easy for you to say. You are only 29."

At that moment Adrian rolled his eyes. "Stylists, please hurry up with those drinks. And child, please, get me something from the stress management stock for Beverly." He looked at Beverly and said, "Beverly, where did you go?"

"I'm right in front of you," she said suspiciously.

He looked around as though he couldn't see her. "Oh, there you are!" He looked her over, head to toe. "Honey, if you get any skinnier, you will be wearing MC Hammer pants and whenever you decide to wear underwear, you will be wearing baggy thongs."

"Ha, ha!" Beverly said venomously. "Everyone wants to do stand up." She rolled her eyes as she angrily crossed her arms and fumed. Adrian rang that damned bell again.

Ashley, gazing off into space as if on another planet, jumped and yelled, "What was that? Are we having church?"

"No, we are not having church," Jan said in a sharp tone.

"Can I have your attention please?" Adrian interrupted. "Let me continue with my daily orientation. So there is no misunderstanding, let me lay down a few house rules. You know I'm trying to bring sexy back, but this is Adrian's, not *Nip/Tuck*. I'm a hair stylist, not a plastic surgeon." He said rolling his neck sister girl style.

"I'm now in the weight business."

"All right!" Beverly declared. "It's about time. I'm looking a little pudgy."

"Jan and Beverly, if you come to my shop twice a week, you are guaranteed to look Fa-Bu-Lous and feel Glam-Ur-Ous. But, having money to buy groceries is de-ba-ta-ble."

We cracked up and Adrian clapped excitedly. He reminded me a little bit of Richard Simmons the way he was jumping around. "We also give preferential treatment to service people and POW's."

"POW's?" Jan quizzed.

"Yes, POW's, Jan. Not prisoners of war. Prisoners of a Weave. A nappy weave is always a 911. At Adrian's we are unisex. We respect all race, ethnicity and keeping it real because of my personal lifestyle, and because many of you are on the down-low, upswing, bi-curious or on the waiting list. We don't use the N word, the ho word, the fag word, the bitch word and we certainly don't use the free word."

Adrian snapped his fingers twice and rolled his neck with attitude. "However, free advice is included in every set, wash and curl. So that is why I'm charging everyone an additional four cents for your issues and my daily two cents."

"Ah, Adrian. Your prices are already too high!" I said. Everybody moaned.

"When this Fa-Bu-Lous experience is over, you're guaranteed to get sexually harassed, or you get your money back."

"Hooray!" Jan screamed. "I need to be sexually harassed."

"Now back to business...when this Fa-Bu-Lous experience is over, you Buckhead housewives ain't got to go home, but you got to get the hell out of here. Ta!Ta! Now carry on!"

The hostess brought us fluted glasses of Cristal champagne. We settled down for an enjoyable afternoon. We looked around the crowded lobby and knew we might as well prepare ourselves for a long wait.

"Relax ladies, I'm getting you set up for your complimentary massage."

"Oh, that sounds so good," Jan gushed.

Adrian sat down among us and began to slyly interrogate us. "So, Buckhead housewives, how's married life?"

I looked around at the other girls. I knew that being as pretentious as they are, they'd all start fronting, with so many ears listening. Sure enough.

"Its just Fa-Bu-Lous," Jan said.

"No complaints here," Beverly said.

"Antonio is a beast, an animal. I can't keep him off me," Liana said, running her hands up and down her body. "Antonio put the Hot in Hotlanta!" Liana accentuated.

"Red Hot Chili Pepper, would you like to be alone with yourself?" Adrian wisecracked. "I don't believe any of you. But, I'll let it go for now." He rose and sauntered to the back.

When he disappeared, Liana looked at everyone and whispered, "Girls, please keep this to yourselves. If Antonio found out I told you, he'd be so upset."

Jan looked Liana up and down with distaste and said, "Mum's the word."

Liana cut her eyes at me. "Girl, I really need you to pay close attention. You're such a Goody Two Shoes."

"I'm no Goody Two Shoes," I fired back defensively. "I'm a wild woman. A sex kitten...if you don't believe me, ask Quentin."

"Ask Quentin? What the hell does he know? You really need better references. Quentin's a 35 year old virgin."

"That's an ugly lie," I protested.

"Whatever, Bridgett, whatever." Liana laughed. "Anyway, girls, I'm such a slut puppy."

"Now why would you say that?" Jan queried with a malicious glint in her eyes.

"Last week Antonio took me to dinner at Pappadeaux Restaurant on Windy Hill. The place was about to close. We took a romantic booth in the back. We had a few drinks. The place was dark and we started acting silly. I was sitting across from Antonio. I put my stiletto heel in his crotch under the table."

"For real?" Ashley came out of her lethargic stupor again. There was nothing she liked better than hearing about the girls' sexual escapades.

"Man, he was turned on. I slid around the booth and rubbed up against him. I stuck my tongue in his ear, while I got some lotion out of my purse. I starting whispering to him and undid his pants and pulled out his thing. Then I put one hand up on the table gave him a hand job with the other as I sat there and pretended to be looking around the restaurant."

"Liana, you slut!" I cried, laughing.

"Poor Antonio, he was trying so hard not to scream, but I remained calm and kept talking to him about everyday things. He was red in the face trying to maintain control. After about three minutes, he exploded like the bombs bursting in air on the Fourth of July!" Liana started to sing, 'A-meri-ca, A-meri-ca.' She broke off and exclaimed, "Damn, I love this country!"

"And ladies, you think that is something...that was nothing. There's more!"

"What?" The girls exclaimed as we all leaned in to hear better.

"Yeah, Antonio couldn't wait to pay the check! On the way home I gave him a little paradise by the dashboard light. I gave Antonio the ultimate blow job."

"What's the ultimate blow job?" I asked, hoping to learn something.

"I used the vowels..."

"Vowels? Ashley interrupted.

"The vowels, ladies. You know, A E I O U and sometimes W and Y."

"I don't understand," I said. Jan and Ashley pretended they didn't want to get pulled into it, but leaned in even farther.

"Well, ladies, get closer. Imagine you have your man's penis in your mouth. Take it as far as you can down your throat."

Jan was uncontrollably wagging her tongue and became frustrated. "Wait, I need visual aids." She shouted for Adrian.

When Adrian hustled back in she said, "Adrian, can we borrow some ink pens? We need five. We need to take some notes."

Adrian looked flummoxed, but quickly complied and returned with five new ink pens, boldly inscribed with the name of the beauty shop. We all pretended to write something until he left the lobby.

"Okay, the coast is clear. Now class," Liana continued, "imagine the pen is your man's thing." She looked over at Jan, who was holding the pen up in front of her face.

"Jan, pretend you are sucking on a lobster claw or a Klondike bar." Jan stuck the pen in her mouth and began sucking ferociously.

"Now that's what I'm talking about! Okay, now form the vowels A, E, I, O, U on the tip of his dick with your tongue. Increase your speed as you get to W and Y. Within three to five minutes, he will shoot up like Old Faithful! Now let me see your tongues!"

At that moment Adrian sprang back into the lobby looking at us with our tongues hanging out and pens in our mouths. "Ladies, what the hell is going on in my salon. You're sucking on my pens! This is Adrian's Beauty Salon, not feeding time at Jurassic Park."

Before he could say another word, a man that had been observing our lesson, rushed over. "Ladies, here's my phone number." He thrust a business card into Liana's free hand. "My wife just doesn't understand me. I think you ladies feel my pain."

Liana looked at the man, then looked at Adrian. I hung my head in embarrassment, and the rest of the girls looked at the ceiling, out the window, anywhere but at Liana and Adrian.

Liana said, "We're sorry Adrian."

"Liana was showing us how to give a man a blow job with the vowels," Jan muttered.

"Red Hot Chili Pepper, don't get Barney the Dinosaur and Big Bird fired. The last thing we need is another minority on the CW Network. That's the very reason they want to ship your people back to Mexico. You don't know how to act, and speaking of going back to Mexico, I can't hide this any longer. I've got to get it off my chest."

"What Adrian?" Liana asked, against her better judgment.

"Liana, I got a bone to pick with your people. I was looking at the news the other day and saw 40,000 Latinos protesting in the street. They were all protesting that Senate Bill 529. Liana, I was so embarrassed that I gritted my teeth and cringed."

"You were embarrassed because they were illegal?" She exclaimed defensively, ready to take on Adrian.

"No, Liana, I was embarrassed because their hair style was illegal. Even Don King and Buckwheat said DAMN!"

We tried to contain our laughter.

"To make matters worse," Adrian continued ignoring us, "I saw jacked up hair in high definition!"

None of us could contain ourselves any longer and we burst out laughing.

"Liana, if you are going to march, make sure you have your 'do' together. Even the Reverend Martin Luther King kept his hair neat. Things didn't get shaky until the Reverend Al Sharpton came on the scene. But Barack saved the day."

"Stop it Adrian!" Jan laughed, but everyone knew that Adrian was on a roll again.

"I saw a Chewbacca starter kit. Check this out, he had the audacity to have his pants sagging. Then I saw a James Brown curl, that didn't look or feel so good."

"Girls, some were even screaming, 'Please, Please, Please.' I know the Godfather of Soul was turning over in his grave. Papa may have a brand new bag, but what papa needed was a brand new hairdo. I was so embarrassed."

I bit my tongue as I uttered, "Adrian you are insane."

"Check this out Bridgett. One of them even had the audacity to be wearing an Adrian's Beauty Salon T-shirt! I couldn't take it anymore. I got on the phone and called the police."

"You called the police on my people?" Liana burst out angrily.

"Not the cops, the fashion police. I'm as open minded as anyone, as liberal as the next guy, but something must be done about the illegal aliens."

"What exactly would you suggest, Adrian," Liana said tightly.

"We don't need the National Guard at the border. What we need to do is control and patrol what they are wearing. Some of them look like a 'hot mess' and made my 'No Ma'am List'. Certain fashions should not be allowed in this country and will you please tell your people to stop wearing white shoes after Labor Day."

Thank God Jan changed the subject.

"Girls, I'm debating on whether I should get liposuction or a gastric bypass. Do you think a woman should go under the knife to please her man?"

"Hell no," Liana exploded, still hot from her conversation with Adrian. "Look at what happened to rapper Kanye West's mother, Donda. She died shortly after surgery. Before that Starr Jones-Reynolds came close to waking up dead. No, no, no, a man should accept you the way you are!"

"I don't see anything wrong with it," Beverly commented. "A little self-improvement never hurt anyone. As for Donda West, I still blame that sleazy plastic surgeon." She turned and looked at herself in the floor to ceiling mirror on the wall opposite her, touching her face. "All men want is a trophy wife or a woman who is eye candy. Men are visual. If you can't get them interested, how the hell are you going to hook them?"

"Jan, ignore Beverly, she's a wannabe Kimora Lee Simmons. You know models and actresses are shallow, dizzy and self-centered," Liana said.

Beverly merely rolled her eyes.

"Can you girls keep a secret?" Jan asked.

"You know we can," Beverly said offended she would even ask.

"I'm also thinking about getting a labiaplasty and vaginal rejuvenation."

Everyone looked equally confused.

"What the hell is that?" I blurted out. "Is that some kind of new dildo?"

"Not quite, Bridgett," Jan said with a laugh. "When women have several births and get older their vaginas get loose and the lips around your vagina become enlarged. The surgery is basically reshaping the genital area to be more aesthetically pleasing and tightens up the vaginal walls so you get more friction during sex. I'd look like a sixteen year old down there."

"Girl, are you talking about shrinking your coochie!" Adrian said, blatantly eavesdropping.

"Let me finish," Jan protested. "When you get older like Ashley and me, sometimes things just get a little loose."

Ashley leaned over to Beverly and whispered, "Child, you know that will take a whole lot of thread." Beverly snickered.

"Did you say something Ashley?" Jan pounced.

"No, Jan. It must have been something I ate that is hard to digest," Ashley said looking at Jan innocently.

"Girl, leave your stuff alone. There's nothing wrong with something that is pre-owned. If God wanted your stuff tight as a drum, he wouldn't have made you bear children," Adrian protested.

"I agree," I interrupted. "A man should accept you the way you are."

"That's right Bridgett." Ashley said maliciously.

"Well, Peter has asked me to lose weight," Jan whined.

"Did you agree to it?" Beverly asked.

"Hell no! With each pound I gain there's just more of me to love."

"Tell the truth, Jan," Liana said jumping up. "If God wanted you to lose weight he would have never made Krispy Kreme donuts.

"I agree!" Jan said triumphantly. "Here is some more advise, never trust a skinny cook, or buy hair tonic from a bald-headed barber!"

ANTONIO

Liana and I were nervous. She looked great! We'd been arguing ever since we left the house.

"Stop it Liana. Please just stop it. Jeez, you sound like a nagging wife."

"I am a nagging wife," She exploded. "It goes with the job and the marriage vows. Tonight I feel like Diary of a Mad Latino Woman!"

She stewed in her anger. "Antonio, I just don't understand you. You use to be so honest, so pure and naïve."

"And so broke," I reminded her.

"You may have been broke, but you had principles and character."

"Huh? Principles and character are on sale at the grocery store right next to the magazine rack. That's right next to where the soup is found and you can get a sucker free!"

She sighed loudly, "*Madicon!*"

"Oh, I'm a faggot now!" I said hotly.

"Did I say you were a faggot?"

"You said it in Spanish."

"Hey, Antonio, if the dress fits, wear it!"

"Liana, please do not speak Spanish tonight. It makes people nervous."

"Okay, okay, whatever."

"Liana, please try to get along with the other wives and please don't go in there with an attitude."

"Who's got an attitude? I'm as cool as a cucumber. I'm just sweet, little Liana from south of the border. I don't have a damn attitude. Antonio, I know how to act around your rich *gringo* friends. All I have to do is smile and agree with whoever you're trying to impress. Or agree with whoever has the most money. Act fake, it's easy. I've been doing it for years. I got it down pat."

I looked over at her and frowned. I never knew what that woman was going to do. "Calm down. Please calm down. Tonight is one of the biggest of my life. Stay loose. Stay charming. Stay witty. Keep your positive energy." I looked at her calmly, "Liana, when this is all over, I'm taking you to anger management school."

"I got your anger management school right here Antonio. *Madicon! Madicon!*"

We pulled into the driveway at Peter's estate. When I looked at my watch, it was eight on the dot. The valet stepped forward as I pulled the car to the entrance and he opened the door for Liana. "Hurry Antonio, on a night like this, it is not good to be fashionably late."

As the valet drove away with the car, Liana hooked her arm through mine. I looked down at her. "Liana, do you love me?"

"You know I do Antonio with all my heart."

"Then please, please be sweet tonight." She rolled her eyes at the heavens. "Okay, Antonio, I will be sweet. I will be so sweet you will think I am Dixie Crystal Sugar. I promise not to speak Spanish and I promise not to have an attitude. But there is one thing I cannot promise."

"What's that?" I replied as sudden dread filled my heart.

"I can't promise I won't laugh if I see those little old ladies with the blue hair. They look like Marge Simpson. They crack me up, especially when I see them sticking food in their purses."

I gave her an angry stare and the mad seemed to go out of her. "Okay, Antonio, I promise I won't laugh since tonight is so important."

I relaxed a little and smiled down at her, "You'd better not." As we started up the steps I leaned down and whispered in her ear. "*Tu eres muy hermosa.*" (You are so beautiful).

She wagged a finger at me and said, "You said no Spanish tonight."

"I promise, that was the last time."

"Antonio, what kind of underwear are you wearing?"

"What kind of question is that Liana?"

"Antonio, please just answer the question."

"Okay, okay, jeez. Hanes. The Michael Jordan collection."

Liana pumped her fist, "Yes! I told the girls you were a real man!"

I laughed and we walked inside.

As soon as we cleared the front door we heard cries of "Congressman Fernando."

"Here, Congressman."

"How are you Congressman?"

We started up the stairs and nodded graciously. The doorman at the entrance of the ballroom snapped to attention as we approached.

"Congressman Fernando, we've been expecting you. Come this way, please." He opened the doors wide and led us to the receiving line. As we walked in, everyone begin to applaud. Liana and I, holding hands, waved to the crowd. Liana smiled and shook hands and exchanged a word with everyone. I had to admit, she looked stunning. Her black, sequined dress fit her in all the right places. Her black hair was swept up in a chignon with a cluster of diamonds pinned along the side. I didn't look too shabby myself; I'd had a tuxedo made last year for these occasions.

Peter and Jan greeted us. "Antonio, Liana, you both look smashing," Peter said.

"Thank you Peter," Liana said graciously.

Jan kissed her on the cheek. "I love your dress. It's very beautiful. Is it Chanel?"

"Merci beaucoup, oui." Liana responded.

"You speak French?" Jan asked with admiration.

"Oui, madam."

Jan looked at Peter. "I must have that dress. I'd look like a million dollars in it?"

I could see the wheels turning in Peter's head and I knew he was thinking "No way in hell!" But he was polite enough not to say it.

A waiter offered us champagne in fluted glasses. Liana and I strolled among the crowd. We were introduced to other VIP's and the women hated all the men's smiles in Liana's direction.

I whispered to Liana, when we had a moment to ourselves, "I didn't know you spoke French."

She looked at me coyly and replied, "There's a lot you don't know about me. But it's all good."

We continued to stroll and then Peter took my arm and pulled me away to meet other members of his group. Jan steered Liana off in another direction to meet the 30305 Club.

There was one lady that stood out in the crowd. It was Senator Ginger Paine. She stood about 5'6," weighed about 125 pounds and had perfectly streaked blonde hair and clear blue eyes. I'd met her briefly at the Capitol Building. She was usually conservatively dressed, but tonight there was nothing conservative about her. She had on a white, layered silk dress that floated around her, and fit where a dress should fit. Her hair curled softly around her bare shoulders. I looked around to make sure Liana wasn't watching me. Luckily, her back was to me and she was engaged in conversation with other Buckhead wives. It was hard to take my eyes off the Senator.

Ginger walked towards me with a cat-like grace and smiled. A subtle scent drifted off her skin that was doing things to my nerve endings. She stuck out her hand. "Congressman Fernando, we meet again," she said in a low, sultry voice. She looked me up and down, assessing me. I could tell she liked what she saw. I have to admit, I liked what I saw too.

A waiter offered Ginger and I champagne. We both took a glass.

"Let's propose a toast, shall we?" she said silkily.

"To what, Senator?"

"To the man of the hour, of course."

As we tipped our glasses, Peter joined us. We all exchanged banter. Ginger was as witty as she was smart. Peter could tell there was a special chemistry between us.

"Excuse me, Congressman, Senator, much as I have enjoyed our conversation, I really must attend to my other guests. Ginger will you see that Antonio is introduced to the people that matter."

Turning to me, Peter said mockingly, "You are in good hands, my friend," and took his leave.

Ginger chuckled low in her throat and put out her arm. I took her hand and linked her arm with mine and we strolled over to meet her friends. When we arrived, everyone stopped talking.

"Antonio, you already know the Governor and the Mayor, but let me introduce you to Senator Hall, Judge Baker and Councilman Clark."

I shook hands with everyone and Councilman Clark patted me on the shoulder. "It's a pleasure to meet you, Antonio." He pulled me close and whispered discretely in my ear. "The gang is a little squeamish about Senate Bill 529. Peter assured us you would do the right thing. Look around this place. Membership has its privileges."

"Don't worry," Ginger assured everyone. "Antonio is practically a member already." She looked up at me with a cattish smile and ran her hand down my lapel in a clearly proprietary gesture.

As we turned away to greet more people, she said, "Your wife is so cute; very plain and unpretentious. A regular Michelle Obama. Do you have any children?"

"No, we don't. Maybe one day we will have them."

"You know, Antonio, with the right woman by your side, there's no telling how far you can go. Take Peter for example, he was a poor orphan. Now, he's one of the richest men in Georgia. You can be just as successful. You have all the right tools. You have the looks, the smarts and the ambition. Plus, you are coming in at the right time. Latino's are in now. They helped cinch the presidency for Obama. The Latinos' time has come. Antonio, catch the wave and ride it to the top."

Her words went round and round in my head. I took another sip of champagne.

She pulled me close. "Power also has its privileges. In order to get something that you've never had, you must do something that you've never done. If you keep doing things the same way, you will get the same results."

"I like that," I replied. "I'll keep it in mind." Before I could say another word, a stunning woman walked over. Ginger smiled at my reaction.

"Antonio, this is my girlfriend, Tracy Collins. She is a federal judge. When we need things fixed, she's our girl."

Tracy extended her hand, "Antonio, I've heard so much about you. I've seen you on television numerous times. You are so much more handsome in person." She gave me a naughty look. "You know, the three of us can have lots of fun." She stroked a finger down Ginger's arm as she said it.

"Now, now Tracy. He's married. He's off limits. You need to detour."

"Highways open and close all the time," Tracy said deviously. "But first you have to pay the toll." Her eyes traveled down to my crotch and lingered suggestively before moving down to my feet.

"Antonio, what's your shoe size?"

The question took me off guard. "Twelve." I replied, puzzled.

"Twelve!" Tracy giggled. "In that case, I would like to issue you an invitation."

"To what?" I asked, swallowing hard.

"A group of us are having a little get together Sunday at Lake Lanier. Peter is letting us use his yacht. We would love for you to come. Trust me, this is a party you don't want to miss. Some of our other VIP friends will be there."

"Okay, I'll tell Liana. I'm sure she would love to come." I looked at Ginger's expression and knew I'd said the wrong thing. What woman wants to hear about your wife when she's trying to get into your pants?

As we moved through the crowd, Ginger purred, "So ambitious, yet so green. There are so many things you must learn. I need to take you under my wing."

"I would like that Ginger. I would like that a lot," I said looking around to make sure Liana was nowhere nearby. I turned around and noticed Peter on the small stage at the end of the ballroom.

"Can I have your attention please?" he said into a microphone. "Can I have your attention?" He paused, and when everyone quieted, he continued.

"First of all, I would like to thank everyone for coming out for Congressman Fernando's celebration. He is the first Hispanic Congressman from the great state of Georgia!"

Applause erupted around the ballroom.

"Is everybody having a good time?"

"Yeah," came shouts from the crowd.

"I know many of you are aware that the Senate is voting Monday on Bill 529. Tonight we have the man who holds its future in his hands. Congressman Antonio Fernando! Antonio, can you come to the stage?"

I shouldered my way through the crowd; people patted me on the back and shouted congratulations. As I passed Liana, she grabbed my hand and kissed my cheek, and whispered, "Do the right thing, Antonio. Our people are depending on you."

I stepped on the stage with a big smile on my face. The closer I got to Peter, the more I felt as if I had lead weights in my shoes. In a split second my life will change for the better or for the worse. I would ensure our future or flush it down the toilet. Before accepting the microphone, I threw both arms in the air. I jokingly formed Richard Nixon style peace signs. Laughter rang out from the floor of the ballroom.

I took the microphone from Peter and let out the breath I'd been holding. When everyone quieted down, I spoke, "I am not a crook and I did not sleep with that girl." The laughter and applause was deafening.

I motioned for everyone to be quiet.

"Seriously, my friends, President John F. Kennedy once said, 'ask not what your country can do for you, but what you can do for your country!' As we go through life every loyal American must ask himself that same question. President Obama said, 'I am not making history, you are! I am proud to be an American. I am proud to be the first Hispanic Congressman for this great state. Much is given, much is expected. This Monday, I plan to do that very thing." I looked around the room. I looked Peter in the eye, and then looked at Ginger. Finally, I locked eyes with Liana. She looked back expectantly. A lump rose in my throat and I hesitated.

"Don't be shy Antonio," Peter shouted. "Don't let political parties divide us. Tell us what to expect this Monday."

I took a deep breath and smiled at Liana.

"Peter, what you and your friends can expect Monday, is..." The words locked in my throat, almost choking me. I had to look away from Liana.

"You can expect my vote to pass Senate Bill 529. We must stop illegal aliens. Illegal aliens should not have the same rights of citizenship. They are draining the resources that belong to this great state and this great country!"

I smiled and threw up another peace sign. Pandemonium broke around me. I slowly looked back to Liana. She stood there, in shock, tears in her eyes. She turned on her heel and disappeared into the crowd.

27

Liana gave me the silent treatment all the way home. Regardless of how much I apologized, or reasoned with her, she ignored me, staring out the window.

When we arrived back home, she turned on me.

"How could you Antonio?" She screamed at me. "How could you turn on your own people? You will destroy the lives of honest, hard working Latinos. I thought you were man enough to do the right thing, but instead you chose your ambition."

"Liana, I did it for us." I cried, defending myself.

"No, Antonio, you did it for you. You did it for your career and for your bourgeois friends. If you had done it for us, you would have stood up like a man and you would have told those rich assholes you were voting against the bill. It would be the right thing to do."

"I wanted to, Liana, please try to understand."

"Antonio, I will never understand." Her eyes were bright with tears. "You have hurt me deeply. You have jeopardized our marriage and our future. I don't even know who you are. You definitely aren't the man I married. I thought we were a team. I thought you would never betray us or our people." Her voice continued to rise. "Maybe we don't want the same thing. I love you Antonio, I always will, but right now, I need time apart. I need space to sort things out."

"Liana, listen to what you are saying…"

"I'm saying we need to separate. How can that be so hard to understand?"

"We don't need to separate!" I replied, stunned. "I made a big mistake Liana."

"You made a mistake you can't correct," she yelled. "You knew what you were going to do way before you went there tonight. You weren't even man enough to tell me! I'm proud to be Latina. I'm proud to be Mexican, even if you aren't."

She turned and ran into the bedroom and started pulling clothes from the closet and drawers.

"Where are you going?" I shouted.

"I don't know, anywhere but here in a traitor's house!"

I tried to hug her and she pushed me away. She pulled her suitcase from the back of the closet and piled the clothes in haphazardly. She stormed into the bathroom, grabbing toiletries as she went and returned to dump them in the suitcase.

"Will you call me when you get where you are going?"

"I don't know Antonio, I don't know."

"Liana, please don't go, sweetheart. I love you."

She snapped the suitcase shut. I tried to take it from her, but she snatched it away from me.

"Liana, if you love me, please don't go. We can work this out."

"No Antonio, we can't work this out." She walked past me. I continued to plead, but it fell on deaf ears. Everything seemed to be moving in slow motion. I put my hand to the door to stop her from opening it; she pushed me away roughly. She opened the door, turned and looked at me. Then she slammed the door behind her and was gone.

I burst into tears. I staggered to the bar and grabbed a bottle and a glass. I sat on the couch, tears running down my face. I poured one glass after the other down my throat. I couldn't even tell you what I drank. When I was totally drunk, I staggered to the bedroom. I looked at the dresser and all the photos on top of it. It seems we had spent a lifetime together.

I pushed my hair off my face, fell on the bed and tucked myself into a fetal position and cried like a baby.

28

The next morning I woke up to the telephone ringing. I had fireworks going off in my head and a mouth that felt like the Sahara. Damn! Why is that phone ringing so loud? I looked at the clock and it read 6:38a.m. I tried to sit up and the fireworks turned into atom bombs. I groped around on the bedside table and found the phone.

"Hello," I rasped out.

"Is this Congressman Fernando?" a female voice asked.

"Yes, it is."

"This is Ginger Paine." Her name brought back a semblance of life to my system.

"Ginger, to what do I owe this pleasure?"

"I was just thinking about you, so I decided to give you a call. Is the little wifey around? If she's near, you don't need to elaborate. Just say yes or no."

"Liana is not here," I choked out, freshly feeling the pain of Liana's defection.

"Hmmm, that's not good. If sweet and faithful isn't there at this hour, it can only mean one thing. You had a fight and she's packed her bags and left you hasn't she?"

"Right Alex, give the Senator 100 on having a fight. Ginger, what a fight it was, short, and to the point."

"What happened?" Ginger asked sweetly.

"I'll give you the short version...Bill 529. I won't vote to abort it. Now I'm a sellout and she is pissed. The end."

"I'm sorry Antonio," she said not sounding in the least sorry. "I didn't think she would take it so hard."

"I think it's a no-win situation. I'm damned if I do and damned if I don't."

"Antonio, I think you need a friend right now. You need to get out and clear your head. And I know the very place. Tell you what; let's do something silly. Why don't you meet me at the Georgia Aquarium?"

"I don't know, Ginger. I don't think it would look good. You know Atlanta is nothing but a big country town. People talk. The last thing we need is an infidelity scandal like the one Mayor Bill Campbell was involved in. When the media got into his stuff, they discovered that not only did he have a wife and a girlfriend, but two more women on the side. The media can be friend or foe. Scandals sell."

"Ah, come on," she persisted. "We are two public figures. They would think we're just politicking."

"No, it's not a good idea. Plus, I've had way too much to drink last night and have the worst hangover."

"Drink plenty of black coffee and meet me there at one this afternoon. I won't take no for an answer." Ginger continued to ride me about it until I finally agreed.

The moment I hung up the phone, I went back to sleep. What only seemed like a couple of minutes had turned into a few hours. When I looked at the clock again it was 11:18a.m. I quickly jumped in the shower. Once finished, I made a pot of coffee and downed several cups. I was finally halfway coherent. I dressed in a tight shirt and a pair of starched jeans. I looked through several fragrances and decided it was a Dolce and Gabana kind of afternoon. I put on my leather banded Cartier watch, grabbed my cell phone and a jacket and left the penthouse.

I walked down the hallway to the elevator. I love living in a penthouse, but it seemed to take forever to get to the garage. When I finally got to the lobby, I told the concierge that if Liana called to patch her through to me immediately. I proceeded on to the garage and got in the car.

I decided to take Peachtree all the way to the Aquarium. I hit the scan button and selected a jazz station. Man, I love jazz. My mood began to lift as I zipped in and out of traffic. With Wynton Marsalis blasting through the speakers, I relaxed and enjoyed the ride.

With minutes to spare, I arrived at the Aquarium. I looked at the clock it was 12:48p.m. The moment I walked in I saw Ginger. She was wearing a pair of skintight jeans and camisole top. I admired her curves and walked over to her. I put my hands over her eyes and said, "Surprise."

"If you are trying to rob me," she joked, "there are cameras everywhere. You'll never get away with it." She turned around and looked me over. "Nice." She felt my biceps and ran her hands over my pecs. My shirt was thin, her touch made my nipples rise.

"Ginger, we are in public," I said, feeling uneasy. "There are cameras everywhere."

She smiled up at me, "Well then, shall we take a tour?"

"Let's do it," I jested. We were both in awe as we moved from one exhibit to the next. There was an incredible number of species of fish, from freshwater to seawater.

"Wow!" Ginger said as we stood in front of a floor to ceiling tank. A stingray had glided up to the glass and launched itself upward, its white underside, sliding up the glass right in front of our faces.

"Be careful. That thing killed the Crocodile Hunter," I joked. "Let me take a closer look," I said trying to imitate his accent.

"Antonio, you are awful!" she said laughing at my lousy impersonation. A school of fish caught her attention. "Run, little fish, run. Here comes the shark. Watch out for Peter!" Realizing what she'd said she turned to me, "Please don't tell him I said that."

29

I found myself having a better time than I expected. We were acting like school kids on a field trip. I could see people whispering and staring.

"Isn't that Senator Paine?" One woman asked her escort.

Another woman said to her husband, "I thought Congressman Fernando was married to a Mexican woman?"

The husband rolled his eyes and said, "Your point is..."

Yet another woman was overheard to say, "Looks like he's married but still looking?"

We ignored their comments as best we could and continued our tour.

"Come here and look at this octopus!" she said excitedly. "He has so many arms. Reminds me of some of the men I've dated."

"For real?"

"For real. I could tell you some stories. In fact, you met some of those octopi last night."

"I can only imagine," I chuckled.

It took a couple of hours to finish the exhibits. I had to admit that, even though I was upset about Liana, Ginger was good medicine. The attraction seemed to be mutual.

"Are you hungry?" I asked.

"I could eat. What's your favorite food?"

"Seafood," I said with a smile as I looked around me.

She gave a delighted laugh when she caught on to my feeble joke. "Mine too. How about Pappadeaux? It's my favorite place for seafood."

"I like it too."

"Since we both drove, let's just take one car."

"That sounds like a winner."

When we got to my car, I opened the passenger door for her.

"I could get used to this. Not many gentlemen left these days."

"Chivalry is not dead."

"Chivalry is not dead, but it is in a coma and needs resuscitation," she corrected.

"Touché."

We decided to go to the Pappadeaux on Windy Hill. We jumped on I-75 North. We bantered back and forth. I was enjoying our lighthearted conversation. Liana only crept into my mind a few times. Carelessly, Ginger laid her hand on my knee. I liked it.

"Did you enjoy today?" She asked, leaning her head back against the seat.

"I sure did. I can't remember when I acted so silly. I remember Liana..." I caught myself. "I'm sorry, Ginger."

"It's okay, Antonio. We are friends. You can be honest with me. I appreciate that."

"But I had a wonderful day. It was just what the doctor ordered."

"Hey, tomorrow Tracy and her friends are getting together at Lake Lanier. Want to come?"

"We'll see," I said.

We soon arrived at Pappadeaux. As always, there was a long line. The moment we walked into the lobby, the maitre 'd recognized us and escorted us immediately to a private booth. Our waitress arrived and asked if we wanted a cocktail.

"No, no!" I protested. "No more alcohol for me. I had enough last night. Would you get me a glass of orange juice, please?"

"I'll have a white wine." Ginger told the waitress. The waitress recited the specials and departed.

Ginger turned to me, "Antonio, the first time I saw you, I knew you had the right stuff. Look at Peter. He rose from poverty to royalty. He's both loved and feared." She gave me a piercing stare. "Sometimes it's better to be feared than loved."

I pondered over her philosophy. The waitress returned with our drinks.

"Are you ready to order, Congressman, Senator?"

"The Pescaro is delicious," Ginger said.

"I like the Gumbo. Tell you what, you order the Pescaro, I'll get the Gumbo and we can nibble off each other's plate."

"Yes, sir," the waitress said, "I'll get your order in right away."

We lingered over our dinner. The more time I spent with Ginger, the less I thought of Liana. Ginger was refined, elegant and worldly. She was a go-getter. I found those traits turned me on. It's funny, some women are attracted to a powerful man, but there is nothing that gets a dick harder than a powerful woman. Oprah, Hilary Clinton and Martha Stewart are all sexy as hell. If I had to make a choice between tits and ass or power, I'd take a woman who has power...I'll take a business suit over mini skirt any day. But if I could find a woman with power, a lady in the street, a freak in the bed and goes to church every Sunday, I'd marry her on the spot. That is as good as it's going to get.

I paid the check and the valet brought my car around. As we passed the customers, many recognized us. Congressman Antonio Fernando! Senator Ginger Paine! We both enjoyed the spotlight. It felt good to have power. But it turned me on the have a woman at my side that was even more powerful. We headed back to the Aquarium.

"Thank you, Ginger. I had a wonderful day. It really was just what the doctor ordered."

"Thanks for coming, it was fun acting like high school kids."

I pulled in beside her car. I opened her car door and she squeezed my hand. Before I knew it, she'd pulled me to her and we were reclined on the front seat, kissing passionately.

"Ginger, someone will see us."

"I don't care. Let them watch." Her large breasts pressed into my chest, her tongue explored my neck. I was getting aroused. But guilt overcame passion. I pushed Ginger away and said, "I can't do this."

"Don't you find me attractive?"

"That's the problem, you're too damned attractive. But I'm married. I sat up and straightened my clothes. "I'm sorry, I think I need to leave. Thanks again for a nice afternoon."

I jumped in my car and left the garage. I pulled into the traffic headed for home. I breathed heavily, trying to calm myself. Ginger is like kryptonite to Superman. I felt weak and out of breath.

I turned on the radio and found a Latin station. Salsa music blasted through the speakers. I car danced and sang at the top of my voice. Daddy Yankee came up next, my favorite Raggateon artist. I rapped along with him and laughed out loud. Yep, I was feeling better.

I pulled into the Buckhead Towers and looked up at the tall building. It seemed like a stairway to heaven. I thought about George Jefferson from that 70's TV series, 'The Jeffersons.' The theme song ran through my head. '*Well we're moving on up. To the east side. To a deluxe apartment in the sky. Fish don't fry in the kitchen, beans don't burn on the grill. It took a whole lotta trying just to get up that hill. Now we're in the big leagues, getting our turn at bat.'*

I looked at the top of the building, at my deluxe apartment in the sky. I asked myself if I really had achieved the American dream? Dreams come with happiness, but right now, all of a sudden I felt sad and lonely.

I pulled into the garage and took the elevator to the penthouse. It was graveyard quiet. The clock ticking on the wall in the kitchen was the only noise I heard.

Normally, the minute Liana heard my key in the lock, she would run to the door, jump into my arms and wrap her legs around my waist and shower me with kisses. She would make me carry her into the bedroom and we would make love. Then she'd fix my dinner. She'd even cut the meat and feed me like a child, piece by piece.

Man, I thought to myself, you don't miss the water until the well runs dry. I looked at our pictures on the mantle over the fireplace. Tears ran unheeded down my cheeks. I remember how we first met. I immediately looked at my cell. I scrolled through the call list. I didn't see her number. I checked the message machine. Nothing from Liana. How could I have been so stupid? I walked into the bedroom and saw our wedding picture sitting on the dresser. I picked it up and kissed her face. I held the frame close to my chest and cried. Oh, Liana, I love you. Please come back. Please come back. It was a mantra I repeated over and over, hoping she'd appear in the doorway.

Still holding the frame I walked back into the living room and turned on the television. There was nothing worth watching on any channel. I switched to DVD and started watching the Jennifer Lopez movie, *Maid in Manhattan*. That was our favorite movie. I switched it off. I couldn't watch it. It reminded me of Liana. What else is there? *Shall We Dance* with Jennifer Lopez. Damn. Liana and I loved to dance together. What else? *Desperado* with Selma Hayek and Antonio Banderas. This is a real man's movie. That should be okay. Ah damn, Liana sure looks a lot like Selma. Liana is so proud to be Latino. Man, my mind was in overdrive. I needed to stop tripping. I watched *Desperado* until I fell asleep.

30

It was Sunday morning. I staggered to the kitchen. Normally, Liana would already have breakfast prepared. Our Sunday ritual was breakfast, church and then we would spend the rest of the day watching old movies and romantic comedies.

At first I hated those 'chick flicks', but Liana made me start to like them. It's amazing how someone enhances or takes away from your life. I tried to do the same things I would do if she were here. I cooked my favorite breakfast. I couldn't face church today. I washed and put away the dishes and watched old movies. After killing about three hours, I dreaded the rest of the day. I was alone and didn't know what to do with myself. I stood at the French doors and looked out over the Atlanta skyline. The telephone rang. Thinking it was Liana I answered it before the first ring was finished.

"Hell...Hello, Liana?"

"No. It's Ginger," she said rather acerbically.

I sighed deeply. "Oh, hi Ginger," I said with evident disappointment.

"Don't apologize, I do understand. Sorry to disappoint you. It's just little, old me."

"I'm sorry Ginger. Rough morning. I am happy you called."

"So am I. I can see it's not a moment too soon. You are about as sad as a fox in an empty hen house. I like to be around happy people. Being sad is a no-no."

"I think you might have dialed the wrong number. I'm having a pity party. No one else is invited. I'm the host and all the guests."

"You're nuts!" She replied with a girlish giggle.

"My life is spinning out of control," I said vehemently.

"It's going to be okay. I take it you haven't heard from Liana?"

"No, I don't know where she is, or what she's doing or if she's even all right."

"Antonio, don't stay at home moping. She just needs time to cool off. You need to get out. Are you up for it?"

"I don't know Ginger, maybe that isn't such a good idea."

"Of course it is. And I have something in mind that may be just what you need. Let's go up to Lake Lanier today. Tracy's party is today, on Peter's yacht. Remember? You really need to meet some of the other guests."

"I don't know Ginger."

"Antonio, don't look at it as a date. Look at it as business. Remember, the real deals are made in relaxation."

We went back and forth and Ginger eventually wore me down. We agreed to meet at the Cheesecake Factory and just take one car for the hour drive to the lake.

Just as I got in the car to leave for the restaurant, my cell phone rang.

"I'm here." She replied to my greeting.

"Wow, you're early."

"The early bird gets the worm."

"But the guy that sleeps late probably owns the worm farm."

She laughed, "Man, that Peter is a bad influence on both of us. Antonio, I'm parked at the back of the parking lot; you'll know my car when you see it. It's not the same as I had yesterday. Look for bright red!"

Within ten minutes I was turning into the parking lot and immediately spotted a bright red Ferrari at the very back. Must be nice. I turned my car over to the valet and walked back to Ginger's car.

She'd saw me coming and got out of the car as I approached. She was wearing a very short black mini skirt, sheer blouse and black stiletto heels. She sat on the hood of her car with her long legs crossed provocatively. She looked just like one of those pin-up girls you see in the men's car magazines. It was definitely one of those shots you see with the expensive car and gorgeous girl and you just know you can never have either one. Ginger was playing dirty poker and she knew it.

"Hello Antonio," she drawled as soon as I got close.

"Hello Ginger." I don't know which turned me on the most, the girl or the car.

She struck an Anna Nicole pose and asked, "You like my car?"

"Man, it's sweet!" I whistled.

"Cost me 250K. Like I told you Antonio, membership has its privileges."

"You ready to go Ginger?" I couldn't wait to get in that car. I walked over to the passenger side.

She gave me a surprised look and said, "So you think you can't handle something hot, fast and powerful?" She licked her lips suggestively.

"I'll be the little old lady from Pasadena and ride on the passenger side." I opened the passenger door with a flourish and hopped in.

As she slid into the driver's seat her skirt rode way up. My eyes bulged. I couldn't help but notice she wasn't wearing any underwear. She was certainly appealing to my basic instinct.

She looked at me coyly and said, "Big bad wolves are ferocious, but a little pussy never hurt anyone."

"Don't let the big bad wolf get you. I will huff and puff and blow your house down." We both buckled up and she turned the key.

We roared out of the parking lot. Heads turned as we flew down the road. We passed Lenox Mall and Phipps Plaza in a blur. We hit Georgia 400. She shifted through the 2nd and 3rd gears as we entered the highway. She hit 4th and 5th, moving in and out of traffic like a race car driver. I looked over at the speedometer. Smooth as silk it rose to 80 mph, then 90. In seconds she'd hit 100 mph. Ginger's hair blew in the wind, her skirt rode even higher. I ogled her legs. We really needed to slow down, in more ways than one, but the bad boy in me told her to put the pedal to the metal. The engine roared, the speedometer shot to 120, my heart pounded. The woman had nerves of steel, she just sat there with a little smile playing around her lips. We passed a sign that indicated that the toll bridge was coming up in half a mile. We looked at each other. A congressman and a senator, a man and a woman. This was our little battle of the sexes.

The speedometer read 130. She popped into 6th. The toll bridge was close. I looked at her again and we hit 150.

I punked out 2000 feet from the bridge and hollered, "Ginger, slow down! You win, you have the bigger balls!"

She suddenly hit the brakes, laughing hysterically. We slid sedately into the toll bridge and she tossed in some coins she'd found in the console.

She looked at me and said, "If you can't run with the big dogs, stay on the porch and bark."

Even though I went out like a bitch, living on the edge turned me on. We rolled on through the tolls and she kicked it up to 80 and let it ride there on cruise control. Ginger reached over and turned on the radio. It was set to a Latin station. "Ah man, Salsa!" she said. She started moving her body to the rhythm and I looked at her in surprise.

"What do you know about Latin music?"

She turned up her mouth. "Well, I know Carlos Santana, Tito Puentes, Hector Laude..."

"Shut your mouth!" I said slapping myself on the knee. "A southern girl who knows Latin music. I thought you good old boys and girls liked country music."

"Antonio, you can't judge a book by its cover. I love jazz, old school, new school. One of my favorite hangouts is Café 290 in Roswell and Londzell Jazz and Blues on Holcomb Bridge Road."

I shook my head in amazement. I had thought she was just one of the spoiled rich girls that had decided to work for a living, but she was smart and ambitious. I smiled to myself and settled back to enjoy the drive, car and woman.

We made it to the lake in record time. We found the marina where Peter docked his yacht and started down the gangway to the slips. The marina was loaded with huge, expensive yachts. We found Peter's slip at the end of the pier and my mouth dropped open. A gleaming 75-foot Azimet Motor Yacht bobbed gently on the water. I handed Ginger up onto the deck and everyone greeted us. A waiter instantly appeared with a tray of champagne glasses. Remembering my headache I sipped with caution. Ginger started working the crowd. I met several other members of Peter's club that I'd not seen last Friday. Everyone patted me on the back. Many said, "We're counting on you, Antonio." Or, "Don't let us down, Antonio." I smiled politely and walked away.

I stepped into the main salon where more people milled around talking. A DJ was set up in the far corner. The salon was lushly appointed with rich leather and highly polished teak furniture. I couldn't help but wonder what Peter dropped on this baby.

Ginger had followed me in and slid her hand over my shoulder, pulling me close. "They are playing our song." She pulled me toward the center of the room and gripped me for a tango. "Let's show them how to do it, shall we?"

She slung her hair back and slid her foot out. I moved, pulled her close and we burned up the dance floor. We dropped hands and moved apart and Ginger's body swayed freely. Men's tongues were wagging and their eyes bulged. I was no slouch on the dance floor. The women were turned on and I worked it. As the music wound down, we moved together and as the final note sounded I dipped her low over my arm. Everyone applauded. We bowed politely. We picked up our drinks and she grabbed my hand and took me below.

We went into an aft stateroom. The stateroom was a beam-to-beam luxury suite that was about as big as my bedroom at home. We were laughing and giggling. The laughter died in my throat when I noticed a table in the center of the room that had a long line of coke laid out. And I don't mean the soft drink kind. Ginger's rich and powerful friends were getting their noses full. They looked high as kites. A judge I'd met previously at Peter's party looked up and saw me. "Congressman Fernando, glad you could make it. Man, this stuff is the bomb! I got it from a drug dealer I just sentenced. Man, I hate to see him go. This is some good shit. Very pure. Oh well, he doesn't need it where he's going."

The group around the table laughed, and I walked over to the table. The judge handed me a rolled hundred-dollar bill. I hesitated, but since I didn't have the angel named Liana sitting on my right shoulder, I decided to give in to the devil sitting on the left shoulder. After all, I'm trying to be a team player. I leaned over and inhaled a very long line of coke. I could feel the burn all the way up to the tops of my eyes.

Tracy ambled over, "Antonio, Ginger, I'm glad you could make it. Antonio, where's your wife?" She smirked at me.

"We had a fight. We are just taking some time off from each other," I said sniffing as I handed the rolled bill to the person standing beside me.

"Oh, that is too bad. There is no drama here. As you can see, we are all happy people."

Tracy pulled out a decorative silver capsule on a long chain from beneath her summer sweater. She unscrewed the top and tapped in some of its contents into the top. She held it to her nose and sniffed deeply. "Ah, man this is good. Try some Ginger."

Ginger took a hit. As she exhaled her eyes became glassy. "Man that's good! Here Antonio, try some." She extended the capsule to me.

She put the capsule under my nose. I took a hit. My eyes widened and the room started to spin. A waiter walked by with a tray full of champagne glasses. I immediately grabbed a glass and took a gulp, hoping to stabilize myself. Watching me, the girls looked at each other and giggled. I couldn't help myself and giggled back. I was feeling good. I finished off the glass of champagne and someone stuck the bill in my hand, so I leaned over for another hit. Maybe I had too much too fast and the room started dip up and down, but I was feeling good. I wanted to move, or dance, or something. I suddenly was full of energy and good feelings that I hadn't had in a long time. I pulled Ginger close to my side and smiled down at her.

"Come on Antonio, we've got a surprise for you. Let's do one more for the road." We took another hit from the lines laid out on the table and then they both pulled me out of the stateroom and down a short hall to a smaller, but no less luxurious, stateroom. As we passed another waiter, Tracy grabbed three glasses of champagne. Tracy closed the door with her hip as Ginger pushed me down on the king-sized bed. I sat and she started nibbling on my neck.

"What are you doing?" I said, gripping her arms, I was confused. On one hand I enjoyed it, on the other all I could think of was Liana. I pushed Ginger away. "I don't understand this Ginger, I don't want to be unfaithful to my wife. Please just back off."

"I just want you to relax." She said, giving me a beguiling look. "It's OK, Antonio, really. Just relax." She thrust a glass in my hand. "Drink Antonio, it'll help relax you." I downed the drink.

They both began to kiss me, pinning me to the bed. Tracy peeled my shirt off and ran her tongue around my nipples. Goose bumps formed on my body. Ginger undid my pants and pulled them off. At that moment my telephone rang.

"Wait a minute!" I said, pulling away from them both. "Someone is calling me!" I searched for my pants and pulled the cell out of my pocket. I was fumbling with the phone, trying to push the receive button, but as I did, Ginger grabbed the phone from my hand and put it to her ear.

"I am sorry, but Congressman Fernando can't come to the phone right now. Please leave your name and number at the sound of the beep. BEEP!" She threw the phone down on the bed.

"Who was that?" My head was spinning wildly.

"I don't know. Whoever it was will call back. All work and no play makes Antonio a dull boy."

They both started kissing me and licking my body. They stripped the rest of my clothes off. I noticed that they had both somehow removed their clothes. They started kissing and stroking each other. I didn't know what was working on me the most, the coke, champagne, or two powerful women kissing each other.

Tracy got on her knees in front of me and took me in her mouth, deep down her throat sucking hard. I thought about Liana, but instead of the cold dash of water that I expected, my thoughts drifted back to Ginger as she pushed Tracy away and took me in her mouth slow and deep, moving up and down, sucking. Each stroke took me to another dimension. Tracy moved to my nipples and sucked and fondled me. I was lost and all thoughts of Liana flew out of my head..

"I love it. I'm about to explode," I moaned.

Ginger removed her mouth and straddled me and slid my throbbing penis into her volcanic walls.

Tracy positioned herself on her knees beside my head and spread her legs, lowering herself to within an inch of my face; I turned my head to her and tasted her essence, pushing my tongue deep.

"Fuck me harder!" Ginger demanded, as she pushed her body down on mine. Tracy was moaning, and caressing Ginger's breasts. I reached up and pushed two fingers into Tracy. She yelled, "Antonio, more baby, more!"

Ginger pushed herself up and down faster and faster and screamed, "I'm cumming, Antonio, I'm cumming. Oh, shitttt!" She moved off me and Tracy pushed my hand away and turned her butt to me yelling, "Do me doggy style, Antonio. Now, now!"

Ginger turned her butt to me and yelled, "Smack me daddy. Smack me!"

I slapped her across her bottom, leaving a red imprint of my hand.

"Harder!" she begged. "I fucked your best friend. I fucked him in our bed." I gave her a hard whack, leaving red marks across her perfect backside.

"I'm sorry!" she screamed, totally into the role-playing, "You weren't there, I was so horny. I needed some, please, please forgive me."

I slapped her across her butt again, all the while pumping hard into Tracy. "Did you like it?" I bellowed at Ginger.

Tracy was coming close and yelled, "Harder, Antonio, I'm so close. I need all of it!"

Ginger yelled. "I didn't like it, I was waiting on you. I gave your pussy away!"

"You slut!" I yelled, smacking her.

"Show me you are a real man," Tracy yelled, matching me thrust for thrust. "Oh God, I'm cumming. Ohhhhh! She pulled herself away from me and I immediately thrust into Ginger.

"Oh God, it's so big, so hard. More, baby more!"

I thrust harder as Tracy gripped my balls from behind, stroking and squeezing.

"Oh daddy, that feels so good!" Ginger screamed as she came.

My heart was thundering like a trip hammer, and I shattered into a climax.

The three of us fell onto the bed like sacks of flour. Tracy lay on one side of me, breathing heavily. Ginger lay on the other, sheened with sweat. That was when I noticed my phone laying on the pillow above Tracy's head, open.

I sat up suddenly grabbing the phone and pushing the girls away. I looked at the number. What is the worst thing that could happen in a situation like this? You guessed it. The caller was still connected and my woman heard every fucking thing. Sweat popped out big as bullets on my forehead and the blood drained from my head.

I lifted the phone to my ear. "Hello, is anybody there?" I said, hoping against hope that there wasn't.

"You fucking bastard!" Liana shrieked into my ear. "You cheating mother fucker! How could you do this to me? I thought you loved me!"

"I do, baby, I do." I tried to calm her. "I didn't know what I was doing, I was drugged."

"You knew damn well what you were doing. You fucked two sluts! I hate you, Antonio!"

"Don't hang up, baby. Please listen to me. Let me explain."

"Explain what Antonio? I heard everything. I've been on the phone since you started. I wanted to hang up, but I couldn't. I couldn't believe what I was hearing. After all we've been through, you could do this? I was calling to tell you I wanted to apologize. I wanted to come home." Suddenly there was dead air.

I got up, sick to my stomach. I looked at myself in the mirror. I was so ashamed. I put my face in my hands and cried.

31

The following Monday, Senate Bill 529 passed. Donald, Jeff and Quentin had met at my house to help me celebrate. We met at my house to watch the announcement on the news. Suddenly the phone rang. I anxiously got up and looked at the caller ID. I let out a loud scream.

"Yes! Yes! Yes! It's Peter," I said shaking uncontrollably. "Peter McCallister," I said running my hands through my hair. I started pacing the floor. "What should I do? I let the phone ring several more times to gather my composure.

"Aren't you going to answer it?" Jeff yelled.

I took one final deep breath and put the call on the loud speaker. "Antonio Fernando." I answered in a professional tone.

"Hello fellows," he said all excited. "Are you watching the news?"

"We are," I replied.

"Well, I have some great news for you."

"What is it?" I motioned for everyone to be quiet. My heart was racing 100 miles per hour.

"You guys are officially members of the 30305 Club!"

"All right!" We all hollered joyfully. We jumped up and down and gave each other bear hugs and hard high fives.

"Hey Antonio, I just wanted to let you know that you did the right thing. You are on your way to the top." Peter said slyly. "Can you take me off the speaker?" I could hear a smirk in his voice. I picked up the handset and put it to my ear.

"I heard about the threesome you had with Senator Paine," Peter said matter of factly.

"Who told you?" I replied, embarrassed.

"Let's just say a little birdie told me."

"Nothing gets past you does it?" I asked grimly.

"Antonio, now that you are in the Buckhead elite, your next step is to make some personal changes."

"What do you mean?"

"Your wife, Antonio, your wife. I don't think she can take you where you need to go."

I was silent, mulling over what he'd said, trying to process what he might mean.

"Antonio, are you still there?"

"Yes, Peter, I am."

"Antonio, the last thing I want to do is break up a man's home or get in a man's personal business, but I know you are like me. A tiger. A real go-getter. To be a king of the jungle, you need a queen who is the same. You don't need a pussycat. If Liana can't run with the big dogs, she needs to stay on the porch and bark."

Anger began to overtake me. Sarcastically, I asked, "So Peter, do you have a woman in mind. Who have you picked for me? Who is this woman that can make all my dreams come true?" I had a sneaking suspicion just who that woman was.

He laughed nonchalantly and then was silent for a moment.

I said, "I know the great Peter McCallister is not afraid to speak his mind."

"Okay, Antonio, since you twisted my arm, I'll fill you in. It's Ginger Paine."

"Ginger!" I said in disbelief.

"Yes, Ginger. It's no secret she has the hots for you. To add to that, she is stepping down as senator and calling for a replacement. Who better to replace her than you? Your name is already ringing in the house now. It can be ringing in the senate with Ginger. With the Buckhead elite and a little money behind you, you will be a shoo-in. Just think of it, Senator Antonio Fernando, a democrat from the great state of Georgia!"

As I listened to Peter lay out his plan, I liked the way it sounded. "Senator Antonio Fernando!" Yeah.

I turned my attention back to Peter. "I know I am dropping a lot on you, so take your time to digest it all. Let it marinate. Your wildest dream is not more than a few inches from your fingertips. Think it over. Call me when you make up your mind. See you later Senator Fernando."

32

PETER

When I hung up with Antonio, I immediately called Ginger. The telephone rang several times before she answered.

"Ginger Paine," she said seductively.

"Hello Ginger. This is Peter McCallister."

"Hello Peter. To what do I owe this pleasure?"

"Oh, I just called to say hello," I joked with her.

"Bullshit Peter. Your telephone goes off every three minutes. A conversation with you is worth a million dollars. I am sure you don't have the time to call me in the middle of the day just to shoot the breeze."

"Ginger, do you really think you know me?"

"Peter, we are two of a kind. Game recognizes game. So what's really up, Peter?"

"I just talked to our friend, Antonio Fernando."

"Oh, you did?" I could hear excitement in her voice.

I deliberately changed the subject. "Have you noticed the weather has been nice lately? Maybe I'll go up to the lake."

"You do that!" she clipped out angrily. "What did Antonio say?"

"Antonio?" I teased.

"Peter, you have thirty seconds to spill your guts. If you don't, this conversation is over!"

"Look at you." I said calmly. "I never thought I'd see the day when a man has Ginger Paine's nose wide open."

"What do you mean?" Impatience tinged her voice. "A man will never have my 'nose wide open' as you so poetically put it."

"Miss Diva, I just hung up the telephone with Antonio. I told him our group of friends is very happy about how he voted on the immigration bill. That was the first step in achieving his wildest dreams. The second step is..." Just to make her squirm I changed the subject again. "I wonder what the weather is like in Paris? I know it's beautiful this time of year."

"Peter, the clock is ticking. 10, 9, 8..."

"Cool your jets, honey. You win. I told Antonio that step two is to dump Liana and, to hook up with you."

"Peter, you bastard. What did he say?"

"Come on Ginger, I know you have the hots for him."

She giggled and said, "What did he say to your indecent proposal? I'll bet he was in shock."

"On the contrary, he just sat quietly and listened. I even tempted him with the idea that you are stepping down as a senator. Once your seat is vacant, you will ask the Governor to appoint him to serve out your term. Then he can run on his own and you'll throw your support behind him. He would be a shoo-in."

"What did he say about that?"

"I think the idea is settling in. I know he likes the idea and the sound of Senator Antonio Fernando."

"Hmmm." She mulled over the idea. "Come to think of it Peter, it does have a nice ring to it."

"Yeah. I told him to think about it and get back to me."

"Peter, you never cease to amaze me. The nerve of you."

"It's not nerves, Ginger, it's balls. You need to have balls these days. I must admit, for a woman, you have balls the size of Texas. I've seen you make some gutsy moves."

"I'm flattered Peter. That means a lot coming from the great Peter McCallister. I learned a long time ago that what keeps most women from getting what they want are their emotions. Too many women equate sex with love, and so many use sex in order to get love. I use sex in order to get paid, to get ahead...and to get power. Where a lot of successful women go wrong is they don't know when to be quiet. Many of them want to have the last word. They view it as a power thing. Some even want to go toe to toe with a man. That's a no-no."

"You need to tell that to Jan."

"When a woman appears to be dominant or aggressive, it appeals to a man's sense to compete. When she appears to be softer, feminine or unavailable, it appeals to his nurturing side, he wants to uplift or protect. With a little softness, a woman can not only get her way, but get a man to do almost anything."

I laughed, "Yeah, you got it all figured out."

"I've had a lot of practice. It's not easy being a woman in a man's world."

"Oh come on, Ginger."

"Peter, whether you want to admit it or not, men love it when a woman dogs them out. They love it when a woman acts like a bitch. It makes their dicks hard. Even with our fling Peter, and I treated you like crap, you loved every minute of it. You couldn't stay away from me."

She bruised my ego a little. "I won't comment on that Ginger. Well, I've got to go, I'll keep you in the loop."

"You'd better Peter, if you know what's good for you. Here is a little extra incentive. If it weren't for a little side action with some of my girlfriends, you and Jan would have divorced years ago."

"Time is money, Ginger. Talk to you later," I said with a grin.

BRIDGETT

"Adrian will see you now, ladies. Please step this way." The hostess said.

Beverly looked at her fingernails. "Honey, my nails look a mess."

"Mine too," Liana echoed.

"There's no way Cujo or Melissa and Joan Rivers are going to invite me to the Red Carpet. I can also forget about the BET Black Carpet, too."

Adrian looked Beverly over, with a smirk on his face. "Like I said, Be-ver-ly, we work on nails and feet, not claws and hooves. This is Adrian's Beauty Salon, not Jurassic Park. Girls, have a seat. Have a pedicure on me."

"Adrian, I know we are going to be waiting for a while," I said. "Do you have anything to read while we wait?"

"Yes, I do. I have the latest *Ebony*, *O*, *People*, *Essence* and one more big surprise that I'm not revealing just yet."

"Give me the *Ebony*," Beverly said cordially.

"I'll take the O," Ashley said.

"I'll take the *Essence*," I said.

"Well, since there's only one left, I guess I don't have any choice," Jan barked. "Give me the *People* magazine."

On the cover was a picture of President Obama with his family. Jan reluctantly thumbed through the magazine but stopped when she came to the cover story. "Oh my," she said.

"What?" I asked her.

She flipped the magazine around and showed me a picture of the President walking along a beach without his shirt on.

Jan smiled lustily and licked her lips. "Girl, although Obama is an inexperienced democrat, he's kind of cute in those swim shorts. And I wouldn't kick him out of bed on a cold winter's night either. You know all the belles in the 30305 would like to get some of that. Michelle better watch out, women across America have their eyes on her man."

Adrian looked around slyly. "Okay ladies, let's take a political survey. By the show of hands, how many of you wouldn't mind jumping Barack's bones?"

Everyone within hearing raised their hand,except for Ashley.

"Okay ladies, hands down," he said laughing out loud. He looked over at Jan and continued, "By the same show of hands, how many of you wouldn't mind seeing John McCain in a pair of Speedo's or want to jump his bones?"

Cries of 'Eeeewwww!' and 'No way!' rang out across the salon. Suddenly Jan's hand shot in the air.

"Me! Me! John is a real stud muffin!" Jan slowly became aware that she was swimming in a democratic sea, totally alone. Embarrassed, she slowly lowered her hand and curled it in her lap as everyone stared silently at her.

Ashley broke the silence, giving us all a cold, hard slap of morality. "Ladies, these men are married. Stop lusting and leave the married men alone."

"Hey, hey," Adrian replied, "there's nothing wrong with wishful thinking!"

Two elderly Caucasian ladies had lifted the dryer hoods to see what was going on and eavesdropped on the conversation.

"Janet, that Barack is a real panty wetter. I wouldn't mind getting some of that myself. I go cuckoo for Coco Puffs," she said running her hand over her flat bosom.

"Me too, Mavis," her friend replied.

Adrian shot them an icy glare. "It's not that kind of party ladies. Barack is not Bill Clinton!"

The salon burst into laughter. Then Adrian threw us a curve ball. "Now for my big surprise, ladies. Not only do I have the latest scoop on Barack, but I've got copies of the new book that is selling out across America, *Desperate Husbands*."

"You have Quentin's new book?" Beverly asked excitedly.

"The one and only," he said giving everyone a foxy grin. "Since that book came out, everyone's been looking at their husbands suspiciously."

"I've heard couples have either gotten closer, admitted infidelity or separated," Jan admitted.

"Some couples have even divorced over the book," Liana said with venom.

"I don't know why everyone is tripping," I said in disbelief. "It's only fiction. I was there when Quentin wrote it. It took months, but I know he just made it all up out of his head."

"Touché, Bridgett," Jan said. "It's a made up story. It's complete poppy-cock."

"The people who believe Quentin's crap are the same people who watch Jerry Springer or Maury, or worse yet, that reality TV show *The Real Housewives of Atlanta*. Rich my ass. Those broads are on a budget. They'd all be in the poor house if it weren't for their economic stimulus check." I jumped in eagerly. "Come to think of it, what happened today? I missed those shows."

"I rest my case," Jan said arrogantly. "No husband in real life would put all their business in the street."

"You Doubting Thomas's, I keep extra copies lying around," Adrian fired back. "Women can't put it down."

The girls looked around the salon and many women were reading the book and whispering with their friends. The hostess arrived and took us to the dressing rooms. We undressed and the hostess gave us a towel and a big pink terry cloth robe. When we'd changed, the hostess escorted us to a private room for our manicures and pedicures.

Adrian cut a sarcastic glance at Liana. "Red Hot Chili Pepper, how is Antonio doing? I thought everything was *muy caliente* south of the border?" He cackled at his joke and said coyly, "Oh, did I say that?"

"Don't you dare mention that *pero's* name to me!" Liana spat viciously, "I hate him. I never want to see him again as long as I live."

"Cool out Liana and take a seat," Adrian said calmly. "Let me get you something from my Anger Management stock."

"Doris!" Adrian screamed like a fishwife. "We have a 911!"

The hostess quickly disappeared and returned with five fluted crystal glasses of champagne.

"I don't understand men," Liana said sadly. "You give them respect, admiration, emotional support, peace of mind, x-rated sex and they still cheat."

"The Lord will fight your battle," Ashley said primly, fussing with her robe, making sure that it was completely closed.

"I never want to see him again. Not after what he did."

"Okay, okay," Adrian said calmly. "Just sit back and relax and let me make you all feel, three words, Fa-Bu-Lous."

Within minutes our faces had been creamed and our hair wrapped in a towel. Our feet were soaking in the whirlpool tubs.

"Ahh, that feels so good," I said putting my toes up to the jets. We sipped our wine and flipped through *Desperate Husbands*.

Liana, looking at the book, exploded, "That sell out!"

"Who is a sell out?" Ashley asked.

"Quentin tells the story of this Latin politician, Ricardo Santiago, who sells out his people. His wife, Alexis, is pissed."

"How come?" Jan asked.

"He is trying so hard to be a member of this snooty country club and he doesn't care what he has to do to get there. One of the criteria for acceptance is to reveal his deepest, darkest secret to a group of men that pretty much run the country club. The other is to vote to pass an unpopular bill in the senate."

"Sounds a bit familiar, doesn't it?" Jan said coyly.

"I'm sure it's just a coincidence," Liana said. "It has to be doesn't it? The guy in the book is on the down-low and Antonio is a lot of things, like an asshole, a lying, cheating dog, but he is not gay."

"Oh yeah!" Jan said sarcastically.

"Like we believe in Santa Claus and the Easter Bunny and Clinton's statement the he did not have sex with that woman!" Beverly blasted her. "He's just on the waiting list."

"I got your waiting list right here, Beverly," Liana said shaking her fist at her.

"She's so sensitive!" Jan laughed.

The girls started singing YMCA taunting Liana.

"Young man are you listening to me? I say young man, you can fulfill your dream. It's fun to stay at the Y M C A! Y M C A! Say it loud."

As Liana gawked, we got up and danced around, wet feet and all and threw our hands in the air making the Y M C A moves.

"One more time!" Jan shouted.

Hearing the commotion, Adrian came back into the room. "That's my theme song. What's all the noise about? Adrian's is an elegant salon, I don't need your noise. We want quiet energy. I decorated in Feng Shui, so please keep it down."

"We just found out Antonio has a booty buddy. He's finally come out of the closet." Jan and Ashley couldn't contain their laughter.

"I'm so happy for you, Liana. That's Fa-Bu-Lous. I know how he feels. It's so hard trying to keep it a secret. Before I came out, I almost had a nervous breakdown. Sometimes you need to forget what others think. Sometimes you need to throw caution to the wind. I'm finally FREE! Now if you all will come this way we'll start to work."

Liana stood up and shouted angrily, "Talk to the hand Adrian! Antonio is not gay! Nor is he on a waiting list!"

"He is still in denial," Adrian snapped back, "Excuse me!"

Liana became angrier than I've ever seen her.

"I'll admit that Antonio can't keep his dick in his pants, but I can say one thing for sure, Antonio is a real man. He wears the Michael Jordan Hanes collection. Not pink panties like that Idaho Republican Senator, Larry Craig. In my opinion, if a man is caught in a bathroom playing footsies with another man, he's definitely gay!"

"I heard that," Adrian responded as he snapped his fingers. "Sit ladies, the pedicurists will get to you in a minute."

"Speaking of gay," Liana said more calmly as she reclaimed her chair, "This sellout politician is also questioning his masculinity, hmmm. I was thinking..." She stopped in mid-sentence with a thoughtful look on her face.

"Thinking what?" Adrian encouraged her. "Are you one of Jerry's kids? Complete the sentence. Get hooked on phonics. Give me a vowel, don't be afraid. Let it all out. In Adrian's there are no secrets. The moment you walked through the door your business became public information."

Liana looked at Adrian, embarrassed. "You know Adrian, I was thinking, if you had one homosexual experience, does that make you gay?"

Adrian looked at her and put his hands on his hips in an exaggerated gesture. "Child, you are worried about the wrong thing. Just because you have a set of expensive golf clubs, does not that make you Tiger Woods. Just because your head is wrapped in a towel, does not make you Osama Bin Laden. Child, just because you have a dream, it certainly doesn't make you Martin Luther King."

Beverly was looking through the book and suddenly burst into laughter. "No, she didn't! Boring!"

"What's so funny?" I asked

"I'm cracking up about this Miss Goody Two Shoes chick, Summer Baldwin, who jumps out of bed and folds her panties and bra right in the middle of hot, passionate sex. She's driving her boyfriend up the wall! She's so anal retentive."

"Anal retentive?" Ashley asked, "The woman is gay? My Lord, she likes it in the butt?"

"No, Ashley. Keep up with the program. Anal retentive means she's obsessed with order," Jan said patiently.

Jan grabbed the book and started flipping though it. "No he didn't! What? The preacher, Pastor Hayes is going to hell. That dirty dog!" She yelled as she read a page. "His poor little wife, Carol, never suspected a thing." Jan looked over at Ashley sympathetically. "It's going to be okay, Ashley. The wife is always the last to know."

"Last to know what?" Ashley asked vaguely, coming out of her self-absorbed fog.

"It's just a coincidence," Jan told her as she flipped her hand at her. "Go on back to sleep, dear."

"Look on page 32, second paragraph," Beverly said.

I turned to that page and read aloud. "Paula was sixteen when we met. She was the first child born in my church. We had an affair for seven years. My wife never suspected a thing. As time passed, my sins didn't stop there. I impregnated two women in the congregation."

"That low-down dirty dog," Ashley said woodenly.

As the pedicurists finished up, we moved to the manicure tables and I said, "It's going to be okay, Ashley. Girl, you have our support. We will help you through this." I patted her on the shoulder.

Ashley tried to force a smile. She read the passage as we all stood by silently.

"That Quentin has quite an imagination," she said.

"I don't know. Fiction is sometimes based in fact," I said.

"Don't get your bloomers in a knot," Ashley said with a little more life. "It's just some made up story about a minister getting girls pregnant. It's all make-believe."

Beverly looked at Ashley intently. "It sounds a lot like your Donald, Mr. Holy and Perfect."

"Never trust a man as far as you can throw him," Liana said angrily.

"Beverly, I know it's been quite a while since you stepped foot in a church, but for us loyal members who attend weekly, a man of God would never do that. There is no way Donald would stoop so low. I'd bet my life he'd never, ever do such a thing." Ashley gripped Beverly's hand desperately.

Beverly pulled her hand away, with distaste written all over her face. "Yeah, right," she said simply. I could see she wanted to say something else, but held back.

"Yeah." Ashley stared at each of us. She had a desperate, pleading look in her eyes. "My Donald would never think of cheating, especially when he has a woman like me. It would be..." she searched for a word "ludicrous."

As we waited for the manicurists to begin, all of us were quiet and feeling pain for Ashley, but unable to do anything. Everyone was secretly questioning her mate's behavior. Ashley thumbed through the book and let out a crazed giggle, desperately needing to shift the focus off of her. "What! Oh no, I guess she was too sexy for herself!"

She raised her head and looked pointedly at Beverly. "It's always the pretty ones that can't keep a man!" she said triumphantly.

Beverly pretended not to hear her. Ashley continued to read, then said out loud, "Uh huh, Right! I certainly agree with Quentin about that."

Unable to contain herself Beverly blurted out, "What?"

"I agree your looks can get a man, but your looks are not enough to keep a man. If you don't believe that, look at actress Jennifer Anniston, supermodel Naomi Campbell, Christie Brinkley and the jury is still out on Jennifer Lopez!"

Liana, scanning her book, laughed out loud. "Ashley, that preacher is nothing compared to this whorish pilot from Capital Airlines..." Liana stopped as she turned her attention back to the book. She read for a moment and said, "I know he didn't say that! After all that, his wife still has the audacity to think she is Miss Ooo-Wee!" Liana shook her head. "If she finds out what he said, his ass is grass! But hey, I'll never tell. I'll take it to the grave!" Liana slammed the book shut with a self-satisfied smile.

"I can't take it anymore! What page, tell me what page!" Beverly shouted.

"Child, it's on page 64. Quentin talks about Bob the Pilot, this playboy type that works for Capital Airlines. The night before his best friend's wedding, he sleeps with his friend's fiancée."

"No he didn't!" Beverly shouted.

"Oh, yes he did. Not only with her, but he slept with every female flight attendant in his crew."

"No way!" Beverly said, fire blazing in her eyes.

"Girl, he even had a threesome in the cockpit. He said making love to his wife was like making love to a log. She just lays there cold and lifeless."

"I thought every man wanted a supermodel," Jan said maliciously.

Ashley picked up where Liana left off. "Girls, check this out. When Bob was asked what movie reminded him of sex with his wife, he said *Gone in Sixty Seconds*."

"That model, Giovanna McNeal, needs to sit down," I wisecracked. "Is foreplay included?"

"I got your foreplay right here." Beverly waved her fist at me. "Please don't hate me because I'm beautiful."

"Beverly, you have to tell Jeff that I flew first class with Transco not so long ago. I think they need to change their motto from 'You'll think you never left the ground' to 'You'll think you never left the ground, because we treat you like dirt'," Jan said maliciously.

Beverly shook her head and gave Jan an angry look. As Ashley and Liana flipped the pages and picked out passages that resembled the other's lives, Beverly exhaled through her teeth and opened her book. As fate would have it, it was now her turn.

"Oh, yes!" She let out a jubilant cry. "So Miss Society was like that in bed." She looked at Jan out of the corner of her eye. "Her husband left all his money to who?"

"What page, who?" Jan asked.

"Page 303. It's juicy!"

We all flipped to 303 and read. Even the manicurists that had just entered the room were quiet as they listened to what we had to say.

Beverly had everyone's undivided attention as she began to read.

His poor wife, Buffy, was clueless. Winston had desires in his heart. He had to have his forbidden fruit. They say once you go black, you never go back.

Although Winston pretended to be racist, you would have never suspected jungle fever. For years he looked at African American women on the sly. He didn't want his society friends to know that in reality, he was a closet Thomas Jefferson.

"Peter McCallister is a closet Thomas Jefferson?" Ashley asked one beat behind everyone else.

We all looked at Jan. She had put down *Desperate Husbands* and was now reading *People* magazine. She changed the subject.

"Star Jones has lost so much weight, she doesn't even look like herself." She cut her eyes at Beverly. "Girl, if you lose anymore weight you can hula hoop with a Cherrio." Beverly rolled her eyes at Jan.

I had continued to read the passage Beverly found. "Check this out!"

"What, Bridgett?" Liana said.

"Page 307, paragraph five, Winston says he wishes his wife would lose some weight. He said when his wife sits on his face he can't hear his stereo!"

We all fell out laughing. I cut my eyes at Jan, but she continued to ignore us.

"Oh my God, this is funny. Winston says that making love to his wife reminds him of the movies *No Country for Old Men* and *Titanic* ! He's just not into you like that."

"No he didn't!" Ashley said with delight.

Jan, unable to stand it anymore, picked up a book. "Okay, what page?"

"Page 309."

Jan slapped open the book and began to read aloud.

Winston knew he wanted to divorce his society wife, but he'd been married for 35 years and unhappy for 34. The only thing keeping his marriage together was love. Not love for his wife or stepchildren, but love of his money. Winston was one of Savannah's richest men. His net worth was estimated at five hundred million dollars. He and Buffy were the toast of Savannah. He knew he was smart when it came to making money, but a total idiot when it came to love. He hadn't had a pre-nuptial agreement signed before he married Buffy. If they divorced, Buffy and her children stood to get half of everything he owned.

"Oh, poppycock!" Jan shouted and plopped the book down.

"Girl, you didn't get to the good part," Liana said to Jan. "Keep reading!"

Jan picked the book up again and opened it back up, leafing through until she got to the right page. She started to read aloud again.

As the phrase 'Yes we can' rang out over the cheering crowd, Buffy gave Winston a cunning look. All the while, Winston thought Buffy only married him for his money. She had pretended to be pregnant. But in reality, she'd had a hysterectomy. She had lured him into her devious web. Her deceit and cunningness didn't stop there. During their pillow talk, she would tell him 'What's mine is yours and what's yours in mine.' But, after their elaborate honeymoon, the mask came off. He soon discovered that his share of what was hers equaled zero. Buffy was broke and needed a bail out.

Stupid, stupid!' he thought to himself. Everything was now at risk. She would never give him a divorce. She was threatening to expose his dirty laundry. Five hundred million was too much to risk. To add to that, his candidate was on his way to the White House. He'd spent millions to get him elected. He was the pride and joy of his people. The hope and dreams for America. The first of his race and just when he was about to cash in on his investment, he knew his wife would expose them both.

Time was ticking away. Winston's back was against the wall. He was desperate and desperate people will do desperate things. Buffy thought she had him by the balls.

"God, this is so juicy!" Beverly screamed, totally involved in the story.

"Take a chill pill, Beverly," Liana yelled. "Let Jan finish!"

Jan gave them both an arch look and continued.

But the rich, southern businessman had a plan of his own. On her thirtieth birthday, his illegitimate daughter, Summer, would inherit his entire empire. At the stroke of midnight, five hundred million dollars would automatically be wired to an offshore account in his daughter's name. Buffy would be left clueless and penniless. His money and his empire would finally be out of her greedy grasp. He would then be free to divorce Buffy with no consequences, and be able to marry his one true love, Kathleen, Summer's mother and an African American stripper he'd met thirty four years ago.

Jan slowly closed the book and laid it gently in her lap. She placed her hands on top of the book and stared at her lap intently, not speaking.

"Oh, Jan!" Liana said maliciously, breaking the silence, "Your man is leaving you and you are going to be dead ass broke. You will have to shop with a layaway plan and be the best dressed woman in the soup line."

Ashley came back to life. "At least there's a bright side!"

"Ashley, what could be worse than being left without a cent to your name?" Jan asked with a red flush creeping up her neck.

"At least you'll have a tight coochie," Ashley said and we couldn't help but laugh. Jan threw us an angry glare.

"Rubbish. I've never worried about getting a man and I'm not going to start to worry now. Women just need to chill. Women get anxious when they hit their 30's, desperate in their 40's and fuck it by the time they hit 50."

"I can't wait to be an old cougar like Jan," Beverly said with a giggle.

"I got your old cougar right here sister. Arrrr," she said sarcastically to Beverly, clawing the air.

35

Adrian walked back into the room with a copy of Quentin's book. He gave us each a cold stare. "Uh huh, I knew you Buckhead chicks were fronting." He sucked his teeth and burst into rib tickling laughter. He fell backwards into a chair.

"What, Adrian?" Jan asked.

"Oh nothing." He picked up the book and continued to read.

"Adrian, I know you don't believe a word of Quentin's book," Jan said, looking at him suspiciously.

"Oh, no girls," he said, gathering his composure. "It's just good, old entertainment. I don't believe a word of it."

"That's right. Good, old entertainment. It's all poppycock."

"Well, I don't really believe it," He said defensively. "But, you have to admit, the characters sound a lot like you ladies from the 30305. And according to the husbands, when it comes to your sex lives, none of you are working with weapons of mass destruction." He jumped up and gave Jan a reassuring hug. "My little Boston cupcake, I didn't know you and Winston were having marriage problems. It seems the wife is the last to know. You poor thing. But, don't worry Jan, I'm not going to let Kathleen take your man!"

"Kathleen is not going to take anybody!" she said, spitting fire. "She's a fictional character."

"Honey, don't be so defensive," Adrian said calmly.

Jan took a couple of breaths. "Peter and I are as happy as the first day we married," she stated smugly.

I couldn't believe what Adrian had said. None of us really believed that we could possibly be the basis for the characters in Quentin's book.

As Adrian lead us into the shampoo room and we settled into the chair and leaned back for washes he continued, "Okay Buckhead wives, settle down. I'm just giving you a word of caution. You should always prepare for war in time of peace." Adrian snapped his fingers and rolled his neck sister girl style. "I've got a solution!"

"We're all ears Adrian," Jan and Ashley chorused.

"The idea hit me when I was watching TNT, the movie channel. I came up with the very thing that's guaranteed to keep any man from walking away. Do you remember the movie 'Misery', with Kathy Bates and James Caan?"

"I don't believe I know that one," Ashley said, perplexed.

"Well, anyway, James Caan plays a famous writer who is on his way up to an isolated cabin for peace and quiet. He's hit a bit of writer's block. On the way he has a car accident. He is lying flat on his back in the snow with two broken legs, moments away from becoming a vanilla Popsicle when Kathy Bates, playing this psycho chick, finds him."

"What happens?" Ashley asks.

"She drags him back to her place. Turns out she's a nurse so she sets his legs. When he gets a little better she wants him to write a book that brings a favorite character of hers, named Misery, that he'd killed off, back to life. This psycho chick felt he was being rude and unfair to her. I mean, after all, she only asked for one small favor for all her tender loving care."

"Well, that sounds like a fair trade," Jan said pompously.

"Yeah, to me too. Any man found half dead in the snow is your man, Beverly," Liana said spitefully.

"Losers weepers, finders keepers. I think it is in the American Constitution. Well, anyway ladies, after a week of TLC, breakfast in bed and every bad sitcom ever shown on TV, he finally figured out he needed to get out of there."

"What an ungrateful man," Ashley said.

"Well, the psycho chick isn't about to let him go until he writes Misery back to life. He's healing up and the only way to make sure he doesn't get up and walk out of there is to..."

"What?" Liana screamed in frustration.

"She cuts off his legs with an axe, just below the knees."

"Oh my God, no!" Jan yells.

"I'm serious as a heart attack. When the movie ended I was inspired to tears. I haven't been so emotional since Obama got elected. Women everywhere can learn from the movie *Misery*."

"Like what, maim men," Liana said sarcastically.

"Duh!" Adrian rolled his eyes at Liana like she was stupid. "The subliminal message was given all through the movie." He snapped his fingers. "Since you are one of Jerry's kids, I'll make it simple. To keep your man from leaving, all you have to do is take him up to your winter cabin and have a car accident. When he's about to become a vanilla or chocolate Popsicle, drag his ass to the cabin and cut off his legs. From that point on, there ain't no way in hell he can walk away."

I couldn't help but shudder at the image.

Adrian noticed and leaned over and said, "Honey, I am speaking metaphorically."

"Lord, please help these retarded souls," Ashley lamented the heavens.

Jan shook her head and said, "You know I don't believe a word of Quentin's book. It's just a story. There is no way in hell a man will turn over a fortune to an illegitimate daughter of an African American stripper. This is the south and it is just not done. Besides that, pre-nuptial agreements don't mean anything. They can be broken in court. So forget it, you've been sitting under the dryers too long."

"You are right, Jan." Ashley agreed, putting on her best 'there's a soul in need' expression. She patted Jan on the back. "It's only fiction. It makes as much sense as *The DaVinci*. It is for entertainment purposes only. Come to think of it, I'm tired of the book anyway. It's just a literary version of the *Jerry Springer Show*."

We all followed Ashley's lead and tossed our books onto a table, but we looked slyly at each other anyway. Regardless of how hard we tried to keep a poker face, *Desperate Husbands* hit home.

As Adrian walked away, he suddenly did an about face, "One more thing ladies. I'd better tell you myself before you read it in *Desperate Husbands* or see it on *Nancy Grace*."

"What's that?" Jan asked, sounding tired and wrung out.

Our hair washed, we moved to the styling area and the stylist got to work, snipping and trimming.

Now that we were in the common area of the salon everyone was listening to Adrian. He dropped his head and said coyly, "There have been many rumors circulated about the truth. But they say the truth shall set you free."

We looked at him through our mirrors and he raised his head and declared. "I am Anna Nicole Smith's real baby's daddy. Little Dannielynn is my love child. I'm going tomorrow and claim all that money. Please keep it a secret." He snapped and rolled his neck like an Egyptian dancer.

Everyone within earshot doubled over in laughter.

36

We were finally primped, manicured, pedicured and styled to within an inch of our lives. We'd gotten dressed and returned to the lobby and were sitting having another glass of champagne while the cashier sorted out our bills. Suddenly the glass doors at the entrance were flung open and a suspicious looking woman, wearing oversized dark glasses, a full-length mink coat and dripping with diamonds, burst through.

"Check her out. Why is she wearing that coat? It's a hundred degrees out there!" Beverly said, sitting up for a better look.

"God, look at that bling-bling. I bet none of them are Harry Winston's, but cubic zirconium." Jan hissed. "I'll bet, my on a budget friends, she got that coat at Burlington Coat Factory. That's some kind of class wearing fur in the middle of summer," Jan said bitingly.

"Stop hating Jan," I said, "You know money when you see it."

The woman was carrying a copy of Quentin's book.

"Isn't there anybody who doesn't have a copy of that stupid book?" Jan wailed.

The woman whipped off her sunglasses as she strode across the lobby. Jan leaned over and whispered, "Isn't that Wanda Smith? You know, the local DJ from the 'Frank and Wanda Morning Show.' She just moved to Buckhead from Gwinnett County."

Beverly peered closely at her. "That's her. Shh! Don't let her know we recognize her."

Wanda stopped in front of Adrian. We all eavesdropped shamelessly.

"Adrian, Adrian!" Wanda wailed in frustration. "I'm going to kill that man of mine."

"Wanda, what happened?" Adrian flung an arm around her shoulder and led her over to a chair near us.

"I was reading Quentin's book and I swear he's talking about my husband. I caught my husband cheating red-handed. Now, my business is all over the street."

"Wanda, stop playing!" Adrian said in surprise. But, you could see the eagerness on his face for some new, juicy gossip. "Just sit right here and let me hang that coat up. Does this thing bite? And why are you wearing it in this heat?"

"No, it's pedigree and I figure I'd better wear it while the democrats are in power! The way the economy is it could be dinner next week."

Adrian rolled his eyes and said, "Doris, we have another 911, bring the Anger Management stock."

Doris quickly returned with a fluted glass. Wanda took it, leaned back and kicked off her shoes.

"Ah, that's what I'm talking about."

"Okay, Wanda what happened?"

We all found ourselves leaning in closer to Wanda and Adrian not wanting to miss a thing.

She noticed and said, "Well ladies, you might as well gather around. It seems like all of Atlanta knows my business. Why do men have to cheat?" She drew a deep breath.

"Because right ain't in them," Beverly answered angrily.

"I knew I should have married an old man," Wanda said. "I should have married an old man like Anna Nicole Smith did."

"Oh, Wanda, that is so nasty," I said making a face. "Somebody told me you could catch something from sleeping with old men."

"You damn sure can, you can catch all the sales at Nieman Marcus!" She laughed bitterly. "Girl, I was such a fool. He told me everything was fine."

"He told you everything was fine? Duh! Don't you know that when a man tells you everything is fine, that's when you need to worry!" Adrian said gleefully. "Child, you would have saved yourself a lot of heartache by snooping through his things."

"All men are peros!" Liana erupted.

Wanda gave her a puzzled look. "You want to run that by us in English, for those of us that are working toward our GED's...what the hell is pero?"

"Pero is dog. All men are dogs!"

"Honey, how do you say homicide in Spanish? What about alibi or the phrase 'be on the lookout' or 'at large'? I'm trying to keep black on black crime down, but that husband of mine's life span is about to become even more limited."

"Come on Wanda, it can't be that serious!" Adrian said, trying to comfort her.

"Adrian, I will divorce him and take everything he has in the process." She whipped a calculator out of her Coach bag.

"Let's see, like Ivana Trump said, don't get mad, get even." She held the calculator up and began to punch in numbers. "His bank account and investments are worth about..." she punched in more numbers. "Oh, yeah, his 401K and savings account...add to that his golden parachute." She punched furiously, "And his real estate holdings..." She frantically punched at the calculator, squinting at it. "Damn, now let me total it all...his net worth is...damn, okay, carry the one. What's zero from zero?" She asked the room at large.

"A big ass zero!" Ashley yelled, suddenly alert.

"Is that before or after taxes?"

"Both!" Ashley shouted triumphantly.

"Damn, damn and double damn! I'm fucked. My golden parachute has a hole in it. I have one foot in the poor house, the other on a banana peel, my hand has grease on it and I'm stuck in a tornado." She fainted.

We tried to revive her. Ashley slapped her face. Liana got an ice pack from somewhere. Jan kept yelling "Wanda, wake up!" Someone finally got some ammonia and put it under her nose. Wanda woke up and pushed the rag with the ammonia away. She pushed Ashley's hand away as she continued to try and slap her.

"What the hell are you people doing to me!"

"You fainted," Adrian said, wringing his hands.

"Oh, well never mind that. Get that woman off of me!" she said pushing at Ashley again, as she tried to administer one more slap for good measure.

Wanda sat up and wailed hysterically. "As God is my witness, I will never be poor again. I will vow to keep the republicans out of the White House. Adrian, all my life I had to fight someone. I had to fight my father. I had to fight my brothers. I had to fight my uncle. Adrian, if that man cheats on me one more time I will kill him dead this time!"

"Wanda, it can't be that serious." He sat down beside her.

"It is Adrian!"

"Didn't we see this scene in 'The Color Purple'? The first part of your soliloquy was definitely 'Gone with the Wind."

"Adrian, this is not about Rhett and Scarlett or Celie or Sofia. It's about me." She pointed two fingers at us. "Until that man does right by me, he's never going to progress," she exhaled sharply. "Unlike you Buckhead wives, I know I am working with a weapon of mass destruction between the sheets."

We rolled our eyes. I thought about taking that book from her and hitting her over the head with it.

"Wanda, let me give you a big hug, Sugar. You just sit right here and tell us all about it. Tell everyone what that bad man is doing to my Wanda." Adrian cooed sympathetically as he gave everyone a delighted look. "They better leave my Wanda alone. They don't know who they're messing with."

"Adrian, I keep choosing one bad man after the other," Wanda said. She shook her head and looked absolutely bewildered. "This is Atlanta. Maybe I need to forget about men altogether. Maybe I need to get me a gay or bi-sexual lover."

"You'll do no such thing," Adrian said soothingly.

"Why not Adrian? Give me one damn reason why I shouldn't?"

"For one thing, all the good ones are taken."

Laughter erupted around the salon.

"Adrian, the Lord, and myself, don't approve of your alternative life style. Why don't you give it up?" Ashley said judgmentally. "Why don't you join the church?" Ashley must have had way too much to drink; everyone knew you didn't mention joining the church to Adrian.

Someone said, "Oh, no!"

Wanda let out a piercing cry, "Fire in the hole, incoming torpedo!" and she grabbed her head and ducked.

Adrian got up in Ashley's face. "I know you didn't just say that! I know you didn't mention the "C" word - church!"

"Yes, join the church! Repent your sins so you can go to heaven," Ashley said, starting to realize maybe she said the wrong thing. She took a step away from Adrian and looked at him stupidly, blinking rapidly.

We all peeped out from our hiding places. A deathly silence filled the room. Adrian calmly reached into the pocket of his bright pink smock and pulled out a large Afro comb. He started to whistle nonchalantly as he walked over to Ashley. She just sat there with a prim, tight-lipped expression on her face. Adrian lifted the comb and popped Ashley smartly over the head with it.

"Ouch! That hurt!" she cried. Everyone breathed a sigh of relief that the crises seemed to be over and started laughing.

"Ashley, how many times are we going to have to tell you to stay out of grown folk's business?" Jan said in exasperation. "Adrian and the Lord have an understanding."

Wanda's head popped up from behind a chair. Adrian reached out, grasped her hand and pulled her to her feet.

"Ladies," he yelled. "This is not *CNN Headline News*. This is a bulldog conversation. No puppies or Chihuahuas allowed."

We all pretended to turn away and mind our own business, but the minute they were seated we turned right back around and continued to listen.

"Adrian," Wanda continued, "my troubles all started when I was reading *Desperate Husbands*. Quentin was talking about this gold-digging woman who only dated men who are rich or famous. Well, anyway, I didn't want to be just another gold digging sister, so I decided to give Joe the Plumber a chance. Why should an average Joe have catfish when he can have caviar? When I met him, he was so broke he was eating wish sandwiches.

"What's a wish sandwich?" Jan whispered to Ashley.

"Two pieces of bread that you wish had some meat between them," Ashley whispered back.

Wanda continued tearfully, "With the competition being so cut throat, you would think my husband would be cool. Truthfully, on a scale from one to ten, he's a two." She paused and looked around at us as we leaned forward to hear her better. "Well, he barely made the draft. He was a last round pick. In my little, black book he was running neck and neck with Boy George, Little Richard and Pee Wee Herman. Girl, I'm serious, I got real problems over here. Before I let him make a fool out of me, I'll kill him. I mean dead!"

"Wanda, get back to the story," Adrian said.

"As I said, you would think he would do right. Knowing that he was about to get traded."

"Hell no, that was too much right! Men are peros!" Liana shouted.

"That's right girl, peros," Wanda agreed. "But Adrian, the good book says that what is done in darkness will certainly come to light."

"Amen, Wanda," Ashley said pompously, sitting up straight as a poker, putting on her holy face.

37

"Ladies, get some business!" Adrian shouted at us, "Now Wanda, how did you find out he was cheating?"

"About a month ago, he claimed he was working late. But when I looked at his paycheck, he was broke before taxes. I mean he was borderline section eight. You know it's bad when the homeless are taking up a collection for you. I thought to myself, my man is not coming home and he is always broke. The toaster and the TV are still here. So, it's obvious he's not on crack. The only other logical explanation is he's cheating. So I hired a private detective. He only confirmed what I'd already suspected. The dog was cheating."

"With who?" Ashley asked.

She looked at Ashley, "Girl, he was cheating with one of those manless hoochies at Holy Faith Church."

"What? No Wanda, I'm sure you are mistaken. Maybe she's from Bishop Eddie Long's church, or Creflo Dollar's church. You know Creflo requires a copy of your tax return before you can be a member."

Wanda shot Ashley an impatient look and went on with her story. "I knew right then the devil wore imitation Prada. I could tell she shopped at the flea market. That same evening, my husband, out of the blue, asked to borrow my car because he didn't have any gas, you know with the gas prices so high and all. So, like a sweet and trusting wife, I gave it to him. I didn't even ask questions. I just gave him the car."

"That's where you went wrong," a nosy woman in the back spat out. "Like mama used to say, you should only trust a man as far as you can throw him."

"Well ladies, my bad," Wanda said tearfully. "I knew with five dollars worth of gas in my car, he wasn't going far. He and his skank were spotted going into the Ritz Carlton. A friend of mine saw them and called me. I had her pick me up and we waited outside until they left and we followed them to Carrabba's Italian Grill. They were hugging and kissing like newlyweds."

"What, girl! He had the nerve to take his skank to a fine restaurant!" someone shouted.

"Ladies, stop hating your fellow female. Would you like it if someone called you a skank?" Adrian said reasonably. "Now go on Wanda, what happened when that little bitch went into the restaurant?"

"My first impulse was to go up to her and pull a Rambo, but that wouldn't be ladylike. I thought about the Terminator or OJ, but then I remembered Johnny Cochran is dead. The glove will fit and they won't acquit."

"Well, what did you do?" Adrian said impatiently.

"I chilled."

"You what!" Jan said, shocked.

"Yeah, chilled. Never let a man know what you are planning. You always plan for war in time of peace. I had my friend take me on home and I waited like a good little wife. When he came home I acted like nothing had happened and we went on to bed and made love like there was no tomorrow. While he was sleeping I looked at his lifeless body, planning and thinking.

"He even had the nerve to call out her name in his sleep! Ain't that a bitch? In my house and he hadn't even paid the rent."

"No, he didn't!" Adrian said, stroking his chin.

"Yes he did. He came this close to waking up dead." Wanda held up her hand with her thumb and index finger less than an inch apart.

"But, I chilled. I thought about throwing hot grits on his ass, but decided me and the kids might need them. I thought about ringing his bell with a cast iron skillet. But I chilled. I thought about cutting his testicles off and slicing them up like bologna and feeding them to him in a sandwich. But I chilled."

"If that wasn't bad enough, the bitch was broke too. She used to call his office on a pre-paid phone."

"No she didn't!" Liana interjected.

"Child, yes she did. But still I chilled. Night after night I chilled. Finally an idea hit me. I knew how to get even and get paid. You know God doesn't like ugliness."

"He surely doesn't," Ashley agreed.

"Well one day, tragedy struck."

"What happened?" I asked surprised.

"He borrowed my car again. He and that skank were on 285 when the brakes went out."

"What!" Adrian clapped his hands with delight.

"The car was totaled."

"That's awful, was anyone hurt?" Jan asked, with a gleam in her eye.

"Oh yeah, the both of them. They hit a pole and had to be rushed to Grady. They were both in intensive care. They just got out. God is a good God."

Ashley threw up her hands and said loudly, "Hallelujah!" Beverly and I looked at each other and giggled.

"Well, being that it was my car the police called me. He tells me that my husband and an unidentified woman were in a car accident because the brakes went out and that they'd both been sent to Grady. I was in shock. The brakes went out in my car. Damn! I loved that car."

"Oh my God, that's awful," Jan said in disbelief.

"But the plot thickens. I was the cops' number one suspect!"

"That's because you're black," a nosy woman commented.

"I don't know," Wanda responded. "All I know is that they hauled me down to the Fulton County jail. They took me to a dark, dingy room and put a bright light in my face. Two cops came in and pulled the good cop, bad cop routine on me."

"For real?" Ashley said.

"Yes, child, they banged their fists on the table screaming 'Wanda, don't play innocent with me.' They kept on saying they know I did it, all the evidence pointed to me. They said I had a motive and no alibi. They said they had the device I used and he pulled out a small screwdriver. I told him the only thing I knew about a screwdriver was that it had vodka in it. That was when I decided to play the race card. I told them I knew the only reason I was there was because I was black.

"The bad cop shouted at me 'Michael Jackson was black and we arrested him.' But, I told him Michael Jackson hadn't been black since the Jackson 5.

"The good cop kept trying to sweet talk me into confessing. He wanted to know how the brakes could go out on a brand new GEO Metro. Well, how the hell do I know! Do I look like a mechanic?

"I tried to keep it gangsta. I was hard as nails. I just told him since he was the cop, he should figure it out. I held up like Lil Kim. I ain't no snitch. But after fifteen minutes of no food, they broke me down. I went out like a real bi-atch, I was crying like Paris Hilton, 'Mama, come get me. I can't take it no more.'"

"Fifteen minutes! You're a real hard case," Liana laughed.

"Fifteen minutes of pure torture. Child, Paris Hilton kept it more gangsta than me!"

"I'm telling you, I couldn't go on. I started yelling, 'I did it. I did it. Officer, I don't know how the brakes went out; I rigged the car so the fucking steering wheel would fall off. Those American cars ain't worth a damn! I can see why those motherfuckers need a bail out. You can't depend on them.' Those cops started laughing so hard they cried. I plead temporary insanity and got off with a little probation."

"All right!" I cheered.

"There is justice in America!" Liana screamed.

"Plus, ladies, I'd insured the car with five different insurance companies. All of them paid off the same policy. Now, you keep that a secret. Everybody's business ain't any business at all."

"No *problema*," Liana promised.

"Well, now, since my husband saw his life flash before his eyes, I'm hoping he'll be as faithful as a puppy, but time will tell. He's working two jobs and he bought me a new convertible Jaguar. This Sunday, we are joining the Holy Faith. The slut doesn't go there anymore. Somebody told her a little voodoo was coming her way and she'd better get out of town."

"Who told her that?" Adrian asked.

"I have no idea," Wanda said innocently, turning her hand up and looking at her nails.

"Well, I'm glad you are coming to the Lord!" Ashley said, throwing her hands up in the air. "God is good!"

"Forget Dr. Phil," Wanda said with a sly grin. She reached into her purse and pulled out a large screwdriver. "Now this is a real murder weapon. Home Depot has saved my marriage! The screwdriver didn't fit so the police had to acquit!"

We all burst out laughing and gave each other high fives.

38

PETER

I walked over to the bar and made myself a scotch and soda. I sipped slowly, feeling the tension drain from my body. I was looking forward to relaxing for a few hours.

I heard the car door slam. I looked out the window and saw Jan's car. Damn, it was Jan. Usually her trip to Adrian's Beauty Salon guaranteed a day of peace and serenity. I took another few sips. I knew the minute she hit the door she'd be horny as hell.

Every time she goes to Adrian's she listens to all those cackling hens boast about their men and their scandalous sex lives. By the time she hears so many stories of sex in the kitchen, sex in a crowded restaurant, sex on the washing machine, sex in the elevator, and who is doing who, she's all sexed up and ready to go. She's going to be ready to rip my clothes off. It wouldn't be so bad except Jan was such a selfish lover. I could even overlook her extreme mood swings if she were an adventurous lover, or thought outside the box.

Since she was going through menopause, it was even worse. I know a lot of women think men like bitches, but that is the farthest thing from the truth. I don't want to sound like a chauvinist pig, but because of a woman's biological makeup, they have to have constant mood swings. So as men, we are programmed to overlook them. Very few men want to go toe to toe with an emotional woman. You get no cool points and it is a no-win situation from the start.

It seems everyone takes the side of the woman. The courts definitely do. Then, everyone else seems to jump on the bandwagon, her family, her friends, her therapist and even the preacher at church. When everyone gets through dogging men out, we even start to think it's our fault. To avoid an argument or confrontation, most men will usually do one of seven things: One, take the code of silence; two, lie; three, agree with everything she says; four, buy things to pacify her or shut her up; five, avoid talking; six, work late and come home late; seven, when all else fails, get a chick on the side.

I had to smile. A chick on the side is guaranteed to boost your self-esteem, guaranteed to get your libido all fired up and bring a new excitement to sex again. It also helps men to emotionally distance themselves if their wives suspect infidelity or precipitates a break-up or divorces them. Like the old saying goes, 'you should prepare for war in time of peace.' The experts may not agree with it, but, hey, it works for countless unhappily married men across America.

What so many women fail to realize, is a man compares what he has to what he sees in the streets. The same thing it took to get your baby hooked is the same thing it's going to take to keep him. When a man gets married, he married the fantasy or the image she projected. A sexy, loving and catering wife, a woman he believes is there to make him happy. So when the woman flips the script, men feel betrayed. If you start off skinny, stay that way. Don't get married and pick up weight. The man feels you have betrayed your implied contract; you know, the one that says what you see is what you get.

"Peter, I'm home!" Jan yelled out seductively in a singsong voice. She walked through the library door and I turned, putting on my game face.

"Darling, I'm so happy to see you. Your hair looks beautiful! That style definitely suits you," I said patronizingly.

She patted her hair, striking a seductive pose. Well, it might have been seductive if I were a man whale. "You like it. It's the Hilary Clinton look."

"I like it Jan."

"All the girls at Adrian's Beauty Salon raved about it."

"It makes you look ten years younger."

She blushed and smiled from ear to ear. She walked over to me and stuck her tongue in my ear. "How was your day Peter? Did you make us lots of money?"

"I did okay," I said nonchalantly.

"Well, how much is okay?" She started her usual rant. "Two hundred thousand, a half million? A million? More? How much Peter?"

Then she grabbed my crotch. "Tell me and I'll make it worth your time."

Men have such large and fragile egos. Even I'll admit my ego was the driving force behind my success and also my downfall. I stuck out my chest. I felt proud as a peacock in full feather, even with her attached to my crotch. "I made two million today. With a single phone call," I said proudly.

"I like the sound of that," she said, running her free hand over my chest roughly. "Two million from one phone call. If those cackling hens at Adrian's knew about my man, all their pussies would be wet."

She released my crotch and started to rub me through my trousers. "Ohhhh, Peter. I love a man with power. I love a man in uniform too, as long it's not prison fatigues."

She grabbed my tie and pulled me upstairs. When we reached our bedroom, she began peeling my clothes off. In the back of my mind I was hoping today would be different. Maybe she'll be open for some adventurous sex, open to some variety. But instead, after all the dirty talk and the big build up, it ended the same way as usual; the same old tired missionary position. Are we having fun yet? Calgon take me away.

As usual, Jan climaxed, totally forgetting about me. So many women feel it is the man's job to make them happy, without giving anything in return. It amazes me. I hear so many women joking about how men are inadequate in the sheets, but if women knew what men say about them behind their backs, they would cringe.

With Jan you can forget about foreplay or adventure. She would always tell me in that thick Boston accent...'nice girls don't suck dick.' After three or four minutes of what she calls marathon sex; she would lie in my arms and talk her ass off. It is really sad that men have to go looking in the street for what they aren't getting at home.

"Oh, Peter, that was great! You are such a stud! An animal! A beast! Was it as good for you as it was for me?" She said pushing me off her before I came.

"Words can't describe how I feel," I replied dryly. She breathed like she'd run the Peachtree Road race in under three minutes. Just like every time before, she flopped over and started to cuddle and talk and talk and talk. Rather than get upset, I just tuned her out.

My thoughts turned to Carla, as they often did. It was the only way I had of getting through the torture of sex with Jan. Sex with Carla was always incredible. What was more of a turn on was that we connected on every level. We connected emotionally, spiritually and personally. What so many women haven't learned is that it's easy to get a man's body or his money, but the grand prize is to win his trust and heart. Only then will he reveal his most intimate thoughts. If a man doesn't talk to you, or open up, he is indirectly saying that he doesn't trust you. He is also saying he doesn't feel that his emotions and feelings are safe with you.

There is always one woman a man will feel comfortable with. A woman he can let his hair down with; a woman that doesn't want anything from him; a woman that doesn't judge him and who will just accept him for who he is. Men would be in heaven if that woman was his mate, but often, it is not.

The woman I felt comfortable with was Carla. We would lie in bed and talk with each other for hours. We used to laugh and play like children. She made me feel like I could do anything, or be anybody. Her body was like a highway, full of peaks and valleys and curves. My body was like a sports car, my heart pounded as I raced to reach the end. I wanted to drive at 100 miles per hour, avoiding all the stops, yields and cautions. I loved to explore her body with my tongue, tasting the nectar of her vagina. Our bodies worked together in perfect harmony. Our bodies were created as a perfect compliment to each other, like a hand in a glove. We were like two instruments playing off each other, the perfect melody, the perfect pitch and the perfect tone. We were two people knowing each others' every move. - predestined calculated, perfected. Every touch necessary, we would crescendo into a feverish pitch. Each climax was the Fourth of July, and then we'd descend into a whisper. Afterwards we'd come back to reality, totally exhausted from our lovemaking.

I would lie awake and look at her beautiful body. She was like chocolate syrup, soft and silky to the touch. I loved the roundness of her butt, her full, beautiful breasts, and her luscious lips. She was a forbidden, exotic fruit that made me want more.

Jan suddenly intruded upon my thoughts. "Peter, are you listening to me? Don't you agree?"

I snapped back to reality. "Agree with what, darling? I'm sorry, I was starting to doze."

"Don't you agree that women should be put on a pedestal?" she said with impatience.

"Uh huh," I replied, still slightly dazed. "I certainly agree women should be put on a pedestal."

"So many men think only of themselves," she droned.

"Yes, how dare they not think about a woman's needs?"

She reached up and kissed me. "Peter, it seems like we agree on everything."

"Yes dear, we certainly do." I couldn't help the sarcasm that crept into my voice. Fortunately she started on another tangent and didn't notice.

I slipped back into my fantasy. I looked down at Jan's bloated body that was twice the size of the body I'd married. She went to the gym daily before we married. Now if someone mentions the word 'Ballys', she shudders and goes into hiding. She is so busy being Mrs. Society she's forgotten how to be a woman.

Jan finally drifted off to sleep. I wondered what it would have been like married to Carla. She was everything a man could want. She was loving, supportive and wanted a family. The only thing she wanted was to make me happy. I should have divorced Jan thirty years ago, and followed my heart. But back then, Carla was the wrong color in the minds of most southerners. I got caught up in what society would think of me. Even though society is more accepting, most people still feel the color of someone's skin still matters. I never thought that the woman of my dreams would exist in another race or color.

But, I can't just blame society. Mostly, it was my own fault. I was young, ambitious and wanted to make a mark in life. I wanted to be in a position to make people feel the same pain I felt growing up in an orphanage. Money gave me that power and control. The people that ran the orphanage told me I would never amount to anything. Both my parents were alcoholics and drug users. They tried to sell me to a drug dealer in exchange for a hit or two. At first, after all the physical and emotional abuse, being taken away by the state was a relief. For some reason I never understood why I didn't end up in foster care, but instead was placed in the orphanage. I remember all the teasing and bullying, and I watched as other kids got adopted. Every time the doorbell rang at the orphanage, I would run to the door, thinking each couple that walked through the door would be my new parents. I dreamed of living in a white house with a mommy and daddy that loved me. I hoped they would buy me a bicycle, but nobody wanted me. Tears formed in my eyes and I wiped them away.

When I turned eighteen, I joined the Army. Two days before my hitch was up, I discovered that my parents had died of a drug overdose. I went to college on the GI Bill, determined that I would never be like my parents. With a business degree under my arm, I walked out in the big, wide world, ready to take it on. I would never be dependent on anyone again, ever. I also swore that no child of mine would ever be without a father.

I discovered I had a talent for real estate. I worked hard and pulled myself up by my own bootstraps. I invested my savings from the army into small real estate holdings. With each payoff, I plowed more money back into investments. Before long, I had become moderately successful and proud of my accomplishments. I began to move in wealthier circles which helped me make more money.

A few years later, I met Jan at the Mayor's Ball. When we met, she gave me that love at first sight bullshit, but I liked the level of society she represented. She liked me for my money. Little did I know at the time, she would end up practically penniless when her husband passed away, and she desperately needed someone to support her extravagant lifestyle. Before her husband was even cold in the ground, she had blasted through any money that was left after fulfilling his debts. She had an eye for younger men, most of whom used her for their own personal ATM machine. I guess I was her next rising star and I was another younger man.

I had just made my first million in real estate. Jan worked hard to ensnare me in her web and I was dazzled by the prospect of walking in the Buckhead Golden Circle. She acted sweet and supportive. To society, we were the perfect couple and she became the perfect wife. She was witty and charming and knew all the right people, and was an active member of the church. Sex between us was incredible.

Shortly after we met, she became pregnant. I was on cloud nine. I was finally going to have the family I'd wished for all my life. The wedding was suitably grand, all the right people attended and every newspaper carried the details. I was so happy that a pre-nup was the last thing from my mind, besides, back then it wasn't common practice.

That's where I'd made my first mistake. Once Jan became Lord of the Ring, everything changed. I'd paid off her debts, and found out she wasn't pregnant. In fact, could not have even gotten pregnant due to a hysterectomy she'd had after her last son was born. To add insult to injury, sex became a weapon to be used as reward or punishment. But, as the saying goes, it was cheaper to keep her.

39

The next morning Jan and I were up early. Maria, our cook, prepared us a delicious breakfast. When we walked into the kitchen nook for breakfast, she was reading Quentin's new book.

"Mr. McCallister, I can't put this book down. All the ladies in Atlanta are talking about it. He's on every talk show and magazine cover. I hear husbands all over this country are admitting their own guilt. They were interviewing Quentin Banks on 'Good Morning America.'"

Jan interrupted Maria, as I pulled out her chair for her. "Yesterday he was on the 'Today' show. He has admitted that since this book came out, a lot of couples have either sought counseling, gotten married, or divorced. A lot of ministers and officials of churches are under attack. Bridgett also told me that since this book came out, Quentin has received death threats." She gave me a piercing look as I sat opposite her at the table.

"What are people getting so upset about, it's only make believe, isn't it? Its just more rubbish."

"That is what I thought too, until I read bits of it. But a lot of what he's saying in the book hits a little too close to home, according to a lot of the women at Adrian's."

"Like what?" I said, suddenly worried about my own indiscretions.

"The part that intrigued me the most was about this rich guy, Winston Dillingsworth, who left his entire fortune to his illegitimate daughter that he'd had with a black stripper."

I had just taken a sip of hot coffee. I choked, almost spewing coffee all over the table. Jan continued as if she were unaware of my near death experience.

"Peter, have you ever heard of anything so ludicrous. I mean, one of our kind would never set foot in a strip club. So please, forget about having a child with a black stripper. Even Jerry Springer wouldn't put such rubbish on his show. Peter, if one of our kind is crazy enough to do something like that, it would be the biggest scandal since Thomas Jefferson."

I could have sworn she gave me a knowing look, but decided Jan wasn't that intelligent. I attempted to play it off, knowing that I was going to wrap my hands around Quentin's throat and choke the living shit out of him. I laughed and said, "Jan, what man of means would be so foolish? Anyway, no sane person is ever going to believe any of that stuff is real," I said that with a lot more confidence than I felt. I know how southerners like their scandals.

"That's exactly how I feel Peter, but, all the girls at Adrian's swore Quentin was talking about you. How absurd right?"

"Completely absurd," I said with a lump in my throat.

Maria poured herself deeper into the book. Even Maria was interested to know how Ricardo voted.

"Maria, could you put that book down and get us some more coffee!" Jan said impatiently. "Imagine, even the servants can't put that damn book down."

As Maria poured our coffee she said, "What a sellout!"

Jan, unable to contain her curiosity asked, "What, what are you talking about Maria?"

"That Latino politician, Ricardo. The Latinos put him in power and the first thing he does is sell out his people! What a *pero!*"

I looked at Maria and rolled my eyes. If Quentin were standing in front of me, he'd be a dead man. But I said as evenly as possible, "Not you too, Maria. Is there anybody in Atlanta that hasn't read Quentin's book?"

Jan answered for her, "It is bad enough that he's on every cover, but there's talk he's going to be on the cover of O. He'll be the first man to ever be on that cover."

If the fellows and I had just kept our mouths shut, none of this would have happened. The only thing we would ever have to worry about is Quentin throwing a monkey wrench in our order at McDonald's. The next time I will leave well enough alone. In the future, when I see a man down, I will put my foot on his neck.

As we finished up breakfast, Jan and Maria continued to discuss the book. They were so involved neither one noticed me get up and walk out. I was shaking. I was so furious and I wondered how the other fellows were handling having our past sins publicly displayed to the world. I dialed Jeff's cell. When he answered and we exchanged pleasantries I said, "How's it going?"

"Not so good. Every since Quentin's book hit the shelves it has been non-stop drama. Beverly and I are arguing. My best friend, Dean, is looking at Clarissa and me suspiciously and employee's at Transco are calling me the playboy of the skies. Now, I think my job is in jeopardy."

"I'm sorry to hear that Jeff."

"Quentin must be stopped!"

"It's a little too late for that. Most of Atlanta has already read the book."

"I talked to Donald," Jeff said with exasperation. "He is really catching it at home and at Holy Faith the rumors are circulating all over. Pastor Cash is getting ready to retire. Donald is next in line, but the congregation is whispering behind his back that he's Pastor Hayes in the book. Pastor Cash has mentioned it in passing, but Donald assured him it is just gossip because of the book."

Suddenly Jeff screamed at the driver in front of him. "Get out of the way, buddy!"

"Peter, I'll call you later. Let me focus on this traffic."

"Okay, big guy. Be careful out there," I cautioned.

40

JEFF

When I finally arrived at Hartsfield-Jackson Airport, my crew gave me the cold shoulder. It didn't take a rocket scientist to figure it out. It was because of Quentin's book. I kept away from everyone until it was time to board the plane. I hoped that with a little luck, all this would blow over peacefully. But any hope of that lasted about as long as the phrase 'I'll love you forever.' The moment I boarded the plane, the flight attendants looked at me angrily. I walked through first class towards the cockpit and I saw that damn book everywhere.

As I passed one woman leaned over to her seatmate and said in a loud whisper, "That's him."

"Who?" Her friend asked.

"Bob the pilot!" she whispered back. "You know the one that can't keep his dick in his pants and sleeps with every flight attendant." I glanced down at them and they smiled suggestively.

One man shouted, "Bob, you're the man!"

Another said, "Bob, can you hook me up?"

Yet another roared, "Bob, can we get a lap dance in first class?"

All I could do was duck my head and continue on to the cockpit. I was happy to close the door shutting out the laughter coming from first class. I was relieved to finally be away from Quentin's stupid book. My co-pilot simply nodded at me as I slid into my seat. I put my headset on and then there was a loud banging on the door.

"Who is it?" I asked.

"It's Clarissa or Allison, take your pick, I'm sure you know me. I'm the flight attendant you screwed in Quentin's book. Open this damn door before I kick it down!"

I pulled off my headset and as I opened the door, Clarissa hauled off and slapped me so hard my ears rang. "You bastard, how could you?"

I pulled the door wider and hauled her into the cockpit. "Control yourself, Clarissa. We are at work and have a plane full of passengers."

"Why should you care about what people think? You didn't care when you told your friends all of our fucking business. How could you do this to me? What in the hell were you thinking?"

"Shhh, Clarissa, calm down. The passengers and crew don't need to know our business."

"They already know our business! Quentin's freaking book isn't just popular in Atlanta, it's popular everywhere. 'Men are dogs' is now a universal phrase. It's the one thing women of all nationalities share."

"Clarissa, I'm sorry."

"Sorry my ass Jeff! If you cared anything about me you wouldn't have told the world about us. Now my husband is looking at me suspiciously. He swears I'm Allison. My marriage is in jeopardy thanks to you. If I don't do something, I will be divorced before the ink dries on my marriage certificate."

"Just calm down and assure Dean the book is fiction. It will soon blow over." I looked at her curvaceous body and I just couldn't help myself. "Clarissa, you know we have a flight to Rio in two weeks?" If looks could kill, I'd be a dead man right now.

She said, "The next time you get some of this, Shaquille will have shot ten for ten from the foul line. Furthermore, your pussy privileges are suspended indefinitely." She slammed the door on her way out.

As I got down to doing pre-flight, my co-pilot looked over at me and waggled his eyebrows at me without saying a word. I opened my mike to speak to the passengers and realized it had been on all the time. Suddenly Clarissa was banging on the door hysterically.

"What now?" I said as I opened the door.

"I can't go out there."

"Why not?" I asked.

"You left the freaking microphone on and everyone on the plane heard everything we said, you fucking idiot!" Slowly I became aware of the laughter and catcalls erupting along the aisles of the plane.

41

ANTONIO

It had been months since Liana and I talked. The first few months I had pleaded with her to come home, but she wouldn't budge. My ego had been raked over the coals and reality finally hit me. Our marriage was over. She was gone forever. I sought refuge in Ginger's arms and bed.

It was Saturday morning and I had spent another night of hot, meaningless sex with Ginger. I guess it's true; sex is better in a happy, committed relationship. Sometimes the worst thing in the world is to get what you want.

I tried to stretch out and relax and felt a lump under the pillow. I felt around and pulled a book out from under the pillow. It was a copy of Quentin's stupid book.

"Ah, man, not you too?" I said. "Is there anybody that doesn't have a copy of this damn book?"

She gave me an embarrassed smile. "It's a good book, lots of scandal. After reading his book, a lot of my friends are keeping their mates on very short leashes."

Curiosity got the better of me and I opened the book. I flipped through the pages and started reading.

"Hm, I agree with that...uh huh, that too."

"Agree with what?" Ginger said as she rolled over to look at me.

"According to Quentin's research, he says the average man thinks of sex about every six minutes."

"Bullshit," Ginger disagreed. "In my personal research I'd say it was more like every six seconds."

I had to laugh. "He says here that while 90 percent of American women say they enjoyed receiving oral sex, only 49 percent reciprocated. American husbands say only 43 percent of their wives were good at it and 88 percent said their mates give it to them with an attitude."

Ginger shot me an odd look, "Oh yeah."

"That's what Quentin said. Sixty-one percent of the husbands surveyed admitted they had cheated and that included emotional infidelity; seeking the advice and comfort of a female friend other than their mates. Fifty percent still think about their ex and 60 percent of the same husbands admitted they couldn't get or keep an erection with the room completely dark. Only 40 percent of married couples make it to their silver anniversary and only 25 percent make it to their golden. Check this out. 60 percent of those same men say they had a replacement in mind, just in case something happened to their mates." I read further in silence, for a moment.

"Now, here's a shocker," I exclaimed in surprise. "Most cheating husbands are engaged in unprotected sex. One out of eight husbands are on the down-low or bi-curious, meaning they are sleeping with both men and women, or wondering what it is like to sleep with a man."

Ginger wrinkled her nose.

"Quentin writes that once men get busted, they abandon cheating altogether. Most men cheat with women that are the opposite of their mates."

"I can believe that." Ginger looked at me slyly.

"It says here most men prefer to hang with blonde women for sex, but when it comes to settling down they prefer dark-haired women. Men think they are more credible and professional.

"Bullshit!" She exploded, smacking me on the arm.

"Hey, I'm just the messenger," I said, rubbing my arm.

There was a chill in the air that had nothing to do with the nip in the air beyond the French windows. I continued to look through the book for lack of anything better to do.

"Hey, check this out, Ginger," I finally said. "Quentin says that in spite of their initial reservations about getting married, 60 percent of the men married because of threats, intimidation, she withheld sex or they thought it would make their mates happy."

"Why would a man do some crazy crap like that?"

I glanced sideways at her. "Because we think it would make a woman happy. It makes perfect sense in the male world."

She let out a strong breath, ready to pounce on me.

"Calm down and stop taking everything so personally," I said placating her. "Sixty-eight percent of men complained their wives are too sexually inhibited and 38 percent lost interest in sex after their wives put on weight."

I hesitated about the next part, but decided to plow ahead anyway. "He says 44 percent of women have thought about cheating, and 31 percent have thought about leaving their husbands. Guess I'm busted. The most popular places men go to cheat…"

"Now I've got to hear this," she smirked.

"Number one is the Internet; two, the gym; three, a sports bar, airport, or business trip; and, four is on the cell phone while stuck in traffic. Married men do the most cheating when running errands for their wives and on their lunch break.

"I wonder who lies the most." She looked at me pointedly.

"Good question." I continued to skim the pages. To my surprise Quentin had really done his research. "Here's the answer. He says men are guilty of telling the most lies, the biggest lies and the most unnecessary lies. But the woman is the master of the game. They pay more attention to details and remember what they say."

"So true," Ginger said cunningly.

"Hell no, I don't believe that!" I said as I read. "It says here most straight men have had at least one homosexual experience."

"I can believe that," Ginger said.

"You can't believe that? Why? Explain."

"Antonio, most of my friends are men. It would curl your hair what they reveal. They tell me things that would make a soap opera seem like the Disney Channel. Antonio, have you ever tried to make a vagina?"

"What? Are you crazy! Make a vagina?" I wasn't sure if I was hearing this right.

"Yeah, Antonio. Have you ever taken your dick and tucked it all the way back between your legs."

I looked at her with a sheepish grin.

"Busted! Sounds gay to me." We both laughed at the visual image.

"Check out what he says about professional and overly successful women."

"Enlighten me." She sounded bored.

"Eighty percent of the men surveyed said the same characteristics that made a woman rich, powerful or successful in business are the same characteristics that make them unsuccessful in relationships. For example, a woman with a dominant or aggressive personality; one that loses sensitivity or compassion; a woman that is never satisfied or has a constant need for a challenge; or a woman with an unhealthy need for adventure or a new rush won't be very successful in a relationship. But when it comes to men with those same characteristics, the need is often satisfied with a new woman or new relationship. I think that's what happened with Ted Turner and Donald Trump."

I thumbed several pages ahead. "This boy has no shame," I said.

"What now?" She sounded positively bored.

"According to the book, money or another woman are the two main things that would break up the relationship of best friends. Five out of ten men admitted they secretly slept with their best friend's wife or girlfriend. One out of two ministers have secrets that they've never confessed."

"No, that can't be, a minister?"

"That's what it says. Most men have at least one hidden porno tape that he watches alone. I don't have one." I looked over at Ginger and winked. "The men that cheat expect their mistresses to be faithful to them. It says a lot of cheating husbands will call their wives to find out where they are if they have a rendezvous with their mistress. Fifty-five percent of the men surveyed admitted they've cheated even when they had a good woman."

"You men are dogs."

"No, we're not. We're just misunderstood." I joked. "Ninety-five percent of American men are mama's boys and 93 percent of these same men regretfully kick a good mate to the curb because their mother didn't like them. Ninety-four percent of American men can't stand their mothers-in-law and 88 percent of men can't stand their fathers-in-law. The only women men really trust are their mothers. Most men believe that if you can find a woman who loves you half as much as your mother then you've found the perfect woman. Ninety-nine percent of American men said they would stop lying, cheating and playing games if their mates would just teach them how to love them."

"Well, I sure would like to know how to do that!" Ginger exclaimed.

42

DONALD

I was excited about being on the Ryan Cameron Show, a popular radio show here in Atlanta. I let out a nervous breath. In spite of his take no prisoner's reputation, I hoped he would show me the same love he showed Michael Vick a while back regarding that illegal dog fighting fiasco. He also went pretty easy on Pastor Thomas Weeks, III, about his wife abuse scandal. As I walked into the studio, he greeted me warmly.

"Hello, Pastor Reynolds, I'm honored you could join us. I've heard so many wonderful things about you."

"The pleasure is all mine, Ryan." I responded, thinking so far so good. I thought this interview just might be a piece of cake.

As his knockout assistant, Elle Duncan, whisked me into the studio and fitted my headphones, I looked at her curvy body.

Hmm, she's a cutie, I thought to myself.

She quickly disappeared out the door.

I looked up, and to my surprise, staring me right in the face was Miss Hard Ass herself, Joyce Littel, the host from the weekend show, *Love and Relationships*.

Lord, how did I get myself in this situation? I mumbled silently.

As the hosts looked at each other with sly grins, Ryan began his intro.

"You are listening to the Ryan Report. Sitting in with me today is our very own, Joyce Littel, and our special guest, Assistant Pastor Donald Reynolds of Holy Faith Non-Denominational Church. The topic today is "Pimping in the Pulpit." Pastor Reynolds and Pastor C. A. Cash are two of the most respected clergymen in the community. The reason we asked Pastor Reynolds to come today is because ever since Quentin Bank's book, *Desperate Husbands* came out, the conduct of some of our most prominent and trusted clergymen have been under fire. Not so long ago, a well known DeKalb County minister, Earl Paulk, was caught in a love triangle that caused quite a scandal."

Littel took over, "He was accused of dating and impregnating several women in his church. Shortly after, other ministers were caught embezzling money from their churches."

Cameron resumed speaking, "Who can forget the drama in the parking lot with Juanita Bynum, who accused her husband, Bishop Thomas Weeks, III of assaulting her? And who can forget President Obama's former minister, the infamous Rev. Wright, and the list seems to go on."

Littel jumped in. "With all the controversy and ministers under fire, loyal church members are looking at their spiritual leaders, and religion itself, in a very unfavorable light."

"I know that's right, Joyce," Ryan said sarcastically. "While a lot of their flocks are barely making it, their shepherds are living lavish lifestyles. Many are wearing two thousand dollar suits and riding around in Rolls Royces and Bentleys. Others are traveling first class or in private jets."

He turned to me and I licked my lips nervously.

"Donald, according to my sources, your wife just received her own little piece of bling bling. A three carat Harry Winston diamond, I believe."

I took a deep breath through my teeth.

He was now on a roll. "I also understand that she is wearing a full-length mink coat. Hey, it looks like you are balling just being an assistant pastor."

Give a brother a break, I thought to myself. I leaned into the microphone and gathered my composure. "Now Ryan and Joyce, when it comes to a minister's lifestyle, there are three sides to every story; the member's side, the minister's side and the truth. Let's get one thing straight, the Bible teaches prosperity. A minister's personal prosperity is the fruit of his labor and the blessing from a prosperous God."

"We'll let that one slide for now Pastor," Joyce cut in smoothly.

"Here is something else that has me puzzled," Cameron said deviously. "What is up with all the VIP seating in so many churches? Most Sundays you can tell the rich people or who is the largest contributor by where they all sit. I thought heaven was free?"

"Heaven is free." I replied more calmly than I felt. "But I guess the ticket cost..."

Joyce interrupted me, adding fuel to the fire. "Do any members who come regularly get frequent flyer miles?"

Cameron interjected, "What about an upgrade to a seat near the pastor?"

I didn't want listeners to hear me lose my cool, so I took a deep breath. "Ryan, Joyce, I don't know about the other churches, but at Holy Faith there are no VIP seats. It is first come, first serve. The wealthy are treated the same as the poor."

Joyce gave me a sly look and I could tell she wasn't buying it. "Pastor Reynolds, I have visited so many of the mega-churches in Atlanta and a lot of them are like billboards. Many of them run commercials for advertising on big screen TV's in the sanctuary before each service."

"And most modern day churches are equipped with ATM machines," Cameron said dryly.

"Well, I must admit, church has changed from the broken-down shacks found along a country road. It is not only a place to get spiritual healing, but many of the mega-churches in the Atlanta area fund programs locally and internationally. Our own programs include feeding the hungry, housing for the poor and the homeless, scholarships, missionary work, real estate investments and we're even sponsoring food and shelter for victims of Hurricane Katrina and the mid-west flood victims. A lot of our programs are sponsored by advertisers and contributors, so of course we let our members know who they are.

"As far as the ATM's, we want our members and guests to concentrate on the word of God and not the money. Ministers want to make it convenient for their members, especially when it comes to tithing."

"Thank you for explaining that Pastor," Ryan said, flipping over some papers in front of him. "Let's go to the telephone lines and hear from some of our listeners. Caller number one, you are on the air."

"Pastor Reynolds, hello, my name is Jena and I was reading that book, *Desperate Husbands*. It made me so upset and suspicious of my husband that I started snooping through his things."

"Jena, they say when you go looking for trouble, you are likely to find it or invent it," I said knowingly.

"Yes, I know Pastor Reynolds. I found that saying to be true," she said sadly.

"What did you discover, my dear."

"What I discovered was that my husband had fathered a child outside our marriage. I even found the receipts where he's been supporting both of them for the past two years. That means he is taking food out of our children's mouths to feed this other family. Now I'm pissed to the highest pisstivity."

"What do you plan on doing about that?"

"I'm as serious as a heart attack about this. I want to know, should I confront him, but then I'd have to confess to snooping."

I quickly looked at Joyce. She had a rather self-satisfied smile on her face. I thought I'd turn the tables. "Joyce, let me ask you this, say you go snooping through your man's private things and you get your feelings hurt by something that you found. Should you bust him at the risk of busting yourself?"

Joyce gave an embarrassed giggle. "You know I'll never go snooping fellows. I trust my man one hundred percent. Don't listen to those haters." Ryan and I both looked pointedly at her and rolled our eyes. She had to come clean.

"Fellows, I know what our male listeners are thinking and ladies, not to punk you out or betray the sisterhood, but I would have to go with the men on this one. You can't get upset with him for being dishonest when you're doing the same thing. Most women will look at snooping as not being that serious. Even the police have a reasonable suspicion law. You may look at him having a family on the side as an act of betrayal—"

I had to interrupt her quickly because it looked like she might be making a pretty good case.

"Jena, you had no right to go snooping through your husband's private things. Being married does not give anyone the license to snoop."

"Jena, you have now created another problem," Cameron said, coming to the defense of all men.

"What are you going to do with this information? Are you going to get angry or resentful every time he touches you? Or, keep your guard up and not give him a fair chance at love?" Joyce quizzed.

"You both are right," I said.

"The method you used in getting this information, Jena, is just as important as the information itself. You breached the issue of trust in your marriage. If you confront him with this, you will only create more friction in your relationship," Joyce said knowingly.

"Right you are, Joyce," I said in admiration.

"Now, Ryan, here's some food for thought. I must warn all men who are listening to the show. Many of you try to be slick and think you are getting away with your dirt, but God knows your heart. The Bible says what is done in darkness will certainly come to light."

"So, Pastor Cash, you are saying I should just let this go and let that man keep on getting away with it?" Jena broke in.

"No, my dear, but you now have to search your heart and find forgiveness for your husband to save two families. He does have a moral obligation to take care of his children. The deed is already done. The next step is up to you. Will you forgive him or not? How will you let it affect your future relationship? You are the only one that can answer that question." I replied.

"Amen, Pastor Reynolds," the hosts agreed.

"So, Pastor Reynolds, I understand that in a month Holy Faith is having its 30 year anniversary," Cameron said.

"That's right Ryan. Pastor Cash will also be officially retiring as our pastor."

"We will be anxious to know who will replace him," Joyce said.

"We have several ministers who have studied under him. But, those are pretty big shoes to fill. Many have called, but few are chosen."

"I'm sure you wouldn't have any problems, Pastor Reynolds," Joyce commented.

"Only the good Lord knows. In fact, the topic for our anniversary sermon will be 'What is Done in Darkness, Will Come to Light.' Of course, everyone in Atlanta is invited."

Elle walked back into the studio and signaled to Ryan and Joyce to wrap up the segment.

I shot her a flirtatious glance, puckered my lips and slyly threw a kiss her way. Catching my drift, she shot me a 'get lost buddy' look and turned her back on me.

Ryan quickly brought me back to reality. "Pastor Reynolds, we are almost out of time. Thank you for coming to the Ryan Cameron show, and thank you, Joyce, for riding shotgun with me."

"Thank you for inviting me," Joyce replied.

"Ryan, before I go," I interjected, "I would like to remind your listeners that they are all invited to our big anniversary celebration one month from this coming Sunday."

"I'm sure all of Atlanta will be there," he said ending the interview. "That was Assistant Pastor Donald Reynolds of the Holy Faith Non-Denominational Church shedding some light on 'Pimping in the

Pulpit'," he chuckled richly. "Okay Elle, let's see what's going on with this crazy Atlanta traffic..."

43

QUENTIN

Stan, the mailman, knocked on my door bright and early. When I opened the door, he was smiling from ear to ear, holding a certified letter. To my surprise, this time, he was loaded with charm and personality.

"Mr. Banks, you have a certified letter from your publisher. I knew it must be important, so I got up early to deliver it to you on time and in person."

I rolled my eyes and quickly took the letter. "Oh, I'm Mr. Banks now. Thank you Stan."

He stuck out his hand for a tip.

"Stan, you must be kidding. I know you're not expecting a tip."

"Sure am, Mr. Big Baller! Shot caller! You are a big time author now and you can afford it. So, give me my tip."

I gave him a sarcastic look and motioned for him to come close. "Ok, here's your tip. In a dog race, put your money on the rabbit. He always comes in first."

He stood there with a sour look on his face. I burst into laughter and slammed the door in his face. Payback is a bitch.

I quickly opened the letter. My mouth flew open. I was staring at a check in the amount of one million dollars. I gasped for breath. I jumped in the air.

I'm rich, I'm rich! Goodbye poverty. Hello prosperity. As I did the running man dance, my broken down hooptie caught my eye through the window. Even covered with pretty colored leaves it looked shitty. I stroked my chin like Simon Legree. Yeah, payback is a bitch and it was time to payback that stinking car. I grabbed my keys, putting the check safely in my pocket and jumped into my hooptie. I didn't stop until I got to Motorcars of Atlanta. As I pulled onto the lot, my abuse caused my hooptie to overheat. It was puttering and smoking. I managed to roll in and park the car near the salesmen entrance. The salesmen were lined up along the window, pointing and laughing.

I ignored them as I got out of the car. I strutted into the showroom. There was a picture of the top salesman, Kyle Witherspoon, on the wall in front of me. I spotted his desk and walked over.

"Excuse me, sir. My name is Quentin Banks and I'm interested in buying a black Bentley Continental GT convertible."

He looked up arrogantly, eyes traveling from the top of my head to the soles of my shoes. He looked out the windows at my still smoking car. He looked at his watch. "I'm sorry, but I won't be able to help you. I have another appointment arriving very soon. I will get Andy Salter to assist you. He just started with us and I'm sure he can use the practice."

The other salesmen cracked jokes and punched at each other about Kyle Witherspoon's snotty dismissal of me.

Witherspoon stood and flagged Andy down. "Andy, we have a live one for you. This gentleman..." He paused and looked at me as if I were something on the bottom of his shoe. "This gentleman wants to trade in that broken down hooptie in the parking lot for a black Bentley Continental GT convertible."

Witherspoon again looked at me and asked, "How is your credit, sir?"

I looked right back at him and replied, "Bad."

Witherspoon said loudly to the room at large, "And he has bad credit, too."

A nerdy looking guy in his early 20's with thick glasses came over and extended his hand. "Hi, I'm Andy Salter. How can I help you?"

"I'd like to test drive a Bentley GT convertible."

The other salesmen smirked as Andy hurried off to retrieve the keys. I stuck my hands in my pockets and wandered around the showroom, whistling as if I hadn't a care in the world. When Andy returned, he escorted me to a beautiful car parked in the first row by the window. He pulled the car out and held the door open for me. I slid into the luxury interior and inhaled the new leather smell. I caressed the wood trim on the console and thought to myself, "Man, this is living."

I put the car in gear and drove off the lot and took it onto the freeway for a spin. I could have been riding on a cloud. I wanted this car! Within twenty minutes I pulled back onto the lot. A nervous Andy and the Cobb County Police met me.

Judging by my appearance and my hooptie, I guess they thought I wasn't coming back. After I'd given the cops my name and showed them my ID, I pulled out my one million dollar check and showed it to the cops and then to Andy. Andy's eyes got so wide I thought they just might pop out of his head. After that, everyone's tune changed.

"Mr. Banks, we've heard so much about you. I'm sorry I didn't recognize you!" one of the other salesmen said. I ignored him.

Witherspoon stepped forward and said, "Mr. Banks, if you'll come with me I'm sure I can work you a much better deal than Andy."

I looked at Witherspoon like he was a dog turd I'd stepped on and told him Andy suited me just fine. His face fell. Bet he was already missing that commission.

After Andy drew up the papers, I whipped out my checkbook and wrote a check for the full amount of the car. Andy was getting quite red about the neck with all the salesmen glaring at him. Feeling sorry for the kid, I wrote out another check, payable to Andy Salter, in the amount of ten thousand dollars. As he looked at the check, he smiled and got even redder. "Here Andy, take this ten K and buy Kyle and those other salesmen a personality, some class, breath mints and new suits at K-Mart," I said loudly.

It was gratifying to see the look on their faces as I strolled out the door, hopped into my new two hundred? grand black Bentley Continental GT convertible and peeled out of the parking lot. I blasted the stereo as I swung in and out of the traffic on the way home.

I love money, fame, success and being a rich asshole.

44

The following day after finishing up with my interviews, I was drained. Why did I have to pick a DJ whose business I had put in the street. He really roasted me. I wondered who the most hated man in America is, Osama Bin Laden, OJ Simpson or Quentin Banks? I think I've gone to the top of the shit list.

I jumped in my car and exited the parking lot. I turned the radio to a jazz station. I couldn't help but think this famous author thing is not what it's cracked up to be. I can now see why people that write books have issues themselves.

I took out my tape recorder and started a to do list. Tomorrow, I'm supposed to piss off the girls on The View. On Thursday, it's Good Morning America, The Today Show and The Jay Leno Show. On, Friday...uh oh, I forgot about The Steve Harvey Morning Show. There were a host of others to do the following week.

Afterwards, let me pencil in making love to Bridgett. That shouldn't take more than about three minutes, tops! I thought to myself, "Man, why couldn't Bridgett be a bad girl? Why does she have to be so inhibited?" It is no use complaining now, she's all I've got. Plus, we make a nice, tired little couple. Before I forget, I need to call my friend and therapist, Pastor Cash at Holy Faith. He's about to retire and I really need to talk to him. It seems since this book came out, my world is really falling apart.

My friends don't trust me anymore, Bridgett is pressuring marriage and to make matters worse, she thinks I'm Lance Shelton in my book. She is also speculating whether her father is alive. Maybe I should forget about being an author. It's not too late. Maybe I can still put that application in at McDonald's. No, can't do that, Calvin is pissed at me too. He sent me a dirty email just last week. I can remember it word for word.

Dear Mr. Banks,

I read your book Desperate Husbands. I really didn't appreciate your putting my business in the street. Thanks to you, I am no longer at McDonald's.

What I do with the milkshakes and hot apple pies is my own damn business. I am sure since your book came out, you're probably full of yourself. In fact, I am sure when you look at yourself in the mirror, you get a hard-on, because you are staring at a great big pussy!

Calvin

PS. I got your hot apple pie right here pal! Take your damn business to Waffle House from now on.

Okay, strike off getting hired at McDonald's. From this point on, I'd better make sure I check my bags carefully.

I decided to call Pastor Cash right away, while it was fresh on my mind. Most men will never admit to going to a therapist, but everyone needs to know whether he is playing with a full deck. Picking up the telephone, I hit speed dial for Pastor Cash's personal number.

"Hello Quentin."

"How did you know it was me? Are you psychic?"

"I'm not a dinosaur, Quentin," He responded jovially. "I have caller ID. How can I help you?"

"Pastor Cash, I really need to talk to you. Every since my book got published, all hell has broken loose. The fellows are angry with me, I'm getting paranoid all the time and my personal life has gone to hell. Even Bridgett is questioning me now. She thinks I'm Lance Shelton and now she thinks her father is alive. Can you see me today?" My request was met with hesitation.

"I don't like snitches," he said humorously, "and right now I'm talking to the Finance Department of the church. Every Sunday, money seems to come up missing. I will get to the bottom of it. But, let me check my schedule. Hmmm, that's full, Hmmm. No, that's taken. Okay, Quentin, I can squeeze you in about 4:30p.m. I promised my wife I wouldn't be late, so we have to make it short. Thanks to you, she is now looking at me and wondering whether I'm Pastor Hayes.

"Thanks Pastor, I promise I won't be late." I hit my last appointment for the day and headed over to Holy Faith. As always, the traffic was horrible. Who taught these people in Atlanta to drive? Ray Charles? I finally weaved, bobbed and took side streets until I was sitting in front of the majestic building that was Holy Faith Non-Denominational Church.

It was Pastor Cash that christened me. The Pastor was like family. Even though my father was the man of the house, my mom and I both knew that he consulted Pastor Cash before he made any major decisions. Now I guess I'm keeping the Banks' tradition alive with a fresh set of issues as to whether money should take precedence over my life, loyalty and friendships.

After parking, I ran into the church and made my way down the long hall to Pastor Cash's office. As always, there was a long line of people waiting to see him. Since I was a little early for my appointment, I stood in the hallway with the crowd, mostly women. It was gratifying to see that most of them had a copy of my book. I shamelessly listened in on their conversations about my book and for the most part the popular opinion was that the book was true.

One woman whispered to another, "I betcha that no good preaching man is Pastor Cash."

"Honey, Pastor Cash is a prince in the pulpit," her friend said defensively. "He's not another pimp in the pulpit."

Another woman said, "I've been a loyal member of Holy Faith for fifteen years and never once has there been a scandal in this church!"

Yet another woman put her two cents in. "I bet that no good preacher is Pastor Reynolds. Every time he preaches, those single women wear those short dresses. Honey, I don't know whether they are coming to church or leaving a nightclub. Pastor Reynolds just sits and smiles and flirts with them all."

One older man asked another man, "Eddie, what do you think? You think Pastor Reynolds is the man in the book?"

"Player, I don't want to think. All I know is someone needs to check up on some of these ministers."

As I listened I kept my head down to avoid being recognized. This was my fault. My ambition got the better of me. But what was I going to do about it now? The damage was already done.

I wondered if exposing myself to Pastor Cash was such a good idea after all. People need to trust and believe in something. They need to believe in someone, but, on the other hand, the church, the word of God and the lives of our clergymen should be pure. They hold the fate and faith of many of us in their hands and their lives should be an open book, untainted. If they are truly God-fearing men, we will know them by the fruits that they bear.

I looked at my watch at the same time as Pastor Cash opened the door to his office. He escorted a couple out and apologized to the crowd in the hallway and slipped me in through the door. Silence filled the air as we sat down. He gave me a fatherly look. You know that look. It's the one he gives you when he already knows the answer, but you don't know he knows the answer. He's just waiting for you to face up and tell the truth. Finally he spoke. I could tell right away we were going to play by his rules.

"Quentin, you know friendship and loyalty are powerful and valuable. Once that bond has been broken, it is hard to ever regain it. Now, I'm going to speak to you man to man. Quentin, you know there are three things that are hard for men to do. To humble himself before another man is the first, second is to admit he needs help or doesn't know something, and third, reveal his deepest, darkest secrets. Once a man admits to any of these things, he wants to feel that friendship, loyalty and secrecy should not be taken for granted. What he reveals should be taken to the grave."

"Pastor Cash, suppose your wife asked you to reveal something that you pinky swore with your friends never to reveal. Does loyalty to your friends supersede the bond and honesty you have with your wife?"

Pastor Cash leaned back in his well-worn chair. He smiled as he looked out of the window. "Quentin, there are two types of loyalty. The first loyalty is for your wife and the second for your friends. Truthfully, one shouldn't be threatened by the other. The Bible says when a man and woman wed he should leave his parents and cling to his wife. His past should become an open book. On the other hand, we all had friends prior to our mates. I firmly believe that as long as it does not affect your relationship with your wife, the secrets that you and your friends share should be kept between the two of you and your spouse should respect that. Usually that's the one men have the most problem with.

"If your mate is nosy and persistently demands to know your friends secrets, just be honest with her. Tell her in a nice way that to reveal their secrets would jeopardize their trust in you. Just like if your friends asked you to tell them your wife's secrets, it would jeopardize the trust between you and her. The two of you have then established boundaries.

"Unfortunately, Quentin, couples don't see it that way. Today everybody is a blabbermouth. I have never seen so many men and women go on talk shows and tell the world their business. Come to think of it, remind me to send the church bus over to pick up Adrian. He's the worst gossipmonger I've ever come across. Quentin, one of the worse things a person can do is to discuss their mate's secrets with family or friends."

"Why is that Pastor?" I asked. "Couples fight all the time, and families and friends take sides. Some couples even break up to make up.

Pastor Cash pressed his fingertips together and leaned his elbows on the edge of the desk. "When the dust settles and the name calling stops, couples put their love spat behind them. On the other hand, family and friends are not as forgiving. It becomes a matter of who gets custody of the friends. The families have already chosen sides. Families and friends are not as forgiving.

"I'm a minister. I've been one for thirty years. After years of counseling men I've found there are three main faults in the male species. One, we have large, fragile egos; two, we can't keep our thing in our pants; and three, we can't stop competing with each other or trying to be top dog.

"After reading your book, a lot of men have turned into blabbermouths. They did it to hide their own sins or to divert the suspicion away from themselves."

"I am sorry, Pastor Cash." I hung my head.

"Quentin, whatever happened to the day when a man's word meant something? A man is only as good as his word."

"I don't know Pastor Cash. Maybe those days went out with the eight track tape, platform shoes and cheap gas."

We both laughed rather weakly.

"Now Quentin, there is no way on God's green earth that I'm going to tell you my business. You don't need to make another enemy; especially one who has a red phone to Jesus."

I rolled my eyes, but he continued on in the same condemning tone.

"I am so happy that you and some of these desperate husbands weren't spies during the war."

"Why?" I asked.

"If you were, we would all be speaking Japanese."

45

I confessed to Pastor Cash that I was really feeling bad about the way I'd treated the fellows. A big rift had come between us and I really missed them. I didn't know how to even begin to undo what I'd done. I'd thought I was being clever changing names and places, but I was just stupid.

"Quentin, you've made a mess between you and the fellows. You need to fix it. You hurt them deeply and created chaos in their lives."

"I know, Pastor Cash, but I don't have a clue how to go about fixing it."

"The sad thing about it is that the moment your book hit the shelves, your friends felt bad about what they had done that they came to me for counseling. They have confessed their sins. But not one of them revealed your business. They understood friendship, loyalty and making a pact.

"I know we all want to be rich and famous, but the method you used to achieve that goal is just as important as the goal itself. I commend you for achieving your goal, but I dislike the method. You climbed over the backs of your friends for money. I can't tell you how to make amends, I can only tell you that you need to, for your own sake."

"I promise I will make it right, somehow." My shame was profound and my stomach churned with acid.

"You do that Quentin."

"Pastor, I have another issue I would like to talk with you about, if I may?" I hesitated, embarrassed.

"Quentin, your intimate thoughts are safe with me."

"Thank you Pastor Cash." I drew a deep breath afraid how to broach the subject, but it was something I had to know, so I foraged ahead. "Is it wrong to masturbate, especially when you have a partner?"

Pastor Cash looked at me sympathetically, with a slight smile on his face. "Quentin, it is a myth that marriage fulfills all of your sexual needs. Masturbation is a totally different way of expressing sexuality. If you happen to get caught in the act, your mate might feel hurt. It might be a good idea to explain, before this happens, to your mate that you sometimes masturbate, but that it has nothing to do with your desire for another woman, but that it is a means of release. By talking about it, she can learn that masturbation relieves her of some of the pressure of having sex when she's not in the mood. Also, by talking it helps to relieve some of her insecurities and hang-ups.

"On the other hand, Quentin, what's good for the gander is good for the goose. Women I counsel admit they also like to masturbate, especially single women. Both single and married women often complain that they don't achieve an orgasm when they have intercourse. Far too often, their mates get upset and insecure when their mates don't have an orgasm. So to keep from hurting his feelings, they masturbate privately."

"Is that the only reason?" I asked, relieved I was normal in that regard.

"No, it isn't. Other reasons woman give me are that they are not in the mood, or they might feel pressure or pain during intercourse, or they have hidden issues about sexual abuse and mistreatment from past partners."

Before he could utter another word, I threw him a curve ball. "Good Pastor, I have a friend who said that his wife breaks out in laughter during sex. Does he have anything to worry about?"

He gave me a keen look, "A friend huh?"

"Yes, a friend!"

"Tell your friend that women express themselves during sex or an orgasm differently. Some scream, some talk dirty, some may contract or claw like a tigress, some may laugh in your face."

"Laugh in my friend's face," I rudely reminded him.

"Okay, Quentin, laugh in your friend's face. Just tell your friend that unexpected giggles, laughter or other outbursts are just energetic releases that the human body uses when it wants to let out what has been building up to an orgasm. Take it as a compliment. Not only is he giving her a mind blowing orgasm, but having a few laughs in between."

"Pastor, I have a couple more questions, then I won't take anymore of your time."

"Fire away, Quentin."

"I have a collection of porno tapes I masturbate by and, please don't take this the wrong way or tell the fellows, but I have a blow up doll. Is there anything wrong with that?"

He let out a deep sigh. "Quentin, stop punishing yourself. Why don't you go ahead and put a ring on Bridgett's finger?"

"I hear what you're saying, and I love Bridgett and want to marry her someday, I just don't want to be pressured into it."

"Okay, Quentin, since you came to me for help, I won't give you a sermon, but a solution. If it makes you feel any better, when it comes to masturbation, you are not alone. But, having a blow up doll may put you in an exclusive club," he said playfully. "Quentin, masturbation is normal and healthy. But a lot of women have told me that they feel rejected, betrayed or jealous about their husband's masturbating. Some even feel rage that they can't compete with their mate's fantasy woman. And, a lot of women feel that porn is a form of infidelity."

"Well, what should a man do?"

"First you have to separate fantasy from reality. Sometimes what we think we want is not always what we need. So try to keep what is real in your life with honest and open communication. Your plain Jane mate can become your fantasy. There's a bad girl inside every woman waiting to be unleashed by the right man, but she needs to feel comfortable and secure in her relationship. With patience and consideration she can become your fantasy woman. This includes being open to exercises, dieting, a complete makeover and even plastic surgery or implants."

"One more question, then I'm off your couch." He looked at his watch pointedly.

"Suppose you are bored with your mate. How do you put some yabba-daba-do back into the bedroom?"

"Remember Quentin that intimacy begins before you enter the bedroom, not afterwards. And it takes two people working together to keep their sex life exciting. To build anticipation, withdraw from sex. Wait until the end of the week. For that entire week, work on intimacy and improving your technique with kissing, cuddling, oral sex, touching, etcetera. Set aside an hour every day in a romantic environment. Light candles and play soft music. Give her a massage without turning it sexual. Talk to her while you do it. Ask her what she likes, what she wants. Then move on to encouraging her to touch herself or masturbate. Watch and see what she does, how she touches herself and for how long. Encourage her to reveal her fantasy. Ask her to reveal what she is wearing and what you are wearing in the fantasy. Allow her to reveal what details she wants. Allow her to take control of your hand, your tongue, your nose or mouth.

Let her show you how to properly use them. When the week is over, you will not only make love to a new mate, but, experience the ultimate orgasm."

"Thanks Pastor, you've given me a lot to think about."

"I'm always available to you. Now, I do have an appointment with the man you love to hate."

"You mean Peter McCallister."

"Yes, he is not only a loyal member, but one of our biggest contributors."

"How did you arrange that?" I asked in astonishment. "Everybody is always trying to get a piece of Peter."

"I like to call it divine inspiration or government intervention," he said happily. "It was during the crash on Wall Street and the government was investigating the CEO's of major companies. I was sitting at this very desk when the telephone rang. I was working on a sermon and didn't want to be disturbed, so I rather reluctantly picked up the phone. It was the IRS."

"What did the IRS want with you?"

"They were asking about Peter McCallister. They asked if he was a member of the church and when I told them that yes indeed he was, they asked if Peter had made a contribution of five hundred thousand dollars. I thought about it for half a second and told them, 'He will now.' Not only did I get the contribution, but I get that amount every year, plus tithes. So I guess he and I are a match made in heaven. Now, Quentin, before you go, I would like for you to do something for me."

"Anything, Pastor."

"The door swings both ways. Before you leave, put on a pair of dark sunglasses."

"Why?"

"I don't know whether it is cool for us to be seen together. I got you in unobserved, but you might not get out that way. I don't harbor turncoats, mama's boys or blabbermouths. I must admit, since your book came out, Quentin, you have really put a few more gray hairs in my head."

He gave me a humorous stare as I stood and pulled my sunglasses out of my pocket.

"Oh, and one more thing, Quentin."

I turned back to him as I reached the door. "What's that Pastor?"

He chuckled and said, "Have you ever thought about moving your membership to another church?"

I called Bridgett after leaving Pastor Cash's office. I hadn't talked to her all day and she was more than anxious to hear from me. She picked up on the first ring. "Hey, baby! I've been thinking about you all day. Every since your book came out, I can never find you."

"Ah, baby, I'm sorry."

"I love when people call me," she said. "I love listening to my *Here Comes the Bride* ring tone. Quentin, have you gone Hollywood on me?"

"Sweetheart, baby," I said jokingly, "we must do lunch! I'll pencil you in."

"Yeah?" she said, a bit annoyed.

"Or maybe I should have my people call your people."

"You are not that serious." She was getting really annoyed now.

"I can't tell." Ruffling her feathers a bit more. "You sure are sweating me. I can't make a move without you calling me."

"Okay Quentin, whatever." Her feathers were on fire now.

"Ah, baby, I was just having some fun. Don't get angry. I'll see you in a couple of hours. I've got some other stops to make. I'm just leaving Holy Faith now. I had to talk to Pastor Cash."

"About what?" She turned serious.

"Oh, nothing out of the ordinary, we talked about loyalty and friendship."

"Was it one of those man things?"

"You know it baby. I'm free now and on my way home."

"Great sweetheart," she said with anticipation. "When you get here, I will have a nice candlelit dinner waiting for you. Afterwards, I will put on some sexy lingerie and then we can get in the Jacuzzi and..." she said seductively.

"And what, baby!" Now I'm getting all hot under the collar.

"You're the writer, Quentin. Use your imagination. Finish the story yourself," she purred.

"Bridgett, what has gotten into you? Since the book came out you've become an entirely different person."

"Well, Quentin, some of those things men said about their wives really hit home. The funniest story in the book is that little, tired ass woman that folds her panties in the heat of passion. I feel sorry for her mate. Man, I hope I never become that boring. See you in about two hours, darling."

I blew her a kiss and hung up the phone, shaking my head in amazement.

46

BRIDGETT

I let out a loud laugh. After reading Quentin's book, there was no way I was going to be that tired ass Summer Baldwin. A suspicious thought hit me. I guess it is just a coincidence that we both folded our underwear during sex. I wonder how Quentin feels about our sex life? I'll never admit to him that everything I've learned about men and sex came from reading books. I really don't have any real street creds. Quentin was my first and only love. Growing up, the subject of sex was forbidden in my aunt's house. She'd caught her husband in bed, years ago, with a girl half his age, after twenty years of marriage. She wasn't inclined to educate in the ways of being with a man. My mother abandoned me when I was eleven to go to Africa to take care of suffering children in the Sudan, so I didn't have her to learn from either. But my aunt is a good woman and I love her. She took good care of me in every way possible.

I decided that when Quentin walked through the door, Bridgett the Diva, Bridgett the Bad Girl and Bridgett the Slut was going to meet him. I jumped in the shower and washed, shampooed and perfumed. After I dried off, I selected a sexy red teddy with pantalets. I wanted to wear stiletto heels that I hadn't worn in a long while. I opened the closet door and searched through my shoes and couldn't find them. I had some stuffed way in the back. There they were, behind Quentin's stinky golf shoes. I pushed his shoes out of the way, and as I did the left shoe rolled over and a small tape fell out. I was sure it had fallen out of one of our pockets. I knew I used a tape recorder for wedding plans when they popped in my head. Quentin used a recorder too, for story ideas. But whose tape was it? I put on my stilettos and popped the tape into my recorder and turned it on as I went into the kitchen to start dinner.

"...reason with her, told her she was drunk. She told me she knew perfectly well what she was doing as she slowly stripped off her blouse and undid her bra. I protested, reminded her about Dean and how she was getting married in two days. She said that was two days from now and this is the here and now. She was winding herself all over me and pushed me down against the nav console and straddled me, running her tongue over my lips. She pushed her breasts in my face. She was hitting me with them like the LAPD was hitting Rodney King. I tried to get away and I was screa..." I shut the tape off abruptly.

"Jeff, you dog," I shouted in disbelief. I couldn't believe what I was hearing. Why was Jeff taping this? Curious, I pushed the tape forward.

"...was getting turned on. Before I knew what was happening, she was down on the floor in front of me unzipping my pants. Next thing I knew, we were all three in the bed together and getting it on. After we climaxed, we drank more wine and began round two. I was totally shit faced. She left and Bill started kissing me." I shut it off again. That was Antonio's voice.

What is going on here? Damn, Antonio was having kinky sex with another man and a woman? He's gay? I continued to push the tape forward and one fellow after the other revealed their stories. When Quentin's voice came up I listened in stunned silence. I pushed the tape forward yet again. I heard my godfather's voice.

"...favorite clubs were Club Cheetah and Magic City. One day, Jan and I had a major blow out. She packed her bags and flew back to Boston with the kids. In the past, when we fought, I was always the one to apologize, whether it was my fault or not. She knew I would do anything to keep the family together. She always used this as leverage. But that day, I didn't care anymore. I was fed up with her insecurities and excessive spending. I wanted out. But, she knew she had me by the balls. Half of my money would be gone before the ink even dried if I tried to divorce her. I was so trapped..."

Peter? In a strip club? My God, there were so many questions tumbling around in my head. What was all this about? I forwarded the tape a little bit and pressed play and my whole world turned upside down.

"... Jeff, but, I had people keeping an eye on her. She was always safe. She wanted to take our daughter with her, but she was happy living with her aunt. Carla didn't want to uproot her. To this day she thinks her father died in an automobile accident."

"Peter, I would never have guessed. I thought you were a racist."

"I'm not a racist, Jeff, I'm a coward."

"Peter, what's your daughter's name?

"Mmmmy dddaughter's name is Bridgett Mmmoore."

"My Bridgett? My fiancée is your biological daughter?"

"Yes, she is Quentin."

"I knew you were very protective of her, but I never in a million years expected that Bridgett was your daughter!"

"Fellows, for once in my life I am going to follow my heart. On Bridgett's 30th birthday, she will inherit my entire fortune. Seven hundred million dollars has been transferred into an account in the Cayman Islands that I set up in her name. She will become the CEO of McCallister Enterprises."

"Don't tell me anymore, Peter. This is too much to absorb."

"Listen, Quentin, get a hold of yourself. You promised to marry her for better or worse. I'm depending on you to keep quiet about this until I can tell her. Okay?"

"Peter, she'll turn 30 in a few months!"

"I know that. All of you have to keep it quiet. Please."

"Peter, the heir of your empire is an illegitimate daughter you fathered with an African American stripper. Talk about an equal opportunity employer..."

"Ouch that hurt, Quentin!"

"Quentin, you are marrying an heiress. You are going to be rich."

"Quentin, Bridgett must never find out. I will tell her when the time is right. I just don't know how to undo so many lies."

The blood drained from my face and I felt hot and shaky all over. Peter is my father? All these years, and he lied to me! I grabbed my head. Surely it was about to explode. The room started to spin. It all made sense now. He was always more a father than a godfather, very over-protective. All those expensive gifts...the job with McCallister Enterprises...it all made sense now. Damn, him. Damn him to hell. I rewound the tape back as far as when Peter started his story. It took several attempts to find it. When I did I listened to the whole story without interruption. I was trembling uncontrollably. I have a father. I didn't know whether to laugh or cry. I wanted to kill Quentin. The words hit me over and over. My fingers became nerveless and I dropped the recorder. I scrambled on my hands and knees to find it. I wanted to throw it through the window. I wanted to hear everything all over again. I didn't know what I wanted.

Terrible, jumbled thoughts piled up inside my head. Quentin had kept Peter's secret from me. But, he put it all out there in a book! I sat, stunned on the couch and cried as I have never cried before.

47

QUENTIN

When I walked in the door, I said in my best Ricky Ricardo imitation, "Lucy, I'm home. You have some s'plaining to do!"

Bridgett sat on the couch, staring at the wall. She slowly turned her head and looked at me. She stood, walked toward me and then suddenly hit me in the chest. "No Lance Sheldon! You have some explaining to do. Like the truth about your "club" and the "pact" you and your friends made!" She shouted right in my face.

I took a step back, then another, until I was backed up against the front door.

She exploded at me, "Why in the hell didn't you tell me Peter McCallister is my father! Why are you a part of this charade?"

I was completely blindsided. I stammered out, "Bridgett, please, let me explain."

"Explain my ass." She screamed at me. "You are supposed to tell me everything!"

I stood staring at her dumbly.

"Your commitment to me should supersede any commitment or stupid oath you made with your friends."

She raised her hand. In it was a small tape recorder. She hit the play button on the side. I listened to Peter as he told his story to us in the club that night so long ago. The cat was out of the bag and about to claw my eyes out.

"I can't believe it Quentin, you told your buddies intimate details about our relationship and our sex life. You even said our sex life was tired and boring! All of you are liars and snakes. Poor Ashley, she worships the ground Donald walks on. She is going to be crushed when she finds out the truth. I'm going to call the girls right now. I'm going to tell them the truth!"

"You will do no such thing!" I shouted. "We took an oath. The only way you found out is because you were snooping through my things."

"Snooping through your things! I thought the tape fell out of either your pocket or mine. I only found it because I was looking for a pair of my shoes and when I pushed your golf shoes out of the way, it fell out. I just played it to see who it belonged to. I wish I hadn't found it. God knows I wish I hadn't listened to it." She burst into tears.

"Quentin, I can't stay here with you. I don't feel I can trust you anymore. You have betrayed me. You have betrayed our commitment."

"Bridgett, let me explain." I plead for my life.

"Explain what, Quentin!" She lashed out. "It's all on the damn tape. I don't believe you honestly love me. Maybe you're in love with the thought of marrying me now that I'm an heiress."

I reached out toward her, but she pushed me back hard. My head bounced off the door. She ran into the bedroom and locked the door. I heard her moving around and heard the thump of a suitcase being tossed on the bed. In a few minutes she reappeared with her suitcase in hand.

I tried again to talk to her, but she held up her hand and said, "Quentin, I need to get away from you with all that has happened. I know now that I can't marry you. I really don't know who you are. I thought we had something really special."

"We do Bridgett."

"I thought I could make you happy, maybe I was fooling myself all along."

She turned and walked to the door and stopped. Without turning around she said, "You know the sad thing about this mess, Quentin?"

"What is that Bridgett?" I said sadly.

"The sad thing about it is that I still love you. But I know that I can never trust you. What is love and marriage without trust?"

"Bridgett, please don't go." The tears choked my voice.

"A woman wants to feel that her man will do the right thing even when she is not there. She wants to feel that he will check himself even in the midst of temptation and even if he knows he can get away with it."

48

BRIDGETT

I picked up the phone to Peter. My fingers were numb and it took several tries before I hit the right numbers. It rang several times before he answered.

"Hello Bridgett!" He sounded happy to hear from me. I knew that would change pretty soon.

"Peter, I really need to talk to you." I sniffed and blew my nose. I was crying buckets and couldn't seem to stop.

"Bridgett, what's wrong? Did Quentin do something to upset you?" Concern charged his voice.

I exploded. The nerve of him. "No, he didn't. But you did Peter!"

"Me?" He asked, completely taken aback.

"Yes, you!" I spat out. "My godfather, the great Peter McCallister. You have hurt me more that you will ever know. I know the truth, Peter. All of it."

"What?" He sounded genuinely surprised, as if he had no idea what I was talking about.

"Peter, I need to see you in person. Now. Can you meet me at Houston's in Buckhead?" I sobbed out.

"Which one honey?"

"The one at Lenox."

"I'll be there. Meet me in the lobby."

I drove with out seeing anything. I tried to compose myself. I wanted to meet Peter head on and be as calm as possible. There were so many things to ask and so much I wanted to say. I rolled the windows down and drank in the cold air, hoping to clear my head.

Peter was my father! Peter was my father! The phrase ran though my head like a mantra. Should I kiss him or kill him?

I fought the traffic for what seemed like hours. Finally I pulled into the Houston's parking lot.

49

PETER

As I hung up the phone, something inside of me was telling me that the day of judgment had finally come. What was done in darkness had finally come to light. Somehow, Bridgett had found out the truth. Now, I was wondering, will the truth set me free or set me up?

I immediately called Quentin. I waited desperately for him to pick up the phone. Finally the answering machine answered. I waited for the beep and began to speak, "Quentin, this is Peter. The message is—I'm fucked. The cat is out of the bag. I think Bridgett knows I'm her father. Call me."

I hung up and cursed the traffic and cursed Quentin. I tried his number several times on the way to Houston's. I kept getting the machine. I left one final message for Quentin before I arrived at Houston's. I said, "Oh well, all the fellows have gotten busted. Why shouldn't you? The day of reckoning is finally here."

I took the North Druid Hills exit to Piedmont. I turned left on Peachtree and within minutes I saw Houston's Restaurant. Recognizing my Rolls, the valet jumped to attention.

Bridgett was waiting for me in the lobby, looking very small as she huddled in her coat. Her hair had been scraped back into a ponytail. She had on dark glasses, but her cheeks were tearstained. The hostess recognized me and seated Bridgett and I immediately at a quiet table in the corner of the restaurant.

The waitress arrived before we were fully seated. Bridgett ordered an orange juice. I ordered a gin and tonic. I knew I was going to need something to brace me up for this. The waitress left the table to fill our order.

"So how is work, Bridgett?" I asked nervously. She took her sunglasses off. I was shocked to see her red, swollen eyes. "Bridgett, what's wrong? What has happened?" I asked, afraid of the answers.

"Peter, I think you already know the answer to that." She snapped at me, staring angrily.

The waitress returned with our drinks. I was saved by the bell, but only for so long. The waitress asked us if we wanted to order dinner. I told her no and waved her off.

I looked at Bridgett and tears filled her eyes.

"Lady Bug, tell me what's wrong." I patted her hand on the table.

"Lady Bug!" she hissed. "My mother told me my real father used to call me that."

I hung my head in silence and waited. She pulled her hand from under mine.

"Peter, why didn't you tell me you were my father? Why did you and Mom lie to me? How long were you going to keep it from me? Would I ever have known, if it weren't for that stupid book?"

I took Bridgett's hand again, holding it tightly. "Bridgett, I'm so sorry. Your mother and I never intended to deceive you. Back then, we thought it best to keep it from you."

"Best for who? You or her? It definitely wasn't best for me." A tear rolled slowly down her cheek, glistening like a diamond in the overhead light. "I guess I'm the naïve, little black girl born out of wedlock from a one night stand with a stripper," she said bitterly.

"Bridgett, don't ever say that again about your mother. I love your mother deeply. I always have. And I love you dearly. You have no idea of the pain I've felt. I wanted to tell you so many times, but your mother asked me not to."

She gave me a look that spoke of the hurt in her heart.

"Bridgett, wasn't I always there for you? Remember your first day at Catholic School? You had never been away from home before and you were afraid. Didn't I go to school with you? I even stayed with you in the classroom. I will have calluses on my butt for the rest of my life from sitting in those PeeWee Herman Playhouse chairs."

A ghost of a smile played around her lips. "Don't make me laugh. I'm very angry at you."

I gave her a proud smile and said, "I even had to re-learn my ABC's just so I could hang out with you. And, who taught you to ride a bike? Who took you to your first dance and who was there waiting for you to come home when you went out on your first date?"

"It was you." Bridgett said in a small voice.

"Lady Bug, I even made the ultimate sacrifice for you!"

"What was that, Peter?"

"I bought every one of your God awful Girl Scout cookies so you would earn a badge and get to go on that trip."

The tears were slowing down and that small smile stayed on her lips.

"Bridgett, if that's not love, honey, I don't know what is. And you don't know how hard it was for me when you went to your first prom with that knuckleheaded geek."

"He wasn't a knuckleheaded geek! Well, he was a geek." She giggled.

"I always thought you could do so much better than him, anyway. You were very popular in high school. Cheerleader, homecoming queen. You could have had any boy you wanted. And you picked the geekiest, geek in high school. What was his name? Lawrence or something like that."

"I don't even remember." She smiled at me.

"Well, anyway, you are my flesh and blood, I will always want the best for you." I squeezed her hand and she didn't try to pull away.

"That's the real reason I want Quentin to succeed. I knew he would, one day, be the man that would marry Peter McCallister's daughter. That's why I wanted him to become a member of the club. That was the reason I hooked him up with that apartment in Buckhead. I have always been your father and acted as your father. I just didn't make it public."

We sipped our drinks and the silence stretched out. Bridgett broke the silence. "Peter, as far as Quentin is concerned, what attracted me to him was that he was always honest. He always told me the truth no matter how it made him look. He was so sweet, so respectful. I didn't care if he didn't have any money. I loved him for himself.

"What really made me fall in love with him was that while the others guys I went out with were trying to impress me with money and expensive presents, Quentin would send me beautiful romantic poems."

"Talk about starving artists," I said under my breath.

Bridgett heard me anyway and jumped to his defense. "Peter, that was the only thing he could afford. A man who writes poetry has a beautiful heart and honest soul. After we started dating he would take me on picnics to Stone Mountain Park. He would read poetry to me and we would watch the laser show. We would look up at the stars and talk about the future.

"I remember one night we were watching the stars, it was then that he expressed his love for me. It was the perfect night. Quentin had just quit his job. When we first started dating, he was a high-powered stockbroker. He talked about how he couldn't give me everything I wanted. I told him all I wanted was him. I encouraged his dream to become a writer. He was—is a good writer. Maybe I'm partly at fault for him selling out his friends." Tears formed in her eyes once more. "Peter, why didn't my mother tell me the truth. Why didn't you marry her? Why were we never a family?"

"Bridgett, there were a lot of things I've had to come to grips with over the years. One was my own ambition. That, and being an orphan. Then there was Jan's deception."

50

"To make a long story short, I met your mother a couple of years after I'd been duped into marriage by Jan. Jan and I had a huge fight and she left and went to Boston, to her family. I decided that this time I was not going to chase her down. That's when I met Carla. Your mother had a way of making me forget all about my problems. I fell head over heels in love with her. Your mother was everything any man could want."

"You remind me very much of her. Some of the things Quentin tells me about you sound like things your mom would do. Carla was such a good listener. Like you. When I talked to her, she would totally focus on me. For the first time in my life, I felt like someone cared about me for me. That's something Jan knows nothing about."

"With your mother I felt like anything was possible, but I didn't reckon on your mother's will. She's a force to be reckoned with. You know, she never asked me for anything. She was fiercely independent, smart. She had a passion to become a doctor. She worked as a stripper, supported her family and put herself through medical school. No mean feat, let me tell you."

"I tried to help her, but she would never let me. I could sneak things in like buying groceries and taking them over to the house. She'd accept that with poor grace, but she would accept them. You can't very well return groceries."

"We'd spent just about everyday together for weeks. I fell deeply in love with Carla and she loved me. One magic night we made love. You are what that love brought forth."

Bridgett listened quietly, her eyes never left my face. I plowed ahead, getting to the painful part. I could feel the tears gather in my eyes.

"Bridgett, after she found out she was pregnant, she walked out of my life."

I looked at her and tears had formed in her eyes too. She whispered, "Why Peter?"

"She didn't want to continue to date a married man, but I told her I'd divorce Jan and marry her. About that time Jan became very ill. I was caught between responsibility to my wife and her children and the woman I truly loved and my unborn child. I pleaded with Carla daily, but she refused to see me. She was wracked by guilt over our affair. In the end, I did nothing. I was too cowardly to just take matters into my own hands and divorce Jan. Because I didn't divorce Jan, there was no way Carla would let me near her. After you were born, she'd let me spend time with you, but she was never there. I loved you from the first moment I laid eyes on you. You were an angel sent by God, but we could never be a family. She eventually finished medical school and moved to Africa."

"Why, Peter, why did she leave me?"

"It was the hardest decision she ever made. I think it was an act of atonement on her part. She wanted to take you with her, but I talked her out of that because I was concerned that you'd be in danger. And you were happy with your aunt."

"I was, but I would have been happier with my mother. I've spent a lot of years thinking she just abandoned me."

I took her hand again. "No honey, she could never abandon you. But, she had this guilt inside her that grew and grew. She went to one of the roughest parts of the world to try and give children a better life, but it wasn't because she didn't want you."

"A lot of people say I look like you," Bridgett said.

"I never announced to the world that you were my daughter. I was afraid it would destroy too many lives, including yours. I kept you near me the only way I knew how by giving you a job at McCallister Enterprises. You excelled at your work. You are a chip off the old block. But, I think those nosy old women at Holy Faith suspected you might be my daughter, although they had no proof other than the fact we look a lot alike. I guess it was hard to put it together with an old southern bigot. Lady Bug, I'm very proud of you, you know?"

Bridgett smiled at me sheepishly. "I must admit, Peter, that you've taken good care of me. I'll give you credit for that."

"What else could I do? I wanted you to have the best of everything. Your mother refused any assistance, so I tried to make up for it with you." I paused and looked at her closely.

"Do you know what's going to happen December 15th?"

"I heard the tape, but a lot of it didn't sink in after I found out you were my father."

"Bridgett, I've been grooming you to take over the company. On your birthday, you will become the CEO of McCallister Enterprises and all my money will be transferred into an offshore account in your name. You will have 700 million dollars."

A dead silence greeted me. She looked at me with eyes as big as saucers. She let out a deep breath. "Peter, it's the end October now. You're talking about only a few weeks."

"That's right, honey. Everything that I have built over the years for you and your mother will be out of harms way. I've already met with the Board of Directors. They all know my decision. They are loyal and trusted friends. The way is paved for a smooth transition. After you take over, I will ask Jan for a divorce. You, Carla and I can finally become a family."

"What will happen to Jan and the boys?" She looked at me with a guilty expression on her face.

"The boys are grown men. They've been freeloaders for way too many years. They are interested only in being players. I've made provisions for Jan. She will be comfortable for the rest of her life if she reins in her spending. The boys are welcome to join the business if you want to hire them, but the free ride is over for them," I said angrily. I hit the table with my fist.

"Peter, I'm shocked. I don't think I can take all this in."

"Lady Bug, I've been planning this for years. You will be fine. I have every faith in you. But everything I feel towards Jan and her children has been building up for years. For once in my life, I have nothing to lose. But come December 15th, I have everything to gain. I am going after the woman I love. I am even open-minded enough to accept my future knucklehead son-in-law."

A cheery smile lit her face. Then she knit her brows in confusion.

"Peter, you told me when your parents tried to sell you for drugs, that you became an atheist. But you attend church every Sunday and you are the largest contributor to the church. What made you do such an about face?"

"You know the story about the IRS. It's public knowledge at Holy Faith, but that was only part of it. When I joined the Army, I was sent to Vietnam. My squad was on an intelligence gathering mission. Somehow my buddy, Blake, and I got cut off from the rest of the troops. Suddenly we were under attack. Bullets rained down on us. Blake and I took cover and returned fire. We could hear our unit in the jungle. They were being picked off. We knew we wouldn't last the night. We exchanged fire for hours and we were exhausted. We were so exhausted that when there was a lull in the gun fire both Blake and I fell asleep."

"What happened then?"

"What seemed like a few minutes was actually a couple of hours. I awoke in a cold sweat. I grabbed my rifle. I was shaking in my boots. I was so scared the Cong could hear my bones rattle. When I grabbed up that rifle, I swung it north, south, east and west. I could see what was left of my unit on a far hill."

"Thank God you and your friend were rescued."

Reliving that memory had brought tears to my eyes again. I knuckled away a tear as it ran down my cheek.

"Not quite Bridgett. Blake was still asleep. His helmet was on his knees. He was leaning on the helmet with his hands folded under his forehead. I nudged him and said, 'Hey buddy, wake up. Our ride's here.' I could hear the choppers coming in. I told Blake he'd be back with his wife and new baby in no time. He didn't wake up so I nudged him again. 'Come on sleeping beauty,' I said. He still didn't respond and I reached over and touched his arm. His body was cold. I laid him back. There was such a look of horror on his face."

"What happened, Peter?" Her mouth was shaped in a little O of fear.

"His throat had been cut and his eyes were gouged out."

"Oh my God!" she gasped.

"There was a note in his mouth. It was written in broken, misspelled English. It said 'We made a choice between the two of you. Your God has spared you.' To this day I still sometimes wake up in a cold sweat after dreaming about that day."

The tears flowed, I couldn't help it. I felt overwhelmed. I could only imagine how Bridgett must have felt.

"How could I continue to be an atheist after experiencing something like that? There's an old military saying, 'There are no atheists in foxholes.' I firmly believe that if you want to stop racism, put two enemies in a foxhole together with bullets raining around them, they will soon realize how insignificant their differences are."

51

BRIDGETT

When Peter and I finished talking, we hugged each other like there was no tomorrow. It was like a piece of the puzzle had finally been put into the right place. The emptiness inside of me had finally been filled. So many questions had finally been answered. As Peter and I embraced, I realized that I was a lot like him. Now I knew where I got my personality. Although I had my mother's last name, I knew I was also a McCallister, Bridgett Moore McCallister. I liked the sound of that.

I thought about everything that had happened. But, there was still one more piece of the puzzle missing; the one that would make me complete. My mother. For the past eighteen years I only knew of her as a picture in the locket I wore around my neck. I wanted a mother. I wanted to be close to her. I wanted to do the silly mother-daughter things, like roll each other's hair and play with makeup. I wanted to go shopping with my mother and have her tell me that dress looked awful or it looked like a million dollars on me. I wanted her to tuck me in at night and read me a bedtime story.

Now that I knew the truth, the anger I'd felt towards Peter had started to heal. But now I needed to know how a mother could leave her daughter to be reared by someone else. Hearing Peter's story about what my mother went through renewed my interest in her. I wanted to see her and touch her. I needed the healing to be complete.

As Peter and I started to leave, I turned and gave him one more hug. It was the hug I used to give him when I wanted a new bike or was afraid of the boogie man. "Peter, I want to see my mother." I looked at him with a little pout. "I need to see my mother if I'm to move forward and take my place at the company. Do you know where she is?"

I knew that would hit him where it hurt.

"I want to see her too." He held me away from him, gripping my arms loosely. "But Bridgett, I made a promise to her that I would never contact her again. Unless I divorced."

I looked at him solemnly. "How do you feel about keeping that promise now?"

"I feel deep in my heart that she still loves me. But if I never keep a promise to anyone else, I'm going to keep it to her and to you. You know, part of the reason she left Atlanta, was me. She knew that as long as she stayed here, she'd just be the other woman. Her belief in God wouldn't allow that."

He ran a finger down my cheek, stopping under my chin. He gently pushed my head up and looked into my eyes. "You are so much like her. She was smart and kind of square."

"You calling me a square?" I said laughing.

"Yeah, I am." He teased. "When your mom finished medical school she graduated top of her class. Did you know that? Quite a few of the top hospitals around the country tried to recruit her. She gave up a lot to join the Red Cross."

"Peter, do you know where she is?" I asked again. "I'm going to see my mother and Sudan is a dangerous place. It would help me if you know where she is so I don't end up roaming around in a minefield. I need to see her and know if she's okay."

He opened the door and escorted me outside. The wind was bitingly cold for this time of year. Brown leaves skittered across the sidewalk.

He drew a deep, bracing breath. "You can't go to Africa, Bridgett. It's way too dangerous. There is a city in Sudan where tens of thousands of people have died and over two million more have been displaced. The US accuses the Sudan government and its backers of committing genocide against the people of Darfur. Of course, the Sudanese government blames the rebels for the atrocities."

"Peter, Mom may need us. How would you feel if something happened to her and you never saw her again?" I could see that my words cut him like a knife and that never seeing her again would be a fate worse than death to him. "How do I even know she's still alive? How do we know she's not somewhere alone and needs our help?"

"Calm down, Bridgett, please," He said softly. "Your mother is fine. She's alive and she is safe."

"You can't know that for sure. You're only saying that to make me feel better."

He hesitated, and then kissed my forehead. "I do know that for certain, Lady Bug. I've known it for years."

"How!" I wailed.

"Because I've had soldiers keeping an eye on her. They've been in my pay since she's been in Africa, solely to protect her."

"How could you possibly pull that off?"

"She thinks that her security is provided by the African government and the Red Cross. But I hired a private security team to make sure she has protection 24/7."

I started to cry again and wiped the tears off my cheeks hastily. "You do still love her, don't you? But, I'm going, with or without your help, Peter. She's my mother and I need her. Every since I was a little girl, you've given me anything I wanted."

"Within reason." He interrupted me.

"Okay, within reason. I don't think seeing my mother is unreasonable. I want you to go with me. I'm asking you for one last thing, Peter. I need my mother."

He wrapped his arm around my shoulder and pulled me close. "All right honey, you win. We'll leave a couple of weeks. Is that soon enough? I know where she is and I will make all the arrangements."

I felt like daddy's little girl. I liked it.

"I love you Daddy."

52

PETER

Still basking in the glow of being called Daddy for the first time in my life, I started for home. It was time to talk to Jan. I felt as though I was walking the green mile.

When I got home Jan was in the kitchen. I poured myself some coffee and said to Jan, "I have something to tell you. You are not going to like it, but I need you to let me finish without interrupting."

She gave me a stern look, "Peter, you know I never interrupt you."

I took a deep breath. "Jan, we've been married for thirty two years. It seems with each passing year, our marriage deteriorates."

"Peter, we have problems like anybody else, but we have a good marriage."

"A good marriage!" I said rather loudly, not believing my ears. "Stop it Jan! You're kidding yourself. We have just been going through the motions. Whatever I do is never good enough. Even therapy hasn't helped. Our marriage is a sham, a miserable excuse for a marriage."

"Maybe we need another therapist?" Jan suggested.

"Enough is enough. No more. Jan, how in the hell can a perfect stranger tell you about me when he doesn't know a damn thing about me?"

"Peter, if you would just listen to me..."

"Jan, for the past thirty years that is all I've done. I listen to you constantly rattling about everything! And it's always about something I didn't do or forgot to do. I tried hard to please you. I worked sun up to sun down. I wanted to make sure you and your sons would never have to lift a finger the rest of your lives."

Jan became annoyed. "Spit it out, Peter. What is this all about?"

"Jan, when I worked all the time for you, you complained I never spent enough time with you. When I took off time to spend with you, you'd tell me I'm too emotionally needy and you needed your space. You've spoiled your children rotten. You have refused to let them grow up and be men."

"Peter, I just wanted what was best for them."

"Your kind of love has made them so much of a mama's boy, that I feel sorry for their future wives."

"Peter, that's a low blow."

"But it's true. You have gotten everything you have ever wanted out of this marriage; money, security, trips around the world, expensive clothes and jewelry, a beautiful home, servants. All I ever wanted was a child of my own and someone that honestly loved me for who I was."

"But, Peter, I tried to give you a child and miscarried."

I let out a wild laugh. "Miscarried, my ass! You were never pregnant; you couldn't even get pregnant. When I met you I revealed all my most intimate thoughts. When a man lies down at night, he wants to feel that his emotions and thoughts are safe. But that was not the case with us."

She turned on the innocent charm. "Peter, your feelings were always safe with me—"

"Oh, please, Jan." I interrupted, applauding. "And the Oscar goes to Jan McCallister for her portrayal of a loving wife."

I ran my hand through my hair. "Jan, you used my deepest thoughts to manipulate and control me."

"Well, then it seems we both got into this marriage under false pretenses." She sneered at me. "You pretended to be someone you weren't, now didn't you?"

"You pressured me into this marriage with deceit," I said desperately. "You knew how much I wanted children and you played on that by lying to me. You had me on such an emotional leash, I couldn't even think straight. You knew I wouldn't even ask for a pre-nuptial agreement. I trusted you." I ground my teeth and cut her an angry stare.

"Peter, I made you the success you are today!"

"Oh please, give me credit for having a brain. It was my own hard work and determination." I slapped the table for emphasis.

Jan burst into tears. "Peter, I've always loved you."

"Stop lying Jan. There is no reason to pretend anymore. You don't love me and you never have. You love what I represent, you love my money and you love your lifestyle. It's not even necessary for me to be a part of it as long as you have everything else."

"That's not true, Peter. I love you with all my heart."

"Okay, since you love me with all your heart, let me call your bluff," I said craftily. "You remember that huge fight we had over thirty years ago and you took off to Boston with the boys and stayed up there for several months?"

"I remember, you were supposed to come get us but you never did. I had to come back all by myself with two children in tow."

Yep, Jan certainly lives in her own little world, I thought to myself. I almost felt that I could enjoy myself telling her about Carla and me just to see what spin she'd put on that. Grimly, I plowed ahead.

"Yeah, well, during your stay in Boston, something happened."

"What are you talking about Peter?"

"I was going through a lot of stress over everything and I started hanging out in strip clubs."

"What, strip clubs!" She covered her mouth in complete surprise. "Did anyone we know see you? Did any of our friends see you going in?" Her voice rose hysterically.

"I don't know and I certainly don't care. That was when I met Carla, a stripper at Magic City."

"Oh my God!" Jan wailed and grasped her hair in fists of frustration. "Magic City! Is this woman trying to blackmail you? Is she trying to take what's ours?"

"Jan, calm down and be quiet! Carla has never asked me for anything. She and I became good friends. We would talk for hours and she listened to me."

"What?" Jan looked at me with a perplexed look on her face.

"She listened to me," I yelled in frustration.

"Peter, you don't have to raise your voice. I'm not deaf?"

"I know that, but would you just listen to me and try to pay attention. I know that is hard for you to do, but please, just listen for once...Carla and I became lovers."

"What! What are you talking about?"

My level of frustration rose until I thought I'd pop a vein. "Jan, Carla and I had a child together!"

She threw her hands up to cover her ears. "Peter, I don't want to hear another word. You fucked a stripper and now you have a bastard child!" She jumped up from the table and kicked me in the groin.

"AHHHH!" I screamed and doubled over in agony.

"You will never, ever fuck anyone else again. Do you hear me! What will people say?"

I managed to straighten up and grabbed Jan by the arms to thrust her back into the chair. I hobbled over to the counter and placed both hands flat, trying to ease the pain.

"Jan, there hasn't been an 'us' for a very long time. It has always been about you and the boys. For once in your life can't you think about my happiness?"

"Well, what in the hell do you want Peter? Whatever it is, I will do it. We can get through this." She started pacing the floor. I put the kitchen island warily between us in case she tried to geld me.

She continued her rant. "It's obvious what the little bitch wants is money. Let's just pay her off. Then we can get on with our lives. I'll fix everything like I've done before. Our friends will never have to find out."

"Jan, you can't fix this one. I don't want to get rid of her and I certainly don't want to get out of it."

"What in the hell do you mean?" She yelled at me, coming towards me.

I gathered my composure, moving around the island to keep her as far away as possible. "I want a divorce, Jan."

"A divorce!" Her eyes narrowed and her body fairly jiggled from her rage. "Are you on dog food or dope? There is no way in hell some fucking gold digging stripper is going to take my man and she can forget about stealing what belongs to me and the boys!"

She raced around the island before I could even move and begin hitting me in the chest.

"You fucking bastard. You lying, cheating, fucking bastard! I've given you 32 years of my life and now you just wake up one day and tell me you want a divorce. You have the audacity to tell me you love someone else, a stripper no less! I will expose you and destroy you, you bastard!"

"Jan, calm down, please." I tried to grab her flailing arms. She clipped me on the chin. I pushed her away from me. "Stop acting like a child. Jan, I love Carla and want to marry her and be with our daughter."

She stepped back into me and slapped me with a strength I didn't know she possessed. My ears were ringing.

"You fucking dog. Who's your daughter? Tell me now, damn it."

I should have kept Bridgett's name out of it, but she'd find out eventually anyway. I guess I thought it was better to go ahead and lay it all out on the table. Before I could stop myself and really think it through, I said. "Bridgett Moore."

"Your daughter is Bridgett Moore. I can't believe this!" Jan got redder and redder in the face. But I refused to let her rattle me.

"Peter, I swear, I'm going to kill you." She started slapping me over and over. I covered my head trying to shield myself from the blows. I finally grabbed her hands.

"Stop it Jan, get control of yourself. We need to discuss this like adults."

"Adults! You get some black woman pregnant and then throw your kid in my face for years. You must have gotten plenty of laughs off that. I can't believe you!" she screamed.

"Fighting is not going to solve anything. I'll get you something to drink."

I went to the library to pour her a stiff gin and tonic. I took a long pull off the bottle for myself as she followed me into the library. She was crying, her fat face bloated and red. Finally, it seemed that most of the fight had gone out of her. She sat heavily on the couch. I thrust the drink in her hand and she downed it.

"Jan, I'm sorry I'm dropping so much on you all at once. I know this is hard, but I—"

"Hard, Peter—"

"Please Jan." I held up my hand for quiet. Amazingly she complied and held her glass out for another drink.

As I mixed it, I talked. "Carla, is out of my life. She has been for years. She went to Africa."

"So she dumped Bridgett and went chasing off to Africa, fine mother you have there," she said sarcastically.

"Carla didn't want to see me anymore after she found out she was pregnant and as long as I was still married. I accepted that. Jan, I never asked you for a divorce. I've suffered in silence for over 30 years. I couldn't even be a father to the only child I ever had and desperately wanted. Carla made me promise not to tell Bridgett I was her father. She didn't find out until tonight. You know she's always thought her father was killed in a car accident."

"I can't believe that a friend of mine turns out to be the illegitimate daughter of my husband. God, how do I wrap my head around this? You know what upsets me the most...that it's 30 years too late to have an abortion!"

Her words hit me like bullets through the heart. She'd gotten a second wind from adrenalin surges and was cranking up again.

"How did she find out? You told, her didn't you? You can't even keep a promise to that whore!"

I tried to touch Jan to calm her. She slapped my hand away and downed her second drink. "Get away from me you bastard. Don't ever touch me again. Regardless of how I tried to change you, you are nothing but orphanage trash."

"She found out from Quentin by accident. She called me, hysterical. I met her to try and calm her down and clarify the situation for her. She was just as upset and shocked as you are."

"Good," she said viciously, "Misery loves company.

"Peter, how could you have done this, do you even know how many lives you've destroyed? How could you?" She put her head in one hand and stuck out the glass with the other. I took it and poured her another gin and tonic. As I passed it back to her she raised her head and gave me a cynical look. "I appreciate your honesty, and I'll be honest with you. Carla and Bridgett will never receive a dime of our fortune. The boys and I are the rightful heirs."

I decided to keep quiet about the fact that Bridgett would be the CEO of McCallister's in a few weeks. Let Jan believe whatever she wished to believe. My best bet was to just lay low for a while and let Jan think she'd won.

Jan considered my silence as tacit agreement and rage boiled up in her again. "You fucking piece of shit. Get out. I don't want to see you again." She threw her empty glass at my head. "I will never give you a divorce. You will never have your freedom. You can forget about ever marrying that little bitch. I will show you who has the biggest balls. I made you and I can destroy you!"

I just looked at her sadly, and then I walked to the door. But I couldn't resist one more parting shot. I stopped and turned and said, "Oh, by the way, while we are being so honest, the character in Quentin's book, Winston Dillingsworth, is me. It's been fun Buffy."

I climbed the stairs to the bedroom with her screaming at me from the foyer. "You bastard, you fucking undercover Democrat. If you wanted a black baby, why didn't you do like Madonna or Angelina Jolie and fly to Africa and adopt one." I heard the library door slam hard enough to knock the pictures off the wall.

53

QUENTIN

The good sisters of the church really put on the ritz for the 30 year anniversary of Holy Faith. Sister Spencer and Aunt Judy worked diligently to make it a memorable event. The church shined like a new penny. Beautiful flowers and floral arrangements were placed throughout the church. The men looked handsome and elegant in their best suits. The older deacons combed their hair over to hide their bald spots. The women were dressed to kill. They had dressed extra sharp trying to outdo each other. Their hats were elaborate and piled high with bows, feathers, and flowers. Some people tried to arrive fashionably late so they could make a grand entrance. The single women had their own agenda. Their dresses were shorter and tighter and drew attention to their most attractive features. They arrived extra early to check out the divorced and single men. The divorced ladies looked at the single women with stern disapproval.

"Look at those little hussies, competing for the men. They surely have no shame. Up in the house of the Lord lusting."

"Forget a man. Who needs one? The same thing that would make them laugh will one day make them cry," one of the divorced matrons exclaimed.

"Jesus is all the man I will ever need."

"I'm too blessed to be stressed."

The single and divorced women's battle lines were drawn and there was a lot of eye rolling going back and forth. The married women proudly drew their husbands extra close. The children were on a tight leash and put their best manners forward. The parents kept belts handy, in case they needed a little reminder. Over in a back pew a mother sat with her two children. She was making sure they understood the seriousness of the day.

"Amy, Michael, you'd better not show out in church. Forget what you see on TV, in our house there is no such thing as time out." She clenched her fist at the kids. "The only thing I know is 'knock out'. I'm from the old school and abuse is my middle name. When I knock you out, I'll call 911 for you. What do I care about going to jail. It would be like a family reunion!"

It seemed that all of Atlanta had turned out. The future politicians were there to praise and be praised, passing out cards to anyone that would pay attention to their politicking. News crews were camped out on the front lawn, while newspaper journalists wandered through the crowd with notebooks in hand. Adrian was even in the crowd, collecting the latest gossip, his purple hair conspicuous. Jeff, Donald and Peter sat in a pew in the second row.

As the praise team came up, the organ started to play. Paul Spencer, the new choir director started everyone to rocking.

"Come on Holy Faith, let's stomp for Jesus. Throw up your hands if you've come to praise the Lord!"

Hands went up everywhere.

"Ain't no party like the Holy Ghost party!"

The church rocked.

"Because the Holy Ghost party don't stop! Come on stomp for Jesus!"

The choir director started to jump and move. Everyone started rocking and applauding. When it came to the choir and music, it was hard to tell sometimes whether Holy Faith was a church or a popular night club. The music reached a soul searing pitch and women cried and screamed as they ran up and down the aisle.

Miss Clark, an overweight, long time member of Holy Faith would start her weekly ritual. She would unexpectedly start shouting uncontrollably. Then she would fall on the women sitting near her on the bench. All eyes would be on her, as the women around scrambled to get out of the way. The male ushers stood on standby to pick her up. It usually took all of them to achieve this task. Miss Clark would usually try to fall on someone she couldn't stand. Holy Faith had started carrying extra liability insurance to cover any incidents that Miss Clark might cause. But I guess the Lord has his hand on everyone's heart, because in 30 years they'd never been sued by Miss Clark's victims. The congregation often wondered if Miss Clark really did feel the spirit of the Lord, or if she was just sweet on one of the ushers.

While the music played and they danced in the aisles, the men threw up their hands in the air and shouted praise. Amen! Hallelujah!

Everyone was relaxed and feeling the Lord when Donald rose and came to the pulpit. He spread his arms open, with his palms up and addressed the congregation. "Holy Faith Non-Denominational Church welcomes you to our 30th anniversary. It gives me great pleasure to introduce our beloved senior pastor..." He turned, indicating a man seated behind the pulpit. "The honorable Pastor Carl Adam Cash." His voice resounded through the church. Everyone stood as applause filled the air.

Pastor Cash walked slowly to the pulpit and propped his hands on each side. Tears filled his eyes. The congregation shouted his name. He straightened and pulled a large handkerchief from the sleeve of his ornate robe and gently wiped his eyes. He then gestured to the congregation to sit. A lump came to my throat as I watched my friend and my mentor stand before me. For years, I had looked at his peppered hair and Godly smile. He was going to retire officially tonight and pass the torch to a younger predecessor. I keenly felt a since of loss. Pastor Cash cleared his throat and began to speak.

"Holy Faith, today is one of mixed blessings. It is a glorious day because we are in the house of the Lord. It is a sad day because today I will be officially stepping down as your senior pastor.

"For 30 years, it is a duty that I have embraced, cherished and tried to perform to the best of my ability. As I look around the church, I see so many familiar faces. Many of you I watched from birth grow into fine people. I watched you stumble and fall. I've officiated at your weddings and cried over your divorces. I've watched you commit your lives and marriages to the Lord. I watched this church grow from a few humble members to the mega-church we are today.

"We are large in number, with new members joining weekly, but we are still a family."

"Don't leave this family," came an emotional outburst from the back pews. "Amen," a young minister shouted.

"I feel that my assistant pastors, and you, the congregation, are all my children. You are and will always be a part of me. However, my replacement can take the family, the flock and my children to the next level!"

Thunderous applause filled the church. The very rafters were rattling.

His glance swept over the assistant pastors that sat behind him.

"As senior pastor of this church, my replacement must be someone the people can trust. They must feel their best interests are paramount."

"Break it down!" The congregation shouted.

"He must never yield to temptation, carnal desire, corruption or pressure from outside influences that may threaten the church."

"Take your time, Pastor Cash," Donald shouted out.

"He will be called upon to counsel members of this church in troubled marriages. He cannot clean the house of the troubled if his own house is dirty! He must have honesty and purity in his life to instill it in your lives!"

"Amen, Pastor," someone in front shouted.

"Holy Faith Church, without further delay, I'd like to introduce you to my replacement, my successor and your new Shepard..."

A collective gasp went through the congregation as we all held our breath in anticipation. The assistant pastors looked at each other expectantly.

"Pastor Donald Reynolds!"

Applause and cheers rang out. Donald rose with a humble smile and shook hands with the other assistant pastors. He walked to the pulpit and embraced Pastor Cash and then kissed him on the cheek.

I leaned over to Jeff and remarked, "Didn't Judas do that to Jesus?" The fellows shook their heads. We knew Holy Faith would never be the same.

Ashley was smiling and waving to the congregation, proud as a peacock. She gave the other wives of the assistant pastors a sly, haughty stare.

"I love you good pastor," Donald said with tears in his eyes. "I won't let you down."

The church applauded and Donald raised his hands to heaven, pride filling him. He had reached a life long dream. He was now a member of the Buckhead elite and the new senior pastor of the largest church in Atlanta. He was now one of the most influential and powerful men in Atlanta.

54

Donald looked at Pastor Cash with a mixture of pride and humility. He turned to the congregation. "Good Pastor and Holy Faith Church, I accept my responsibility as Senior Pastor of Holy Faith Non-Denominational Church! I will assume my duties with the same leadership, pride and commitment that you have given us in the past, Good Pastor. I know the pulpit is a place of honesty, integrity, sacrifice and trust." Pastor Cash patted Donald on the back and returned to his seat behind the pulpit.

"Holy Faith, let us turn to the Bible. It states that whatever is done in darkness will come to light. As we go through life, far too many of us wear a mask."

"Amen Brother Reynolds," an elderly woman witnessed.

"Far too often, we pretend to be something that we are not."

"Preach the truth!" Pastor Cash shouted.

"We wear a mask on our jobs. We wear a mask with our families, our friends and even our loved ones."

"Don't bite your tongue," a divorcee yelled. "Tell it like it is!"

"Daily, our television is plagued with scandals from the White House, to Wall Street and to the pulpit. We see Presidents and CEO's of large companies indicted from cooking their books to stealing millions and billions of dollars from their trusted employees. Now they are crying to the President and the government for a bailout!"

"Speak the truth and shame the devil!" Miss Clark shouted.

"We have seen scandals in the White House and among our trusted lawmakers. Not too long ago a trusted Governor from the great state of New Jersey decided to come out of the closet. A powerful Republican from the great state of Idaho was caught playing footsies in the bathroom with his john. If that wasn't bad enough, Illinois Governor Rod Blagojevich was busted trying to sell the senate seat made vacant by President Obama."

"Bring it home," Pastor Cash encouraged.

"A powerful congressman was accused of an inappropriate relationship with a 16-year old. Shortly after that scandal raised its ugly head, Evangelist Juanita Bynum and her husband, Bishop Thomas Week III, blew a million dollars on their highly televised wedding only to have their marriage fall apart when she accused her husband of assaulting her in a hotel parking lot."

"The devil is a busy child," Sister Spencer shouted.

"Holy Faith, just because you call out the name of Jesus, it doesn't really mean you know the man! Everything that shines is not a dime."

"Hallelujah Brother," a woman stood and applauded.

"Go ahead with your bad self, Donald," a man cheered.

"I am so proud to announce that while so many churches are under attack or investigation, Holy Faith has never had any scandals."

"No one can serve two masters," a woman in the back yelled.

I looked around in awe. I wondered how he could deceive so many honest and trusting people. Everyone was buying into his speech.

"Scandal is everywhere!" Donald thundered. "You might fool yourself, you might fool your spouse, your family or your friends, but you cannot and will not fool the Lord!"

A chorus of "Amen" rang out. Women got up and cheered.

"What a hypocrite," I whispered, slouching down in the pew.

Pastor Cash stood and applauded. "Come on with it, Pastor Reynolds," he shouted.

"You see Holy Faith, what is done in darkness will certainly come to light." The single women hung onto his every word.

"Church, when ministers and other clergymen yield to temptation it becomes even more detrimental."

"Amen," a man said.

"You see, the House of the Lord is supposed to be the last refuge."

"Preach the truth, Donald," one of the assistant pastors said.

"That is why as your pastor, it is my responsibility to stand for what is decent, good and pure!"

The assistant pastors stood and applauded. Donald's voice echoed over the applause.

"Holy Faith, if you can't trust your minister, priest or rabbi, who can you trust?"

"Break it down," someone yelled.

"Men, if you can't trust your minister alone with your wife, who can you trust?"

"Hallelujah," an elderly woman screamed.

Everyone stood. Deafening applause filled the sanctuary. As he motioned for everyone to be seated, an obviously pregnant woman and her husband walked toward the pulpit. Donald totally ignored them and I expected a bolt of lightening to hit him at any moment.

"Now, Holy Faith, one of the biggest problems that we have in our marriage is trust. Far too many men and women don't trust each other."

He gave the men a judgmental stare. "Men, how can your wife trust you when you are on the down-low, bi-curious, leading a double life or cheating on your wife?"

"Talk to the men, Donald," a woman shouted.

"Men, we are supposed to set an example. How can women trust us when we are doing so many ungodly things?" He shot another judgmental stare around the sanctuary.

"Single women, far too many men are just wolves in sheep's clothing." Applause and pandemonium erupted.

He flashed a confident look around the congregation. "Don't worry good sisters. What is done in darkness will certainly come to light."

The man and woman had stood patiently in front of the pulpit, but now they spoke. Donald looked down, as if he'd just seen them and paused.

"Pastor Reynolds, you are going to bust hell wide open!" the husband shouted.

"You are no man of God. You are a pimp in the pulpit. You are nothing but a wolf in sheep's clothing!" The wife shouted.

A rumbling noise broke out throughout the congregation, as everyone turned to their neighbor questioning what it all meant. Pastor Cash stood and walked to the pulpit to stand beside Donald. Donald hung his head and gripped the edges of the podium.

The woman turned to the congregation. "My name is Angie Brown. Donald and I have been sleeping together for the past twelve years. What he has done in darkness has most certainly come to light!"

Angie turned sideways to the assembly and pulled her dress tightly against her protruding belly.

"I told my husband, Wayne, everything. I didn't leave out any details. So ain't no use denying it Donald. You are busted."

Pandemonium swept the church. Donald started to stutter as he tried to discredit her. "Young woman, what would make you come to the House of the Lord and lie? The devil must have taken over your mind!"

"The only devil that took me over is you Donald Reynolds." She turned to the congregation again, "Since I was 16-years old I've been his mistress. At first you told me you would leave your wife, and I waited because like a fool I believed you. Then you introduced me to Wayne and when we got married I wanted to break it off, but you held our affair over my head and threatened to tell Wayne. I found out you had other mistresses on the side. I should have realized that if you would cheat on your wife, you'd cheat on me!"

"Oh my God!" an elderly woman cried out as she clutched at her seatmate.

Angie continued with venom. "Look at you standing in the pulpit like your are all of that, acting like the thirteenth disciple." She raked Donald with a pathetic stare. "You are supposed to be a man of God. You could have been another Bishop T.D. Jakes, Joel Osteen or Billy Graham, but instead, you've damned both our souls to hell."

"Angie, stop lying in the House of the Lord!" Donald yelled in desperation.

"Who is lying? I am telling the truth. I asked the Lord to forgive me and I asked my husband to forgive me." She looked around angrily, "Your new leader has impregnated me. In two months, I'm going to give birth to twins."

"Stop lying!" Donald thundered and banged his fist on the pulpit. His face was contorted in rage. If he'd had a flaming sword he would have looked just like an avenging angel. A really, really mad avenging angel.

Angie's husband jumped to her defense. "It is no lie, Pastor Cash and he knows it. Pastor Reynolds is not who he pretends to be. Here is all the proof you need." He held up the box containing a DVD. "Here is a disk, an X-rated disk he and my wife made together."

The congregation looked back and forth at each other whispering. When I looked behind me I caught a glimpse of Adrian's purple hair. Ashley jumped up from a half faint and yelled passionately, "Tell them it is not so Donald. Tell them you are a man of God!" She burst into tears and collapsed back into her seat, covering her face with her hands. "Please," came a muffled plea. "Please, if for no other reason, tell everybody the truth for our marriage's sake."

During the commotion another woman fought her way to the front. "Holy Faith, Pastor Cash, my name is Nicole Peterson." She shouted above the noise. "I'm another of his mistresses. Donald Reynolds is not fit to lead us. He has also fathered my child. My baby is due this spring. In fact, I met him hanging out at the Cheetah Club."

Ashley moaned and fainted. The women sitting around her started fanning her and whispering furiously among themselves. Other members had started to leave, mother's put their hands over their children's ears. "I can't believe this," a mother shouted as she herded her children toward the sanctuary doors. "Holy Faith is a den of iniquity."

Donald stood with tears in his eyes. Pastor Cash took the microphone. "Could I have your attention, please? Attention, will everyone please sit down! I promise you I will get to the bottom of this. Lies, dishonesty and deceit have no place in God's House."

He looked at both the pregnant women and Angie's husband. He summoned the loyal church sisters, "Sister Vivian and Aunt Judy, could you take these women and Wayne to the waiting area at my office?"

As he looked around the congregation, the look of so many hurt, shocked and disappointed members brought tears to his eyes. "The Bible says 'let he who is without sin cast the first stone.' Holy Faith is about honesty and trust. Right now, I want to get to the bottom of this. Are there any more members present who feel that they have been wronged by Pastor Reynolds? Please come forward now."

The church members looked about the sanctuary, as one by one, several young women rose from their seats. "Oh my God!" one woman screamed. "Some of those girls are underage!"

More people got up to leave, threatening to move their membership, no longer wishing to be a part of Holy Faith.

Pastor Cash stood in shock as six young women approached him. But he remained remarkably calm. "Aunt Judy, take these young women to the waiting area, as well, if you please. Please call the medical staff for the young women. Also, please call our attorney and call the local authorities." He turned to Donald. "Pastor Reynolds, please close your Bible and leave the pulpit. I want you to go to my office."

Donald hung his head in shame as he and Pastor Cash moved down the steps from the pulpit area. When they reached Ashley, Pastor Cash quietly instructed the women with her to take her to one of the more isolated sitting areas and get some medical attention for her.

Only a few people had actually left the church. They sat stunned in the pews, whispering back and forth to each other. Pastor Cash handed Donald off to one of the elders and returned to the pulpit. He watched as

Donald and Ashley were escorted through a side door and then he turned to the remaining congregation.

"Please, may I have your attention?" Pastor Cash pleaded. As the whispers died down and the congregation turned to him, he continued. "Church was set aside today to be a joyous occasion, a time to renew our vows and converse with the Lord. It was supposed to be a time to glorify in the Lord. But it has turned out to be a time when skeletons have come out of the closet. What was done in darkness has truly come to light. But Holy Faith, I promise you that I will restore your faith again.

"A lot of you are new members and new in Christ. When scandal hurts the church or when there is a pimp in the pulpit, it hurts or destroys the faith of those looking to believe in something or someone.

"To the members and visitors that are still here, the Spirit of God is strong, but sometimes the flesh is weak. For the past thirty years, I have always preached to follow the spirit, not the man. The evidence against Pastor Reynolds looks overwhelming, but I will get to the bottom of this. In one week, I will let you know Holy Faith's decision. I would like to thank everyone for coming out today. To my guests and loyal and faithful members, I am so sorry. To my deacons and to the elders of this great church, please meet me in my office."

Jeff and I looked at each other, speechless. But we were thinking the same thing. What was going to happen when our own dirt came to light, would it set us free or set us up?

55

DONALD

I nervously walked into the pastor's office. I had never been so embarrassed in all my life. My head was pounding and sweat was popping out all over me. My heart pounded so hard I thought I was having a heart attack.

Pastor Cash entered his office a few minutes behind me and sat behind his desk. He reached up and took off his collar and wiped his face with a large handkerchief. I stood, unable to even think.

"Donald, please take a seat." I nervously sat down and he gave me a sympathetic stare and took a deep breath.

"Donald, I'm in shock. I don't know what to think. I know being a man of God is not easy. Everyday temptation is presented to you. Everyday lies and rumors are told about you and accusations are always made against you. But I never expected scandal in my house."

"I know Good Pastor," I said timidly, "I know."

"Your life should be an open book. It should be able to withstand public scrutiny." He paused for a moment.

"Right now, what's done is done. If I'm going to defend you or stand up for you I want you to tell me the unfiltered truth regardless of how ugly it is."

He got up and poured me a glass of water from a pitcher on his credenza. I drank nervously. I cleared my throat. I tried to conjure up a strong voice, but all that came out was a childish squeak.

"First of all Pastor, I didn't voluntarily step down from Divine Baptist Church. I was forced to step down or go to jail."

"Please explain, Donald."

I took a hard swallow. "What happened was I got caught up in a love triangle with an underage member. Angie Brown."

I told him all the details right up until the time Angie had disappeared from the hotel room with that damned disk.

Pastor Cash asked questions and kept my rambling tale on track. I told him about breaking it off with Angie but going back to her like it was a sickness in me. "Pastor, I couldn't let her go. I would often misinterpret the Bible and use the word of God to manipulate or control her."

When I finished, Pastor Cash looked at me from across his desk. He steepled his fingers beneath his chin and asked. "What about Ashley. Didn't she ever suspect?"

"I think Ashley suspected, but she never confronted me about my affairs. She just looked the other way and prayed to God that one day I would stop.

"Pastor, as the years passed, Angie turned into a beautiful young woman. In an effort to atone for my sins against her, I introduced her to her husband, Wayne. He was a doctor, and came from a wealthy family. He was so grateful he gave the church twenty prime acres of real estate. We built a church that could hold 15,000 people.

"When construction fell behind, I used Ashley's money and Wayne mortgaged his properties and dug even deeper in his own pocket to help keep us from going under. I felt so bad, Pastor. He wanted to make my dreams a reality and I couldn't keep my hands off his wife.

"Each Sunday, I preached before a standing room only crowd. The church grew and my influence grew, and the devil tightened his hold on me. My lust and my temptation grew."

"How did you lose your ministry, Donald?"

"About six months after the new church was built, four women accused me of sexual misconduct. I was even accused of coercing them into having sex with visiting evangelists."

"Did you do it?"

"Yes, I did," I said hanging my head.

"Pastor Cash, it seemed that Satan had me in his grip. I was spinning out of control. Ashley and Angie weren't enough. I wanted variety. One of the women I had my eye on was the daughter of a church elder. She was about fifteen. She wanted to be a model. She was certainly beautiful enough. I'd known her family through the church and one day her parents came to me for counseling. After several sessions they brought their daughter to me. She developed a crush on me. I was very attracted to her. She was a model student, a cheerleader at her high school. I talked to her about her family problems and she grew dependant on me. We became very close."

"How close?" Pastor Cash asked.

"She started wearing those short skirts and high heels and flirting with me. I know it was in all innocence on her part. She was just coming into womanhood. I used that. I would take her to Piedmont Park and have sex in the back of the car. That was our thing. I would often ask her to stoop down so she couldn't be seen. We loved to have sex in the back of South DeKalb Mall or in back of the school. Even at the church graveyard.

"One night our luck ran out. We were at the high school and I'd given her a little alcohol."

"You gave alcohol to a minor?"

"Yes, I did. She had begun to pull away from me and become distant and difficult. I think she was regretting our affair and realized how wrong it was. I thought the alcohol would help her relax, but that night I think guilt overwhelmed her. So I forced myself on her."

"You raped a minor?"

"I didn't think of it as rape. We'd been having an affair for months. I convinced myself that she had initiated it by flirting with me. But, yes, I forced her. I was about to pull up my pants when a DeKalb police officer knocked on the window. The window was fogged up so we were able to get our clothes back on. I rolled down the window and he asked to see my ID. He shined the light on both of us. She sat with her head forward, her hair shielding her face. It turned out he was a member of my church. I told him I was helping her with a personal problem, but he wasn't buying it. She never looked up or said a word. He asked her if she was all right. She looked up then and he asked her again if she was okay. She told him she was fine. Finally the officer left."

"What happened to the young lady?"

"After the cop left, she started slapping me and crying. She kept screaming that I'd raped her. I finally got her calmed down and took her home. I told her she needed to keep this quiet because I was her minister. I used the same tricks with her that I used with Angie. Quoting the Bible and telling her it was her idea. Brainwashing her really. I never saw her again after that. She refused to come to church and eventually her parents stopped coming. Time passed and I thought it was over. She went on to become a supermodel. She is married to another of my closest friends. He never suspected a thing. I didn't have the heart to tell him that I was the cause of most of the problems he has with his wife."

The pastor gave me a sorrowful glance.

"What's the young lady's name, Donald?"

I hung my head again and cleared my throat. Tears began to flow again and I wiped my eyes with my fingertips.

"Beverly Montgomery, sir."

I broke down and cried like a baby. "Oh God, I have brought such shame to the pulpit!" I wailed in misery. "Lord, please forgive me!"

The pastor came around his desk and embraced me. "Donald, it's going to be okay. Right now you must confess your sins before God, before man and ask forgiveness."

"There's more Pastor. I have to tell you this now. Stories started circulating about me around the church. Beverly's father found out and threatened to sue the church. I paid him off by my stealing church funds and mortgaging everything Ashley and I owned. That was when the church finally asked me to resign or face criminal charges. Pastor, I stole money from Holy Faith too. I was planning on paying it back before you found out. I needed to buy Ashley a diamond ring and mink coat."

Pastor Cash sat down heavily on the edge of his desk and ran his hand over his face.

"Donald, of all the churches in Atlanta, why did you choose Holy Faith? You know I don't allow mess like this in my church."

"Good Pastor, I knew you were truly a man of God. I was hoping that you could rid me of my demons. You became a father to me. You saw the good in me and believed in me. I just couldn't tell you about my past. I was so ashamed. A lot of members from my old church followed me here, including Angie and Wayne. I thought that since so many people had faith in me, since you had faith in me, I could rise above my past. But I couldn't." Tears threatened to choke me. I took a deep breath.

"Good Pastor, I'm so sorry. I will make it right. I promise, I will make it right."

56

The minute I arrived home all hell broke loose. Ashley came at me with a cold slap that threw me off balance. My head was ringing like church bells. "You hypocrite, Donald, I can't believe you!"

When I recovered I noticed that three vases were broken and shattered lamps lay everywhere. There were three packed suitcases sitting next to the door. Ashley was out of control. I sought refuge in a corner.

"I've never been so embarrassed in all my life! This is what I get for being faithful to you?"

She threw another vase. I cowered in the corner and covered my face from flying glass. She stepped in and backhanded me across the face. Then she grabbed me around the throat and started choking me. "You dog, I hate you!" She screamed wildly.

I tried to pry her hands off me. "Ashley, stop it, please stop!" I cried desperately. "I'm so sorry. Please listen, please hear me out!"

I pulled her hands behind her back. I took a deep breath to get some air. "Sweetheart, please listen. Sit down."

"Oh no, Donald. I don't want to hear anymore of your lies. I'm leaving you. Now let me go." She twisted out of my grip and stormed to the door. "I'm going to Sister Spencer's house. I want as far away from you and this house as I can get! For all I know you screwed those harlots in the bed you shared with me."

Out of the blue, she ran towards me and kicked me hard in the balls. As she ran to the door she screamed, "Try and fuck a bitch now." She left the door standing wide open as she picked up her suitcases and left.

The cold air spilling in from the door revived me slightly. I crawled to the door begging, "Ashley, please come back." But she was already pulling out of the driveway. She almost hit a car that passed her in the street. The car turned in the driveway and the fellows got out. They came into the house and saw me lying on the floor.

"Donald, what happened here?" Jeff said as he helped me to a chair.

"I think she broke something," I said cradling my balls.

"Are you okay?" Quentin said.

"I'll live man."

"What happened, Donald?" Antonio said as he looked around at the wreckage.

"Sweet, little Ashley blew a fuse and kicked me in the balls." I coughed a few times to ease the pain. I turned my back on the fellows to check for any major damage. "Everything is still in one piece," I said turning back around. I tried to walk off the pain. "Since I'm up, do any of you want a drink?" I said in an agonized whisper.

Quentin declined, but Jeff and Peter wanted a double. Jeff walked over to help.

"Man, what in the hell were you thinking, Quentin?" Jeff blasted. "Why did you have to put all of our fucking business in the street? Now the whole damn world knows our dirty laundry."

"Look how fucked up Donald's life is right now," Antonio interjected. "He's going to be the lead story on every news station and front page news. CNN and Nancy Grace are going to have a field day!"

Jeff yelled angrily, "Whose going to be next Quentin, who is going to be publicly humiliated next. Me, Peter? You can rest assured it damn well isn't going to be the great Quentin Banks."

"Fellows, I'm so sorry," Quentin said quietly.

"Sorry my ass," Peter said spitting fire. "It's too late to be sorry now."

"I promise I'll make it up to you," Quentin pleaded.

"How can you make it up to us?" Peter clenched his fists. "It is too late to close the barn door, the horses are already loose."

Jeff turned on Antonio. "It's all your fault, Antonio!"

"My fault!" Antonio exclaimed.

"Yeah, your fault. You and your blind ambition. It was you who convinced us to participate in this charade. We only did it to help you out." Jeff looked at Antonio coldly and then hit below the belt. "You sold out your own people, so what the hell do you care about your friends?"

Antonio jumped in Jeff's face, angry. "I know you are not talking about selling out. I have known your sorry ass for ten long years. I noticed all of your women are light, bright and damn near white. Before you found Beverly you dated predominately white girls. There was not one dark-skinned sister in your stable. You are color struck and have a problem being black!"

They got closer, clenching their fists. "So you say I'm color struck?" Jeff snapped.

"Hey man, I just call it the way I see it. A hit dog always barks. Since the gloves fit, I can't acquit – OJ!"

Peter jumped in between them. "Cool out on the testosterone. This is not a pissing contest. Right now, all of our balls are in a sling."

Still fighting among themselves the fellows moved to the door and walked out. I could hear them arguing all the way down the walk. Then car doors slammed, and the engine started up and they were gone.

Pressure was building in my head. "Lord, how did I get myself in this mess?" I mumbled to myself.

I walked about the mess that was my living room. "Think Donald, think. There has to be a way out of this." I felt as though I was walking my last mile. I had no idea what tomorrow would bring, although I was fairly sure the police would be involved. I threw my glass at the mirror, completing the carnage.

I sank to my knees in the rubble. "I've lost everything," I cried. "I've lost my reputation, my position, my wife and I may even be brought up on criminal charges." Hearing myself say it out loud hammered my position home.

I slammed down a couple more drinks and the room started to spin. I swiped the stuff off the couch and laid down. I just wanted to escape into sleep. The moment I got horizontal, I passed out.

57

What seemed like hours of sleep was only about thirty minutes. I needed something to drink and I needed to think. Somehow I had to get out of this mess. I poured myself a vodka and tonic.

The doorbell rang. I looked at the clock. It was 11:13 p.m. and dark as pitch out. Who could that be? Thinking one of the fellows forgot something I looked out the window and didn't see anybody. I walked over to the door and looked out the peephole. Nobody was there.

I turned and started to go upstairs when the doorbell rang again. I staggered back to the door. "Who's there?" I asked. When there was no answer, I looked out the peephole and saw the silhouette of a woman. I strained my eyes and Ashley came into focus.

I eagerly open the door. "Baby, sweetheart, you came home!" I started to kiss her, but she roughly pulled away. As she came into the light I could see her swollen, bloodshot eyes. She'd been crying and drinking, heavily.

"I'm so sorry," I said as she closed the door. "Can you ever forgive me? Those other women didn't mean a thing. I love only you."

"That is not what you said on the little porn flick you made with that whore. You're a liar Donald. Everyone in the whole church saw it. I can never show my face there again. I'm so embarrassed."

I tried to comfort her. "Calm down, Ashley, please let's talk."

"How could you Donald? How could you do this to us? I gave you fifteen years of my life. I tried to be the perfect preacher's wife to you. I gave up my dreams to nurture your dreams. This is how you repay me? You tell someone who hadn't done anything for you that you can't stand making love to your wife. How long have you been feeling that way?" Tears flowed down her face. "If that was a problem," she sobbed, "All you had to do, Donald, was talk to me."

I walked over to her and tried to touch her.

"Keep your hands off me," she spat, jumping away. "I can't stand for you to touch me. That DVD you made goes around and around in my head. You had your face between another woman's legs, for God's sake. You are a sick, dirty bastard. I want to puke. I hate you! I hate you!" She looked crazed, her eyes swinging from one side of the room to the other. She licked her lips constantly.

"Ashley, I am weak. The devil got a hold of me! Please, baby, calm down."

She spoke angrily, but coherently. "Donald, do you know what the sad thing is? I never once cheated on you. I had many opportunities, but I took our marriage vows seriously." She shook her head violently from side to side. "I took our religion seriously. Donald, what happened to you? I thought you would be a great man. But instead of being a prince in the pulpit, you were just another pimp in the pulpit."

Her body swayed, as if she was standing on the deck of a pitching ship. She reached into her purse and pulled out a gun and pointed it at my chest.

The blood in my veins froze. "Ashley, what are you doing? Put down the gun baby." My feet finally moved and I backed away, holding my hands up in front of me. "Someone may get hurt, baby."

"Someone may get hurt?" She chuckled eerily. "Donald, so many innocent people have already gotten hurt and it is all because of you. I know two wrongs don't make a right, but two wrongs do make us even. You are not going to damn anymore of God's children to hell. You will go there alone. Goodbye Donald, say hello to Satan for me!"

I watched her pull the trigger in slow motion. My heart pounded and I saw my life flash before my eyes. It was not a good life.

Hot fire ripped through my chest and I smelled the acrid stench of gunpowder. "No Ashley! No!" My mind shouted, but no words ever left my lips. The impact of the bullet hurled me against the couch. I put my hand to my chest. I could feel the hole. My blood covered my hand. I looked at the ceiling and started to cough. I was dying. With every last bit of strength I had in me I whispered, "Ashley, please call 911."

She stood over me, staring. Her eyes were bright with a crazy light. She raised the gun again and pointed it at my head. I couldn't say anything; my life was running out of me. She pulled the trigger. God must have had his hand on both of us. The only sound was the click of an empty chamber. She looked at her hand clutching the gun as if it didn't belong to her and slowly released the gun. It fell to the floor, hitting the carpet with a dull thud. She turned and walked to the telephone and dialed 911.

58

ASHLEY

"Is this 911?" I sobbed hysterically.

"Yes, it is. What is your emergency?" The operator said calmly.

"This is Ashley Reynolds. I am the wife of Pastor Donald Reynolds of Holy Faith Church. I'd like to report a shooting." I could hear my toneless voice. I felt devoid of emotion. I knew I'd just shot my husband, but I was completely disconnected from it.

"Ma'am, who has been shot?"

"My husband. He's been shot."

"What is your address, ma'am?"

West Paces Ferry Road. Two doors down from the Governor's mansion."

"I have someone in route to you now, ma'am."

"Thank you, please hurry."

"Ma'am, the police are on the way also. Do you know who shot your husband? Is the assailant still there?"

"Yes, ma'am. The assailant is still in the house."

"Ma'am, try to get to a safe place in the house. I will stay on the phone with you until the police arrive."

"I'm not in any danger. I shot my husband." I broke down into tears finally. "I'll be here when you arrive."

"Ma'am, the police will be there in five minutes." I became aware of the wail of sirens. "Ma'am, are you there?"

"Yes, I'm here."

"Ma'am, you need to put down the gun, do you understand, put the gun down."

"Yes, I understand."

"Okay, have you put the gun down?"

"I dropped it on the floor. I don't know where it is."

"That's fine ma'am. Go to the door and open it slowly and step outside and raise your hands."

I put the phone down and walked to the door, doing what the emergency operator requested. I saw a dozen police cars and emergency vehicles, pulling haphazardly on the front lawn. Cops jumped out of their cars and moved behind their cars with gun drawn. I raised my hands high in the air. I looked behind me at Donald. He was clutching his chest, his breathing strained and ragged. The police ran up the stoop and pulled my hands behind me and cuffed me. The EMTs ran in the house and started working on Donald.

As they locked the cuffs around my wrist I asked Donald, "Why did you have to do that to all those other women? Why?"

59

DONALD

We were in the ambulance rushing down the interstate. The siren wail was a mournful sound in my ears. The ambulance hit a bump and I started coughing. I felt a new wall of pain hit me.

"We're losing him." I heard a voice say.

The ambulance screeched to a halt in the emergency bay at Grady Hospital. I thought to myself that I didn't want to die. I started making deals with God. "Oh, Lord, please forgive me. I don't want to die. Give me one more chance and I promise I will change."

They unloaded me from the ambulance. A doctor jumped on the gurney and started resuscitation as they rolled me down a long corridor to a medical room. I felt the shock of a defibrillator burn through my chest. I could feel my spirit leaving my body. I looked down upon a scene of utter chaos as the staff rushed around my body, trying to restore life. I could see the doctor leaning over me, pushing my chest up and down. He was fighting to save me and I could hear him talking to me. "You are not going to die on my watch. Do you hear me? Lord, don't let this man die a sinner. I forgive him. Please God!"

I noticed a small gold cross bouncing on the end of a chain as he pumped my heart. I felt peace for the first time in a very, very long time. I felt myself being pulled down a long tunnel. At the end of that tunnel was a brilliant white light. It was warm and welcoming. I wanted to go to the light more than I've ever wanted anything in my life. I could see someone sitting on what appeared to be a throne. I knew that if I could just get to that throne, all my troubles would be over. Golden angels surrounded the throne. Beautiful, serene faces beckoned me to peace. There were many people waiting at the feet of the omnipotent being seated upon the throne. My spirit came close to him. A golden light shown from him and bathed my spirit in tranquility. A voice touched with the song of God said to me, "Donald, it is not time. You have much work to do. Go back. Make peace with your brothers and sisters and sin no more."

I was pulled back down the tunnel and found myself in the room where the doctor still worked frantically over my body. I felt a sharp tug and then I heard the beep of the monitors.

"He's back." I heard someone say in astonishment. Totally exhausted the doctor slumped over my body.

"Thank you Lord," he said simply.

I fought to open my eyes. As the room swam into focus, I looked in the eyes of Dr. Wayne Brown, Angie's husband. He gave me a weak smile and said, "Welcome back, Pastor."

I was weak and my throat was parched. I could barely croak out the words. "I'm happy that you are a bigger man than me. If the shoe were on the other foot I think I would have let you die." Tears ran from the corners of my eyes into my hair. They felt like angel kisses. I forced my arm up and clasped Wayne's hand. "Please forgive me for the hurt and pain I have caused you and your wife."

He looked down at me, compassion softening his eyes. "You are forgiven brother. You once had a head full of knowledge of God. Now, you have a heart full of knowledge of the Lord. You are now a God-fearing man."

60

ANTONIO

I woke the next morning after that debacle at Holy Faith with a hangover. Donald was immediately on my mind. "What were you thinking Donald?" I thought to myself.

As I prepared my breakfast, I turned on the TV in the kitchen for the news.

"Hello, this is Brenda Wood, with an exclusive. Scandal in the pulpit...Donald Reynolds, Assistant Pastor at Holy Faith Non-Denominational Church was rushed to Grady Hospital last night after suffering a gunshot wound to the chest. His assailant, his wife of fifteen years, Ashley Reynolds, was detained by the Fulton County Police.

"His wife has been closed mouthed about the motives behind the shooting but our sources have revealed that the shooting happened following revelations that Pastor Reynolds had fathered children by two different women from his congregation. He is listed in stable, but critical condition after undergoing surgery.

"Ashley Reynolds was released early this morning on a fifty thousand dollar bond. Pastor Cash, senior pastor of Holy Faith was not available for comment.

"This incident follows on the heels of the scandal that occurred at Holy Faith during their thirty year anniversary celebration..."

I stood in shock. Ashley shot Donald! The phone rang and I picked it up.

"Antonio, this is Quentin. Are you watching the news?"

"Yeah man, I just heard it." My telephone began to click, indicating another call. "Hold on Quentin. I've got to answer the other line."

I clicked over and answered. It was Peter.

"Antonio, are you watching the news?" he asked. "Did you hear about Donald?"

"Yeah, I've got Quentin on the other line."

"Call me back as soon as you're finished with him."

"I will Peter." I switched back to Quentin. "You still there?"

"Yes Antonio."

"That was Peter. He just heard about it too."

"Antonio, I am so sorry," he apologized again. "I feel that everything is my fault. If I hadn't betrayed you guys, none of this would have happened."

"Quentin, I am angry at you, but it is not entirely your fault. We are all at fault. If we hadn't put ourselves in that position to begin with, it would have never happened. We acted like a bunch of desperate husbands. Right now, we have to put our personal differences aside. Donald needs our help."

"Hey man, meet me at Grady?" he asked.

"That's a plan." I hung up the phone and called Peter back and told him to meet us there.

I was searching for my car keys when the doorbell rang. "Who could that be at a time like this?" I threw open the door and the mailman stood there with a letter in his hand.

"Are you Antonio Fernando?" he asked.

"Yes." I said abruptly. "I am."

"I have a certified letter for you. Please sign right here."

I took the envelope and signed. Tearing off the card and handing it back to the mailman I saw that the letter was from the law firm of Meyer and Roberts. I quickly opened the envelope. Inside was a letter from Liana.

Dear Antonio,

I feel that I can no longer live a lie. I feel that we don't want the same things right now. All I wanted and ever wanted was your love. Right now, I feel that the best gift I can give you is your freedom. I want you to pursue your dream. I guess I will do the same. I'm just sorry that our dreams are on opposite sides of the fence now. I want to go on with my life so I am asking for a divorce. My attorneys will serve you with the necessary papers within a couple of days.

Liana

The word divorce hit me in the face like a cold slap. I stumbled over to the couch and cried.

I must have dozed off. When I woke up an hour had passed. "Oh my God, I'm supposed to meet the fellows at the hospital." I found my keys, jumped in the car and headed out for Grady Hospital.

When I arrived at Grady, I double-parked and ran into the building. I asked the receptionist where I could find Donald.

"Pastor Reynolds is in ICU on the sixth floor." I quickly thanked her and rode the elevator up to the sixth floor. When I got to Donald's room, all the fellows were there. They looked like they were attending a wake. Donald had on a full oxygen mask forcing air into his lungs. There were IV tubes running from both arms. There were monitor wires running from underneath his gown in all directions, and machines were beeping. Underneath his gown was a big pad of dressing where they had performed the surgery to remove the bullet Ashley had plugged him with. He was awake, but in obvious pain, in spite of the morphine drip. His gray face was skeletal and the smile he gave me was more of a grimace.

"Hey man, what took you so long?" He said lifting the mask to talk.

"Sorry Donald, I got stuck in traffic. Man, you are hurting. Why don't you ask them to turn that thing up?" I said, indicating the morphine.

"Ah, no man, I need to feel some pain. Otherwise how would I know I'm alive? It's a small price to pay for the things I've done."

"So how are you feeling?"

"I'll live. I really made a mess of things. Am I being roasted in the media? I am a disgrace to the Lord. My church-going wife tried to kill me, but besides that everything is great.

"It's going to be okay Donald," Peter said.

"Yeah, I'll live but right now I don't know if that's a good or bad thing."

"Don't talk like that," Quentin said. A tear formed in the corner of his eye and ran down his cheek. "You will make it through this. The Bible says this too shall pass. God has forgiven you."

"The Lord may forgive me, but what about man? They are talking about bringing me up on criminal charges. There's a lot of pissed off people out there."

Peter said, "Fellows, I think it's time we go. Donald is getting tired and needs his rest."

We made our farewells to Donald, but his eyes had closed and he'd drifted off to sleep.

I looked at Peter and Quentin. "I have some bad news, guys."

They both looked at me with concern. I took a deep breath and ran my hands through my hair.

"Liana asked me for a divorce."

"I'm sorry man," Peter said, placing his hand on my shoulder. "We are a sorry bunch aren't we? I told Jan I wanted a divorce and I told her about Bridgett."

"Oh man, we are in a pickle," I commiserated.

The nurse walked in and told us it was time to leave. As we boarded the elevator, we talked about Donald's dilemma and how messy our lives had become.

"Fellows, if our situation wasn't so sad, it would be funny," Peter joked.

"I would love to laugh to keep from crying," I interjected. "We were once bound by friendship, but now we are bound by fear and scandal."

Jeff let out a long sigh. "Looks like we are the poster boys for the 30305. Quentin picked the right title for his book. We truly are a bunch of *Desperate Husbands.*"

61

JEFF

I went straight home after I left the hospital. Beverly met me at the door. She had been an emotional wreck all week.

"Jeff, did you hear what happened to your friend, Donald?"

"Yeah, I just came from the hospital. Donald is doing okay, considering."

"I can't believe it," she said hysterically, "Ashley actually shot him. She isn't a killer. She wouldn't hurt a fly!" Beverly wrung her hands nervously.

I kissed her gently on the cheek. "The doctor said he's going to be all right. The worst is over. Now he just has to heal."

The TV was on in the living room and I settled in to watch the news. Beverly came in and sat on the opposite end of the couch. I surfed through the channels and Donald was the lead story on all the local channels and a few of the national ones.

Beverly was watching me. I began to grow uncomfortable under her gaze. She was looking at me suspiciously. Finally she said, "A lot of people are saying that Donald is Pastor Hayes in Quentin's book."

"I think everyone is upset over nothing," I said as off-handedly as I could.

"Upset over nothing? Are you kidding Jeff?" She exploded at me. "A minister's wife tries to kill her husband and you call that nothing? He impregnates two women of his congregation and you call that nothing? It just so happens that the minister's best friend gives sordid details of what happened in his damn book just before everything hits the fan. Jeff, that is more than mere coincidence."

I got up and went to the bar to make myself a drink. Beverly came up behind me and grabbed my collar. "Jeff, tell me the truth. Are you Bob, the pilot, in Quentin's book? Is that book based on the past exploits of all of you? Did you all make a secret pact not to reveal these scandalous secrets?"

Okay, it was now time to pay the piper. Will the truth set me up or set me free? I poured a large measure of Jack Daniel into a glass and watched the amber liquid swirl around. I sat on a bar stool and looked at Beverly levelly.

Beverly had worked herself up into the rant and rave stage. "Stop lying Jeff. The gig is up. You are busted. Now tell me the truth. Are you Bob?"

"Beverly, please don't ask me that. A lot of people will get hurt."

"A lot of people have already gotten hurt, Jeff. Your best friend almost got killed. I already know about the tape. Bridgett has it. She wouldn't tell me what was on it because of loyalty to Quentin, but the truth is there. But she did tell me about the things Quentin said about her. So why don't you tell me and make it easier on all of us."

"Get real, Jeff. You guys are all partners in crime. If he spilled his guts, I know the rest of you did too. So, are you going to tell me the truth or do I have to find out about my husband like Ashley did? Please spare me the embarrassment."

I took a long gulp and felt it burn its way down. "Sweetheart, you are asking me to betray my friends. You are asking me to break a promise I made to them."

"Well, nobody else kept their promise did they? Look at Quentin. He put everybody's business in the street, and made a ton of money on it. He gave up every fucking man in the United States. I don't understand man's logic. He rats you out, but you remain loyal. But I'm not asking for you to tell me everyone's secret. I just want to know if Bob the Pilot is you?"

I gently took her hand. "Beverly, the damage is done."

"If you tell me the truth, I won't get angry," she encouraged.

I knew that was a set up if ever I heard one, but I had no option but to come clean. She jerked her hand from mine and crossed her arms belligerently across her chest. Her foot tapped the floor impatiently. I listened to the rhythm of the tapping and it started sounding like a death march.

"Okay, Beverly. You win. I'm Bob, in Quentin's stupid book. I screwed my senior flight attendant."

"I knew it!" She erupted. "I knew it was you, you bastard." She slapped me so hard I felt it all the way down to my toes.

"How can I ever trust you again? Get out, Jeff, just pack your bags and get the hell out of here."

"But honey, you told me you wouldn't get mad."

She gave a sarcastic chuckle, "Jeff, in life, sometimes the truth will set you up. You've betrayed your wife and now you've betrayed your best friend. Speaking of friends, if I were you I'd be very careful of who you called a friend."

"What are you talking about?"

"Just what I said. Be careful who you call a friend."

Curiosity burned inside me over that one. "If you have something to say why don't you just spit it out? I don't have the patience for oblique comments."

"Jeff, it is something I don't want to talk about," she snapped.

"Ooooh, I hate it when someone does that!"

She began to shake as if she were freezing. She hugged her arms tightly around herself and tears welled in her eyes. I became very concerned about her.

"Beverly, tell me what's wrong. Are you okay? Talk to me." I said as I gripped her arms. I tried to comfort her. She put her hands over her face and sobbed.

"I can't tell you. I promised I'd never tell anyone, but I can't forget the past."

I held her tighter, trying to shelter her from whatever storm was brewing inside her. "It's okay, baby."

She buried her head in my chest. Faintly, her voice muffled, she began to speak. Frankly, I was prepared for almost anything but what she said.

"Donald raped me."

"What?" I held her away from me. "I know you are not serious!"

"Donald raped me, Jeff."

62

I was incredulous. On one hand it couldn't be true, but I knew in my heart of hearts that on the other hand, it very well could be. I moved Beverly over to the couch and we sat. Tearfully, she told me the story of when Donald was the Pastor of the church she went to as a teenager.

When Beverly finished telling the details of her assault, I wanted to kill my best friend. To hell with loyalty. I could have happily put another bullet in him if he'd been standing in front of me. I couldn't believe Donald's complete lack of restraint. I know I encouraged his exploits and laughed at his stories. But, damn, this is my wife we're talking about. He should have told me and let me beat him to a pulp years ago. If a man can't control himself, he definitely shouldn't control others and this was a man the church looked to lead them through the tricky waters of life.

"Jeff, that experience has affected every aspect of my life. Our marriage suffered, my walk with the Lord suffered. Jeff, I know from reading that damn book that you were tremendously affected, because every time you made love to me, I relived that rape. You became Donald. All I could do was grit my teeth and pray it'd be over soon. I'm so sorry, Jeff."

"Sweetheart, I wish you could have come to me long ago, instead of telling me this now."

"Well, I've had to understand it myself first. Donald was your friend. I didn't know what to do, so I said nothing."

The more she talked the angrier I became. I clenched my fists and I could feel the muscle in my jaw working from gritting my teeth. I was glad Donald was in the hospital because I wanted to make sure Donald stayed there a good, long time.

"Jeff." Beverly whispered to me. "I don't want you to tell anyone about this. I'm trusting you to keep my secret. What is said between a man and his wife or vice versa should be kept strictly between the two of them."

I reached for her and hugged her tight, with more feeling than I'd felt in a long time. For the first time in my memory I wanted to protect this woman, but I didn't have a clue how to go about it.

"Jeff, I need some time alone. I have a lot of things to sort out. Will you leave, please?"

I was dazed. I didn't want to leave under the circumstances, but oddly enough, I understood Beverly's reasoning. I just prayed that time would heal the wounds.

Reluctantly, I packed a bag and went to Quentin's tiny apartment.

63

When I arrived at Quentin's, Peter was already camped out on the couch. I threw my bag on the floor next to Peter's.

"Why aren't you at your apartment in town?" I asked Peter.

"It's full of VIP's that came in for a conference," Peter said, as he carefully tore the top off a bag of peanuts.

It was a real Kodak moment. Three guys crammed into a tiny apartment, wifeless. It was something to see. The great Peter McCallister crashing on a broken down couch.

"Peter, you really went out like a punk. Who is really wearing the pants in your house? You or Jan?"

He pulled back the covers exposing his underwear and grabbed his crotch. "I got your punk right here, pal."

Quentin was sitting at the kitchen table. His head was in his hands. "Fellows, I am so sorry. I had no idea."

"Quentin, if you apologize one more time, so help me, I'll pimp slap you. Just give me a blanket and don't wake me up in the morning."

I made myself a pallet on the floor and settled in. I could barely stretch out my legs.

"Quentin, if I threw down a handkerchief on this small ass floor you'd mistake it for wall to wall carpet. Just think, not that long ago, like twenty minutes ago, I was in a posh Buckhead crib. I may have been miserable, but at least I was comfortable. But no, Top Gun couldn't leave well enough alone. I had to tell my business to a John Grisham wannabe. Instead of upholding the male code of silence, what does he do? He sings like a canary!"

I gritted my teeth. "If that's not bad enough, my wife tells me she's been raped by my best friend. Instead of me taking pleasure in beating the living shit out of him, I have to turn the other cheek because his wife got to him first. Shit!"

"What?" Quentin said.

"Yeah, Beverly just told me Donald raped her when she was a teenager. She's carried this inside her and never said a word. Shit!" I exclaimed again.

"Jeff, it's your own fault," Peter replied popping another peanut into his mouth.

"My fault?" I said with anger boiling to the surface. "I just tried to do the right thing!"

Peter laughed bitterly. "I know you didn't just say you were trying to do the right thing. Jeff, sometimes doing the right thing is the wrong damn thing to do."

I rose up on one elbow and looked over at Peter. "Is your brain not getting enough oxygen because of a stuck peanut?"

"Damn it, Jeff, you should have lied."

"Are you saying that honesty is not the best policy? Am I hearing you right?"

"No Jeff." Peter said patiently, "Honesty is a foreign policy."

"Man, you are talking smack."

"Haven't you ever wondered why some men stay married forever and other marriages barely manage to get off the ground before they crash and burn?"

"No Peter, I really haven't, but since we're on the subject I suppose you are going to enlighten me?"

"Well, the guys who have been married for ten years or more adopt the 'Desperate Husband Rules.'"

"Okay Peter." I said, propping my head on my hand.

"Rule number one, what she doesn't know won't hurt her or you. Rule number two, when in doubt - lie. Rule number three, you are only wrong if you get caught.

"Men didn't fault Bill Clinton or New York's former governor, Governor Spitzer, for their indiscretions. They faulted them for getting caught. What the hell were they thinking? When your wife says she needs to talk, apologize immediately. Usually what is going to follow is something you forgot to do or need to do."

"Uh huh, uh huh." I said with exasperation, but nodded my head in agreement.

"Jeff, it is a big no-no to go somewhere fun without telling her. Once you are married, you can forget places like Hawaii, Paris, Rio or Rome with your buddies. If you happen to go on a business trip to places known for beautiful, exotic women and she asks you if you had any fun, the answer is always, no, I worked like a dog and I thought of you every day."

A sly grin creased my face and I thought to myself that this old geezer has game.

"Jeff, you should never come home feeling good after a night out with the fellows. This is a dead give away that other women were involved. Marriage, unhappiness and agony go hand in hand. If you want to feel good, you should get yourself a dog and stay single."

"I totally disagree," Quentin butted in. "I think marriage should be based on honesty."

Peter and I looked at him angrily. "Jeff, did Quentin have the audacity to use the word *think?*"

"He sure did."

"If you were thinking..." Peter yelled.

"We wouldn't be in this fucking mess!" I screamed.

"If we want your lame ass opinion, we'll ask for it!" Peter said in a low voice.

Quentin put his head down on the table and mumbled. "Sorry, I was only trying to help."

"Help my aunt's fanny." Peter said. "If I'm in the woods fighting a bear and the bear is beating the crap out of me, don't help. Give the bear a knife." He was breathing heavily. "Where was I...?

"Oh yeah...Rule number four for a long, unhappy marriage. If she asks you 'does this dress make me look fat', the correct answer is always no. She could look like Moby Dick but the answer is always no. If she insists, tell her that her butt isn't too big at all, but that the stupid designer made the dress too small in her size." Peter laid back against the pillow and threw his arm across his forehead blocking out the dim light from the ceiling.

"Now Jeff, other important rules to follow are to get your lies straight, those who have the gold make the rules, marriage is a misunderstanding between two fools and have your alibi together."

Peter let out a big yawn. "That is all for tonight. I'm going to sleep. Good night and don't let the divorce lawyers bite."

64

The following morning I was up bright and early. The floor and my back had been at war all night. Peter was already in the only bathroom. It seemed like it took him an hour to get out. I sat on the couch pressing my knees together and seriously considering the bushes outside. "Come on Peter, I need to pee and I have to be at the airport by 9:00a.m."

"I'll be out in an hour," he yelled through the door. I could hear him gargling.

"Man, you never know people until you live with them."

I checked my watch and it was 7:18a.m. "Peter, I'm going to be late. What's going on in there?"

"I'm brushing my teeth. I have to brush each one 40 times."

I'm not real good with math without a calculator, but since he had 32 teeth I figured he'd be in there for a while. Who came up with that crazy ass rule anyway, Barney the dinosaur or the gay tooth fairy?

"I'll be out in a minute. Cool your jets. Do a few calisthenics!" He shouted around the toothpaste in his mouth. "Loosen up. You are too stressed. Go to anger management classes."

"No, you didn't go there," I fired back.

After 45 minutes of trading insults and watching the world float by on a full bladder, he finally exited the bathroom.

"It's all yours big boy."

I almost knocked him down getting to the bathroom. After I took a fifteen-minute pee, I jumped in the shower. The water was cold.

"Quentin, there's no hot water. Just Peter's hot air!" I hollered.

"I heard that!" Peter yelled back.

"Sorry, Jeff," Quentin yelled. "Peter must have used it all. Take a cold shower, it is good for you."

"Bullshit!" I exploded. "Why don't you get a new crib. You sure as hell can afford it now. You got a 200K Bentley parked outside and you still live in this dump? Is this ghetto fabulous or what?"

It didn't take me long to finish my cold ass shower. I shaved and brushed my pearly whites quickly, dressed and ran out the door. I jumped into my Porsche and headed out to I-20 East for the airport. As always, the drive was bumper to bumper. I was pissed off at Quentin, Peter and Donald, but a more pressing problem was how to get Beverly back. I'd never seen her so upset and I didn't know what to do to fix things. Maybe giving her a little space and time would do that and things would get back to normal. As I thought about it, I turned on the radio. I selected an oldies, but goodies station. "Good Morning Atlanta, this is Tom Joyner. Here is a blast from the past. Michael Jackson and 'Who's Lovin' You'..." The music cued in and I listened to the words, probably for the first time ever.

> *When I had you*
> *I treated you bad and wrong, my dear*
> *And girl since, since you went away*
> *Don't you know I sit around*
> *With my head hanging down*
> *And I wonder who's lovin' you.*

Those words hit me like a cold slap and I thought to hell with cooling off. If I don't do something quick, another man may get my stuff. I turned down the radio and called Beverly. The phone rang several times before she answered it.

"What do you want Jeff?" she said wearily.

"I really need to talk to you, honey."

"About what Jeff? About screwing your best friend's fiancée? About how I lay there like a log when we have sex? About you being insensitive when your wife told you about being raped by your friend? Or maybe you want to talk about you, the big asshole I'm now wondering why I ever married?"

Her words cut through me like a hot knife, and I could only bite my tongue. What else could I do? I got busted big time. So I had no choice but to listen as she dragged my ego over hot coals.

"Beverly, I'm sorry. I messed up."

"Jeff, I don't want any of your lame ass apologies. I've had it with you and I've had it with this marriage."

I swallowed hard. "Please, Beverly, you don't mean that."

"Yes I do Jeff. All I want, at this time in my life, is a man I can trust, a man that wants me and only me."

Silence filled the phone. Finally I said, rather lamely, "Maybe I picked a bad time to call sweetheart."

"Sweetheart! I know you didn't just call me sweetheart. How many other bitches do you call that? How many other woman have you fucked from here to Rio? Jeff, it's over. I've got to go, Jeff. I've got a doctor's appointment. I need to get checked out to make sure you haven't passed some disease on to me."

She hung up abruptly. I sat there listening to dead air. I finally flipped my phone closed and turned the radio back up. My stuff is raggedy I thought. What the hell was I thinking? Why did I cheat when I had a good woman at home? Why didn't I try with her, try to understand that there were some other issues underneath her lack of response. Why didn't I try to be a better man to her? Why did I always go looking in the street for what I could have had at home? I started making deals with God. "Lord if I get Beverly back, I will never sleep with another woman. I'll be a good husband. I'll go to church every Sunday."

I didn't want to listen to any more oldies and punched in V103.

"Hi, this is the Frank and Wanda Morning Show. I'm Frank Ski..."

"And, I'm Wanda Smith. Our special guest today is Pastor C. A. Cash from Holy Faith Non-Denominational Church."

Frank jumped in, "All of Atlanta is talking about the scandal that erupted at Holy Faith. Our prayers go out to Pastor Reynolds, who is still in the hospital recuperating. You may remember Atlanta, two days ago Pastor Reynolds was allegedly shot by his wife Ashley. No one knows the reason for the shooting..."

"Frank, I think the reason is fairly obvious to any woman. He got two women from his congregation pregnant. That would upset me a little bit."

"Wanda, let's talk to Pastor Cash. Pastor Cash, let's not pull any punches. Is Pastor Reynolds guilty of the accusations leveled at him by women from your congregation? What are his victims planning to do? Will he be brought up on criminal charges? Is the infamous Pastor Hayes in Quentin Banks' Book *Desperate Husbands* really modeled after Pastor Reynolds?"

65

PASTOR CASH

The hosts and the audience waited anxiously to hear my response. I cleared my throat. "Frank and Wanda, before I answer these questions, I want to thank everyone for coming to our 30 year anniversary. Please reserve passing judgment until all the facts come out.

"Instead of answering your questions, Pastor Reynolds asked me to call him as soon as I got here. He wants to address any questions you might have."

As Nina, the producer, connected Donald's hospital room, the callboard lit up like a Christmas tree. Donald answered the telephone.

"This is Donald Reynolds," he said weakly.

"Hi, Donald, this is Frank Ski from V103. I'm calling from the Frank and Wanda Morning Show. We have Pastor Cash in our studio and our telephones are ringing off the hook. We are trying to get to the bottom of the accusations made against you. The main question everyone wants answered is, are you guilty of impregnating those women of the church?"

A graveyard silence filled the air. The listeners continued to call in. In a faint voice, Donald answered. "Sadly to say, I am. Angie Brown and I have been carrying on an affair for the past twelve years. And yes, the babies she's carrying are mine. I sat down with her and her husband last night. I am willing to do anything, financially or emotionally, to get them through this. Their needs and the needs of the children are my main concern.

"I would like to take this opportunity, however, to apologize not only to the members of Holy Faith Church, but all the people I have hurt along the way. The Lord says that vengeance is mine. Shortly after the incident at Holy Faith, my wife, Ashley shot me. After all the years of lies, public humiliation and infidelity, she snapped. She had a breakdown and shot me in the chest. She called the medics and police. When they arrived they arrested her. On the way to the hospital, I coded, and I died."

"What happened?" Wanda asked, mesmerized.

"When they pulled me out of the ambulance, I was dead. The doctor at the hospital worked on me to exhaustion, reviving me. Listeners, know this, so many church-going people put their trust in their ministers, but your minister is not going to get you into heaven. You must know the Lord yourself, in your heart, as well as in your mind."

"Amen to that," Wanda said quietly.

"I saw my body on that gurney in the hallway of the ER. I saw that doctor, working so hard, never giving up, as he frantically tried to revive me. I was pulled towards a warm, bright light. A magnificent being was at the end of that light. I met my maker and he told me I had to come back. He told me I had a lot of work to do and a lot of people to heal because of my actions. But I just wanted to stay in His light and face my punishment. But I had to atone for my sins."

"So what happened then?" Frank asked.

"I came back, then I opened my eyes and looked into the doctor's face. I was completely shocked," Donald said humbly.

"How come?" Wanda asked.

"The doctor that had worked so hard to save my life was Angie Brown's husband. Good Pastor, Frank and Wanda, I don't know of any greater love a man can show than for a man to give up his life for another."

Pastor Cash spoke, "Or for a man to save the life of a man that defiled his wife. Donald, if the shoe were on the other foot, would you have done the same for him?"

A long silence stretched across the line. "To be perfectly honest, before this experience, I don't think I could have turned the other cheek.

"Good Pastor, I've been a minister for most of my life, but I never truly knew the Lord until that day. The day that I died." He paused. "I met a man that lived God's word in every respect. How many of us can say that? I couldn't and can't. But, from this day forward I will live my life for the Lord. I am asking your forgiveness Atlanta and for your prayers. I most humbly ask Ashley for her forgiveness. Second to God, she is the one I have hurt most.

"Pastor Cash, you have not only been my mentor, but you've been like a father to me. You told me over and over that a man isn't able to clean up someone else's house if his own house is dirty. You told me that if a man couldn't control himself, he should not control others. When you told me these things, you had no idea what sins I had committed.

This is why, Pastor Cash, I am resigning as pastor from Holy Faith Church.

"Donald, don't you think that is a little drastic," Frank said.

"No, it is something I have to do. I can't be a minister with the sins I carry. Pastor Cash, I want to ask a big favor and a big favor of the Holy Faith members."

"What is that Donald?"

"When Holy Faith has its baptismal, I want to rededicate my life to the Lord. I've learned, finally, that the truth will always set you free. Only lies will set you up."

"Amen, Donald," Wanda said, sincerely.

"Sometimes men lie to protect women from hurt, harm or danger. But it's the lies that hurt and harm. By telling the truth, you protect those you love from all those things."

"All the men out there, I hope you are listening to this," Wanda warned.

Donald's voice grew weaker, the interview was taking a toll on him. "One more thing," he said, pain coloring his voice.

"Yes, Donald, we're listening," Pastor Cash said kindly.

"I'm sure you all have read Quentin Banks' book, *Desperate Husbands*. You probably have already guessed that I'm Pastor Hayes. In order for Donald Reynolds to be reborn, Pastor Hayes must die. I am also asking all those people I have hurt to be present at my baptism. I want each person that I've hurt to submerge me in the water. By baptizing me, it will renew their faith in me and the Lord."

"Pastor Reynolds, I will be honored to do so."

"Thank you all for your time." Donald's voice was tired and scratchy, barely audible.

"Let us go to the telephone lines," Wanda said. "Judging from the number of calls on the line, Atlanta has something to say about sex and scandal in the pulpit. Caller one, this is V103."

"Hi, this is Nicole Peterson. I am a loyal member of Holy Faith. I was one of the women abused by Pastor Reynolds. My baby is due soon. At first I was furious with Donald. I even thought of committing suicide or having an abortion. But a child is something beautiful even though it was conceived out of an unholy act. I'm happy he asked for forgiveness and found salvation. Through my own personal walk with God, I found the courage and the strength to go on. Donald wasn't totally to blame, I knew the man was married and I slept with him anyway. Whoever can turn the other cheek is truly a better person. It's his wife I really feel sorry for. I will be at Holy Faith's baptizing next month."

"Thank you Nicole," Wanda said. "Caller two, you're on the air."

"My name is Kim. I'm a member of the church too. Pastor Reynolds is not the first minister to get caught with his pants down. Look at the PTL guy, Jimmy Baker, and Jimmy Swaggart. What about all those priests in the Catholic Church molesting young boys. How about Earl Paulk, or that minister in DeKalb County. He was accused of sleeping with women in his congregation too. Even the Nation of Islam leader, Elijah Muhammad. He was married a long time, but still managed to have thirteen children by seven different women. I guess men will be men, they all make mistakes. We forgave Bill Clinton, so we can forgive Pastor Reynolds too. At least Pastor Reynolds isn't trying to cover it up. Thank you for letting me have my say."

"Caller three, you're on the air," Frank said.

"My name is Carl. I've been a loyal member of Holy Faith for fourteen years. I think it is a disgrace what Pastor Reynolds did. This is one of the main reasons why so many men are turned off with preachers, churches and the Lord. If they are not hustling for money, they are sleeping with the women. I knew he was up to no good when he was on Ryan Cameron's show. Like I said then and I'm saying it now, game recognizes game."

"Thank you Carl. Okay Atlanta, we only have time for a few more calls. Caller four, you're on the air," Frank said.

Dead silence greeted them.

"Hello, caller four, are you there? We must have lost the caller. Let's go to line five..."

At that moment a timid voice came across the line. "My name is Ashley Reynolds. I'm Donald's wife."

"Ashley, are you okay?" Wanda asked, concern lacing her voice.

"I'm all right," Ashley responded quietly. "I've been listening to the show every since you started. I called so many times but couldn't get through. I started to hang up this time."

She paused, mustering up her courage. "I just want to say to Donald, I'm so sorry I hurt you. I wanted you to feel the same hurt and pain that I felt for so long. The time Donald and I have been apart has made me realize that he made a mistake. Sins aren't little or big. Each sin is punished equally in the eyes of God. I asked the Lord to forgive me for my actions, like I forgave Donald for his. Pastor Cash, I want to ask a favor too."

"What is that Ashley?"

"When you baptize Donald, can you do the same for me?"

"I will be honored, Ashley," the pastor responded joyfully.

The producer broke in saying that Donald was back on the phone. Frank quickly connected him.

Donald's voice came over the speaker, more refreshed than before. "Ashley, I forgive you for shooting me and I'm not pressing charges against you."

"Well, I think we need to let Donald and Ashley talk privately, so Frank, if you could hook them up on a private line, we need to move on to other calls," Wanda said.

66

JEFF

"Okay, Atlanta, we have time for two more calls," Frank cautioned. "Caller five, you're on the air."

"I can't believe what I'm hearing. Are you people nuts? Everybody is just going to wave a magic wand..."

I tuned the caller out. Hearing Donald's sincerity and humility made me want to call in. I dialed the radio station, knowing that I didn't have a snow ball's chance in hell of getting through, but God must have been listening in, because I got through on the first try and the call screener put me right through when she found out who I was.

"Caller six, you're on the air."

"Pastor Cash, this is Jeff. I'm also a member of Holy Faith. I was listening to the show and I commend Pastor Reynolds for coming clean. I can't point a finger at him because I've got a few skeletons in my own closet. But the reason I'm calling is because I want to set the record straight."

"Make your peace, Jeff," Wanda said.

"The Lord blessed me with a beautiful, smart, classy wife. For so long I have not only lied to her, but I also cheated on her. Worst of all, I was completely insensitive to her needs. I destroyed my marriage, all because I wanted to do whatever I wanted, never giving a thought to my wife. All she wanted to do was make me happy and love me. She desperately wanted a child, but I didn't have time and didn't want to be tied down. I didn't want the responsibility of being a good man, a good husband, or a good father.

"Not too long ago, I told a friend some very intimate secrets about my wife and me. Unknowingly, my secret ended up in a book called *Desperate Husbands.*

Wanda broke in, "So you're that no good pilot who is sleeping with all the flight attendants! Frank, this is that guy that cheated on his wife and his best friend with his fiancée!"

"Wanda, let him finish," Frank said in a serious tone.

"Good Pastor, I betrayed our bedroom. I betrayed her trust. Fellows, take it from me, what is said between a man and a woman should stay between the two of them. Now I'm alone and have only myself to blame. I'm a victim of my own lies and games.

"Beverly, if you're listening, if I could turn back the hands of time, I would. I would go back to when I promised to love, honor and forsake all others and start over living those words with my heart and soul. I didn't know what I had until you told me it was all over."

"Oh my God, that is so sweet," Wanda gushed.

I was overcome with emotion. My voice broke with unshed tears. "As men, we often bring a lot of grief on ourselves. We think the grass is greener in someone else's backyard. All I had to do was to water and nourish my own grass. It could have grown to be just as beautiful."

"So true," Frank agreed.

"Donald, if you are still listening, Beverly told me what you did to her. I know Beverly, I promised not to tell this, but I'm in for a penny, so I might as well be in for a pound. Donald, you need to know that I know. Donald, I really wanted to kill you when I found out. But, I must forgive you. I can't ask for forgiveness myself if I'm not willing to forgive others.

"Good Pastor, I want to rededicate my love and fidelity to my beautiful wife, Beverly Montgomery. I'm no longer a desperate husband, but I am desperate for my wife to return to me. I desperately want to rekindle the marriage we once had and desperately want to start a family. If someone should ask me if I could do it all over again, would I marry Beverly, the answer would be an unequivocal yes. Without a doubt, I would marry you again.

"Beverly, if you are listening, will you marry me, again?"

"Atlanta, I know I said this was our last call," Frank said. "But I've read Quentin Banks' book. I am curious to know how the real Bob the Pilot's story is going to end. Will Beverly call it quits, or will she have a change of heart?

"Beverly, if you are listening, please give us a call. We want to know. Are you going to be a runaway bride or are you willing to jump the broomstick with Jeff one more time? The clock is ticking. Give us a call at 404-898-8900."

"While we wait on Beverly to call, here is a classic Luther Vandross song, *A House is not a Home*," Wanda said smoothly.

The minutes ticked by as I waited with the phone clutched in my sweating hand. The song finished playing and Wanda returned to the air, "That was *A House is not a Home* by the late, great Luther Vandross. I think that was an appropriate song considering our topic for today has gone from scandals in the pulpits to homeless husbands. Atlanta, I just got word that we have another caller on the line. Let's hope it's Beverly Montgomery."

A lump the size of Texas formed in my throat as I waited. Anticipation fairly crackled over the line. Wanda connected the caller and said, "You are on the air."

There was only silence over the airwaves.

"Hello, caller, are you there?"

My heart skipped several beats. I could feel it bump against my breastbone when it kicked in again. My mouth suddenly went dry.

A small voice finally come over the radio, "Frank, Wanda, Pastor Cash, this is Beverly."

A collective sigh of relief could be heard all across Atlanta. Wanda said excitedly, "Beverly, thank you for calling the Frank and Wanda Morning Show! We can't wait to hear what you have to say."

"I was so hurt when I found out that Jeff had revealed the intimate details of our sex life to his friends; I was also angry and hurt that he'd slept around and cheapened our marriage. I felt like that was the ultimate betrayal. The man I heard today was not the womanizing Jeff that once was.

"The man that called in today was the sincere man that asked me to marry him all those years ago. But Jeff, in order for me to come back, you will have to really mean that you want to commit your life to me and you will have to submit your life to the Lord. You go to church, but God is not in you. Once you rededicate your life to God, I will have no problems submitting and committing my life to you.

"Pastor Cash, I want you to baptize me along with my husband. Only then can I feel safe in rededicating my heart to Jeff."

"Beverly, I would be so honored to baptize you."

Beverly burst into tears and I could hear her heart wrenching sobs. "Donald, I forgive you for what you did to me."

Pastor Cash spoke, his voice filled with gladness. "Thank you Beverly. The burden and shame have been lifted!"

"Pastor Cash, I have taken back my power!" Beverly said victoriously. "What Donald did no longer hurts me and I no longer feel the shameful burden. I will be back in church after a ten year absence."

The studio erupted into cheers. I cried as I watched the drivers of all the other cars sitting in Atlanta's biggest parking lot share Beverly's victory.

67

BRIDGETT

Quentin and the girls tried to talk me out of going to Africa, but it was no use. My mind was made up. The morning that Peter and I were to leave for Africa, I finished packing and then sat and had a cup of coffee. I reflected over all the drama and heartache of the past week. I was about to meet my mother for the first time since I was eleven years old. The car to take me to the airport arrived. I washed my cup, picked up my bag and left the house to begin a new adventure.

I met Peter at the airport and we boarded our plane. We took our first class seat and sat holding hands, enjoying the hustle and bustle of people settling in for a long flight. During the flight we talked about the future, about Carla and what we might expect. He told me of his conversation with Jan about the divorce. We slept, ate and talked some more about his plans with my mother.

We finally landed in Al Khartum. We exited the plane to heat and dust and noise, only to be shoved through Customs as quickly as possible. Then we were hustled through the confusing maze and the airport to get on a small puddle jumper that would fly us to Al Fashir.

Peter's friend, Dr. Ebu, from the consulate, met us upon our arrival at the small structure that called itself an airport. He had arrived with an armed militia. His entourage quickly gathered our bags and whisked us through customs and before long we were comfortably ensconced in his home in the city.

Dr. Ebu's cook had prepared a delicious dinner of curried chicken, dirty rice, yams and native fruit. My first introduction to African cuisine was a wondrous experience. We said our grace and dug in. After we had eaten, Dr. Ebu told us of my mother's years in Africa.

"Bridgett, your mother was a godsend. We receive aid from many humanitarian and charitable organizations around the world, but it is still not nearly enough for the care of over three million people. Carla has been instrumental not only in getting additional assistance, but in making the world more aware of our cause."

I smiled, my heart filling with pride at my mother's accomplishments. As he talked, I began to see my mother not as a woman that abandoned her child, but as a woman that saved thousands of other children.

"The only salary your mother will take is just enough to get her by for her daily needs. Everything else goes to medical supplies and medicines. Because of the political uncertainty in the region and the continuous fighting we receive only a fraction of what we need. But I have seen your mother face down men hardened by war just to get them to smuggle in vitamins for her children. They are, how do you say it, like putty in her hands.

"How much do you need?" I asked.

"At last accounting, it would take about forty six million US dollars to build basic medical facilities, get medicines and supplies and hire medical staff on the most basic level. We receive only a third of that. With the violence escalating and budget restraints, the UN may have to cut back what we receive now by half."

"How will you make up for the loss?" I asked.

"We will do what we always do. Make do with what we get. Your mother is very clever, she will stretch supplies as far as she can. If a western hospital saw some of the things your mother does, such as rewashing soiled bandages in a pot of boiling water over a wood fire, they would be appalled. We do what we have to do. This is a country ravaged by war. Carla constantly pleads with the UN and the Red Cross and other humanitarian organizations to build a hospital here, but with the corruption, fighting and governmental red tape, that is almost impossible.

Peter sat at the table, deep in thought. Exhaustion was etched into his face and he had very little to say.

"Your mother has a shelter about fifteen miles from here. It is not much to see, but many displaced woman and children depend on it daily just to survive. I will take you there first thing in the morning. Well, now that we have finished dinner, I am sure you are both exhausted from your long journey."

I was excited to know that my mother was so near. But, I was also scared to death about tomorrow. I didn't know what to expect. Would she even recognize me? I'd asked Peter if he'd kept in touch with my mother. He told me that at first he'd sent her reports about me with pictures. But she moved around a lot in those first years and mail was iffy at best. Eventually he'd stopped sending her anything since he has no idea whether it had been received. In the last few years, when she had settled in the Darfur region, the mail system was even worse and he had gotten out of the habit. He said that he probably could have gotten reports to her through the security agency he'd hired, but even that might prove problematic.

The following morning we rose at six. Peter and I both had a bad case of jet lag. In spite of our exhaustion, we were anxious to get started. Breakfast was served to us in our rooms and we were supplied with military fatigues to wear. When we walked outside, an armed unit from the African peacekeeping force was waiting outside as our escort. They all stood stiffly at attention.

"Dr. Ebu, do we need to have armed security?" I asked.

"I'm sorry Bridgett, but we do. There is always danger at every turn. The camouflage gear I gave you will make the rebels believe you are part of the UN peacekeeping force. They are less likely to attack you."

We loaded up in a military truck, sitting side by side with the troops on hard benches in the back of the truck. A camouflage cover was buttoned down tight to the sides and the back flap was pulled down before we drove off. The covering didn't allow much air to flow and it was stifling hot. The dust, however, found its way into every little opening, leaving a film over us, and the supplies we shared the space with. As we passed through villages, tears came to my eyes, and not because of the dust. Peeking out a small opening in the flap I saw so many children standing along side the road. They were covered with dirt and flies, their little bellies distended from malnutrition. Some farm animals roamed freely among the villages, starving from lack of food.

"You Americans don't realize how blessed you are. What you waste in a single meal would keep one of these children fed for a week. Your fabulous restaurants throw away the food we wish we had."

"You are right, Dr. Ebu. We are a spoiled country."

"I also watch CNN. My heart goes out to those illegal aliens who want the same opportunity that you Americans have. Peter, didn't I read about a Senate Bill that made felons out of the illegal aliens that your state passed?"

"Yes, there was such a bill.

Dr. Ebu looked sad. "So many families torn apart. A lot of hard working immigrants will have to go back to their own countries."

Peter just listened quietly, rocking slightly with the motion of the truck. He seemed to be gathering himself for what lay ahead.

Dr. Ebu continued, "I know they are there in your country illegally, but if a man is starving, should you not feed him? If he is jobless, should you not give him work? I guess in your country you can only feed him or give him a job if he is an American citizen, or legal?"

I understood the point Dr. Ebu was making. His country was overrun by outcasts from other countries and still they struggled to help them, regardless of where they came from.

As we drove slowly through the open areas I noticed many people walking out of the city. Everyone waved at us to stop.

"Stop Dr. Ebu," I pleaded. "Please stop."

"Bridgett, we cannot," he cautioned, "I know your heart goes out to my people, but it is too dangerous. We have no place to put them anyway."

In spite of the fact that we only traveled fifteen miles, the trip took several hours. The roads were congested with people and wagons and animals. We traveled slowly to avoid hurting anyone, but it also put us at risk. We finally made it to Riyach, a refugee camp in western Darfur. As we pulled up to my mother's shelter, we saw a long line of people waiting outside for food. Volunteers worked tirelessly to accommodate the starving people. Dust and flies were thick and the smells were overpowering.

I saw a tall, stately woman walking down a lane between knock up buildings built from scraps of wood. She was surrounded by people and more gravitated towards her. She was wearing a military T-shirt with camouflage cargo pants and a dog tag and a small silver locket around her neck. A stethoscope was also draped around her neck. The pockets on the legs of her pants bulged with foil wrapped bars. She passed the bars out among the children around her.

I immediately knew who she was and drank in the sight of her. Her hair was longer than I remembered, scraped back into a ponytail, and her face had deeper angles and planes than when she left Atlanta, but I knew her. She strode among the weak and the sick and the hungry. She'd stop and touch a shoulder or shake a hand. She would squat down among the dirt and debris that littered the camp to talk to someone or listen to their hearts and check their eyes. This proud, strong, beautiful woman was my mother.

Looking at her was like looking at a darker version of myself. Tears formed at the corners of my eyes. I couldn't tear my gaze away from her. Peter took my hand and helped me down from the truck. We slowly moved among the people toward her. We were both speechless as we watched her touch and smile at the people as she passed.

"Peter, it's my mother," I said needlessly. I started to run to her, but Peter held me back.

"Bridgett, it's been a long time since she has seen either of us. It feels strange just springing up like this. Maybe we should have called or written to her, or sent smoke signals, something. We can't just reappear in her life after all these years." I looked at Peter. His gaze was serene, in spite of his hesitation, as he looked at my mother. "She is so beautiful. Just the way I remember her." He turned to me, suddenly he reminded me of a teenager getting ready to go on his first date. I had to laugh at his nervousness. "Bridgett, I don't know what to say!"

"Just say what's in your heart Peter."

"Bridgett, we can't just show up. Let's get in the line and work our way over to her. We can put a strategy together. Since we're wearing hats, let's just pull them down over our faces. We can pretend to be soldiers and strike up a conversation with her."

We put on our sunglasses and pulled our hats down and started working our way through the crowd. It took us nearly an hour to get to her, but soon I stood face to face with my mother.

Peter just stood there, struck dumb so I said, "Dr. Moore, you have a lot of people today."

"A lot of people!" she said in disbelief, looking around. "This is the lightest day I've ever seen. Normally it takes about five hours to feed everyone. My heart goes out to these people." Again, she looked at the crowd that surrounded her, compassion softening her eyes. "So much pain." Then she looked Peter and I up and down. "I haven't seen you around here. Who are you with?"

Caught totally off guard, I blurted out the first thing that came to mind. "UN Peacekeeping Force."

Peter chose that moment to finally talk and said, "Delta Force" at exactly the same time.

My mother laughed, "Well, which is it?"

"Both," Peter said.

I gave him a sharp look. He took the hint and shut up.

She shot us both a suspicious stare. "What are your names?"

"Summer," I said without thinking. "He's Lance."

My mother gave a slight nod, but said nothing, as a small hand tugged at her pants leg, momentarily distracting her. She squatted down beside the small boy as he babbled something I couldn't understand to her. She kissed his head and reached into her pocket and handed him one of the bars. Peter took the opportunity to say out of the corner of his mouth, "You told her Quentin's name from the book? Out of all the assholes you could have picked, why that one?"

"Shh, don't blow our cover."

She stood and turned back to us. "Well, Summer, Lance, welcome to Darfur and my humble home."

She and I talked about the camp, while Peter stood and stared idiotically at her. I know she probably wondered why the peacekeeping force would let an imbecile into its ranks. She kindly said nothing, although she occasionally cut her eyes at him as if making sure he didn't do something stupid. When she started filling bowls and passing them out to the waiting people, I helped her. I wanted to hug her so bad. Never have I met a woman with so much love and strength.

After everyone was fed, she beckoned Peter and I to follow her to a large tent. "Church is about to start." She gave us an inviting smile. "Would you care to join me?"

I elbowed Peter in the side. "Lance and I wouldn't miss it for the world!"

69

A crowd had already gathered, and she escorted us to the front and made room for us on a crudely built bench. There did not appear to be a priest or minister present. My mother made her way up front and started speaking to the people. We listened with swelling pride as she spoke plainly and simply about God and love, faith and forgiveness. Peter wiped his eyes under his sunglasses. She seemed to be the only hope in a world gone mad. She was a savior to the children that would probably never grow to see adulthood. I prayed with her for help and peace to come to this region. The values we once held so dear no longer seemed important. All this suffering had changed Peter and me.

When the short service was over, Peter and I again sought her out. She came up behind us unexpectedly and said, "So, Summer and Lance, I see you are still here. It is getting late, shouldn't you two be getting back?"

"Well, no." I reassured her. "The UN sent us to make sure you had all the help you need."

"I'm truly blessed to have so many people who care about this cause."

"Where are you from Lance?"

"Chicago."

"And you Summer?"

I said, "Alabama." It was the first thing that entered my mind.

She looked at us suspiciously. I don't think Peter and I were doing a very good job at undercover work, as he liked to call it. My observation was proved true with her next statement. My mother is no slouch.

"If you two are going to help me out, I need to know that I can trust you with my life."

Peter and I looked at each other guiltily. Her expression became stern. "Tell me the truth. Who are you?"

I knew we were busted. We had gone as far as we could go without revealing ourselves. I slowly took off my hat and sunglasses and looked her in the eyes. She gasped when she saw me, a fair-skinned look-alike. She stood speechless. Peter slowly removed his hat and sunglasses and lifted his head to face her.

"Oh my God, it can't be!" she shouted joyfully. "Peter, Bridgett! I must be dreaming. What are you doing here? Why the charade?"

Her knees buckled and I caught her and helped her onto a crude bench nearby. That was the first time I had touched my mother. I kept hold of her arm, I couldn't let go. I needed that contact. Peter pulled out a small bottle of water he had been carrying in his pocket and handed it to her.

"Here honey, drink this." He gently helped her lift the bottle to her lips. She swallowed deeply and began to cry. I sat beside her and put my arm around her shoulders, but she turned to me and threw her arms around me and squeezed me so tight I couldn't draw a breath.

"I honestly thought I'd never see you again, my baby girl. It has been such a long time," she whispered in my ear. She pushed me away from her and held me at arm's length. "Look at you, all grown up and so beautiful. Oh, thank you God!"

A stunned look passed across her face. "I should have known it right away!"

"Known what?" I asked.

"Summer and Lance! I was given this book called *Desperate Husbands* by one of the military guys that was here. That's two of the characters in the book! I loved that book but I think Quentin is a knucklehead."

"Yeah, well I know the author," I mumbled.

"You do? Well, isn't it a small world. How do you know him?"

"I think I might be engaged to him."

"Now that's an odd way of putting it, honey." She brushed the hair back off my face and looked at Peter. "What does she mean by that?"

Peter exploded with laughter. "It's a long story, but rest assured that everyone else in America thinks he's a knucklehead too."

I watched my mother looking at Peter. There was no doubt in my mind that those two were meant to be together. She looked at him with all the love and tenderness that I imagined they'd shared thirty years ago.

70

PETER

Carla gave me an affectionate glance. "You two should be ashamed, pulling that stunt on me." She touched her hair. "I must look a mess."

"You are still the most beautiful woman I ever saw, Carla. I don't think you've changed at all."

"How is Jan doing?" she said abruptly.

"I guess she's fine. I haven't seen her for a while. We're getting a divorce." I tossed out as casually as I could. Something told me this was going to be a pivotal moment.

"A divorce," Carla said, seeming to roll the idea around in her mind. "I'm sorry to hear that Peter."

A brief silence passed between us. Bridgett looked off into the distance allowing us as private a moment as we could hope to have surrounded by so many people.

"Truthfully Carla, it's been coming for a long time. Jan and I should have divorced years ago. We have both been unhappy for a very long time."

Carla seemed to make her mind up about something, but didn't share her thoughts with me. Abruptly she changed the subject.

"What brings you to Africa?" she asked quietly.

I gave her a long, loving stare. "To do something I should have done thirty years ago."

Again, she changed the subject, obviously deciding she didn't want to go in the conversational direction I was trying to steer her.

"Where are you staying?"

"At Dr. Ebu's house in Darfur."

"I know Dr. Ebu. I sometimes stay there myself if I need to be in the city. He's been a blessing every since I've been here. He and his military have always made sure I was safe."

"You have your own bodyguards?" I probed.

"I guess you could say that. Every since I've been in Africa I've had someone with me wherever I go. Now I know how Whitney Houston feels. But they're good guys. Never intrusive and always helpful. So I can't complain."

"Which Whitney are you talking about? The 'crack is wack' Whitney or the 'new' Whitney?"

"Don't be ugly Peter. We all go through changes in life."

Amen to that I thought, but I apologized and changed the subject. "Carla, have you eaten. I noticed you didn't eat a thing when we were feeding the people."

"I was so busy serving them, I forgot to eat."

"Well, Bridgett and I haven't eaten since breakfast and that was hours ago. Why don't we all go and find something?"

Carla led us to a small building that was half tent and half crude shelter. Inside was a kitchen of sorts that produced all the food that was fed to the masses. The food was very plain and simple, consisting mostly of rice and a few local vegetables thrown in, but it was as nutritious and filling as it could be under the circumstances. There was no seasonings to improve the bland flavor, but if these people could eat it, then so could I. We helped ourselves to a small bowl each.

After we ate, I rolled up my sleeves and jumped in to help in whatever capacity I was needed. I hauled water, peeled potatoes, swabbed down the tent that was used as an infirmary. I helped feed the never-ending line of people that poured into the camp by the minute. I stuck plasters on children's boo-boos and washed small hands when Carla directed me to.

It was quite an experience for me to wait on others for a change. All my adult life it had been the other way around. I'd snap my fingers and I had whatever I wanted. But to serve these people was an honor I can't even begin to describe. I yawned widely and stretched my aching back, but no matter how tired or sore I was, I still felt energized by giving of myself. It was a great joy to serve others.

By the time she finished giving medicine to the sick, the sun was going down. I could see that Carla was as exhausted as I was. Carla had talked with Dr. Ebu sometime during the day and had decided to go back with us to his house. I knew she wanted to be near Bridgett for as long as she could. I decided to make arrangements with Dr. Ebu to have Bridgett and I transfer our living quarters to the camp later in the week so that we could stay near Carla, and continue to help at the camp.

71

BRIDGETT

I will never forget the ride back to Dr. Ebu's house. I had so much catching up to do that I bombarded my mother with question after question. The more I found out about her, the more I wanted to know.

"This camp and the shelter have been the most rewarding experience of my life," my mother said reflecting. "I've had a few relationships off and on but nothing serious. I never got married, nor do I have any other children."

"Why is that Mom?" I asked.

She gave me a loving smile. "When I had you I knew I couldn't duplicate perfection."

I laughed and blew her a kiss.

"I'm for real, look here." She pulled the silver locket from inside her shirt. It was identical to mine. She opened it and showed me the same pictures that mine contained. "I've never taken it off. It's my good luck charm. It keeps me safe from, Jason, Freddie Kreuger and vampires."

She looked around, peering intently into the dark corners of the truck. "Must be working. I haven't seen any of them since I got here."

We burst into laughter. "Mom, you are a trip."

She stared at my locket. She reached out and opened it with a slight smile on her face. "Your father gave me both these lockets the day you were born. He told me that as long as we had these lockets, we'd be a family." She touched my father's knee and looked at him. "Peter, where is yours?"

He pulled it from underneath the neckline of his T-shirt. "I haven't worn this in years. I was afraid Jan would find it. I kept it locked in my safe at the office. I took it out every day and looked at the pictures." He stroked the well-worn surface with his thumb, as he had done everyday for thirty years. Peter kissed us both and gave my mother a squeeze.

"Bridgett, I hope that for all these years, you didn't believe that I didn't want you. I wanted to bring you with me, but now I realize you wouldn't have thrived here. It was God's calling that brought me here, and you were happy with your aunt, weren't you?"

"Mom," I said seriously, "for a long time I did think you had abandoned me. I kept those feelings to myself. I cried for you on so many dark nights. I missed you more than I can ever say. But, as I grew up I had Auntie and I had Peter. They helped me to understand what you had to do. It didn't always make it easier, but those feeling of being cast aside kind of went away. I was so angry with you for a long time. Now I see what God wanted you to do. I'm okay. I grew up happy, and I love you."

"I'm glad you came to understand. I was struggling with the love I had for Peter. I knew he was trying to make his mark in the world. He desperately wanted to have the life he dreamed of when he was in the orphanage and I knew it wouldn't have happened in that time and place with a black woman and child. The temptation for me would have been too great to ignore."

"But he loved you," I said, all choked up.

"I know Bridgett. I loved him too, but it would have never worked. It wouldn't have worked for me, because of my belief; and it wouldn't have worked for him because the sacrifice would have been too great. When you were born, I made him promise not to reveal he was your father to protect him. I told you your father died in a car accident to protect you.

"I'm happy that it all worked out and that you now know the truth. I wanted him to tell you eventually, when the time was right. I didn't expect that blabbermouth fiancé of yours to tell the whole world in his stupid book. Why didn't he come with you?"

"I didn't really ask him to. But he's probably hiding out somewhere. He's got a lot of people pissed at him."

"He needs to be hiding," Mom said angrily. "Even the men in this country are mad at him. I've heard talk of cutting his tongue out, then slapping him with it. Men's secrets should be men's secrets."

I giggled at her response. "Right now, Quentin and I are having some trust issues, but we are working through them."

"Oh yeah, I know first hand about that!" Mom cut her eyes at Peter, who adopted an innocent expression.

"What? What! What did I do?"

Carla laughed, "You were born a man." She poked him in the ribs.

When we arrived at Dr. Ebu's, we washed up and a late supper was laid out. The contrast between the simple luxury of Dr. Ebu's house and the squalid conditions at the camp stood out sharply in my mind. Apparently the same thought crossed my mother's mind.

"Africa is such a beautiful country. But, some of the corrupt people have made parts of it so ugly. Bridgett, death and starvation are a part of everyday life. People are hungry. AIDS is a widespread epidemic. Sometimes I think my contribution is useless and I'm just beating my head against the wall."

"On the contrary, Mom, what would these people do without you?"

"I just get so frustrated sometimes that I think about jumping the first thing smoking back to the good old U. S. of A. When I first came here, I was so green and naïve. For years, it was just heal one person at a time. Eventually I realized that I had to work on a much larger scale to even begin to make a dent in the problem. Believe me, this whole venture has been a huge learning experience. I never in my life thought I'd be capable of raising hundreds of thousands of dollars for medical supplies. But no matter how hard I work and how much money I get, it's never enough." Carla put her hands to her head. Frustration was evident in every line of her body.

"Carla, what would make an appreciable difference?" Peter asked.

"What we most need is a hospital, but that is just a dream."

We talked for a few more minutes, and then my mother excused herself to go to bed. After she'd left us I whispered to Peter, "Mom has such a good heart. Wouldn't it be great if we could help her?"

Peter smiled at me with the same indulgence he did when I was a kid. "I would love to, but how... besides donating money?"

A gem of an idea took root in my head. "A hospital!"

"A hospital?" he said loudly.

"Shh, don't wake Mom. A hospital, Peter. I know Dr. Ebu said it was impossible because of the corruption, but what if it all came from an outside source, administered by a corporation, rather than the government? Dr. Ebu could assist you in getting the necessary clearances, couldn't he?"

"That's a great idea Bridgett, but there's one small catch."

"What Dad?"

"In a few of weeks, I'm going to be penniless and no longer CEO of McCallister Enterprises. I wouldn't have the time to effect this decision before the new CEO took over my office. Only a CEO can make that decision."

"Well, who's going to be the CEO...Oh my God, that's me!" A big smile shone from her face. "Building a hospital can be my first executive decision!"

"It would be a great tax write off, plus the publicity would be a great boost to McCallister's image and stock."

I smiled as I thought to myself that 'being the man' may not be so bad after all.

72

The next morning we were out the door and headed back to the shelter. As Peter and Carla joked with each other, I could tell the bond between my parents was growing stronger.

"Peter, remember the time we took all those kids from the church to Six Flags?"

"Oh yeah, how can I forget?" He chuckled and looked at me. "We were on the Scream Machine and I threw up on the kid sitting next to me."

I burst out laughing thinking about the suave and sophisticated Peter McCallister even throwing up, much less on a kid.

I watched the sun come up through a slit in the camouflage covering over the truck. The golden glow painted the stunted growth and open dusty fields in glowing colors. Even the shanties we passed along the way took on a beauty that belied the ugliness that surrounded us. The back of the truck grew warm and dusty. I leaned against Peter and dozed off.

The jolt of the truck stopping, jerked me awake. Our day had begun. We worked feverishly all day, following Mom's directions and doing whatever else was necessary. It was never ending. Soldiers, volunteers, even the sick, pitched in and helped in whatever capacity they could. People constantly poured into the camp. Sometimes only a handful, sometimes they came in by the truckloads. There was laughter and there were tears. Children smiled and ran, or sat and suffered. It was heartbreaking and immensely rewarding.

By the time we all climbed back in the truck for the long, bumpy ride home, Carla had fallen asleep in Peter's arms. While she slept we broached the subject of a hospital with Dr. Ebu.

"I think that is an exciting idea, Mr. McCallister. I'm sure that through contacts I have in the government, we can get the necessary clearances. Under your company's administration, we could sidestep some of the more corrupt officials, but you must understand there will be required payoffs to the right people to make this happen. I know of a site closer to town that can accommodate such a building. It already has a well and electricity can be run easily, but power generators must be installed since our services are not the most reliable." The ideas kept coming and in his excitement, we were able to map out a loose plan.

"Dr. Ebu," Peter said quietly. "There is one stipulation."

Dr. Ebu looked at Peter, crestfallen, as if seeing his dream go down the drain.

"No, no," I said, holding out my hands, hoping to alleviate his fear that the hospital won't happen. "It won't affect the hospital."

He looked from me to Peter in confusion.

Peter said insistently, "the only stipulation is that Carla must never know we are behind the construction. When it's complete, we want to name it in her honor."

Dr. Ebu let out a pent up breath and smiled broadly. "I think my people can keep the secret." He gave me a sly look, "just don't tell your knucklehead boyfriend."

I rolled my eyes at him. "Is there anyone who doesn't know about the damn book?"

"I don't know about that Bridgett, but even African women are keeping their husbands close. Do you know how many words there are for dog in all African dialects?"

73

PETER

Bridgett and I stayed in Africa about six weeks. She talked to Quentin daily. By the time we were getting ready to leave, plans for the hospital had been drawn up and Dr. Ebu was making rapid progress with the clearances, greasing the right palms and stroking the right egos. The paperwork was moving ahead slowly.

Bridgett's birthday was celebrated quietly at Dr. Ebu's house. She was happy that she could celebrate it with her mother. The transfer of funds went off without a hitch and Bridgett was officially named the new CEO of McCallister Enterprises and the Board of Directors gave their blessing.

The hospital would be a reality. Carla was excited about the hospital finally becoming a reality even through she remained unaware of McCallister Enterprises' involvement. Dr. Ebu "arranged" for her to be appointed chief administrator.

"Peter, this hospital is a dream come true. It will bring hope to so many people. It seems like my blessings never stop. I can only wonder what other miracles and blessings may come."

I gave her a squeeze and blinked at her innocently. I took her gently by the chin and tipped her head up to me. "Carla, the last few years have been one big struggle."

"Struggle?" she looked at me in disbelief. "Peter, you are one of the richest men in Georgia. The word struggle is not in your vocabulary."

"Well, yes, financially I've done well, but Carla, for the past thirty years, I've been..." She stopped me with a finger to my lips.

"Peter, don't..."

I paused, having to force the words out. I didn't know if this was the right time or not, but I foraged ahead, deciding to let the cards fall where they may.

"Carla, I still love you. I've always loved you."

She stood there frozen. I got down on one knee. A little puff of dust rose up as I landed stiffly.

"I'm not going to lie to you or to myself." I awkwardly pulled a small box from my pocket. I'd been carrying that box around since we left Atlanta and the velvet had rubbed bare on the corners. I stared up at her face and opened the box, revealing a 5-carat, flawless white diamond ring set in platinum. "Carla, I'm asking you to be my wife."

The shock was evident on her face. Her eyes grew wide, but she didn't take the ring. She ran her hand through my hair.

"Peter, you never cease to amaze me. The ring is beautiful, but..."

"But what Carla? I love you and you love me," I said in desperation.

"Peter, I do love you, but it has been such a long time. A lot has happened. I'm not the person you knew thirty years ago. I found the Lord and I'm dedicated to serving him and serving others." She gestured around the camp. I followed the movement of her hand and noticed several children standing close by watching us intently.

"Peter, I'm not the kind of woman you need. You love money and power, being a part of society. I love the smile of a child who goes to sleep properly nourished. I feel rich only when I save the life of an expectant mother, or save a child from a life of slavery or abuse. I am not the person you used to know."

"Carla, you are a better version of the woman I fell in love with. Please, accept the ring and think about it." I rose stiffly to my feet. "I have to leave today. Will you come back with me? I need you and Bridgett needs you."

Carla looked at the ring and hung her head. She scraped the toe of her boot through the dirt thoughtfully. When she looked up at me, tears were running down her cheeks. "No, Peter. I can't. The people here need me more. Even if I wanted to, I know I can't leave right now. This hospital is so important. I need to be here to make sure it gets built. I'm sorry, I can't keep your ring."

She closed my fingers around the box. I was speechless and I felt as if someone had pulled the rug right out from under me. All the dreams I had of being with Carla were going up in smoke.

74

BRIDGETT

When Peter and I boarded the plane in Al Khartum, he looked like a broken man. I ordered drinks for us. After the flight attendant had returned with our drinks and left us alone, I asked him what was wrong. He stared silently out the window and sipped his drink. He turned to me, with tears in his eyes.

"Peter, what is wrong, please won't you tell me?" My anxiety level rose. "My woman's intuition is telling me something is very wrong. Are you feeling all right?"

He rolled his eyes. "Have you ever thought maybe your intuition is wrong? Maybe it's time for a tune-up."

"Well, for the past thirty years it has never failed me," I persisted.

"Okay, okay, I do have something on my mind."

"Thank God, it's just something on your mind. I was afraid you might have gotten ill or something."

"Not ill in that sense, no."

"So what's going on? Spill it Peter."

"It's your mother."

"What about Mom? Is she all right? Something hasn't happened that you didn't tell me about has it? God, Peter, what's going on?" I was ready to start tearing my hair out.

"I proposed to her."

"What! Yeah! It's about time. When's the wedding?" Excitement rose in me. I started thinking right then and there about a double wedding. That would be the best wedding ever!

"Hold your horses. She turned me down."

I know my face fell. "Oh, I'm sorry. Maybe she just needs some time to think about it. You can't expect her to drop everything she's familiar with and jump back into a world that is basically foreign to her."

"I can and do," he said stubbornly. "It happens in movies all the time."

"I know you're joking. But joking aside, Peter, this is real life and a woman needs to know the man is sincere and that her emotions are safe. You have done very well financially; you have everything money can buy, but spiritually, you are a mess. You are so used to people catering to you and kissing your ass..."

"Hey, kissing my ass is a good thing."

"Peter, you had Quentin, Antonio, Jeff and Donald selling their souls just to get into your stupid club. Don't tell me you aren't used to people jumping when you say jump. But Mom is not that type of person. Your money is not going to impress her, unless it comes in the form of medical supplies. The only way you're going to totally win her heart is spiritually. She's not going to commit to you until you commit to God."

"How did you get to be so smart?" He tapped me under the chin, affectionately, but I knew what I'd said hit home.

"Dad, be real with yourself. The only reason you joined Holy Faith was because of political connections and it made you look good."

"You're right Bridgett. I guess I haven't been any better than Donald or Jeff when you get right down to it. I've been a hypocrite far too long. Another stumbling block is Jan. She wants blood. The only thing I own is the mansion, a few stocks and a couple of pieces of property."

"Be honest with Jan, I'm sure she'll understand. It's not the quantity of time you've been married, but the quality. You told Mom you were going to get a divorce, but you're not divorced yet. Do you think that might have had something to do with her turning you down? Why should she believe that anything would change? If you truly want to win my mother's heart, your actions must be consistent with your words. It's time to put up or shut up."

"Again, how did you get so smart?"

"Hey, I watch 'The View'!"

"I think you're right, Bridgett. As soon as we get to Atlanta I'll take care of that situation. It's now or never. Oh, by the way, have you talked to Quentin lately?"

"Yes, I talked to him just before we left. He's picking us up at the airport."

"What's up with you guys now?"

"When I left, I really didn't like the person that Quentin had become. He was turning into a rich asshole." I cut my eyes to Peter. "Don't you just hate that kind of person?"

He dropped his head to hide a smile. "Oh, yeah, I know the type well. Some of them can be real pricks."

"But you know what? I think Quentin has changed. I think the time we've been apart has been good for the both of us. He's talking about getting married now, instead of avoiding the subject."

"Well congratulations. Have you set a date?"

"It's not official yet. We still have a lot of things to iron out. I want his proposal to be something he feels, not given because of threats or intimidation. I want it to be heartfelt and given freely."

"You are wise beyond your years, daughter."

"Africa taught me that, father."

We fell silent for a while. Peter seemed lost in his own thoughts and I didn't intrude. The drone of the plane's engines soon had me drifting off to sleep.

The smell of food brought me to wakefulness and I realized I was starving. I'd dropped several pounds in Africa, and while I loved the country, the food in the camp left a lot to be desired.

After we'd been given our dinners, Peter decided to play devil's advocate and asked, "Bridgett, since you are now an heiress, don't you think you should have Quentin sign a pre-nuptial agreement?"

"What for Dad?" I said angrily. "I know Quentin loves me for me. I would never ask such a thing of him."

"But what about your fortune. You need to protect it."

"Screw that. A pre-nuptial agreement is telling him that I don't trust him. How can a relationship last if you go into it without trust?"

"Where have I heard that before? Do you think Quentin feels the same way? I mean, what if the tables were turned and he had the money and you didn't?"

"He has money now. And yes, Quentin would feel the same way. You know that! Plus, with the success of his book, he's just signed a multi-million dollar deal for two more books. In fact, just the other day, he told me what is his is mine. I feel the same way. I wouldn't think of asking for a pre-nup."

He smiled at me proudly and said, "Bravo Bridgett, you never cease to amaze me!"

75

QUENTIN

I was waiting for Peter and Bridgett in the baggage claim area. I saw them as they walked through the custom's gate. I ran over and picked Bridgett up and swung her around. I've never been so happy to have my hands on her. I kissed her hard.

"Baby, I'm so happy to see you. I thought you'd never get here. How's your mother?"

I looped my arm around her waist and looked at Peter, but he pretended to ignore me. I decided to test the water.

"Hi, Peter. Welcome home. Thing's haven't been the same since you left. Did you enjoy Africa?"

He gave me a cold stare. "It was different," he said, not encouraging dialog.

"Did you see any of your ancestors?" I inquired jokingly.

"No," he replied.

"Come on big guy. I know you found at least one McCallister with an afro. Come to think of it, you and President Obama could be related."

Bridgett and I chuckled, but Peter got pissed. "Everyone wants to do stand-up." He grabbed me by the collar. "Okay, Quentin, I've had all I can stand of you. It's you and me, outside, man to man. This ass whipping has been coming for a long, long time."

Bridgett was appalled at Peter's behavior. She jumped between us, pushing us apart.

"Can you guys chill out on the testosterone? How about a peaceful homecoming? Okay?"

"Okay," Peter said, jerking his arm away from Bridgett and straightening his jacket. "Quentin, you got away with it that time, but being my future son-in-law doesn't earn you a free pass. The moment you get out of line, I will whip your ass."

I just couldn't seem to let it go, so I tried to aggravate him further. I snapped my fingers and rolled my head sister girl style like Adrian does and said, "Okay, Billy Bad Ass. You are so sexy when you are angry. You look Fa-Bu-Lous." I snapped my fingers again.

Peter clinched his jaw so hard I could see the muscles bulge out.

"How's Donald doing?" he asked sullenly.

I figured I'd pushed my luck far enough and answered amicably, "He's out of the hospital and back home. The church and his victims are not going to prosecute. Pastor Cash stepped in with the police, so between him and Antonio, I think the police will let it rest, too.

"Thank God," he said.

"The charges against Ashley have been reduced. The police won't overlook a shooting, you know. But, Pastor Cash and Antonio intervened and the prosecutor knows both of them. The state reduced the charges and gave her community service, which she'll work out at Holy Faith. Jeff and Beverly have gone on a cruise and are planning on renewing their wedding vows. As for me, well, I've been missing my baby. And Bridgett and I are sort of unofficially engaged, for real this time."

"I know, she told me," he said dryly as he rolled his eyes.

"So, Peter, can I call you Dad?" I laid my head on his chest.

He pushed me away roughly. "Only if you want to get beat like the *Passion of the Christ*."

Bridgett got between us again and said, "Dad, stop threatening my fiancé, will you?"

"Quentin, can you take Bridgett on home. I'm going to run by and see Jan."

76

PETER

When I left the airport, I called Jan. She was shocked to hear from me. Although our conversation was less than pleasant, she agreed to see me. When I arrived at my former home, I was reluctant to ring the doorbell. It had been over a month since I'd seen Jan. I forced my hand up to push the button.

She threw the door open and said politely, "Hello Peter, darling. Come in."

I was surprised to see Jan. Apparently she'd had extensive plastic surgery. Maria was busy setting the table and I could smell food cooking.

"You are just in time. Maria has prepared a mouth watering meal for us. It's your favorite, giant lobster."

Jan was dressed very seductively, showing off a new, but still ample figure. She wasn't near her high school weight, but she did look better than I remember seeing her in a long, long time.

I took a seat at the dining table and Jan offered me a drink. I accepted a scotch and soda from her. I wondered what she was up too.

She handed me the glass, spun around proudly and said, "So, Peter. What do you think? I've had a gastric bypass, a tummy tuck, liposuction, breast implants, a labiaplasty, Botox and a Brazilian butt lift. I think I could work as a stripper at the Cheetah Club." She laughed sarcastically. "Oh, I'm sorry, you've already had one of those."

"You look great Jan," I said dully, refusing to rise to the bait.

"Thank you Peter. Actress Kirstie Alley has nothing on me. Now here is the good part. My new body only cost you about one hundred thousand dollars," she cackled.

"One hundred thousand," I shouted. "I could clone another human being for less!"

She looked taken back by my outburst, but continued as if I hadn't said anything at all. "I also need another fifty thousand."

"For what, Jan!"

"I have this new personal trainer and he is at my disposal any time I want him."

"Whatever, Jan."

Jan sat down at the table and unfolded her napkin across her lap. "How is Bridgett doing?" she asked innocently.

"She's fine."

"How did she take the news?"

I couldn't figure out Jan's angle. Was she fishing for something, or was she trying to hold on? "Bridgett is fine. She was shocked to find out I was her father, but we are developing a good father/daughter relationship. We just got back from Africa today. We went to see her mother."

"Peter, it's so nice to see you embrace your little colored family. Are you sure you're not related to Barack Obama?" she tossed out sarcastically.

Before I could respond, Maria came in with the serving tray.

"Jan, let's enjoy a nice dinner and talk about this afterwards."

Silence prevailed as Maria served our plates. After she had gone, I bowed my head for grace. Jan sat stiffly. I looked up at her without raising my head. She reluctantly bowed her head. Although we were both members of Holy Faith, we'd never said grace before. It was something I had learned from Carla and intended to carry on the ritual.

"Oh, Lord, who art in heaven, bless this food and the cook that prepared it. Help us to walk in the path of righteousness and become more like you. In Jesus name, Amen."

Jan and I both raised our heads and nibbled at the dinner before us. The silence stretched out to the breaking point before Jan inquired politely about Africa. "So was Africa nice?"

"It was and it wasn't," I replied, equally politely. "Going there changed my priorities. I never realized how truly blessed I was until I saw children dying in a refuge camp because they were starving to death. I realize now that money, power or prestige is not a blessing, but the blessing is that we can change our lives for the better. Bridgett and I saw so many starving people, many of them dying from AIDS. The children..."

"Peter, can we change the subject?" she said arrogantly. "I'm trying to eat my dinner. Didn't you say once that for thirty dollars a day, you can adopt a child in a third world country? I've got the perfect solution."

"What is that Jan?"

"We'll send them one thousand dollars and feed everyone in the zip code," she chuckled at her joke. "You see Peter, I'm not as insensitive as you think I am. If they don't have food, let them eat cake!"

Not believing my ears, her words spun around in my head. This woman that I'd been married to for over thirty years had no clue about what life is really like. To be perfectly honest, before I met Carla and ended up in Africa, I didn't either. But I had an epiphany. Living in America, you can't help but get caught up in the rat race. Some people actually believe that the one with the most toys, wins the game. In reality, those who uplift their brothers actually win. I smiled at my sudden enlightenment.

Once the ice was broken, Jan babbled on in her usual manner, and I tuned her out in my usual manner. Thoughts swam through my head. It was time I stopped being a coward and just tell Jan. I wanted to get on with life and I wasn't going to do it sitting here eating lobster and listening to Jan prattle about her society nothings.

"Jan, I will give you everything I have to get out of this marriage," I blurted out, surprising even myself.

Jan stopped eating, with the fork halfway to her mouth. I could see a light go on in that empty head of hers. I know she was thinking that she had me by the balls now. To the old Peter McCallister, money was not everything; it was the only thing.

Jan sat her fork down on the plate with a clink and looked at me coldly. "Does that little bitch mean that much to you, Peter? Is being married to me so unbearable?"

I decided to walk on eggshells until I was able to extract my hand from the lion's mouth. "It wasn't bad Jan, but I feel we have gone as far as we can go. I really want what's best for you and your sons. They're all grown up and you have your own life. I just want a little happiness for myself."

She just stared at me and for once, didn't speak.

"Jan, I have given you thirty two years of my life. I have tried to make you happy. You've never had to lift a finger. Your sons have always gotten what they wanted. Now it's time I think of my own happiness. I deserve some happiness."

Jan started prattling about her personal trainer as if I hadn't even spoken. I slammed down my wine glass, breaking the stem. I watched the wine soak into the tablecloth. It reminded me of my life. It just disappeared right in front of my eyes, leaving nothing but a damp spot. I really needed to get some balls.

"Jan, let's cut to the chase, this marriage is done. Stick a fork in your personal trainer, your day at the salon, the latest fashion craze and whatever else is your interest. The fat lady has sung."

To my surprise, instead of crying or getting upset, she seemed to have a sudden change of heart.

"Okay, Peter. What are you offering for thirty two years of marriage?"

"Let me think about it a second. I told you I'd give you everything I had to get out of this marriage. Well, Jan, I'm no longer CEO of McCallister Enterprises. My money and most of my holdings were signed over to Bridgett on her 30th birthday. But I can still raise about five million in cash. I'll gladly give you that, plus this house, the house in Hilton Head, and the house in Martha's Vineyard. I'll even throw in the yacht."

She was smiling like a fox. "Keep it going Peter."

"When everything is liquidated, you'll walk away with twenty million."

"Peter, you never cease to amaze me," Jan smirked. "Just when I thought I had you all figured out, you do something totally unexpected."

"Jan, I'm offering you twenty million to get out of this marriage."

Her smile slowly morphed into the 'Grinch grin.' "Hmm, that is not so bad. A nasty divorce can go on for months or even years."

She knew I was giving away the farm, or what was left of it anyway.

"There's one more stipulation."

The greedy gleam in her eye was replaced by one of suspicion. "What Peter?"

"I don't have to pay alimony and I get to keep the condo at Buckhead Towers."

"Anything else?" she said, not agreeing or disagreeing.

"I get to keep the Range Rover, the other cars belong to you."

"Okay Chaka Zulu, you have bought your freedom. You are now free to marry your African Queen." She couldn't contain her joy. "I'll call my lawyer tomorrow." She paused and cast me a look from the corner of her eye. "The Caribbean is so nice this time of year." She clapped her hands twice. "Atlanta is really starting to bore me."

Curiosity overcame me. This was way too easy. There's got to be some shit in this game. But before, I could respond to her statement, a well-built Hispanic man strolled down the stairs. He moved to Jan's side and put an arm around her waist. They smiled deviously at each other. So Jan's bought herself a new boy toy that's half her age. That little witch.

"Oh, where are my manners?" Jan cooed. "This is Manuel Alvarez. He is my new personal trainer." She ran her index finger down his well-muscled chest.

"Hello, Manuel." I did not offer to shake hands.

"*Hola*, Peter." He didn't offer his hand either.

"I'm sorry Peter, he can't speak a lick of English, but he's very skilled in so many other areas." She chuckled devilishly. "I just helped him get his green card. I couldn't let him go back to Mexico." She caressed his arm, grinning up at him. "Some aliens we need to keep in the good, old U. S. of A."

"Yeah," I said, rolling my eyes. Those two deserved each other. I had a feeling he was going to help Jan spend a lot of her money very quickly. The woman never did have a lick of sense.

"Yeah," she said, rubbing his youth in my face. "Manual will make sure the weight stays off me."

Manual stood there looking back and forth between us, grinning and flexing his muscles.

"I'm thinking that since your nominees for the 30305 Club are on shaky ground, maybe I'll nominate him for the next candidate. Maybe he can even be the next Hispanic congressman for the great state of Georgia."

As he grinned seductively at Jan, I thought everything that glitters is not gold and everything that shines is not a dime.

When I walked out of the house, I took a deep breath. Freedom never smelled so good. The cold winter air washed over me and lifted the burden I'd carried for so long. I was flat broke, but I was free. For the first time in my life I felt happy. When I got in the car, I pulled out my cell phone and called Bridgett and the fellows. They all congratulated me.

When I finally reached the condo, I called Carla. After a long series of pops and crackles, an operator came on the line and answered in a thick African accent that I could hardly understand. She put me though to another line with equally bad reception and someone finally answered the phone. "Who would you like to speak to?"

"Carla Moore," I shouted.

"Carla Moore is at the hospital site. The lines are all busy but I will keep trying."

I waited for another eternity and I was finally put through. I heard Carla's greeting from half a world away.

"Carla, it's Peter!"

"Peter!" she said excitedly. "Is everything okay?"

"Yes, darling. Everything is better than okay. In fact, things couldn't be better. I went to see Jan," I shouted into the phone.

"You did?"

"She's agreed to give me a divorce."

"Oh, Peter, what have you done?" she cried. "I don't want you to do that on my account."

"Sweetheart, this has been in the making for a very long time. For thirty-two years I have lived a lie. I'm not going to do it anymore. I love you and I want us to be together."

"Peter, you are putting an impossible burden on me. I cannot be responsible for you divorcing your wife."

"You are not responsible. I have been planning this long before I came to Africa. Don't I deserve to have a life? Carla, I have something to ask you. It's very important to me." I could almost see her shy away from the phone thinking I was going to ask her to marry me again. "Next week I'm going to be baptized at Holy Faith. After seeing you again, my heart is under the conviction that I need to rededicate my life to God. I know you and I will never have a chance to be man and wife unless I commit myself to the Lord, but more importantly, I need to do this for myself. I want you to be there. I want your support.

"Carla, I hope you will come. If you do, I know that we will have a chance. If you decide not to come, I will leave the past in the past and never bother you again."

"Peter, you've given me a lot to think about."

"I guess I have. Please, don't think I'm pressuring you. I know that love should be given freely. I don't want you to give me an answer because you feel pressured or intimidated, or out of guilt, so I will leave it up to you. The baptism service will be January 6th, starting at noon."

"Peter, I will think about it. Just know that no matter what happens, I will always love you. You gave me a precious gift with Bridgett."

My heart felt heavy that she didn't agree right away to come to Atlanta. I would have to accept her decision, whatever it might be. I changed the subject and tried to lighten the conversation. I didn't want to break off the call. I wanted to hear her voice.

"How's the hospital coming along? How are the children?" I asked her.

She became excited again, talking about something so near and dear to her heart. I wished she could muster that excitement about me.

"The hospital is moving along rapidly. It's hard to believe. I am so blessed that it has happened so quickly. I'm so thankful that we are finally getting the help we need. Everyone is pitching in to help. Even the sick get out there and help. But AIDS is spreading so fast, everyday there are new cases coming in. So many people are dying that I might have been able to help if the hospital were completed."

"Just do what you can Carla, help is on the way."

"You know what is funny, Peter?"

"What, darling?" I asked, my heart breaking from the pain.

"We still don't have a name for the hospital. Everyone just refers to as the New Hospital. Dr. Ebu said that we will christen it once it's completed." She paused for a beat, "You and Bridgett really shocked me coming here."

"I was excited to see you as well."

"I thought I'd never see you or my daughter again," she said sadly. "I keep a picture of the both of you by my bed."

My love for this woman overwhelmed me. Tears threatened to spill. "Carla, please come to my baptism. I really want you to be my wife."

"I would love to say yes, Peter. I just have so much to think about. So much has changed."

"Just think about it Carla. You don't have to make a decision now."

"Okay, Peter, I will think about, but I can't promise anything."

"That is all I can ask Carla." It occurred to me that if she didn't come, I would never see her again.

"Peter, I know this call is costing you a fortune. I'd better let you go. There are patients I need to see. Take care of yourself."

"I will. Carla, I will always love you. No matter what."

She hung up the phone from her end quietly, without saying anything. A lump came to my throat. I wondered if I made a mistake. Did I give up too much without a guarantee?

I took a deep breath to ease the ache in my heart. Love is all about taking chances, isn't it? That is what faith is. Taking that first step onto a stairway you can't see. It's the substance of the thing you hope for, but is not yet seen.

I poured myself a drink and walked out onto the balcony. The skyline of Atlanta was breathtaking. Lights sparkled like jewels as far as the eye could see. I had one hundred and eighty degrees of freedom spread before me. There was a time when I wanted to own it. Now, I just wanted one woman to be a part of my life.

78

ANTONIO

The divorce was final. It seemed strange that Liana wasn't here. She went on to get her degree and took a job at the Immigration Department in Washington, DC. Soon after, she started lobbying for the reformation of the immigration laws. With a new president, there was so much hope in the Latin community

Every once in while, when I turned on CNN, I would see her speaking to a demonstration in front of the White House. Today I was watching her lovely face fill the TV screen, the cold turning the tip of her nose red. She was making a speech.

> *"...Hispanics did not come to this country to get welfare. Nor did they come to get free medical care or free education for their children. Latinos came to this country to work hard, do their fair share and become law abiding citizens."*

Applause and cheers filled the air around her. I was so proud of her. She sounded like the person I used to be, full of fire, full of dreams, and standing up for what was right. I used to look in the mirror and feel pride. I had made a difference. Somewhere down the line I lost all. What was right had become a gray area in my mind. I couldn't tell the difference between black and white anymore. I thought of myself with the same disdain that other people showed me.

I still called Liana occasionally, but I was just shooting myself in the foot. She was always cordial, but distant.

Ginger and I were now a couple. It didn't feel as good as I thought it would, but somehow I was too apathetic to do anything about it. We were seen at the right places, with the right people. Just as Ginger had promised, she stepped down as senator. With her endorsement, I was appointed by the governor to take her seat although I had yet to be sworn in. But, I had grave misgivings. Being a senator was not as wonderful as I thought it would be.

I felt attraction to Ginger, but I still loved Liana. Everything comes with a price. Ginger's price was marriage. She often reminded me that if she's happy, everyone is happy, but if she is sad, then everyone had better watch out. I have found this to be so true.

Before I knew what hit me, Ginger was announcing our engagement. "What the fuck happened?" I thought to myself while driving to work. Man, I really need to talk to someone about this. A light went off in my head and I snapped my fingers. I decided to call my friend, Joyce Littel?

If anybody knew about relationship drama, it was Joyce Littel.

I whipped out my cell and dialed her private cell number. The phone rang several times.

Come on Joyce, answer the phone. I have some real issues going on. After five rings, she finally answered.

"Hello Joyce, this is Antonio Fernando."

"Antonio, it is so nice to hear your voice. Congratulations on your pending wedding. I received my invitation the other day."

"Thank you, Joyce."

Hearing the melancholy in my voice, she asked, "Antonio, what's troubling you?"

"A desperate husband is what's wrong. Joyce, I have sold myself to the highest bidder and I've lost the only woman I ever truly loved."

"I'm so sorry Antonio. What can I do to help you?"

"Joyce, you know my humble beginnings."

"Yes I do. You have done very well for having so many strikes against you."

"All I can remember is poverty and despair. I remember how the *gringos* use to look down on us everywhere we went. The only job my mother could find was working as a maid or picking fruit. I saw my father work himself into an early grave. He worked his fingers to the bone to put food on the table. Sometimes things were so bad all we had was a pot of beans to eat all week. I can remember my mother and father going without food to make sure my brothers and sister and I had enough to eat. Before my father died, he made me promise to finish school no matter what it took, so that I could give my mother the life he wasn't able to provide.

"Well, I made good on that promise. In fact my brothers and my sister are all college graduates. I finished law school at the top of my class. I became the only Hispanic attorney in a prestigious law firm in Atlanta, and the first Hispanic congressman for Georgia. Peter and Ginger offered me the opportunity of a lifetime. They would make me a senator if I divorced Liana and married Ginger. Joyce, I am so ashamed of what I've become. Now, I see Liana on TV and she has become the person I used to be."

"How so, Antonio?"

"She became a person of honor, principle and integrity. I lost all those things. She spoke out against Senate Bill 529. I went along with Peter and voted for it. Joyce, I'm so ashamed of what I am."

I could hear her sigh into the phone. "Antonio, rehabilitation and recovery first begins with acceptance of your responsibility, then with an apology to those you have hurt. Then you must chart a new course or direction. Do you understand that?"

"I hear you Joyce. Right now, I don't know what to do."

"Antonio, the great Martin Luther King, Jr. once said 'No man can ride your back when you are walking up straight.' Your problems came because you failed to be a man and walk up straight. But, most of all, you need to be very careful what you ask for, you just may get it." "Joyce, I wish it were that simple. If I don't marry Ginger, she and Peter will destroy me. And, she's already sent out invitations."

"The price of ambition," she said knowingly. "Antonio, I remember when I was one of Liana's bridesmaids. Pastor Cash and I talked about your marriage. We truly believed that you two would be one of those marriages that lasted a lifetime."

"So did I, Joyce."

"Antonio, get your power back. The reason Ginger has you by the balls is because you haven't been true to yourself or the people that depended on you."

"What should I do?"

"It is very simple really. Tell Ginger the truth. Be the man you once were."

"What about Peter and the 30305 Club?"

"I wouldn't worry about that if I were you. My sources on the street tell me Peter's past has also come back to haunt him. He is now facing his own demons."

What Joyce said made a lot of sense, but it was easier said than done.

79

The next evening I took Ginger to the Blue Point restaurant. It is an elegant restaurant in Buckhead. I figured breaking up in public would keep it civilized. But, man, I was so wrong...

"You bastard. You ignorant wetback! I gave you the chance of a lifetime. I will destroy you. Ginger Paine doesn't get mad, she gets even. Go back to your little wifey." She threw a glass of water in my face. "You are through in this town and you can kiss being a senator goodbye."

As I wiped my face with my napkin, I said, "Ginger, can't we at least try to be friends."

"Friends!" She laughed evilly. "Friends my ass! When I'm finished with you, you will be lucky if you can find a job picking fruit."

The diners at other tables had all stopped eating and were openly watching us. The murmurs from them grew steadily louder as they enjoyed our performance. I was embarrassed. So much for being civilized.

The next day I called a press conference. Every media and network was there. News of the previous evening at Blue Point had already hit the airways, so this promised to be a media circus. CNN's Nancy Grace had me up against the ropes. "So, Mr. Fernando, are you saying that you were originally against Senate Bill 529?"

"Yes, I was."

"Poppycock," she said as she tightened the screws. "Mr. Fernando, your vote was the deciding vote for passing it."

"Yes, it was, but I felt pressured." Sweat the size of bullets was popping out and running into my eyes. I was scared to death of this woman. "I came to this country with nothing and I wanted more than anything for my people to be proud of me. To be accepted as an equal, to achieve my goals, I lost so many of my values along the way."

"That's an understatement," she said, giving me that piercing stare for which she is so famous.

"I compromised my principles. I lost my honor and respect. To make matters worse, I also lost a good woman that I truly loved; my wife, Liana.

"My father told me once, that if a man's word is no good, he is no good. Because I have not been honest with the people that trusted me, I am resigning as your senator."

"That is the very least you can do," Nancy Grace said, smiling coldly.

"Right now, I am breaking the chains that bind and control me. No man or woman will ever again ride my back. Because this time, I promise the Hispanic community, if you ever trust me again with your livelihoods, lives and dreams, I will walk up straight."

When I arrived home, I fixed myself a drink and turned on the TV. My resignation was the lead story in every newspaper, radio station and TV station across the country.

"Hello...I'm Monica Pearson. This morning, in a strange twist of fate, Antonio Fernando, the first Hispanic Senator from Georgia, resigned. The governor recently appointed Congressman Fernando to the senate seat recently vacated by Senator Ginger Paine. Senator Paine had endorsed Mr. Fernando to fill her position. Mr. Fernando has not yet been sworn in, therefore is not officially a senator. However, the governor has released a statement saying that he will authorize a special election to fill the vacate seat.

"Antonio Fernando made headlines earlier this year when he was a key player in the passing of Senate Bill 529 in the House. The bill declared all illegal immigrants as felons and allowed the state to punish and fine companies hiring them.

"Mr. Fernando gave an emotional apology to Latino's everywhere and said that he had made a mistake in voting for the bill. Standing by is Jovita Moore at the Georgia Capitol."

"Hi, this is Jovita Moore. Thousands of Hispanics are here today at the capitol marching in support of Mr. Antonio Fernando.

"I am speaking to Julio Garcia, a legal immigrant from Honduras. Mr. Garcia, what do you have to say about Mr. Fernando's sudden resignation."

"It took courage to do that. He is a big man to admit he is wrong." He laughed delightedly and continued in his thick accent. "I wish Alberto Gonzales had the same courage, instead of being forced to resign. In my opinion, Antonio is still a man of the people. He's the kind of man we need to lead us and represent us."

"Thank you, Mr. Garcia," Jovita commented as she turned to a young lady standing nearby. "Miss Quintero, what is your opinion?"

"My name is Alejandra Quintero. I am a Latin American citizen. Antonio made mistaks, but we want him as the leader."

Applause and cheers rang out from the crowd around the speakers.

"Monica, I have interviewed Hispanics all over town today and everyone says the same thing; Antonio is still their man. If you listen and look in the background, you can see banners with his name and people are chanting his name over and over...Monica, wait a minute." Jovita hesitated and then turned toward the crowd behind her. "We have just gotten word that Senator Ginger Paine, who has offered her resignation as senator, has requested that her resignation be reconsidered. We will keep you posted on this bizarre twist."

The cameras cut back to Monica in the newsroom.

"Of further interest in Congressman Fernando's story is that he and Senator Paine were due to be married. Reports indicate that they were seen last night at a local restaurant having an argument. Witnesses to the incident report that Mr. Fernando broke off the engagement. Now to other news around the state..."

I exhaled loudly. I guess it was too late now for regrets. My delusion of grandeur was over. I thought about calling Calvin at McDonald's. Maybe he could get me a job.

It had been months since Liana had divorced me, but the following day I got the surprise of my life. The most unlikely of campaign managers called me and volunteered her services.

"Liana!" I was so happy I shouted at the top of my voice. "I'm so glad you called!"

"I saw you on Nancy Grace yesterday. It brought tears to my eyes. The man, yesterday, was the Antonio I used to know. That's the man I want to see get elected to the senate."

"You do? But I resigned." I asked befuddled.

"I do. That is why I called. You need to run against Ginger since she's thrown her hat back in the ring. You have so many people who still believe in you and are willing to support you." Her voice rose with excitement. "We don't have any time to waste, Antonio. I will be back in Atlanta tomorrow. Pick me up at Delta Baggage Claim at four-thirty."

"Liana, I will be there with bells on. Thank you for what you're doing."

"No *problema*, Antonio. See you tomorrow!"

The moment we disconnected I let out a whoop of joy. "Thank you God!"

If I ran against Ginger, I wouldn't have to worry about satisfying Peter. I could be my own man and stand up for the principles that I believe in. With Liana behind me, I couldn't lose!

I started doing the running man dance, and then did a split like the godfather of soul, James Brown. I feel good, like I knew that I would. So good. So good. I got you. When I got up from the floor, I realized that I now needed a tailor.

80

Liana's flight was right on schedule. I waited with a bouquet of a dozen champagne roses. I was jumping up and down like a teenager on my first date. As each passenger drifted into the area, my anticipation increased. Finally I saw her. Her hair was longer and she had picked up a few pounds, in all the right places. I screamed loudly, "Liana, over here." I waved the roses like a banner.

She saw me and smiled. I ran toward her and picked her up in my arms, swinging her around, and showered her with kisses. The roses enveloped us both in their scent.

Liana laughed, but said sternly, "Put me down, Antonio." When her feet touched the ground she straightened the jacket of her suit. I thrust the roses in her hand, which she tucked up under her left arm as she stuck out her right hand. She said, "How are you doing Mr. Fernando." I looked at her hand, openmouthed, "You're looking a little skinny. Isn't Ginger taking good care of you?"

Suddenly I understood. "Ginger and I are over."

"Oh, that's too bad," she said in one of those 'what did you expect' tones. "I have two bags Antonio, would you get them for me? We have a lot of work to do. We only have two months to get ready."

I collected her bags and I hauled them to the car. I think she'd packed bricks in them. When I got them stowed in the trunk, I helped her into the car and pulled out of the parking garage. On the way to Buckhead, we glanced at each other, but didn't really talk. I was nervous and didn't know what to say. Finally, after the silence had stretched out long enough I asked, "How do you like being an advocate, Liana?"

"It's okay. The hours are long and the pay is not great, but it is rewarding. It brings me joy when our people get their green cards and find employment. Kind of like hitting the lotto."

I couldn't take it anymore, so I decided to jump in feet first. I had wasted too much time, and I wanted things back the way they used to be. "Liana, I messed up big time. I destroyed the best thing that ever happened to me. It's been months that we've been apart. I've had a lot of time to think and reflect on what I'd done."

She just gave me an innocent look.

"I'm not the Antonio you used to know. I'm a better, wiser version. If I am fortunate enough to recapture your heart, this time I promise you I will cherish it, value it and never put anything or anybody before you."

She looked out the window, hand propped under her chin. It was like déjà vu. Finally she spoke, "Antonio, we have plenty of time to talk. Right now, let's concentrate on kicking that bitch's butt."

Over the following week we hit the campaign trail. We must have interviewed on every television station from Atlanta to Savannah. In each city we were met by thousands of Hispanic supporters in the streets. My chest swelled with pride when I heard Liana speak to the masses. Her words gave me a reality check. I looked at the small children on the shoulders of their parents and I saw the hopes and dreams of the future. Many of the parents were illegal immigrants. They wanted nothing more than a better life for themselves and their children. With each speech we gained both Hispanic and non-Hispanics supporters.

Ginger was hot on our trail. She put the dirty in dirty politics. She was a master mud slinger and her battle cry was "Antonio Fernando has no place in Washington, DC."

The 30305 Club applauded and cheered Ginger. Liana and I just gritted our teeth. We knew we had a fight on our hands. However, the fellows joined our campaign team. Peter was a changed man. He joined Liana in managing our campaign. Since leaving his wife for an African American stripper, Jan made sure he was on the club's shit list. Ginger not only smeared my name, but brought Peter's name into it every chance she got, reminding everyone about his fathering an illegitimate child.

Ginger's last speech tried to burn Peter's character when she said, "Birds of a feather flock together. Peter McCallister presented himself as a man of principle, a man of honor and integrity. He is a fraud, because in reality, he is an undercover Thomas Jefferson."

Although Georgia had already made Bill 529 a state law, we took our fight to Washington, DC.

81

After weeks of campaigning and spending long hours working, Election Day finally arrived. The votes were split and the rumors were flying. The general word was that Ginger was a shoo-in. I even expected that Peter's reputation would be hurt by all the accusations, but, to my surprise, he laughed it off.

"Antonio, my boy, when you are in the public eye, no publicity is bad publicity. Just make sure they spell your name right. I've been in worst dog fights and I trust Georgians to see through Ginger's lies." He gave me a confident look. "Remember, any man can grab the bull by the balls, but it takes guts and commitment to keep hanging on to them."

The evening of Election Day, we all gathered at a hospitality suite at the Ritz Carlton and watched the returns on TV. For hours, we had watched the numbers. Ginger had edged ahead, but the final tally was a few minutes away yet. The weather was unseasonably warm and we had the balcony doors open to admit the breeze. We all sat tense and waiting. The news stations had started bringing in the latest numbers.

"Hello, this is Amanda Davis...the ballots are in and the race for Georgia's senatorial election is close. We are moments away from naming Georgia's next Democratic Senator. The hopefuls, Antonio Fernando and Senator Ginger Paine are neck and neck. We will now go to Lisa Rayam, live at the Ritz Carlton."

Lisa was in the ballroom surrounded by cheering supporters. People were milling around waving flags and bouncing loose balloons around. "Hi, I'm Lisa Rayam." She touched her earpiece and listened for a moment. "Thanks to an overwhelming last minute turn out from the Hispanic community, the race is finally over! Georgia's next Democratic Senator is Antonio Fernando...that's right...Antonio Fernando is Georgia's first elected Hispanic Senator! We haven't seen this kind of energy and excitement since the election of President Obama!"

The room behind her erupted in cheers. My campaign motto was 'We Can Do It.' A swelling chant of 'We Can Do It', Yes We Can' grew in volume.

In the suite, we all stood and embraced each other, smiling broadly. Several volunteers burst through the door to escort us to the ballroom. Once again, I was the hope and dream of so many people. I would never turn my back on my people again. I vowed to myself to take the responsibility very seriously. I was proud to be an American, but most proud of being a Latino, who would spend his life seeing that others will have the American dream.

As I stood at the podium, looking out over all the people that helped me get elected, a lump formed in my throat. I cleared my throat and tapped the microphone. While I waited for the crowd to quiet down, I looked behind me at Liana and thought about that night so long ago when I betrayed her trust. I smiled at her and she smiled back. I turned to the front and said, "Only in America can a poor boy from nowhere rise from poverty and achieve prosperity." The crowd cheered.

"America represents the hopes and dreams of people of all ages and nationalities. Although we are of different races, religions and ethnic origin, we are more alike than we are different."

The crowd roared.

"Now, one of the biggest decisions that each taxpaying American must make is what to do with twelve million illegal aliens. Many of you say that illegal aliens have no rights, but all of us have the right to want a better life."

The applause was thunderous.

"In the not too distant future, President Obama must search his heart and decide what to do with so many people searching for the American dream. I will work for those people to see that they can become American citizens and achieve the American dream!"

The noise of hundreds of voices could be heard chanting, "We Can Do It, Yes We Can!"

Liana totally surprised me by throwing her arms around my neck and kissing me soundly. The cameras flashed and the cheers increased in volume until I thought my head would split.

Peter yelled out, "Senator Fernando, make your first big decision as Georgia's first Hispanic Senator."

I politely motioned for the crowd to quiet down. Within seconds the noise was muted to a dull roar. I looked at Liana and said, "Liana, may I please have your hand?"

She looked at me suspiciously and reluctantly slid her hand into mine.

I looked deeply into her eyes. "Liana, someone once said, behind every successful man is a good woman."

The women on the floor applauded.

"Every since I pulled your hair twenty years ago, I knew you were that good woman. But, I let you go because I was blinded by my own stupid ambition."

"Antonio, what are you doing?" she whispered.

I gently put my index finger to her lips. "Latin community, Ginger Paine was right! Washington DC is no place for a hypocrite or a sell out! I promise never to be one again!"

My name was shouted over and over by every person in the ballroom.

"I have made a lot of mistakes, but it would take a fool to keep doing things the same way and expect a different result."

Peter applauded loudly and shouted, "Tell the truth Antonio, tell the truth!"

"I made a mistake in my career and I made a mistake in my marriage." I looked out over my supporters. "As you probably guessed, the sell out politician, Ricardo Santiago in the book *Desperate Husbands*, was modeled after me. Liana, in that book, Ricardo was asked if he had it to do it all over, would he marry his wife again?"

I paused and looked around the ballroom. Expectation hung in the air as if everyone there was holding his or her breath. I reached into my jacket pocket and pulled out an engagement ring and pushed it onto Liana's finger, stopping at the first knuckle.

"Claim your bride!" Someone in the audience yelled.

I looked at Liana, "Will you complete my American dream? You made me a happy, complete man. Will you marry me?" I pushed the ring all the way on her finger and lifted her hand and kissed it. "Barack has Michelle and I have my Liana."

The women cheered. The men clapped. I shouted over the rising noise. "Liana, for the rest of my life I will love, honor and cherish you!"

Liana stared at me with a stunned expression on her face. The women were screaming, "Give him a second chance."

She smiled shyly at me and then threw her arms around my neck and yelled, "Yes, yes, Antonio, I will marry you again!"

We kissed and again the cameras flashed. The balloons held at the ceiling of the ballroom were released and rained down around us. Confetti showered the crowd. Everyone cheered. Liana whispered to me, "Antonio, this is the happiest day of my life." She wiped tears from her eyes. As we turned back to the crowd, we both noticed Ginger Paine had entered the ballroom. Liana gave me a mischievous look and said, "There is something that would make me even happier."

"What's that baby?"

She said, "Please forgive me for what I'm about to do!" As I looked at her in confusion, she bounded off the stage and walked across the ballroom to face Ginger. "Miss Paine," she said in a sweet voice. "There is something that I have owed you for a long time!"

"What is that?" Ginger said arrogantly. TV crew and cameramen jostled their way through the crowd to reach them. The audience pressed in close.

Liana smiled broadly and turned to the media. "I have a front page story for all of you as my first official act as the Senator's wife."

She turned back to Ginger, pulled back her arm and gave her a knockout right square on the jaw. Ginger fell back into the arms of a reporter.

Liana exploded, "Bitch that was for sleeping with my man!"

I put my hand over my eyes to hide my expression. I was trying very hard not to laugh. When she climbed back onto the stage I said, "Liana, tomorrow you are going to anger management classes."

Adrian jostled his way to the front of the crowd as the police arrested Liana for assault. He went with me when we went to bond out Liana. As they brought her from the room where they held her, Adrian couldn't help himself. "Well, well, if it isn't Rocky Balboa! Run Mike Tyson, you too Evander, Liana, just made bail and she's hungry for a title fight."

As I tried to contain my laughter, Adrian wouldn't let up. "Girl, do you think Michelle Obama would have showed her ass like that? First Lady Michelle wouldn't be caught giving someone a right across the chops." He put his hands on his hips and rolled his head sister girl style. "Michelle would have given that little bitch an uppercut, then a south side of Chicago beat down. Girl, if I had known you were like that, I would have called Don King, then Pay-Per-View and sold tickets. We could have called this showdown 'Babes Brawling in Buckhead.'

"With me as your manager and Evander as your trainer, we can have the fight game on lockdown." Adrian snapped his fingers and rolled his head sister girl style. "Girl, you are working with weapons of mass destruction."

Liana was getting a little hot under the collar. She waved her hand in Adrian's face and said, "Talk to the hand, Adrian, talk to the hand. I've got your Babes Brawling in Buckhead and your weapons of mass destruction right here and it's *muy caliente*."

Adrian snapped his fingers and rolled his neck again. "As I said before, and I'll say it again, that is the very damn reason we want to send your people back to where they came from. You still don't know how to act." He sniffed loudly and stuck his nose in the air.

We crossed the parking lot to the car and Adrian continued to throw jabs at her. He wouldn't let up until Liana gave me a strained smile.

"What is that I see?" Adrian asked, "Is that a smile?"

Liana bared her teeth at him.

"I guess a cross-bone smile will do for now. At least it's the first step towards your rehabilitation." He snapped and rolled again as I opened the back door. Liana pushed Adrian roughly into the back seat and laughed.

82

PETER

I arrived at the church and went to the usher's room behind the baptism pool to change into my robe. Donald and Ashley were already there, and Jeff and Beverly came in a few minutes after I did. We were still waiting for Quentin and Bridgett.

Aunt Judy, Sister Spencer and the rest of the sisters had made the church shine once again. The parking lot was full. Cars, buses and people lined the road. Old members had returned, and new members were joining. Some folks came just to be nosey. I have to admit that after the scandal with Donald, I was surprised to see so many people there.

Although Holy Faith was a mega-church, it had a country church appeal. Even the rich and famous or the uppity people didn't mind throwing their hands in the air and shouting hallelujah. Jeff, Beverly, Donald, Ashley and I were standing by the door waiting for Pastor Cash to start the service, when Quentin and Bridgett slipped in. It brought joy to my heart to see Quentin rededicate his life to the Lord. Although he was still a knucklehead, I was glad to have him as a son-in-law. I continued to scan the crowd, looking for Carla. She hadn't called me, so I had no idea if she was coming or not. Maybe I was crazy to think we had a future, but I hadn't given up hope yet.

There was a feeling of reverence in the church I had grown to appreciate. The singing itself was enough to keep me coming back. I also enjoyed the people testifying, it takes a sincere person to reveal their sins before strangers. I have always said confession is the first step to rehabilitation, now I believe it.

Pastor Cash rose from his seat and walked to the pulpit. I looked at his smooth brown skin, his serene expression and realized how much I admired him. He was dressed in a long white robe similar to the one I wore. Everyone came to life and applauded.

"Let the church say Amen!" Pastor Cash thundered.

"Amen." The church witnessed.

"Today is truly a glorious day," he said with excitement. "Today is a time to put away our old life; a time to put away our past and look forward to the future. As I look around the church, it brings tears to my eyes. Not long ago, scandal rocked Holy Faith Church. Many of you questioned your leaders, your God and your Faith."

Amen's rose from the congregation.

"After that unfortunate incident, the church congregation dwindled down to just a few hundred members."

Cameras panned the crowd. The faces of people of all nationalities and ethnic backgrounds flashed on the big screens mounted over the pulpit. I still scanned the crowd for Carla.

"As I look around our church, I am happy to see our numbers growing again. I'm happy to see so many young people here. They are our hope and our future."

"Preach the truth, brother," rang out from the crowd.

"They are our dreams for a better tomorrow." He dropped his voice and intoned solemnly, "Young leaders and clergymen, try not to repeat the same mistakes that your parents and church leaders have made. Each generation should grow a little bit taller and become a little bit wiser."

Hallelujah's rose from the congregation.

"Parents, set the example. Make sure your children want to do as you say, as well as do what you do."

Applause filled the church. "Tell the truth, Pastor," shouted an elderly gentleman. Several older kids rolled their eyes.

DONALD

The Pastor motioned for everyone to quiet down and be seated. "Donald and Ashley, will you come forth to be baptized? But before I submerge you, will his victims please come forth?"

Ashley and I left the usher's room and stood side by side holding hands. Beverly slipped out the door and walked to Pastor Cash. Angie, Wayne, Nicole and her husband and a handful of others emerged from the pews and approached the pulpit.

"Pastor Reynolds, before I baptize you and your wife, would you like to say anything?"

"Today, Holy Faith," I said in a trembling voice, "It is a glorious day. Not only for me, but for my wife and the people that I have hurt. Today is a time of reflection, forgiveness, rededication and rebirth. As I look around the church, I am happy that God not only spared my life, but also rescued me.

"Today, I not only get a second chance at love, but a second chance in the eyes of man." I looked at my victims one by one. "To my victims and their mates, let my baptism be a renewing of your faith in God and in me."

Pastor Cash and I ascended the steps to the pool and entered the water. He submerged me in the water and I felt cleansed. When he lifted me from the water, I knew my sins were gone. I looked at my victims, the water on my face mingling with my tears, "To you that I have hurt, I am so sorry."

I handed Ashley up the steps to Pastor Cash and she entered the water. When the pastor lifted her, she was smiling.

The pastor then called Jeff and Beverly and they each had their sins cleansed.

PETER

Jeff and Beverly emerged from the pool with a look of happiness on their faces. They clasped hands as they retreated to change into dry clothes.

The cameraman continued to pan the crowd, showing many teary eyes on the TVs. I continued to look for Carla. With a sinking heart, it became obvious to me that she wanted to leave the past in the past.

Pastor Cash called Quentin and Bridgett to the baptismal pool. I looked at Bridgett, proud of her, and smile weakly. She gave me a reassuring smile back.

As Pastor Cash accepted them into the pool, he said, "Quentin, after reading your book, I'm tempted to baptize you twice."

A chorus of laughter rang out from among the congregation as they were submerged one by one.

The pastor looked around and said, "Do we have anybody else that wants to renew their spiritual walk? Do we have anyone else who wants to leave their comfort zone and step out on faith?"

The cameraman again panned the crowd. "Don't be afraid. Tomorrow is not promised to anyone. It is not important what man thinks of you, we need to worry more about what the Lord thinks of you."

I felt conviction in my heart and sweat popped out around my hairline. I couldn't hide any longer. My day of redemption was finally here. I left the usher's room and walked out towards Pastor Cash. As I walked out, the congregation applauded.

"Come forth Peter McCallister. Rededicate your life to God. The Lord is calling you today. Peter, before you renew your walk with the Lord, would you like to say a few words?"

My heart jumped into my throat, but I pushed myself forward. I quickly took another look around the congregation looking for Carla, but I'd already given up hope.

"Holy Faith, I am proud to begin my walk with the Lord. The Bible says that it is easier for a camel to go through the eye of a needle than it is for a rich man to get into heaven."

"Amen," the church agreed.

"Although I have been a member of this church for twelve years, I've always felt like a visitor. I only came to church to see and be seen by the right people. I never really knew the Lord. I tried to bargain, buy or negotiate with the Lord."

"Speak what is on your heart," Miss Clark shouted.

"I guess I thought that if I gave large sums of money, I could buy my way into heaven."

"What have you realized now?" Pastor Cash asked.

"I've learned that your personal walk, your actions and your deeds are the only things that get you into heaven."

"Amen," the congregation chorused.

"Good Pastor, I never knew the Lord until now. I had a head full of knowledge about God, but not a heart of knowledge of the Lord."

"Speak your heart," Sister Spencer shouted.

"Not long ago I met someone who made me want to know the Lord. She found happiness, not in material things, or what she had, but in the love and blessings she was given. This woman loved the Lord and in order for me to give her my love, I needed to change my life. I was hoping she'd be here today, but I guess she decided not to come."

"What's her name?" Pastor Cash asked.

"Carla Moore," I said proudly.

He leaned towards the microphone and said loudly, "Carla Moore, are you here today? If you are, please stand up."

Everyone looked around and the gossip ladies went into overdrive. "Didn't Peter McCallister just leave his wife?"

"Now he's sniping under another women's skirts?"

"The devil is busy, Emma."

No one stood up and my biggest fear suddenly became a harsh reality. Carla had moved on with her life. A brief silence settled over the church. In that silence I heard the faint noise of the outer doors opening and closing in the vestibule. A small hope bloomed in my heart.

I looked at Pastor Cash and shrugged my shoulders. "I am ready to renew my vows to the Lord," I said.

At that moment I heard the voice I most longed to hear in the world say, "I'm here Peter. I'm here." I looked up and there was Carla entering the sanctuary. She was dressed in traditional African attire. She was colorful and beautiful. She ran to the pulpit and threw her arms around me. The entire congregation stood and applauded. Bridgett ran over and hugged her mother from behind. I looked at the congregation and said proudly, with tears of happiness in my eyes. "Holy Faith, I would like to introduce you to someone that I have kept secret for the past thirty years. This is the woman that I have always loved and the mother of my daughter, Bridgett Moore McCallister. Dr. Carla Moore!"

Tongues started wagging. An elderly African American woman in the back, that was hard of hearing, shouted to her seatmate, thinking she was whispering, "I've been telling you for 30 years that gal had some white in her. She's too high yeller to be all colored. Look at that flat butt, that ain't no colored woman's butt."

"Shh, be quiet Deirdra," her seatmate shouted back in her ear.

"Be quiet nothing, Emma, look at her, she is the spitting image of her daddy."

"No, no, Deirdre, she looks just like her mama."

Ignoring the congregation, I got down on one knee in front of Carla. I reached into the pocket of my robe and removed the worn velvet box that held the ring. I opened the box and the cameraman zoomed in on the five-carat ring. Its brilliance was hugely magnified on the TV screens. I could hear one woman say, "Ohh, child!"

Deirdra yelled out in her whisper, "That's the kind of man I need! I'm tired of these broke ass and broke down men trying to holler at me!"

"Shh," Emma hollered back. "Remember we are in the House of the Lord."

"But look at him," Deirdra shouted back. "That colored woman got his nose wide open."

"Girl I used to be like that thirty years ago!" Emma yelled.

"Down in Alabama, I was a little home wrecker myself. Forget sex in the city, let me tell you about sex in the Civil Rights Movement," Deirdra shouted. "I'd love to put some whipped cream on Barack, tie him down and make him scream, 'Yes we can, yes we can.'"

"Girl, hush your mouth! That is too much information! We've done overcome, don't let your mouth set us back," Emma yelled.

"I don't know but she done hit pay dirt!" Deirdra yelled.

"Shh, y'all know we are in the House of the Lord," a woman sitting next to Emma said.

"Honey, the Lord knows what time it is," Emma yelled.

"I might just have to get me a fine white man. George Clooney makes my panties wet!" Deirdra shouted.

An elderly man wearing very thick glasses jumped in on the conversation. "You two fine colored women don't need a white man. I got money and a new Caddy. I'll break you both off a piece of my social security check."

"Methuselah!" Deidra shouted, crossing her arms over her ample bosum, "Pleassssse!"

Emma started fanning herself rapidly.

Once Deirdra and Emma expended all their conversational skills and the congregation settled down from the excitement, my nerves kicked into overdrive and my knee was starting to hurt. But, finally my heart and my mouth decided to act as a team. Carla and I both had chuckled over the two old ladies, but now she looked back at me with serious eyes. So I took a leap of faith and threw caution to the wind.

"Carla, will you make me the happiest man in the world? I'm asking you to marry me."

The women stood and cheered.

"Carla Moore, make me an honest man," I pleaded

"You go boy," someone shouted.

I was getting a little tired of the interruptions, but remained on my knee, waiting for Carla's answer.

Bridgett couldn't contain herself any longer and said, "Mama, say yes. Please just say yes. Then we can be a family."

I slipped the ring on her finger. I started to get up and my knees locked up. Bridgett pulled me to my feet. I took Carla's hand and kissed it, then held it up for the congregation to see. The ring threw sparks of color everywhere. People were on their feet, applauding and cheering.

Bridgett hugged me tightly. For once in my life I felt a passion and a bond that I had never felt with Jan and her children. I finally had my soul mate.

Suddenly Carla loosened her grip on me and turned to look me in the eyes. "Peter, I need to know something first."

"What's that Carla?"

"Okay Peter, I want to know if you will allow someone to love you? Since your parents abandoned you, you've never given a woman a fair chance."

"Carla, I'm not an angry man anymore. God has given me a second chance."

"Peter, can I trust you with my heart?"

"You can Carla. Just give me the opportunity to prove it."

"Can I trust you whether we are together or apart?"

"Yes, sweetheart."

"Infidelity is not just a physical act, but begins in your thoughts."

"Baby, you can trust me. You're the only woman I've ever wanted."

"Peter, are you sure?"

"Carla, I've never been more sure of anything in my life!"

"Peter, when I get married, it will be forever. Divorce is not an option."

"Carla, I want to be with you the rest of my life."

Our faces flashed on the TV screens. If I didn't know this was real life, I would swear it was a soap opera.

"Peter, can you devote yourself to one woman? Will you come to Africa and live in a humble hut?"

"Yes, Carla, I will, as long as you are by my side. I would live in a ditch. I've had money and mansions. They mean nothing now. But I've spent thirty years without you and I don't want another minute to pass that you are not by my side."

She stood silently, looking at Bridgett as tears ran down her cheeks. I didn't know who was hurting more, Bridgett or me. We both wanted Carla to make up her mind without coercion or pressure.

"Peter," Carla said, "One of the biggest obstacles we will face is that we are of two different races."

"I don't care what people think of me!" I exploded. I turned to the congregation. "Holy Faith, I've loved this woman for thirty years! I want her in my life!"

For once, the congregation was so quiet you could hear a pin drop. Even Deirda and Emma had shut up.

"Carla, all I know is that I love you."

Still she remained silent.

"Carla, hasn't it ever occurred to you that your soul mate may exist in another skin color other than your own?"

Church fans fluttered rapidly. A voice rang out from the congregation, "Child, he got a point there. Love comes in all flavors!"

Another said, "Look at Halle Berry and her new white man."

Still another voice yelled, "Sometimes you need a little milk in your coffee."

Emma shouted out, "I think I'll get me a white man!"

The elderly man with the think glasses yelled, "You don't need to do that. I'm still available. My name is Rock!"

Emma rolled her eyes at the man and shouted, "Father Time, I'm looking for pimp juice, not prune juice!"

The tension that had gripped the congregation suddenly dissolved as everyone laughed.

Carla gave me a piercing look as I gazed soulfully at her. I could see the wheels of her mind churning, struggling to make sense of it all. She'd flown half way around the world to be here. That told me that she still loved me. So why wouldn't she give me an answer?

Carla reached out, placing her hands on each side of my head, weaving her fingers into my hair she pulled my head towards her. She leaned forward and looked sternly into my eyes, her nose inches from mine.

"Peter, you better listen to me and listen good. If you do me wrong, this earth will not be big enough for you to hide. With God as my witness, you will come up missing!"

The church exploded with shouts, laughter and cheers. Carla shouted to be heard above the pandemonium, "YES PETER, I WILL MARRY YOU!"

She kissed me soundly.

Bridgett threw her arms around both of us and we cried uncontrollably.

Pastor Cash restored order and turned to me.

"Peter, are you ready to be cleansed of your sins?"

"Oh, yes, Pastor Cash. I am so ready!"

We entered the pool and he submerged me in God's water. I felt the water flow over me and felt my past and my sins wash away. Pastor Cash lifted me and I climbed the steps to exit the pool. I'd no sooner put my foot on the bottom step coming down, when Carla barreled into me.

She grabbed me and held me tightly. When she stepped away, she was soaking wet down the front of her dress. I grinned at her and was overcome with happiness. Quentin, Donald, Ashley, Jeff and Beverly gathered around us. They all hugged me, then Carla.

Donald unexpectedly walked to the microphone.

"Good Pastor, for so many years, you have been a teacher, a counselor and a mentor." He paused and wiped his eyes. "Pastor Cash, as my mentor and my friend, please don't retire. Please."

His words touched the Pastor. Tears sprang to his eyes. The congregation all cheered in agreement. He pulled out a big white handkerchief and gently wiped his eyes. Everyone near the pulpit grabbed him and hugged him, saying encouraging words and pleading with him to stay as our spiritual leader. The band played and the choir sang. Everyone hugged his neighbor.

Pastor Cash stood at the pulpit and motioned to everyone to sit. When the audience had quieted down, he cleared his throat and spoke.

"Holy Faith Church, for so many years you have shown me so much love. When the Lord called me into the ministry more than 30 years ago, I answered with gladness in my heart. Today I heard the pleas of young and old. As I look around the sanctuary, I see so many familiar faces. I was at the hospital when many of you were born. I was at the hospital with many of you when your loved ones departed. And many of you I have baptized."

"Amen, Pastor Cash!" a woman yelled.

"A while back, I felt my time was drawing to a close. My wife, Barbara, told me to step aside and make room for a new generation. But now, after hearing your voices, I realize my time has not ended. A new challenge has begun.

"You say you need me. Holy Faith, I will once again, answer that call. I WILL BE YOUR PASTOR!"

The band played exuberantly and the pastor did the holy dance in his pulpit. The children ran to the pulpit to hug him. Echoes of praise rang out. It was a joyous day at Holy Faith.

"Emma!" Deirdra shouted. "You can find the devil at any church. We might as well stay here!"

85

Two weeks later, the pastor performed his first triple wedding. Bridgett and Quentin, Antonio and Liana, and Carla and I were married. Jeff announced that Beverly was pregnant with twins and she was going to start her own modeling agency in Atlanta. And shortly after the wedding, Carla and I left for Africa.

Dr. Ebu met us at the airport and we drove straight to the hospital. It was now about ninety percent complete. As we approached the hospital, people had lined the streets and were cheering us. There seemed to be hundreds and hundreds of people, old and young and everything in between. They were the people Carla had touched with her love. They called her name over and over.

We pulled up to a platform that had been raised in front of the two-story building. Dr. Ebu and I escorted Carla up the steps to where several governmental dignitaries waited. A ragtag band occupied one corner and struck up a discordant tune. Carla looked around and said, "Peter, what is this? What are all these people doing here?"

"You'll soon see," I said calmly.

"Peter, did you have something to do with this?" She asked as tears came to her eyes.

I took her hand and turned her to face the hospital. "Carla, this is your wedding present, this hospital, which is so desperately needed."

Carla put her hands to her mouth and looked at me with wonder in her eyes.

"Just wait a moment. Dr. Ebu, if you please!" I said.

Dr. Ebu walked over to the sign that had been affixed above the doors. It was covered with a sheet that had a rope attached to it. He grasped the rope and tugged sharply. The sheet fell away to reveal the sign. It read Moore-McCallister Hospital in bright red letters three feet high.

Carla stared, openmouthed, at the sign. She turned to me, the tears spilling down her beautiful face. I opened my arms to her and she ran to me, burying her face in my chest. The people cheered and children overran the stage, hugging Carla around the knees. My heart was filled with love. A dream had become reality and hope filled the hearts of the people. The joy was priceless.

After christening the hospital, Carla and I went to our new home. I had Dr. Ebu arrange for us to buy a small house near the hospital. It was plainly furnished, with little luxury, except for a new double bed. The house had been cleaned, the sparse furniture arranged and the cupboards minimally stocked by Dr. Ebu's staff. We had sporadic electricity and one small fan for air conditioning. Carla and I consummated our marriage in that little house, in Africa, far from every thing that I was familiar with. I had never been so happy. My life now had meaning and purpose. I'd found my happy place, like Jan's expensive shrink had advised. I was no longer a member of the 30305 Club and I rejoiced.

86

QUENTIN

So there you have it. This is how Quentin Banks, a one time, down and out writer and his friends, Donald Reynolds, Antonio Fernando, Jeff Montgomery and Peter McCallister became members of the ritzy 30305 Club, and how in the process we all became desperate husbands.

As I reflect back on that often hilarious, sometimes tragic year I can't help but think that is was funny how we all worked so hard to get in the 30305 Club, but I thank the Lord we were able to get out.

Bridgett and I are planning a second honeymoon, but first I had one last interview to do for the 'Michael Baisden Syndicated Radio Show.' I ran into the studio with five minutes to spare before airtime.

Michael Baisden met me in the lobby and gave me a brotherly hug, then shoved me into the studio and hooked me up with the headphones. Then we were on.

"Hi, this is Michael Baisden, the Bad Boy of radio. Welcome to Love, Lust and Lies. Our guest today is one of the most hated men in America. No, not Osama bin Laden. I'm talking about public enemy number two – Mr. Controversy, Quentin Banks, author of the book everybody is still talking about, *Desperate Husbands.*"

"How are you doing Michael? Thanks for inviting me to your show. Hey, I want to commend you on spearheading the Jena Six situation. I'm sure those teens would never have gotten out of jail if it weren't for you bringing this injustice to light."

"Thank you Quentin. Just showing the young brothers some love."

"Keep up the good work, Michael."

"I will Quentin. Now, I understand that since your book came out, a lot of couples have looked closely at their mates."

"Yes, they have Michael. In fact, this book also made me pop the question to my girlfriend, Bridgett."

"Damn man, what did she have on you?"

"It was by choice. Getting married was the best decision I ever made. I would encourage every man to do it."

"No, No! Sometimes a man needs to know when to quit. After reading about all that drama in your book, I'll stay happily single."

We both laughed.

"Man, I've been getting the word on you, Quentin. It seems you've caused a lot of commotion with this book. I heard you have been receiving death threats."

"Yes I have, Michael."

"Quentin, when I heard you were coming on my show, I decided to come to work with a bullet proof vest on."

As I fidgeted in my seat, I accidentally knocked my book off the counter and it hit the floor with a loud BLAM.

Michael flinched and said, "What was that Quentin? Was that a gun shot?" He looked wildly around the studio.

"Relax, it was only a book hitting the floor."

"Whew. Glad that bullet didn't have my name on it. I don't want to end up like Tupac or Biggie Small."

"Don't worry, you're safe with me. I've got your back."

"Quentin, a lot of men have told me that the reason *Desperate Husbands* hit home was because it brought to light the fact that there are things that men will tell a perfect stranger before they will tell their mates."

"The fact is, wives ask their husbands to tell them the truth, when in reality they can't handle it," I said sardonically.

"Give me five on that brother," Michael jested.

"Michael, as you and I both know, when a man becomes desperate, he has run out of options."

"I couldn't agree with you more." The host nodded.

"Very few men want to leave a good woman," I commented, "And trust me, a good woman is hard to find."

"So true, Quentin, so true."

"The reality of it is, Michael, when a man actually gives up he will take a code of silence, try separation or start cheating. The very last option is, of course, divorce."

"Hey man, that's too much drama for me."

"*Desperate Husbands* is full of men cheating, lying and bad mouthing their wives. In reality, what I discovered, is that another person can't destroy your marriage from the outside, it's the two people in the marriage that are to blame. A marriage is destroyed from the inside."

"Amen to that brother."

"Another man or woman sees there is unhappiness or weakness in the ranks so they exploit this vulnerability."

"I agree with you man, your trash is someone else's treasure," the host said knowingly.

"Michael, what makes a man desperate is the lack of five essential needs."

"They are?"

"Respect, admiration, emotional support, peace of mind and great sex."

"Give me another high five on that man!"

"When I wrote this book, I did a lot of research. I studied statistics, ran surveys, read everything I could get my hands on about relationships. I didn't leave any stone unturned. One survey was done with a thousand women that said they were happily married. I asked two simple questions. Most of these happily married, educated, professional and successful women received an F."

"How so, Quentin?"

"How about we have a little fun Michael? I'll give the women in your audience the test and we'll see what happens."

"You're on man. The microphone is yours."

"Okay, ladies. Here's the Desperate Husbands Challenge."

"Come on and let's do it America!" Michael said.

"All right, Michael. First question is, out of all the years you've been married, when was the last time you told your husband that you appreciated him?"

"I guess you struck a nerve Quentin. The caller board is lit up like a Christmas tree. Caller one, you're on the air."

"Hello, my name is Dorthea. I'm grown, sexy and live in Washington DC. I tell my husband everyday that I appreciate him. He's a wonderful father, lover and in twelve years of marriage he's never once cheated on me."

"Dorthea, you are a queen among women and your husband is truly a king."

The calls continued to poor in. We talked with as many women as possible. When Michael finally cut the calls, I had the results of my informal survey ready.

"Michael, out of the women we've just surveyed, as in my original research, 95 percent of the callers have never told their spouses they appreciated them."

"Ladies, I'm sitting here with my foot in my mouth. Ninety five percent of you need a marriage tune-up. If you remember, one lady in Buckhead said that the last time she told her husband she appreciated him was when the price of gas was thirty-two cents a gallon."

"Ladies, what is going on?" I said.

"Apparently nothing but the rent," Michael joked.

"Okay, here's the second question. When was the last time you asked your mate what you could do to make him happy?"

Once again, the caller board lit up completely. We listened to woman after woman answer the question. When Michael stopped the calls, I quickly tallied up the percentages.

"Again, Michael, 97 percent of the successful women received an F."

"Quentin, it seems as though we have a lot of desperate husbands all across America."

"We sure do. Another thing I learned when writing this book is that the hardest thing for a man to do is humble himself before another man or admit he needs help."

"You know how our egos are!"

"Michael, it's even harder for men to show weakness, emotions or sensitivity. As a result, like you said, most men cry in the dark. To every single or married women listening to the show, it is easy to get a man's body or money, but the grand prize is winning his heart and the ultimate prize is to win his trust. Only then will he reveal his most intimate thoughts. I discovered some other astounding information."

"What is that, O Great Relationship Guru?" the host jested.

"When I listened to men complaining and moaning about their mates, after a separation, breakup or divorce, most men secretly admitted they wanted to get back together with their mates."

"Quentin, we have a caller on the line for you. Okay, caller, you're on the air."

"Hi, Mr. Banks, this is Calvin, your old buddy that used to work at McDonald's. I was really pissed off at you when you exposed me and got me fired, but I forgive you. Listening to you today, I realize that you are not the SOB everybody thinks you are. It takes a big man to humble himself and admit he is a jerk."

"Thank you Calvin. That is something I learned firsthand."

"Quentin, I'd also like to apologize for the email I sent you. Reading your book helped me with my own personal relationship. Thank you for expressing how men honestly feel. I get so tired of reading those books and seeing those movies by those male bashing women. I'm sure America can't wait for your next book."

"Okay, Calvin, thanks for calling in. Well, Quentin, we're almost out of time," Michael said.

"Before I go Michael, I learned a few things while researching my book that I would like to share. One, if you have a good friend, cherish that friendship. Two, if you have a good woman, protect that love and fight to keep it."

"I agree Quentin. I love you man."

"I love you too, Michael. Remember men, a promise is a promise. It doesn't matter who you made it too."

"Is the great Quentin Banks eating humble pie?"

"Yes, and I mean a big slice of it. Michael, I betrayed some guys who I am really close to."

"Ah, Quentin, you betrayed the brotherhood?"

"Yeah, I did. Even though I was wrong, not once did my friends stoop to my level."

"Your friends are one in a million."

"They sure are, Michael. So to Jeff, Antonio, Peter and Donald, I'm sorry. I know two wrongs don't make a right, but let me put my own business in the street so you can feel we are even. First of all, the character Lance Shelton, in the book is me."

"Why Quentin, you little Peeping Tom. You're the one who used to masturbate while looking at women through a keyhole. Damn, Quentin, I'll never give you a high five again."

"Yeah, well sorry about that. I just hope that now maybe men and women can start healing among themselves. Women must realize that a man will only do what they let them do. A man can't make a woman totally happy, he can only add to or take away from the happiness she already possesses. Women, stop pressuring men to marry you. Give him a choice of becoming a father, instead of you making the choice for him. If the man wants you, nothing can make him go away. So ladies, stop making excuses for men and their behavior. Allow your intuition to save you from heartache and stop trying to change yourselves to fix a relationship that is not meant to be. Keep in mind that your looks may get a man, but it is not enough to keep a man. Slower is better and don't live your life for a man before you know what makes you happy."

"That's good advice Quentin, anything else we need to know?"

"Ladies, if a relationship ends because your man was not treating you with respect, then heck no, you can't be friends. A friend wouldn't mistreat a friend. Don't settle if you feel like he is stringing you along, because he probably is. The only person you can control in a relationship is you. I have told women over and over again, avoid men that have a bunch of children by a lot of different women. He didn't marry them when he got them pregnant and you can't expect it to be any different for you."

"Right you are Quentin," Michael said.

"Ladies that enjoy the company of married men…if he cheats on his wife, why do you think he is not going to cheat on you?"

"Ladies, all men are not dogs and you should not be the one doing all the bending. Learn to compromise. It works both ways. Most of all, do not jump immediately into another relationship after a break-up. You need time to heal."

"Quentin, I tell you, some of my female listeners are carrying so much baggage I think they are Samsonite."

"I agree Michael, a woman should never look to a man to complete her. A relationship consists of two whole individuals that compliment, not supplement. Let him miss you occasionally. When a man knows you'll always be available to him, he'll take you for granted every time."

"Yeah, baby, turn up the heat!" Michael said.

"You can only receive love when you give love. Nothing will change until you change. And quoting the unforgettable words by America's first African American president, 'It's time for a change.'"

"Quentin, all my female listener's should be on your couch."

"Well, I don't think my wife would appreciate that. I also learned, Michael, that couples should never have to go looking in the street for what's staring them right in the face at home."

"Men across America, I hope you are listening," Michael said.

"Yeah, the grass always looks greener on the other side. Let's forget race altogether because you may find the person of your dreams just might exist in another race and most of all, what is done in darkness will come to light."

"Uh oh. I hope not," Michael said. "I want to leave the past in the past."

"Troubled couples, also keep in mind that your mate may not be perfect, but they may be perfect for you. And finally, if you fail to communicate, or reinvent your relationship, there will always be desperate husbands and desperate housewives."

"I couldn't have said it better myself, Quentin." Michael said knowingly.

We gave each other high fives and Michael signed off the air. As I unhooked myself from my headset, Michael sprayed his hand with disinfectant. He looked up at me and said, "Quentin, I still have issues about you masturbating in the bathroom."

The End

Statistics in Chapter 37 were done in a three-year cross racial study with 1000 husbands, ages 21 to 50, in twelve major cities.

These major cities are:

Atlanta, GA
Manhattan, NY
Los Angeles, CA
Chicago, IL
Washington, DC
Miami, FL
New Orleans, LA
Cleveland, OH
Boston, MA
Detroit, MI
Philadelphia, PA
Baltimore, MD

COMING TO A BOOKSTORE NEAR YOU

Don't miss Britten Wilder's upcoming novel, "A God-fearing Man (When Life, Love and the Lord Aren't Making Sense)"
...A story of one man's incredible journey in finding love, hope, faith and redemption after Hurricane Katrina.
Check out the excerpt from the upcoming novel.

A God-Fearing Man
By
Britten Wilder

What if the very thing you were taught and believed was the very thing that had wrecked your life? My name is Paul Spencer. I was born in Birmingham, Alabama. As long as I could remember I was a God-fearing man. My mother took me to church every time the doors were opened. She would constantly recite Mark 11:24 to me.

'Whatever you ask the Lord for in prayer, you believe that you will receive it. Then you shall have it.'

But as my mother drowned before my eyes in the Hurricane Katrina floodwaters, I prayed to God to save her. When He didn't, I lost my faith.

There isn't any God! Just ask those folks down in New Orleans and on the Gulf Coast. How can a merciful God inflict so much pain and suffering on so many innocent people? How can a merciful God allow old people to die in their basements, and little children to die in their sleep? From this point on I'm turning my back on life and love and I'll never step foot in another church again.

It was Sunday, August 28, 2005. It was my mother's birthday. We were on our way to New Orleans, Louisiana to visit her sister, Gertrude. They hadn't seen each other in almost ten years. It was about six thirty in the morning, and the day was building towards a beautiful, cloudless day. We had left Birmingham earlier that morning in the darkness of the night. I was driving a brown, broken down, old hooptie. The car had no air conditioning, the radio faded in and out and the exhaust sputtered gas fumes every other mile or so. To this day, I'm still not sure how we made it. As we got closer to New Orleans, we passed a road sign that read, New Orleans, Louisiana 10 miles. Mama screamed with excitement. "Nawlins' another ten miles, I can't wait to see Gertrude. In a few minutes we'll be wrapping our lips around Gertrude's prize winning gumbo!"

As we closed in on the city, the sun suddenly hid its face. Dark clouds were rolling in. The day rapidly became dark and overcast. Little did I know of the hidden fury that was hot on the heels of those rain clouds.

I dropped Mama off at Gertrude's church. She squeezed Mama so hard I thought she might break her in half. I was reminded of that movie 'The Color Purple' where Celie and Olivia are reunited after years apart.

I jumped back in my car and I was on my way to the French Quarter. When I got there, I met up with some of my buddies and we roamed the Quarter and got sloppy drunk. I don't remember much about that, but somehow I ended up crashing in Robert's room. I awoke the next afternoon with camel dung coating my mouth. I scratched myself and rolled out of bed. My boxers were sticking to me from sweating in the oppressive heat. The humidity lay across my shoulders like a wet blanket. I didn't remember it being this bad when I was a boy.

Then I heard someone scream, "Hurricane Katrina is hitting the Gulf Coast."

"Oh my God! I've got to get to Mama..."

A story of male/female relationships and one man's incredible journey in finding love, hope and faith after Hurricane Katrina.

About the Author

Bold, fresh, informative and uplifting – nobody creates excitement like author, relationship counselor and life-coach, Britten Wilder.

As the author of numerous best selling books, Britten Wilder's sold out relationship seminars have taught couples how to simplify their relationships, rekindle passion, reinvent their marriages and side-step the headache and heartache of contemporary relationships.

This knowledgeable author has studied relationships in ten different countries. Britten Wilder is the 'go to guy' for many major celebrities, a sought after relationship consultant for some of today's hottest publications, as well as an unforgettable guest on major talk shows around the world.

Contact Information

Don't miss the chance to meet this charismatic and entertaining author, Britten Wilder, in person.

If you would like to book author, Britten Wilder, as a guest or speaker for your show, organization or media event, please call us today at Premier Entertainment at 800-305-7948 or contact us in writing at Premier Entertainment, 269 S. Beverly Drive, Suite 500, Beverly Hills, California 90212, ask for Jerry Collins, Publicist/Agent or by email at Info@BrittenWilder.com.

If you would like information regarding the cities where Britten Wilder's upcoming promotional tour "For Women Only" will be held, please log onto www.BrittenWilder.com.

Or if you would like a personally autographed copy of *Desperate Husbands* or a sneak preview of Britten Wilder's highly anticipated upcoming release, *A God- Fearing Man (When Life, Love and the Lord Aren't Making Sense)*, please call us today at 800-206-3934, extension 3265.

For a personal message or comments, please call 800-206-3934, extension 3266, or email the author at www.BrittenWilder.com.

Premier Publishing

Prior Releases

Don't miss your chance to order Britten Wilder's sizzling prior releases.

'Understanding the Games Men Play'
(Self Help)
IBSN # 0-9662124-2-8
$13.95 per book

'Is It Love or a Big Misunderstanding'
(Self Help)
IBSN # 0-9662124-4-4
$14.95 per book

'Getting and Keeping Your Mate Trained,
Whipped, Faithful and on a Leash'
(Self Help)
IBSN # 0-9662124-1-X
$15.95

Interview and Relationship DVD, for $10.00 per copy.

Send Check or Money Order to:
Premier Publishing
3651 Peachtree Parkway
Suite E159
Suwanee, Georgia 30024

Add $4.00 to the purchase price
for shipping and handling.